# Phantasm

## THE EXILED

Harleigh Beck

Editor: Nice Girl Naughty Edits
Proofreader: Traversingfiction
Cover: ArtistaGráfico Cover Design

*Revised October 2024 — formally part of The Exodus Series

# CONTENT INFORMATION

This dark romance contains adult content. It is not intended for readers under 18.
Remember, it's fiction! This author doesn't condone the darker themes in this book.

**For content information, follow the link below.**
https://harleighbeckcontentinfo.carrd.co/

# CHAPTER ONE

## CECILIA

"I hope you know how reckless this is."

Ignoring the head of the house and our inside spy, Mrs. Jones, when she whispers in my ear, I reach for another glass to polish on the large table. It glints by the time I'm done. Mrs. Jones means well, but I won't rest until I've exacted my revenge on the Exiled for the death of my father. If I had my way, I'd burn the entire secret society to the ground—that's how deep my hatred runs—but Rome wasn't built in a day. I need to pick my battles carefully, and the Dukes are a good starting point. Tomorrow is Hell Fire Night. A ten-hour period once every five years where all crimes are legal in Bozeman for Exiled members. Nothing is off the table. Not even murder. And it's happening here, in this extravagant cottage. Naturally, I needed to scope out the place beforehand. Mrs. Jones was kind enough to sneak me in under the pretense that I'm part of the hired staff responsible for prepping the cottage before tomorrow's event, which is why I'm polishing glasses, dressed in a maid's outfit, feeling ridiculous.

"You're on your own," Mrs. Jones says, moving away

from me when voices drift from the hallway. "If Mr. Sinclair or Delacroix asks, I've never seen you before."

"Relax," I reassure her as I reach for another glass. It soon sparkles. "They're too self-absorbed to pay attention to the paid staff."

Unimpressed, Mrs. Jones huffs. "You underestimate Mr. Delacroix. He's observant, not to mention dangerous, and I dare say, out of all the Dukes, he's the cruelest. There's not a kind bone in that man." She straightens when two men in pristine suits enter the room.

My eyes lift without consent, and I'm caught in the frostiest, bluest eyes I've ever witnessed. While I've seen photographs of Mr. Delacroix, they don't do him justice. But don't let his good looks fool you. Mr. Delacroix is a monster. A cold-hearted, evil monster incapable of empathy.

For all of five seconds, I allow myself to admire his sharp jawline, piercing eyes, and broad shoulders inside that expensive suit that probably cost more than the average mortgage payment. A blush creeps up my neck as I squash any sexual attraction I feel for the man involved with the secret society responsible for my father's disappearance.

I'm mortified at finding him even remotely attractive—a man old enough to be my father. I drop my gaze and spend the next few minutes polishing champagne glasses like my life depends on it. Mr. Delacroix and another Duke, Nathaniel Sinclair, retreat to the study across the room. Much to my pleasant surprise, the door is left ajar, and I feel Delacroix's eyes on me the entire time, but I don't lift my gaze. Not once.

Earlier, I mapped out the cottage, trying to be as inconspicuous as I could while pretending to vacuum pristine carpets and dust antique gold-framed mirrors. There are security cameras everywhere, but some are more obvious than others, like the one currently aimed in my direction. The

Exiled takes security seriously, but I already know that. I also know that Mr. Delacroix is seated behind his desk, watching the security cameras on his monitors while Sinclair discusses business. My ears strain to listen. Why does the table have to be so far away from the study? If only I could get closer.

Sinclair's rich laughter drifts through the doorway. Delacroix mutters something before he rises from his seat, rounds the desk, and leans his shoulder against the doorframe. His imposing presence instantly suffocates the room, and I feel his eyes burning into me like molten lava against my skin.

I keep my head lowered as I place the glass on the table, careful not to let the tremble in my fingers show. Heart pounding, I pick up another glass by its fragile stem.

Why is he staring? Maybe it was naïve of me to think I could go unnoticed, because no man has ever ogled me so openly before. I feel naked beneath that hard stare.

"I'd like a word in my office, miss." He pushes off the doorframe, expecting me to follow.

I finally look up. Delacroix is back behind his desk, sans his suit jacket, his sleeves rolled up past his elbows to reveal tanned, corded forearms.

Sinclair eyes me curiously. I'm in deep shit. This is not how I planned today to pan out. I was meant to scope the place, learn as much as possible about the layout, and then report to the others. I was not meant to catch the attention of Darian Delacroix himself. This is bad news.

After placing the glass and cloth back down, I enter the office with my nerves on edge. Two sets of eyes study me from head to toe. One with curiosity and one with suspicion. Sinclair clears his throat. "I've got business to attend to." He brushes past me in a cloud of bergamot and vanilla cologne, adjusting his circular glasses on his way out.

Delacroix watches me coolly without a change of expression. His eyes rake down my body and then return to my face. "I haven't seen you here before. What's your name?"

"Cecilia," I reply. It takes tremendous willpower to keep my tone friendly. There's a letter opener beside his tumbler of whiskey on the desk, and I try not to eye it while entertaining fantasies of ramming it into his throat.

"Cecilia?" he mirrors, waiting for me to follow it up. When he waves an impatient hand, I blurt the first lie that enters my head.

"Cecilia Taylor."

One of his dark brows rises. "Cecilia Taylor?" His tone is cold enough to rival the Arctic's temperatures, and judging by the slight tic in his jaw, he knows I'm lying. He spins the letter opener with a finger. "You look very familiar, Cecilia. How old are you?"

I swallow hard, clasping my hands behind my back to hide my tremble. "I'm twenty-five, sir."

His eyes penetrate through my lies. I'm burning up beneath that glacial stare. "You don't look old enough to be twenty-five. How long have you worked here?"

"Today's my first day." It's best to stick close to the truth. Mother taught me that. Though I'm only twenty. But I must not, under any circumstances, let Delacroix know my real age.

"Is that so?" He rises from his chair, unfolding like a predatory lion, his long, powerful legs eating up the distance between us. Delacroix moves with purpose, every shift of muscle highlighting his impressive physique, a work of art created by a vengeful god. I try to swallow my fear when he stops before me and openly sweeps his eyes over my face with an indifferent look. A smattering of a beard covers his sharp jaw, and the crow's feet around his eyes add to his allure. He also smells good, with hints of warm cardamom and tonka bean.

Reaching out, he fingers the white lace collar on my dress. "You were eavesdropping on my conversation with Mr. Sinclair, were you not?"

I open my mouth to deny it, but he takes hold of my jaw in a firm, unforgiving grip, reminding me yet again of how dangerous he truly is. I've heard the rumors. Darian Delacroix enjoys instilling fear in people.

"Were you not, Miss *Taylor?"*

"Yes," I whisper. There's no point lying to him about this. Something tells me he could smell it a mile away if I tried.

He hums, his touch softening. "You're an exquisite, curious little thing, aren't you? Tell me, why are you here?"

I can't think when he trails his fingertips over my jaw. "I was hired to clean…sir."

His lightened touch never falters, even when he warns, "If I find out you lied, Miss Taylor, I'll destroy everyone you've ever loved. And it will be my pleasure."

To my utmost horror, my lashes flutter when his fingers trail the curve of my neck. How can I be so affected by a man I hate? A man belonging to the secret society I'm here to destroy.

Delacroix slides his hands into his pants pockets. "Take off your clothes."

My eyes flare as I choke on air. Did I hear him correctly? Surely, he didn't say what I think he said. "Excuse me?" I blurt.

"Strip."

A one-word command.

He watches me with unveiled disinterest. I get the distinct sense this is a test of loyalty. Delacroix, one of the most feared Dukes of the Exiled, has killed for less. No one says no to him if they want to live to see another day.

My heart pounds harder as I reach for the zipper at my side and slowly lower it. The door is open, but not for long. Delacroix leans into me and pushes it shut. Then he steps back and waits for me to strip out of the dress. His heady scent is everywhere, like a spell cast by an evil sorcerer.

When the zipper is down, I slide the dress off my freckled shoulders. A shiver raises the hairs on my arms as the slight chill in the air licks my bare skin.

Delacroix keeps his attention on my face, scouting for weaknesses or a hint of betrayal. Anything that'll give me away. The dress pools at my feet, and I stand before the monster of Bozeman in only my white lace panties and bra. I'm shivering, but not from the chill in the air or the freezing temperature in his eyes. I wet my lips, and Delacroix slips his hand from his pocket to finger my bra strap.

"You look so familiar," he muses, the backs of his fingers brushing against my goosepimpled skin before he rips the strap with a hard yank.

A gasp escapes my lips. My tits bounce free, achy and heavy. I whimper when he palms a full breast. "My staff is carefully vetted, Miss Taylor, by none other than myself." He tweaks my pearled nipple, and heat swirls low in my core.

My pussy clenches with my need for this dangerous man, whom I've vowed to kill tomorrow when the law is on my side. I don't have a weapon at my disposal, so it would be foolish to try until I'm prepared.

My gaze slides past him to the letter opener on his desk. If only I could sink it deep into his side and watch him bleed out, but I can't kill him now unless I want to face a hefty jail sentence. This time tomorrow night, however, he and any other fucker in this building is fair game. It'll be my own funeral, too, but at least I'll die knowing I tasted revenge.

"I recognize that look in your eyes." His smoky, dark voice—like whiskey and cigars—warms me from the inside. "You're plotting my death."

A yelp escapes me when he lifts me by the waist as though I weigh nothing and carries me to his desk. My back meets the paperwork and Delacroix tears my lace panties from my body and stuffs them in his back pocket. Without hesitation, he wrenches my legs apart and stares at my shaven pussy. I can't believe I came here in disguise with the sole intention of scoping out the place before tomorrow night, yet now I'm splayed naked on Mr. Delacroix's desk like a buffet. Even if I want to say no, I can't. It would blow my cover. Sure, Delacroix is suspicious, but he doesn't consider me a threat—yet. I'd be dead if he did.

A hint of heat enters his eyes as he rakes them over my body. And then he reaches for the letter opener and uses it to trace my parted lips. "I saw you eye this up."

My chest is heaving by the time he drags the letter opener down the curve of my chin and over my throat, pausing at my racing pulse point. "Were you planning on using it, by any chance?"

I hold my breath as he digs the sharp tip into the skin.

"You'd be dead before you could reach for it."

"You shouldn't underestimate me, sir." It takes everything in me to speak steadily.

A hint of a smile touches his lips, almost like my response amuses him.

The letter opener continues its journey down my body, and he asks, "What's your real name, *Cecilia?*"

"I told you my real name," I croak, and he pauses, but I don't dare look away from his intense stare.

Something darkens his expression before he places the sharp tip between my breasts. A shiver takes over my body as he slides the blade to my navel and threatens with a whisper, "It wouldn't be the first time I've gutted someone alive, miss. Word of advice: don't lie." Tossing the letter opener to the floor, he spears my slit with his tongue and grips me by the hips to hold me in place.

I throw my head back with such a loud moan that it borders on a scream. I have no shame. Since I'm here, in the enemy's lair, I might as well enjoy his brand of poison. Delacroix's skilled mouth and tongue feel divine. Not that I have a lot of experience to compare. I've only had sex once, and it was over before it started. Sex has never been something I've been interested in until now. Always too busy planning my revenge on the Exiled to waste time on bodily pleasure. But now that Delacroix fucks me with his tongue—owning me in ways I never knew possible—I can't stop the embarrassing sounds escaping my parted lips. He licks and sucks and nibbles until my thighs shake. Rocking my pussy on his face, I chase my orgasm.

I'm just about to come all over his tongue when he rips himself away and plops down on the desk chair. The way he sits, with his elbows on either armrest, makes him look like a regal, bored king. "What's your name, Cecilia?"

"Wha-at?" I stutter, barely able to lift my head. My clit pulsates almost painfully. Delacroix's lips and chin are wet with my arousal, but he makes no move to wipe himself clean. Instead, he gestures to me, impatient. "What's your name? Your *real* name."

"Taylor," I insist, closing my legs.

"Did I say I was done with you yet, Miss Taylor?"

When I stare at him blankly, he lifts his stubbled chin. "Spread them. Let me look at your greedy cunt."

Christ… I knew he was a dangerous man, but I never realized what a filthy mouth he possessed. It shouldn't surprise me. A man like him at the top of the food chain has no shortage of willing pussy. I open my legs and place my bare heels on the table's edge.

As he looks down at my cunt, I fight the urge to hide. I can see the outline of his big cock through his pants, and my parched mouth waters in response.

One thing is for certain: I will never tell the others about this. I hate this man. At least, that's what I've always told myself because it's true. Though, when he licks me off his lips, I can't stop myself from whimpering.

"Tell me your real name, sweetheart, and I promise to ruin you for all other men. I can see how much you want to come. How needy you are." To prove his point, he leans in and swipes his finger through my slit. And then he sucks it clean and hums with masculine pleasure. "Sweetest pussy I've tasted."

When I remain quiet, he stands up, slides open the desk drawer, and removes a gun. My eyes widen as he puts my ankle on his shoulder and nips the skin with his teeth while trailing the gun down the length of my leg all the way to my soaked cunt. His eyes bore into me the entire time, daring me to beg him to stop. When he bites me again, I gasp at the sharp pain. "You're a brave, stubborn little slut, aren't you? Either that or a fool." He darts his tongue out and swirls it over my ankle. The gun presses against my opening, but if anything, it arouses me more. I feel empty.

There's a distinct click, and I know he's removed the safety. Fear pumps through my pounding heart.

"Your name." His deepening voice is both a seductive purr and a threat.

I push up onto my elbows. "Pull the trigger, and you'll never find out, *sir.*"

Where is this bravery coming from? Darian Delacroix is a ruthless Duke known for his savagery. He didn't become a Duke by being a good guy or an outstanding citizen. Underneath his pristine suit and expensive Rolex is a man without a heart.

His eyes lock on mine, and he bites down hard on my ankle. When he speaks, his soft lips ghost my abused skin. "Careful with that attitude, or I might want to keep you. And that, sweetheart, would be a fate far worse than death. I like to break pretty things like you."

"I'm sure you have plenty of lovers you can torment. If you don't mind, I'd like to go back to cleaning glasses." *Or run far away.*

His devastating hint of a smile is back. I almost whimper again—almost. Fuck me, this man is perfection. I watch, mesmerized, as his tanned hand and long fingers dig into my thighs, bruising my skin and leaving marks I know will last for days.

"Drop the act. We both know you're not part of the hired staff. You snuck in here to snoop around. I saw the security footage. Naughty girl. The moment I laid eyes on you, I knew I had to return here to spread you naked on my desk. Such perfection needs to be tarnished." He peppers kisses on the inside of my leg, devouring me with his eyes on his journey to my throbbing pussy.

I watch him suck on each pussy lip with such devotion that by the time he finally grazes my clit with his teeth, my entire body trembles.

Releasing a moan, my tits quiver with my next heaving inhale. It feels so good I almost forget the barrel pressing against my entrance.

"I have two options," he says, dragging his tongue from my pussy, all the way to my left breast. His warm, skillful mouth envelops my nipple, and he pulls the rosy bud away with his teeth while watching me from beneath his dark lashes. It hurts, but the pain is laced with pleasure, too. "I can either kill you now," he says, "and let it be over with, or feast on your dripping cunt until you're coming all over my face, before I put a bullet between your brows." Sucking on my tit, he palms the underside with his big hand. "Either way, you're dying tonight for your insolence."

I yelp when he flips me over and digs the gun into the back of my head, but I'm not able to process my options before he's giving me another order. "Spread your ass cheeks for me."

Shame heats my skin as I dig my fingers into each cheek. Behind me, Delacroix unbuckles his belt and pulls down his zipper one-handed. I'm insanely curious, but with the gun digging into my skull and his threats hanging in the air, there's not much I can do but keep my eyes locked on the closed door.

"What was your plan, Miss Taylor, when you snuck in? Were you going to kill me today or tomorrow during Hell Fire Night? I'm a Duke, sweetheart. You'd get yourself tortured and murdered."

He's jacking off. I can hear the sound of skin-on-skin behind me. Now, I really want to peek.

He chuckles breathily and digs the gun farther into my skull. When he grunts, I almost whimper with increasing desire. I shouldn't be this turned on by his threat and carnal urges. He's a sick monster. A devil in human skin. But my body has other ideas.

"I can't decide if I should be impressed or enraged."

"Maybe both," I bite back, glancing over my shoulder,

seeing his arm move rapidly. I face forward again as a shot of liquid desire shoots straight to my core. I've never known arousal like this, never been this consumed by it. My pussy has its own heartbeat.

Just then, warm cum covers my back hole in quick spurts, and Delacroix groans as he milks his dick. The next squirt of cum rains over my lower back, hot and sticky. I'm still holding my ass cheeks apart, obedient to a fault, as his release drips between my legs.

I slam my eyes shut when he smacks my hand away and squeezes a handful of my pale cheek.

"I like seeing this ass covered in me. Such perfection." He rains three hard slaps in quick succession before flipping me over and hauling me to my feet. Gripping my chin with his full palm, he digs the gun into my temple, forcing me to look at him. "Here's what will happen. You have ten seconds to get your shit and leave the property. And you better run far fucking away, sweetheart, because when the hour strikes ten tomorrow night, I'm going to hunt you down, fuck every hole you have to offer, and then finally kill you so fucking slowly that you'll be begging for death."

He shoves me away, pocketing the gun and collecting the letter opener off the floor.

I slump in relief, albeit on shaky legs.

He checks his Rolex before reaching for his suit jacket draped over the back of the desk chair and sliding it on. "Nine and counting."

I don't wait around. I grab my shit and bolt.

# CHAPTER TWO

## DARIAN

"Bingo," I whisper, leaning closer to the screen and zooming in on the photograph. A rare smile graces my lips when Sinclair knocks on the doorframe.

"Should I be worried?" he asks, adjusting his circular glasses. "I can't recall the last time I saw you smile." Without invitation, he enters my space and sits across from me—formidable and larger than life in his pressed suit and designer glasses. "Who died?" Interlacing his fingers on his stomach, he kicks his expensive Berluti Oxfords up on the desk and crosses his ankles. I'm too intrigued by the mysterious little intruder to be annoyed by Sinclair's apparent lack of manners or the patch of dirt on his soles. We both know he likes to push my buttons.

I turn the screen. "As soon as I saw her face, I knew she looked familiar."

"Who?" Sinclair points over his shoulder. "The help you plucked from polishing duty? I must say, I was surprised. It's not like you to act so impulsively. I was beginning to think you were a born-again virgin."

I ignore the amusement in his voice. "Does she not look familiar to you?"

Sinclair puts his feet on the floor and leans closer to study the photograph of Cecilia. "Since when are you into working-class girls? I thought they were more up Beaumont's alley."

My jaw twitches at the mention of my arch nemesis. "Since I took one look at her and realized she is Cecilia van der Meer."

That gets his attention. He straightens in his seat. "*The* Cecilia van der Meer?"

"The one and only."

"You found her."

"*She* found *us*," I reply. "Katarina van der Meer's daughter grew up."

The girl is careful—I'll give her that. She went to great lengths to cover her tracks. It took a quick phone call to my best investigator and a large sum of money to find out everything there is to know about her after she was hidden from the Exiled to keep the family's legacy and fortune safe. Seems she grew resentful of the events during a past Hell Fire Night when her father disappeared after he declined a very generous offer for his daughter and disrespected the King. Why else would she be back? If not to seek revenge?

I turn the screen and bring up a different article my investigator sent me. Sinclair frowns when I show him it. "Antichrist? What the hell is that?"

"Looks like van der Meer has teamed up with a well-known rebel group that has a history of attacking Exiled members on Hell Fire Night. There are plenty of rebel groups, but this one is particularly pesky. It's all being swept under the rug, of course." I lean back in my seat, waving a dismissive hand.

Sinclair rolls his eyes and rakes his fingers through his silver hair. "So where is she now?"

"I sent her on her way."

He blinks at me and then laughs, but it dies just as fast. "You're serious. Why did you let her go? Are you feeling okay?" He sits forward. "Do I need to call an ambulance? Did *the* Delacroix let a pretty woman go after she snuck in here to snoop around? I've never seen you think with your dick before."

"Please," I say with a scoff, "don't be ridiculous. I'm giving her a head start." Sinclair watches me slide open the drawer to retrieve a warthog mask. It's an ugly golden thing. Tossing it on the counter, I smile darkly. "Tomorrow night, I hunt."

Sinclair chuckles, placing his ankle on his knee. "I rest my case; you think with your dick. I'm proud of you. Always knew you had it in you. Though I must say, I never realized how much you like to play with fire."

I don't react to his mediocre humor. "You know as well as I do that Beaumont will show his face when he gets wind of van der Meer's daughter. Their fortune is dwindling fast, and the Exiled has been hunting for her for a long time. Beaumont will do just about anything to get in good standing with the King."

"Oh, the rivalry." He smirks. "You torpedoed their ship like the Britannic after you went to great lengths to interfere with their weapon trade late last year so you could swoop in and pick at the remains. Don't pretend you don't love watching them sink."

"I enjoy it immensely. Beaumont has been a thorn in my side since day one. Which is why I can't let him get his hands on van der Meer's daughter."

Sinclair stands up and walks over to the minibar. "This has nothing to do with a shapely pair of legs and green doe eyes or your hatred for her father?" He pours himself a tumbler of whiskey, his eyes on the task. "If you wanted to kill this woman to cut off Beaumont's last chance of resurrection within the Exiled or to avenge your family, you would've killed her without hesitation when you had the chance. Instead, you let her go. I know you, Darian. You've always liked a challenge. This petite woman has balls big enough to sneak in here to snoop around in broad daylight. Not only was it courageous, but it was also reckless. When was the last time anyone stood up to you? Your reputation precedes you. Let's not forget that she's forbidden fruit and a woman you should stay far away from if you have an ounce of survival instinct."

"What are you saying?" I ask, bored with this conversation. The chair creaks beneath my weight as I ease back and drum my fingers on the armrests.

He takes a sip of the amber liquid, appreciating the expensive alcohol at his disposal. "Beaumont might indeed try to track down this woman, but his desperate death throes do not explain why you defiled the poor thing on your desk."

I roll my eyes.

Smirking at me from behind the rim of his tumbler, he takes another small sip, letting the smoky flavor mature on his tongue before he swallows it down. "I've known you your whole life, Darian. You don't act impulsively, and you don't date women below your own tax bracket. You keep your affairs out of the public eye and refuse to take a wife. Yet this young woman was moaning loudly enough to make the gardener blush mere minutes after I left this room." His smug smile irks me. "She broke in here, ballsy as hell, which caught your interest, whether or not you're willing to admit it.

Even more so when you realized that she looked familiar. You're intrigued by this woman. Intrigued enough to betray the Exiled."

I try my hardest to ignore my eye twitch while watching him drink. Sometimes, I hate how observant he can be and how much he loves watching me squirm like a worm on a hook.

"It's okay," he says, shrugging. "We've all chased pussy."

"I'm not chasing pussy."

"No?" Placing his drink down on the bar, he saunters to my desk, retrieves the warthog mask, and inspects it. "Since you're so set on playing with fire, you should wear this when you fuck her face-first into the dirt tomorrow. Make her choke on a leaf or two. Women dig that nasty stuff."

He tosses me the mask and walks out, but not before he turns over his shoulder and winks. "Oh, pull her hair. You'll thank me later."

My eyes roll again. "It's a hunt, Sinclair. I'm killing her, not fucking her," I call out after him. Today was a blip on my radar. I won't give in to such carnal urges again. Sure, I threatened to fuck her after I chased her down, but I won't. I'm excited for the hunt. That's all. Not her taste, sweet moans, or fiery attitude.

Sinclair pops his head back inside with a mischievous smile big enough to earn him a part as Pennywise in the next adaptation of Stephen King's *IT*. "If van der Meer is still alive after Hell Fire Night, your Bugatti La Voiture is mine."

I wave him off without a second thought. "Deal. Now, find out who let her in. Someone helped her, and I want them brought as sacrifices to the party tomorrow."

He shakes his head, chuckling. "What do you take me for? A Commoner? I'm out of here. Business to attend to."

Before leaving the room, he taps the doorframe and says, “Hey, Darian?”

“Hmm?” I’m distracted, leafing through paperwork.

“I look forward to taking your Bugatti for a spin the day after tomorrow.”

I flip him off, but he’s already gone.

# CHAPTER THREE

## CECILIA

Ten of us are gathered in the Antichrist's stronghold, an old large Victorian house on the outskirts of town, which has been my home for the last couple of years.

I'm packing away the blueprints on the dining room table when Lauren sidles up beside me. "You did good. We have a much better idea of the layout."

I side-eye her as I reach for the folder of information about the King and the Dukes who make up the Exiled—all the big players. Beneath them are the Lords and Commoners.

I want the juicy steak, unlike the others who are happy going after the bottom feeders. Why take out a Commoner when I can aim a lot higher? While the King is as untouchable as the king of England, the Dukes don't have the same ironclad security detail.

"Thanks," I reply, placing the folder in the bag.

"You're hiding something," she says as she rests her hip against the coffee table.

I reach for the zipper. "Why would I be hiding something?"

Lauren watches me closely before crossing her arms and shrugging. "You've acted shifty since you got back."

I hate how perceptive she is. Always has been. We first met years ago through an online forum, and she introduced me to Greta, Keith, Carlo, and the others. That's how I found like-minded people with a vendetta against the Exiled. While we have different motivations for why we want to cause a dent in the Exiled's bulletproof armor, we have one thing in common—we've all lost someone on Hell Fire Night. Grief is our uniting force.

"I'm not acting shifty," I say, cursing the blush creeping up my neck. I've not had time to shower yet because things have been busy around here. Every time I move, I smell him on me—a hint of cardamom and tonka bean.

Lauren's gaze burns into me, and then she puts her hand on mine to stop me from assaulting the bag in my quest to zip it closed. "What really happened when you were gone?"

Why does she have to pry? I'm already suffocating with shame. What does it matter that I let one of the Dukes eat me out on his desk? I had no choice but to let it happen. Men like him…they're Dukes for a reason. No one says no to them.

*But you enjoyed it.*

I squash that voice. "Nothing happened," I say. "One of the Dukes noticed me—"

Lauren gasps, and my blush deepens. I keep my head lowered. I promised myself I wouldn't tell anyone, but Lauren can see right through me. "He brought me into his office and…"

"And what? Cecilia? What did he do?" Lauren whispers to stop the others from overhearing.

"We…" I gesticulate impatiently, wishing for her to figure it out by herself so I don't have to spell it out for her. It's already awkward enough. "You know…"

Her eyes grow as wide as saucers, and her mouth pops open. Two long seconds pass before she blurts, "No… You didn't." A strangled laugh fights its way through her vocal cords.

I finally get the bag zipped up. Thank fuck for the small wins. "I wasn't in a position to say no."

"So you did what?" She follows me out of the room. "You had sex with him? A Duke? The Enemy?"

We stop in the hallway, waiting for two guys to walk past. "What was I going to do? Turn him down and risk blowing my cover?"

"You liked it." A wide smile spreads across her lips, but then it dies. "That was dangerous, Cecilia. He could have killed you on the spot."

"Well, he didn't. I'm not dead." Turning on my heel, I ascend the staircase. Lauren is hot on my heels. I won't shake her now that she's curious.

"What if you were followed here?"

"I didn't blow our cover."

"Are you sure?"

No, I'm not. Delacroix knew I snuck in, and he was perceptive enough to call me out on my lie when I told him my name. Not even my friends know who I am, and it will stay that way. My parents would turn in their graves if they saw me now, but I'm done spending my life hiding to protect my father's fortune. I don't care about my family's bloodline or their old money. I care about revenge. About doing as much damage as I can to the secret society. No one should have to feel the grief I've experienced. My father's disappearance was swept under the carpet as if he never existed. Never mattered. It's bullshit. The killer is still out there, breathing.

It ends now.

I pause on the top step. "I'm sure. Don't worry. I know how to cover my tracks, Lauren."

She looks unconvinced as she watches me stride to my bedroom and shut myself inside. Once the door is locked, I collect my laptop from the desk and make myself comfortable on the bed. Light rain smatters against the window while the laptop powers up. Restless, I tap my coffin nail against the touchpad.

Memories of Delacroix's heated eyes invade my thoughts. Pesky, unwelcome thoughts that I wish I could incinerate. I still remember the sensation of his sharp stubble against my bare thighs, which makes me tingle in places I shouldn't. How can my body betray me like this? It pisses me off. I want him dead, his eyes plucked from his skull. So why am I recalling how it felt when he came all over my ass and back? The sounds he made. And how—despite his threat to kill me—I welcomed his brutality and got off on it. This is one of the men responsible for my father's disappearance. For all I know, he could be *the* one behind the attack.

I shake off my racing thoughts. It doesn't matter. The Exiled needs eliminating. If we kill them all, we will eventually catch my father's murderer.

My gaze drifts to the rivulets of rain on the glass, but it's too dark to see outside. Even so, I can't shake the feeling of being watched. A packet of sour laces is wedged between two empty coffee mugs on the bedside. I pick it up, slide out a lace, and bite off a large piece. *Christ, that's why the packet has the word 'sour' written in capital letters on the front.* I always forget. Do I even like these sweets? Yes, I do, but I also don't. Much like my sexual encounter with Darian Delacroix today. I liked his tongue on my pussy, yet I also hated every minute of it.

I open the web browser and type in his name. Pictures

flood the screen. He even has his own Wikipedia page. Pretentious asshole. It almost hurts to suppress my eye roll, so I don't even try.

There are lots of photographs of him alongside important society members. Mustached men in expensive suits and their dolled-up-to-the-nines wives. He's especially close to that womanizer Nathaniel Sinclair, whom I saw earlier today. Further research shows they went to Harvard together. Interesting. Something else that's interesting—though it absolutely shouldn't be—is the fact that I can't find pictures of Delacroix with other women. I don't know why my heart does a weird little flip. There's no reason for it.

Closing the lid on my laptop, I bend over the side of the bed to retrieve the duffel bag from underneath. I haul it onto the comforter and unzip it to reveal an arsenal of weapons. Guns and knives of all shapes and sizes.

There's a knock, and Keith enters, shutting the door behind him. He glances at the bag on my bed and the gun in my hand, and then he slides his hands into his pockets. Keith is in his mid-fifties, with brown, silvery hair on the longer side—he's forever running a hand through his locks to keep them off his forehead—and hazel eyes laced with the guilt he can't shake after losing his younger brother to Hell Fire Night two decades ago. We rarely talk about our personal lives, so I don't know him that well. From the little I can gather, he grew up with a strong sense of responsibility for his brother, and it broke something inside him when he failed to protect him. Keith is one of the few founding members who fought in previous Hell Fire Nights. They started this rebel group and then welcomed me years later with open arms when I sought them out online.

"How do you feel about tomorrow?" he asks, crossing the room and taking a seat at the edge of my bed.

I study the gun in my hand, wondering if Lauren ratted me out. I doubt it. Keith would be fuming if he knew what happened in that office. "As ready as I'll ever be."

He studies me for a moment and then sighs. "We've never attacked the nest directly."

The "nest" is the word we use for the rented cottage where the party will take place. It's mandatory for the Exiled members to attend. In other words, it's a nest, and we plan to smoke it out. I've always believed in hitting them where it hurts. Go straight to the source. It's ballsy enough that they won't see it coming because they think they're safe in their little luxury cottage with the best security money can buy while they destroy families and futures.

I gnash my teeth. Keith notices and removes the gun from my hands. Once it's zipped back inside the bag, he sits so that he's facing me on the bed. "I'll tell you what I've told the others—you can back out. A lot of people will die tomorrow. Our own men included. No one will blame you if you change your mind."

"I'm not backing out."

I've waited too fucking long for this.

He stares at me for a moment. "We're doing something we've never done before. Attacking the nest is not only reckless, it's a suicide mission. Once we enter that building, we're not getting out alive. You have to be one hundred percent certain before you come with us tomorrow."

"I'm certain." There's a bite to my tone, and he responds with a tightened jaw. Keith took a shine to me early on. Shame he's like a father figure and thirty years older than me, or I might have explored my sexuality before sending myself into an early grave. "I want revenge as much as you do," I continue. "It's all I can think about."

"I know." He doesn't sound happy. "The anger we feel…

it's poison. A miserable existence. We only feel alive again for ten hours every five years when we can water the seeds of our anger. If I have learned one thing, the relief I feel when I kill one of those entitled motherfuckers is short-lived. Like scratching an itch. But it returns sooner or later, and I'm tired of scratching."

In the ambient bedside light, his eyes gleam with a rare show of emotion. "I know what I'm walking into tomorrow. I'm fine with it. I've spent the last twenty-five years angry, but you're young, Cecilia. You have your whole life ahead of you. There's still hope for you."

"My family is dead because of them. Trust me, there's no hope for me."

He reaches out and puts his hand on top of mine. No more words are spoken. With a squeeze, he stands up and walks out.

"Hey, Keith," I call out as he's about to exit through the doorway. When he turns, I lift my shoulders. "Tomorrow, we get our revenge."

He smiles weakly. "Goodnight, Cecilia. Get some rest."

---

I DON'T SLEEP. I doubt any of us do. What we've waited and planned for is only hours away. I'd lie if I said I'm not nervous, because I am. I want to succeed—I really do—but the odds are stacked against us. Despite this, I knew the risks when I suggested we attack the heart of the Exiled. It's our best shot. Maybe it's our *only* shot. For one night, the members gather beneath the same roof for the party of the quinquennial, bringing offerings, like some sacramental ritual, to the gods of unmeasured wealth and power. It's not an opportunity that comes around often, so we need to be there instead of intercepting members on their way to the party. We need to be at the heart of it, and if we're lucky, the King might show.

It's my turn to get tattooed, so I take a seat at the kitchen table. Lauren, an undergrad nurse, is in charge of the procedure. It's not something I'm excited about, but we can't gain entry to the property without a barcode tattoo.

Lauren is swabbing my wrist when Carlo hands us all our masks to wear tonight. Mine is a cougar. I turn it over in my hand, wondering briefly what Delacroix plans to wear. The Dukes will be easy to spot with their gold masks. Ours are black—the color of Commoners—to make us blend easier.

"Not gonna lie, this will hurt like a bitch," Lauren says. A sharp pain follows, and I suck in a breath. Luckily, it's a quick procedure. She wipes away the excess ink and then pats me on the shoulder, which is my cue that she's done.

Not all of us are going to the nest tonight. Most of the others are hunting in the traditional sense by attacking members on their way to the event when they're at their weakest. Months of planning and staking out members have brought us to tonight. Everyone knows their role. We're as prepared as we'll ever be.

After tonight, the lucky few survivors will start the process again in preparation for the next Hell Fire Night.

My mood darkens when I allow doubts to sneak in. A part of me knows we're not the first rebels to attack the Exiled on Hell Fire Night, and we won't be the last. This event has historical roots. It's tradition and a display of wealth, power, and influence. Tonight is when they flaunt their power.

*Look what we can do. We can murder your entire bloodline for shits and giggles and make the evidence disappear. We're above the law.*

Returning to my room, I change into the black silk

evening gown I bought for this event. It has a slit that stops mid-thigh—perfect for grabbing my weapons in a hurry—and a plunging neckline. I'll regret my six-inch heels later, but the effect isn't lost on me as I slide my feet into them now. One glance in the mirror reveals a young heiress to one of the largest fortunes in the country. I belong in their world as much as the other Dukes. We're equals where wealth is concerned, and if they hadn't killed my parents, I would've been a member of the Exiled. Promised to one of their sons.

I'm torn from my thoughts when Lauren whistles in the doorway. She's dressed to the nines, too, in an emerald gown with a mermaid skirt. "You look smoking hot."

I turn away from the mirror and unzip the bag of weapons on the bed. "We need to blend in tonight. Unless we dress like royalty, we won't make it through security."

Lauren stays silent while I strap knives to my thighs. I'm not going down without a fight. The Exiled won't know what hit them. "Are you…worried about tonight?" Lauren asks, pushing off the doorway, heels clicking on the floor.

"No," I reply, checking the safety on my gun. "Greta and Keith have prepared us well. We know what we're doing."

"I've been thinking," she says as she comes to stand beside me. "What if the Duke you seduced comes after you tonight?"

"I know he will. He told me as much."

Her eyes saucer, but I wave her off and reach into the bag to grab her a weapon. She accepts it and parts the slit in her emerald skirt to put the gun in the holster. "Don't worry," I reassure. "He doesn't know we're attacking their cottage tonight, which means he won't be there if he was serious about hunting me."

A slow, knowing smile tugs on her mauve lips. "Mr. Delacroix will be chasing shadows."

# CHAPTER FOUR

DARIAN

Live music streams from the main room, but it's all pretentious to me. Orgies, live acrobatics, and a fight club. Sacrificed humans suspended from the roof and bled into tiered wine goblets. Unnecessarily messy and unhygienic, if you ask me. I even saw a room where naked people were covered in body paint.

A shudder runs through me at the mere thought of messing up my freshly pressed Italian suit. No, thank you.

I turn away from the large window overlooking the trees outside and the cobblestone path leading to the entrance. My quick scan of the security footage on the computer screen reveals nothing out of the ordinary. A helpless woman is being nailed to the wall by a group of masked Lords, another group of people are engaged in an orgy on the top floor in plain sight of anyone walking past, and Elijah—Sinclair's son—is pressing the thumbprint scanner to unlock the torture room on the second floor. I eye his offering—a young lady unlucky enough to have caught the eye of Sinclair's sadistic offspring. I don't feel sorry for her because that would require empathy, and my black heart has no room for such pesky things as emotions.

I'm circulating through the numerous security cameras when the door opens, and Sinclair walks in, nursing a tumbler of whiskey. "I always knew you were a bore," he says, "but even back in our Harvard days, you used to be more fun than this. Have you killed anyone tonight?"

I ignore him, clicking buttons. Sinclair is undeterred. Getting on my nerves is one of his favorite pastimes.

He parks his ass on my desk, disrupting my perfectly aligned pencils, and then because he can't help himself, he lifts one of the spheres on my Newton's cradle and releases it. I don't even know why the fucking thing is there. The clinking sound reminds me of Captain Hook whenever he hears a clock ticking. That's me now. Fighting an eye twitch while Sinclair grins like the devil.

"You didn't bring an offering." He tuts. "The King will be displeased. You know I like you, Darian, but even I might have to bring the popcorn when he chops you into pieces for showing such contempt for our precious traditions."

With a snort, I stop the pendulum from swinging. Ah! Blissful silence. Well, except for the ruckus outside my office. "I won't lower myself to such"—I wave a hand at the door and the riot outside—"carnal urges."

"Carnal urges?" He chuckles, sipping his whiskey.

"Besides," I say, zooming in on the screen and searching the crowd of newcomers, "I have brought an offering."

My statement sparks Sinclair's curiosity. "You have? Who? Don't tell me you have some poor, unsuspecting local tied up in your trunk like last time. Remember? You considered yourself above all this, so you kept the poor girl in there for hours until you had no choice but to present her or risk pissing off the King. You basically tossed her at his feet and told her to gnaw off her own fingers or die." Shaking his head, he laughs. "Underneath your crease-free suits, obsessive desire to remain in control, and inability to smile, is a pure-bred psychopath."

"Done with the dramatics yet?" I ask, checking the security camera in the next room. She's around somewhere. The security intel I put on her yesterday told me she was en route here, which was such a pleasant surprise after I was preparing to go through the effort of hunting her down myself. "And no, she's not tied up in the car." As I turn the screen, Sinclair studies it, and I point to a woman in an animal mask in the corner of the room. "Looks like my little cougar is about to start a war."

I better intercept before she opens fire on the Exiled members and gets herself killed. No one lays a finger on her except for me. No one else gets to watch the life drain out of her big eyes.

"Is that Miss van der Meer? Wow. I don't know…" Sinclair says, not even attempting to tame the amusement in his voice. "Seems a little stalkerish, don't you think? The unattainable Darian Delacroix gives in to his *carnal urges* once, and now she's back for seconds." The ice clinks in his tumbler when he inhales the last of the whiskey. "You must give good head if she's willing to traipse into the lions' den. I'm proud of you." He claps my shoulder. "She's even gone to great lengths to blend in. Who's the inside spy that provided her with member masks? I bet she even has a barcode tattoo on her wrist to gain entry."

I'm smirking, unable to tear my eyes from the screen as she flips her blonde locks and scans the crowd. "We're about to find out. Now, if you excuse me." I straighten up and smooth my tie before opening the drawer and removing my warthog mask. My pulse heightens seeing it.

Ever since I laid eyes on van der Meer sneaking around the cottage—looking as inconspicuous as a drunk pirate in a jewelry store—I've salivated for the hunt, which is a first. Sinclair is right—in previous Hell Fire Nights, I've simply plucked someone off the street, tied them up, and left them in the trunk until it was time to present them to the King or whoever else cared enough. The offerings are an inconvenience, but tradition requires us to bring one, so I have no choice but to comply.

Tonight is different. The King must not under any circumstances find out who Cecilia is. I'll have to present her to my most loyal and trusted friends amongst the Dukes—members I know won't blabber.

A sliver of excitement zaps through me at the security footage. I bet my CEO position that van der Meer's creamy thighs beneath that silk skirt sport more weapons than the local dealer's shop. My dick sure likes that thought.

I glance down at my growing bulge, confused by my reproductive organs' eagerness to engage in procreation. Sex is yet another inconvenience and a weakness. I put up with my secretary, Miss Sanders, for precisely fifteen minutes on Monday mornings at 10 a.m. when she sidles in on her knees between me and the desk to service my needs. But even then, I curse my body for requiring such a release. So color me intrigued when Miss van der Meer waltzed into my territory with no care in the world for her own safety.

She's a dangerous vixen who needs to be eliminated. I, Darian Delacroix, refuse to drop my guard for women. Yesterday's incident was a temporary lapse of sanity, but it won't happen again. I'll eliminate the threat before the Exiled finds her.

"Are you staring at your dick?" Sinclair's smooth

whiskey voice drags me back from the black hole that seems to be my racing thoughts.

Flustered, I clear my throat, while my eldest friend snickers into his tumbler. He tips it back and proceeds to crunch on the ice.

*He really is a wild boar in a jungle.* With a shake of my head, I reach for my suit jacket on the back of my chair and then slide it on. "Where's your offering?"

Sinclair winks. "Don't you worry, my friend. She's well taken care of."

"You wouldn't know how to look after a houseplant." I sail past him, sliding my mask over my face and typing a quick command to my security.

***Darian Delacroix:*** *Bring them in. Not a scratch. Leave Miss van der Meer.*

"Remember what I said about pulling her hair when you fuck her," Sinclair calls out behind me when I open the door. He puts the tumbler on the desk. "You might as well give me the keys to your Bugatti now."

Sinclair pulls on his own mask and follows me out of the room. I ignore his persistent presence as I pause on the second-floor balcony overlooking the open space below. I spot her immediately, surveying the crowd and checking out her first targets. I like that she's not irrational. She calculates and takes her sweet time.

"She's a stunner," Sinclair says beside me. "No wonder why you shoved Jesus aside to let your dick take the steering wheel yesterday. You better bring her in before the others find out she's here and inform the King."

I shoo him away, making him laugh as he strolls off on the hunt for someone to beat to death with his bare fists. Unlike me, he doesn't mind blood splatter on his suit.

I refocus on the stunning blonde with sharp eyes taking in her surroundings. Her black dress hugs every curve.

A quick sweep of the crowd confirms my suspicions; I'm not the only male in the room who undresses her with their eyes.

An irrational spike of possessiveness courses through me. I'm white knuckling the banister when a masked man in a suit walks past behind me, dragging a crying, naked woman by her hair.

Stepping back, I merge effortlessly with the shadows, watching him haul her up and throw her over the banister. Screams erupt below as she slams into the gyrating crowds, and then he walks past me in a black mask.

A Commoner.

I'm not even surprised. Members that far down in the ranks often behave like wild animals.

Our eyes meet, and he inclines his head as a sign of respect. I sneer, disgusted with the lack of self-control he showcased when he threw that woman over the banister. While it's a night where lawlessness is expected and even celebrated, it brings forth the weak.

I whistle for him to stop, and he draws to a halt, glancing over his shoulder. I gesture impatiently, and the moment he turns, I remove the gun from my inside pocket and plant a bullet in his heart. He drops like a sack of potatoes, clutching his bleeding chest, crimson pouring from between his fingers.

I pocket the gun and then walk past, cursing the single blood fleck on my cuff, though my annoyance doesn't last long because halfway down the winding staircase, I catch sight of her again. She's ethereally beautiful and a regal queen in her own right. Her mother was a vision, but Cecilia van der Meer is more than beautiful. It would be an insult to call her something so trivial. Cecilia is a weapon to bring down men like myself, and my own weakness, where she is concerned, must be destroyed.

# CHAPTER FIVE

## CECILIA

Lauren fidgets beside me while we scout the crowds for targets. We only get a very short window to create as much damage as possible, so we need to ensure we're in a prime location before we open fire on the members. Carlo and Keith disappeared into the crowds earlier.

It was surprisingly easy to get in. Once the barcode tattoos had been scanned, we were let through and handed a glass of champagne upon entering.

*Champagne that probably costs more than I can even imagine.* While I'm tempted to sip it, I don't want to accept anything gifted here. This organization, this event, is behind my parents' deaths.

I'm discreetly pouring the drink into a large plant when warmth envelops my back, and a deep baritone speaks into my ear, "Is my champagne not to your liking, Miss van der Meer?"

*That voice.*

My blood freezes to ice at the mention of my real name. How did he find out? I straighten up, pretending I'm not quaking on the inside. "Your champagne? It's funded by your little boys' club, is it not?"

As I turn around, I am confronted by his expensive pressed suit, a warthog mask that covers half his face, and piercing frosty eyes. His cardamom and tonka bean scent invades more than just my senses when his lips pull to the side in a dirty smirk that's all sex.

He takes the flute from my hand and passes it to a waiter without breaking eye contact. "The champagne was my contribution to tonight's event. I had it imported directly from France. The champagne you used to water the plant costs 1.6 million dollars per bottle."

"So you have a lot of money. Impressive." I let my gaze wander, but I'm shaking on the inside.

"Is that sarcasm?"

When I pin him with my eyes, I'm struck by the intensity in his. "Wow. Not only are you rich, but you're smart too."

"What can I say? I'm a catch."

Light laughter bubbles up from my chest before I can stop it. I try to push past him, but he steps in my way, towering over me with his six-foot-three frame and deadly smirk. "Bachelor of the year, several years running."

"Good for you." This is my opportunity to reach for my knife and stab him, so why am I hesitating?

"What I can't figure out"—he fingers a strand of my hair, causing my breath to catch—"is why you're back, Miss van der Meer. This is a dangerous place for an orphaned heiress like yourself."

The mention of my deceased parents has years of suppressed anger rushing to the surface. I push on his chest, but he's as immovable as a mountain. When he still doesn't shift, I part the slit in my dress and grab my gun, but I'm stopped by his hand on my wrist. Surprised, I glance up.

"Allow me," he says, sliding the gun from the holster strapped to my thigh. My throat dries up at his sensual, slow touch. Who knew retrieving a loaded weapon from a holster could be so sexual? Delacroix takes his time removing it, brushing his fingers up the inside of my thigh, and I swallow hard, eyes locked on his smirking mouth. I never knew teeth could be sexy, but those sharp incisors look threatening in the dim light.

The moment his fingers curl around the gun, I lift my eyes to his and fight a shiver. Delacroix is fucking me with his dark gaze.

The weapon slides from the holster slowly, and he uses the gun to brush a lock of hair away from my brow and then places it in my hand. My heart pounds hard as he guides the barrel to his chest, right over his heart.

Leaning in close, he whispers against the corner of my mouth. "Put a bullet in my heart, Miss van der Meer. It would be a mercy, for you have me under your spell."

*Who talks like that? What is he? A duke from Shakespearean times?* His spicy scent drugs me as much as his warm breath against my parted lips. He places a kiss at the corner, and my heart threatens to break free when his prickly beard brushes against my chin.

*Christ...* I gulp, my knees growing weak. We stare at each other, suspended in a bubble of sexual tension and something else. Something unspoken and dark. In my mind's eye, he slams his sinful lips to mine, kissing me senselessly while stealing the breath from my lungs with strokes of his tongue. In my mind's eye, I pull the trigger and clutch his blood-soaked shirt to keep his knees from buckling from beneath him. In my mind's eye, he bleeds out in front of me.

A commotion startles me from my haze, and I look behind him to see Keith open fire on the crowd. Piercing screams and chaos erupt as people scatter. It happens in slow motion and reminds me of fireworks.

Delacroix shields me with his body, forcing me behind the large plant pot. He exudes calm as he aims and shoots three times.

Keith collapses to the marble floor, clutching his bleeding hand, while men dressed in sharp uniforms storm the room to haul him away.

I try to rush past Delacroix, but he digs the gun into my forehead and forces me deeper into the shadows until we're shielded by the plant.

"You're not going anywhere." His arctic eyes deepen in color as he plants his free hand over my mouth. The cool wall is at my back. There's no escape. I try to reach for one of the knives strapped to my skin, but he rams his leg between my thighs, and the pressure against my clit has a whimper brushing against his big palm.

"Your friend made a mockery of my hospitality tonight, Miss van der Meer. You see, I knew you were heading here before you even stepped out of the Antichrist's stronghold." When my eyes widen, he tightens his grip on my mouth and grinds his thigh against my damp lace panties. "I knew your plans, sweetheart. I knew and still let you and your friends enter these premises unharmed."

It dawns on me then that I brought my friends to their deaths. What happens next is my fault. We were naïve and thought we stood a chance at taking the Exiled by surprise—and it would have been worth the sacrifice if I hadn't foiled our plans by catching the eye of a monster. As I drown in his bottomless ocean, I know he'll never let me go.

"Now," he whispers, dragging his thigh across my damp slit, "what am I to do with you, little troublemaker? Or are you a thrill seeker?" His eyes burn into me. "You seem to enjoy danger. Here's the thing: danger comes with a hefty price."

If he didn't keep his hand firmly clamped over my mouth, I would tell him to fuck off. Since that's not an option, I settle for letting my eyes speak for me instead. Judging by his dark chuckle, the fury amuses him. Those sharp canines reappear, gleaming in the shadows. His hint of a smile is breathtaking.

An exhale escapes through my nostrils, and I whimper, a puddle at his feet. Noticing, he shifts his hand from my mouth to my throat and wraps his long fingers around me, seductive and threatening. My life is in his hands. As he squeezes, I gasp, trapped between his hard body and the wall, pinned like a butterfly by the reaper.

"Such a delicate little thing," he murmurs, eyes on his hand around my throat. "So breakable." I feel him caress my pulse point, my skin burning beneath his corrupt touch. He applies pressure, and my clit pulses almost painfully. Delacroix is a weapon. A deadly hurricane. A firestorm.

Darkness invades the edges of my vision as I claw at his wrists, gasping for a sliver of breath.

Just as fast, his touch disappears, and he pulls me away from the door, guiding me through the crowd with a possessive hand on the small of my back. There's no point fighting him. I'd be dead before I could reach for a weapon. Besides, my advantage of surprise is gone. The truth is, I never had it. Delacroix knew I was here all along. He was never chasing shadows. No, he waited for his prey to walk willingly into his trap before he showed his cards.

His fingers burn the small of my back as we walk up the winding staircase to the second floor. He moves like a king—a man who commands power and respect.

Commoners and Lords lower their heads as we pass, but the man at my side ignores them, his attention on me. He's not looking in my direction, but I know he's aware of my every inhale.

We enter an office, a vast space with a desk and a separate seating area. Large wing-backed chairs face an impressive fireplace with intricate carvings. Not an item is out of place. Music pulses through the walls, disturbed by voracious laughter and the occasional fearful scream.

I can't look away from my friends near the window, each flanked by a massive security guard. Keith's injured hand is bleeding profusely, and so is his kneecap. There's duct tape on his lips, and his arms are tied behind him. He's staring straight ahead, refusing to make eye contact with anyone. Delacroix is an excellent shot, so it's not lost on me that he kept Keith alive. But why? He's not capable of mercy.

Carlo bleeds from a cut on his lip, his right eye swollen shut. He's trying to remain brave, but every time the security guard shifts behind him—however slight—he flinches. Lauren is the only one crying, her loud sobs adding to the tension.

Delacroix crouches in front of me and trails his warm fingers from my ankle to my thigh, pausing to palm the back of my knee and bring it to his lips. His touch is gentle, like a lover, but he can't fool me. There's a darkness within him that can't be leashed or tamed. He's unpredictable and dangerous.

He lowers my knee and relieves me of every weapon strapped to my legs except for one—a butterfly knife strapped to the inside of my thigh.

Our eyes meet as he rises and hands the weapons to a masked Disciple who whisks off just as fast. It's a test, I realize, as he saunters to the bar and proceeds to remove his mask and pour himself a glass of bourbon. He's curious to see what I'll do. Am I gutsy enough to use my weapon?

The liquid splashes against the sides as I try to catch

Keith's gaze, but his jaw clenches. They must wonder why I'm not tied up like them, with a burly guard behind me. I ask the same thing. My fingers itch to grab the knife and hurl it at Delacroix—God knows my aim would ring true; I've practiced long enough. But it would be foolish. Delacroix would punish not only me, but my friends.

The minutes tick by while he types on his phone and sips his expensive bourbon without glancing in my direction. It's another mind game. I try not to fidget.

*Throw the knife.*

*Do it.*

"These are your friends, are they not, Miss van der Meer?" He pockets his phone and swirls the tumbler, watching me from beneath his dark lashes. Taking a long sip, he says, "I'm curious. Do they know who you are?" His steps carry him closer until his mysterious scent swirls around me like the electric summer air before a storm. I greedily fill my lungs with his poison. He's close enough now that his heat warms me through his dress shirt. I smell the bourbon on his breath when he tips my chin up with his fingers.

I jerk away, but he tightens his grip, touching me like I'm already his. "Do they know you're one of us?"

"I'll never be one of you," I hiss.

He falters then with his fingers on my jaw. I stand my ground, allowing him to remove my mask. A disciple materializes and takes it. Delacroix keeps his sole attention on me, skimming his thumb over the swell of my bottom lip. Everything he does is a sensual act—from how he touches me, looks at me with those frosty eyes, or allows his bourbon-scented breath to dance across my lips—but I'm not stupid. His touch could force pleasure or pain. It could give life or snuff it out.

"Wrong," he says, sounding so self-assured I want to

punch him square in the nose. "You're already one of us." Cupping my chin, he touches me with reverence, whispering secrets with his gaze. "You can spit fire at me all you want with those big eyes, but it doesn't change who you are, sweetheart."

I suck in a breath when he releases my chin. His powerful shoulders shift beneath his dress shirt while he circles me. Every time he walks behind me, the hairs on my neck stand on edge. Delacroix seems even bigger. I feel so small next to him, and it's both exhilarating and infuriating.

As he sizes me up like a predator, I stand my ground with my chin tilted high, refusing to look weak. A man like Delacroix could smell it a mile away if I lowered my guard. My pride is my greatest weapon. Surely, I must have cards to play, or why are my friends and I alive? He could have killed us downstairs to make an example out of us, but I have something he wants. A weapon I can yield. But what? I'm glancing in my friends' direction when the door opens and a group of men enters. Three of whom wear gold masks. They line up against the back wall with their hands clasped in front of them.

*Dukes.*

I've heard about this. Witnesses. They're here to witness Delacroix present his offering.

A cold sliver of panic coils my insides. This is bad news. I pause when I spot the last man in the procession. Father Faulkner. So the rumors are true—his pockets are full of corrupt money. Cheeks flushed with anger, my chest tightens. This is the same priest who married my parents.

Sweat beads on his forehead as he greets Delacroix, casting a few worried glances toward my friends, looking anxious. I reach for the knife in my slit, ready to bulls-eye him between the brows.

Delacroix turns in my direction. "Miss van der Meer."

I straighten, the skirt falling back into place.

"No need to look so worried. These gentlemen are my closest allies. I'd trust them with my life. You can rest assured that the truth won't leave this room. You have my word." He sweeps his hand toward my friends. "You were a good girl and brought my offerings to the party."

*No, no, no.*

Three heads swivel in my direction. I can't even look at my friends.

"That's not... I didn't—"

Delacroix sucks out the oxygen in the air as he walks up to me and cups my chin. He pierces me with his eyes, then whispers so only I can hear, "You're not in a position to fight me, miss. It's in your best interest to accept your defeat with grace. Your friends' lives rely on your cooperation. Defy me, and I kill them without hesitation. You don't want their blood on your hands, sweetheart. Do you?"

I set my jaw. Fuck him if he thinks I'll roll over and let my friends think I betrayed them, but then… What other choice do I have?

Delacroix's smirk grows. "Good girl."

I jerk my chin away as he steps around me and slides my hair away from my neck in a possessive touch I feel down to my toes. Everything about him is calculative. He takes his sweet time, eyeing my friends from behind me before leaning down to press a hot kiss against the curve of my neck.

I shiver at the feel of his lips and clench my hands. Why does his touch have to feel so nice? Why is the threat behind it so delicious?

He straightens up and walks away, leaving me in the wake of his enticing cologne and tingling kiss on my neck. With his hands behind his back, he saunters to my friends, and Lauren yelps when he grabs her chin, tilting her face left to right, inspecting her like cattle at a market. I want to hurt Delacroix, but all I have are my words, so I hiss, "Don't touch her."

Ignoring me, he moves down the line until he stops in front of Keith. "You must be the leader."

Keith meets his disgusted yet lazy gaze head-on, his nostrils flaring as he tries to reign in his emotions.

"That wasn't a smart move you pulled."

Keith spits at him.

Gasps ring out around the room, but the Dukes at my back remain deadly silent. My heart beats so hard I struggle to breathe. Delacroix accepts a tissue handed to him by one of the Lords and wipes his shirt clean of spittle while chill-inducing screams filter through the walls, and then he hands it to the Disciple, who bows before retreating into the background. "I believe you're familiar with our traditions, Mr. Turnbull," he says, proving that he's done his research. Proving that he made true to his promise to hunt me. "I should kill you for your insolence alone, but I respect tradition, so you'll get to choose." He pauses for effect. "Join the Exiled or die."

Keith turns red with fury. "I will never join the Exiled."

"Very well," Delacroix says, dismissive, as he turns away and inclines his chin to one of the Dukes behind me. "Mr. Vanderbilt. He's all yours."

The man behind me steps forward, and the guard behind Keith shoves him to make him move. I rush to Delacroix. "What are they doing? Where are they taking him?" Frantic, I try to get to Keith, but Delacroix blocks my path. "Mr. Vanderbilt has offered a hefty sum for your friend."

"Paid you?" I try to move past him again. They're nearly at the door. "Keith!" I shout.

Delacroix leans in close. "Mr. Vanderbilt has a penchant

for torture. He'll cut your friend into tiny pieces while he's still alive and drag his death out for hours, maybe even days."

"Days? But Hell Fire Night—"

"Mr. Vanderbilt is one of the richest men on the planet. His bank account ensures he'll never see the inside of a prison cell."

With my adrenaline pumping, I fling myself at Delacroix in my bid to get past, but he grips my shoulders and hauls me back, proving yet again how much stronger he is than me. "You can stop this, Miss van der Meer."

Strands of wild hair tickle my lips as I breathe harshly. He's still holding me by the shoulders while I flick my eyes between his, trying to make sense of this horror in my panicked state. "What do you mean?"

"I've seen Mr. Vanderbilt's demon in action. There's no worse death. But you"—he sets me on my feet and brushes my hair away from my brow—"can give him a fast, dignified death."

Keith roars in the background as he wrestles with the guard. Another one joins in, and the sound of his furious shouts breaks something inside me.

"Okay," I hear myself whispering. "I'll do it."

Warm fingers caress my cheek. Delacroix looks like the devil himself. He smiles slowly, soaking in his moment of victory, and then he glides his eyes past me as he calls out, "Mr. Vanderbilt. You can keep your money."

I can't look him in the eye anymore. He's playing a sadistic game, and I want no part in it, yet I know it's Hell Fire Night. Traditions must be honored. There's no room for mercy. If an Offering chooses death over a chance to join the Exiled, no amount of begging on my end can change the outcome. Keith has made his choice.

Mr. Vanderbilt grumbles but lets the guards drag Keith

deeper into the room. They toss him at my feet. The guard delivers a hard kick to his side, and I wince. All the while, Delacroix studies me closely with that small, sadistic smirk of his.

"Van der Meer has offered you a swift death," he explains. He must see the question in Keith's enraged eyes, because he continues. "Her real name is Cecilia van der Meer, daughter of Charles van der Meer. The sole heir to one of the largest fortunes in the country. She's also one of the youngest Dukes in the Exiled now that her parents are out of the way. Though she's not yet ready to admit she was born one." He winks. "Judging by your surprise, she failed to divulge such important information. Don't worry. Many have tried to find her." Turning, he captures me with his cold gaze. "None have been successful. Until now."

I hold my breath when he enters my personal space and says loud enough for everyone to hear, "Kill him." Then he's gone, and I'm left staring at Keith. When he looks up at me, I want to drown in my own shame. I didn't lie to him—I just didn't tell him the truth of who I am, either. I never told a soul. They wouldn't have looked at me the same if they knew I was a Duke's daughter. A fugitive on the run from the Exiled.

Lifting my head, I scan the gathered members. Empty eyes peer back at me from behind gold and black masks. Gunshots ring out outside the room, but I barely flinch at the sudden sound. Tonight is the devil's night. Death and mayhem are his love language.

"Miss van der Meer," Delacroix warns from somewhere behind me. "Last chance."

Mr. Vanderbilt is watching me from his spot near the doorway. He's a round old man with a beer gut and a sweaty, bald head. His beady eyes salivate at the thought of torturing my friend to death. It's that thought that finally kicks me into action. I won't get a second chance. Death is the only way out.

"Cecilia," Keith says, momentarily drawing my attention away from the slit in my dress. "It's okay."

Two words of forgiveness. A mercy I don't deserve.

In a swift move, I pull the sharp knife from the holster and slice his throat. It's an out-of-body experience. Over in seconds. Blood gushes from the gaping wound.

Lauren is screaming behind me, but I barely hear it above the thumping in my ears. Keith gurgles, a river of crimson pooling around my feet, growing larger by the second. I step back out of instinct.

Keith topples over, and silence falls in the room before Lauren breaks it with another anguished, heart-wrenching sob. My chin wobbles, but I manage to keep the tears at bay, even as the bloodied knife trembles in my hand.

Delacroix's voice sweeps over my skin like a heated breath. "Now, Carlo. Your turn. Join the Exiled or die?"

# CHAPTER SIX

DARIAN

Miss van der Meer is staring down at the still-bleeding corpse on the ground. The knife in her hand clatters to the floor, and she takes yet another step back. I was insanely curious to see if she had the guts, but I knew deep down that she did. Call it an inkling. A woman like her needs a backbone to claw her way back into our world. And here she is, making her daddy proud.

"Impressive," I drawl, glancing over my shoulder. "You barely flinched."

Her eyes snap up. "Shut up," she snarls. "You sick bastard."

"Take him away," I order the Lords, then return my attention to Carlo. Unlike his stoic leader, the man is shaking in his boots. Pathetic. He would be as useless to the Exiled as a wet rag, but tradition requires offerings. "What's it going to be?"

He watches Keith's corpse get dragged out of the room, leaving a mess behind for the cleaners to sort out. They know the drill—remove the blood stains from the wooden flooring or get fired. I arch a brow when he looks at me again.

"I'll join," he says, trembling.

"Tsk. Tsk." I clasp my hands behind my back and stroll casually over to Cecilia. "Not so fast. How familiar are you with our traditions?"

Carlo looks around the room for help, confused.

"You've done a poor job of preparing him, Miss van der Meer," I whisper in her ear on my way past, and then I slowly walk back over to Carlo. "You have to prove yourself worthy."

"Worthy?" Hope flares in his eyes.

I almost roll mine. If he thinks I'll ever allow someone as weak as him into our ranks, he's sorely mistaken. He'd barely be suitable as a Commoner. Not when he's already proved himself to be a traitor.

"Munro and Legrand!" I bark.

Two of the Commoners step forward, obedient to a fault, and bow, speaking in unison. "Yes, Duke."

"Fight Mr. Moretti to the death."

Behind me, Cecilia draws in a sharp breath. A smile plays on my lips, but it disappears just as fast when I focus back on Carlo. "You want to live? Prove it."

His guard unfastens his restraints while Carlo blubbers nonsense to my non-existent humanity. The guy still hasn't caught on. While I consider the Exiled beneath me, I still don't feel a shred of empathy for his cause. Or anyone else's. Hell Fire Night is nothing more than an inconvenient event that I must endure for a greater cause, such as unlimited money, power, and revenge.

Cecilia is behind me now, digging her nails into my arm. "Please, stop this." I shrug her off, but she's undeterred. "You can stop this, Delacroix."

I peel her off me, repulsed by the crack in her façade. "Pull yourself together, miss. I detest weakness."

"You're a monster," she hisses behind me, and I whirl on my heel, close enough for our chests to touch with our next inhales.

"You brought them here," I remind her. "You knew your friends would die tonight, and you gladly sacrificed them for your agenda."

"But not like this."

I flit my gaze between her eyes and her tempting mouth. "Ah! You wanted to go out in a blaze. Kill as many Exiled members as you could." She looks away. "Would that have been a dignified death?" When she remains mute, I finger a lock of her hair. "There are no dignified deaths. At least this way, your friend has a fighting chance."

Her gaze clashes with mine, fire on ice. "Against two of them?"

"I never claimed to play fair." Smirking, I release her lock of hair and slide my hand into my pocket. "Now, let's enjoy the show."

If looks could kill, I'd be six feet under. No woman has looked at me with such hatred before. Cecilia's eyes positively burn. "I'll kill you," she snarls. "So help me, God, I will deliver your death one day soon."

"Let's keep the pillow talk for the bedroom." I leave her to fume as I take my place by Sinclair.

He hands me my warthog mask, and I slide it on. "Quite a show you're putting on for Miss van der Meer's benefit. I'm intrigued and a little alarmed. What's your plan, Darian?"

I lift a shoulder, eyes on Cecilia. "I've decided Miss van der Meer's last breath won't suffice. She's an annoying itch that demands scratching. I'll hide her in plain sight. No one has to know she's here."

Sinclair chuckles, sliding his phone from his pocket. "What's the Bugatti's horsepower?"

Ignoring his bad humor, I flick invisible lint off my suit jacket. "I want revenge against her father. I want *everything* she has to offer. Her family's money, her family's legacy, and her heart and soul. I won't rest until she's broken beyond repair. I want to crush her little beating heart in my palm."

"Easy there, tiger." Tapping on his phone, Sinclair whistles. "It says here it has 1497 horsepower. Impressive."

My eyes roll. Of course, he isn't listening. The guy has a one-track mind. I jerk my chin to one of the guards, silently telling him to ensure my little thrill seeker doesn't try to step in to rescue Carlo. He's on his own.

While Carlo and the Commoners begin the mindless ritual of circling one another, I check my Rolex. The Dukes beside me exchange money, betting on the winners.

I couldn't give a shit about the death match in front of us. Not when my latest obsession is watching the scene unfold with tears in her eyes that won't fall. She's too proud. I wish to see a tear kiss her cheek, but she blinks them back before they spill over.

That's when I vow to do everything in my power to make Cecilia van der Meer cry. Few things in life are priceless and precious. Cecilia's pain is right at the top of valuables.

A commotion explodes. The two Commoners attack Carlo in unison, kicking his ribs and kneeing him in the face. It's an unfair fight. Carlo stands no chance against trained Commoners—the brawn of the Exiled. But Cecilia needs to be taught a lesson. I have grand plans for her, and they all require her submission.

Lauren openly sobs, but not my Cecilia. No, she's still watching, like she's here but also far away, and I yearn to reach deep into her psyche and pull her back.

I glance at the fighting men. Commoner one is stomping on Carlo's leg, and the other is digging his fingers into his eyes, blinding him. It's a bit much, to be honest, but whatever amuses the masses. Tonight is all about entertainment.

Sinclair glances at his expensive watch.

"Somewhere better to be?" I ask.

"Warm pussy, Delacroix. You should try it."

I peer at Cecilia again. She lifts her gaze and levels me with a look so dark and intense that my dick thickens. Her fury is palpable, like a sweet aroma in the air. Oh, I'd pay good money to cut this charade short and ram my dick down her throat. I bet she feels amazing when she's clawing at my thighs to catch a breath.

"Keep lying to yourself," Sinclair says, with another one of his signature chuckles. "You're hard for the heiress. Careful there, my friend, or Miss van der Meer will break you instead."

"Don't be ridiculous. I'm unbreakable."

The Commoners are now stomping on Carlo's head. He's already dead, but they won't stop until I give them the signal.

"Don't be cocky. They claimed the Titanic was unsinkable, and look how that turned out."

When I lift a hand, the Commoners instantly step back, covered in blood and brain matter. With another dismissive flick of my hand, Carlo's broken corpse is removed from the premises. I cast an appalled glance at the smeared blood streaks. This place better reek of bleach when I return tomorrow. Maybe I'll ask them to fumigate the place while they're at it.

Cecilia stands taller when I eat up the distance between us with determined strides. Defiant to the end. A royal queen without a crown. I haven't known her for long, but her strength has already impressed me. While her friend Lauren sniffles and cries, Cecilia cuts me into pieces with a dismissive glare. I decide there and then that I love seeing her look at me like I'm the monster beneath her bed. I'll soon be the monster *in* her bed.

"And so, there were two," I say.

She follows me with her eyes as I walk past her to Lauren. The poor girl is quivering, terrified.

When I pause behind her and pat her hair, she begins to cry all over again. Why is she even here? Has she no backbone at all? I doubt she would've had it in her to pull the trigger on the members here tonight.

I smirk at Cecilia over her head. "She's pretty."

"Leave her alone," she bites out, showing her cards, her hands trembling at her sides. I continue patting Lauren's hair, ignoring the annoying scent of hairspray and cheap perfume. Cecilia cared about the others, but Lauren is her weak spot, and it thrills me to see her so tense.

"How about a trade."

"A trade?"

I hum, playing with the curly strands, my focus on the task. "A life for a life."

Cecilia inches closer, curious. "I'm listening."

*Of course, you are.* I suppress my smile. "Marry me tonight, and I'll let your precious friend live."

She draws to a halt. Her face pales.

"Your life for hers." I fist Lauren's hair and pull hard, making her cry out. "Give your life to me, and your friend gets to see another sunrise."

Cecilia bounces her eyes between Lauren and me, unsure. I see the moment determination sets her jaw, and she nods once like it's a done deal. "I'll marry you."

"Excellent," I drawl like a villain, then curl my finger at Father Faulkner to join us. "You heard the lady. Marry us."

He scrambles forward. "Yes, sir. Of course, sir."

I never take my eyes off my future bride, who's about to

sell her soul to the devil. Why does a spark of excitement shoot through me, and why am I gripped by a sense of possessiveness when I imagine calling this woman mine? I refuse to explore it, but she'll belong to me minutes from now.

Father Faulkner fumbles with the Bible he brought, his pores dripping sweat. He's a disappointing sight to behold.

"Anytime today," I bark, and he jumps several feet into the air. Pages rustle. He mutters something incoherently under his breath. Sinclair smothers a laugh with a cough.

I'm seconds away from putting a bullet in his head, when he finally reads from the book.

"Dearly beloved, we are gathered here today in the sight of God, and in the presence of family and friends, to join together Darian Delacroix and Cecilia van der Meer in holy matrimony…"

I tune out the rest of his speech.

"What the fuck are you staring at?" Cecilia hisses, barely tolerating my presence.

"My beautiful bride, of course. At least pretend you're happy."

She snorts, revolted. "In your wildest dreams, asshole. If it weren't for my friend, you'd be the last man on earth I'd want to marry."

"I know," I reply, unbothered by the vitriol spewing from her sinful lips. "Why do you think I kept her alive? I knew you'd sacrifice yourself." I can't quite hold my smirk back.

The priest clears his throat, looking at us pointedly.

"Sorry. I got distracted. My bride is bewitchingly beautiful."

Cecilia kicks my shin.

Smothering a laugh, I reach for her hand. "I, Darian

Delacroix, take thee, Cecilia van der Meer, to be my wedded wife, to have and to hold, from this day forward."

"Now it's your turn," the priest tells her, waiting expectantly.

Cecilia takes one look at Lauren and then she stands tall and sacrifices herself. "I, Cecilia van der Meer, take thee, Darian Delacroix, to be my wedded husband…" The rest of her speech becomes background noise.

The moment Father Faulkner declares us husband and wife, I trail my lips to her ear and whisper darkly, "And so the devil took a wife. Welcome to Hell, Mrs. Delacroix." I seal it with a firm kiss.

She clutches my suit jacket in a bid to push me away, but her hands simply rest against my chest as though she can't quite summon the strength to fight me. I break the kiss, slip my hand into my pocket, and toss Sinclair my car key. He catches it one-handed.

"The Bugatti is all yours," I say.

His rich laughter bounces off the walls.

Now to the part where I piss off my new wife…

"Mr. Visage," I call out.

The Duke steps forward, glittering eyes staring expectantly at Lauren from behind his goat mask.

"Take your Commoner away."

He goes to grab Lauren, and my wife stiffens beside me. "You said a life for a life. You promised not to hurt her," she says, beating my chest like a wild animal when Lauren is being dragged, kicking and screaming, out of the room.

I wrestle her into submission, digging my fingers into her arms and bruising her creamy skin. "Not a hair will be harmed on her head. You have my word."

She tries to peer around me at the door as Lauren's

screams echo down the hallway. Such a dramatic addition to the Exiled. "But he—"

"She belongs to Mr. Visage now."

Cecilia's eyes clash with mine, wide and terrified. She really does feel a sense of responsibility for her friend, so why did she bring her here tonight? It could only lead to death. Cecilia knew it. At least, this outcome is a step up from rotting inside a pig's stomach.

"Belongs to Mr. Visage? What do you mean?"

"She's his Commoner. He paid a hefty price for her. Don't worry, he won't kill her."

She jerks free from my grip and steps back. "Do tell, *husband.* What does Mr. Visage want with her?"

"She will serve his needs the way he sees fit."

"She will what?" she shrieks.

I roll my eyes at her theatrics. The others file out of the room, leaving me alone with my seething wife. "She's a Commoner now. The lowest rank in the Exiled. She's Mr. Visage's property, so providing that she behaves, she'll go unharmed."

"And if she doesn't behave?"

I don't bother with a response as I walk to the bar. She's a clever woman; she can read between the lines. It will be in her friend's best interest to scrub Mr. Visage's pristine floors, suck his cock between morning meetings, and say, 'Yes, sir,' to all of his demeaning demands. But at least she's alive and in one piece.

"How could you do this? Money had already exchanged hands before they entered this room. You planned this."

I pour a glass of malt whiskey and swig it like it's soda. God knows I need a stiff drink. "You shouldn't be so predictable, Mrs. Delacroix."

She bares her teeth, making me snort a laugh into my drink. She's such a feisty little thing.

I can't wait to spread her legs again. Nothing is more thrilling than taming such a vicious creature.

Where are these thoughts coming from? I've never entertained the notion of pleasuring women before, never cared for their presence, but I have to admit that it's a tempting idea to replace the fury on my wife's face with post-orgasmic bliss. I bet she would be far more pliant if I shoved my tongue in her tight pussy.

"I should also mention before I forget…" I pour more whiskey into the tumbler, and Cecilia hikes a hand on her hip. "If something were to happen to me—should I die unexpectedly—Mr. Visage will see to it that your precious friend dies a slow, painful death. Consider yourself warned, wife. Don't try anything stupid."

"You think I'm going to accept this?" she spits. "That I'll just roll over and take it? You can't treat me like this."

"You're my wife. I can treat you however I see fit." Downing the last of the whiskey, I shrug out of my suit jacket before undoing the cufflinks and rolling my sleeves up my arms. "Come here."

She hesitates, watching me like a dangerous animal in tall bushland. She's not wrong. "I think I'll stay right here."

I hum, drawing out the tension, while my wife tries not to fidget. I notice her watching the veins in my arms bulge, her nipples budding underneath the thin silk. It's more exciting than it ought to be to have her undivided attention on me, which is why I need to find my equilibrium again. I can't let this mystical creature waltz into my life and flip it upside down. Women don't bring me to my knees. I won't allow for such simple desires.

Pushing off the bar, I saunter to her and grab the back of her neck. She gasps in surprise as I propel her forward and slam her front against the desk. Pens go flying, and so does her dignity when I flip up her dress to expose the curve of her ass. I give it a firm smack, causing Cecilia to cry out and rock forward.

"If I tell you to do something, you do it. You're my wife now, Mrs. Delacroix. You will obey me." I dip my hand inside her panties and glide a finger through her slit. "You're wet already. What turned you on this much? Seeing your friends die, or our verbal sparring?"

She hisses through her teeth but stays down. "I hate you!"

"I can certainly feel how much you hate your husband." I sink two fingers inside her tight cunt and keep her down with my free hand around her neck. "Your pussy seems to disagree with the sentiment." Her skin flushes when I pump my fingers. "Hear those wet sounds, Mrs. Delacroix? That's your pussy's love language."

"You're an asshole," she grinds out, making me chuckle.

I slip my fingers out and smack her pussy. "Be good for your husband."

"You should have married someone else if you wanted a compliant wife. I'm going to make your life a living hell—"

Releasing her neck, I drop to my knees behind her and silence her tirade with my mouth on her sopping cunt, sucking on her pussy through the damp fabric of her lace panties. A strangled moan escapes her.

I've never cared for cunnilingus before. But as I slide her panties aside—greeted by her pink folds and dripping juices—there's nothing I've ever wanted to taste more. I'm ravenous as I dive back in, spearing her with my tongue, gripping her hips.

"Oh, Christ," she chokes out, rocking back against me and seeking more friction. "Darian…"

My name on my wife's lips must be the most addictive sound I've ever heard. Sinclair's voice warns me somewhere in the back of my mind that my ship is taking on water, but fuck if I care. I'm eating Cecilia's pussy like a starved, rabid animal.

I lick, bite, and suck, growling against her. The apocalypse could happen, and I would be none the wiser. I wouldn't even care.

Cecilia moans so loudly that I'm surprised security hasn't rushed here to see what's happening, but it's Hell Fire Night. I could be tearing her limb from limb and no one would care.

"Yes, yes, Darian," she whines, gripping the table's edge. "More. Fuck…"

I'm bruising her hips with my tight grip and painting her with my marks. I can't get enough. Cecilia begins to shake as I fuck her with my tongue—fuck her like it's my cock tearing through her tight pussy.

I briefly wonder how many other men have had the pleasure of feasting on what's mine. I make a mental note to have my PI look into it.

My wife won't even know they all met an untimely death. I'll have their records wiped, and it'll be like they never existed.

Cecilia is trembling now, ramming her pussy in my face.

She looks back over her shoulder. "Aaah! Darian."

Then she comes, and it's a beautiful thing to behold. She moans and writhes, fighting to get away, to get closer. I lick her through it, lapping up her slick arousal.

When her breathing returns to normal, I stand up and tighten my tie as I lick her off my lips. Then I lean over her and press a button on the intercom. It crackles, and a masculine voice says, "Mr. Delacroix?"

"I need a cleaning crew in here pronto."

Cecilia shoves me off her, growling, "Fucking asshole."

Ah. Married life. Such bliss.

# CHAPTER SEVEN

DARIAN

I never saw myself marrying. Never entertained any of the countless women who batted their lashes at me. The idea of putting up with a nagging, high-maintenance wife, whose life purpose is to drain my bank account, never entered my radar until Cecilia. My quest for vengeance is rotting away in the dank darkness, and I'd almost given up hope of finding Cecilia until she waltzed into my life like a head on a silver platter.

I have a pep in my step as I enter the gym. Sinclair is already on the treadmill, his gray T-shirt drenched with sweat between his shoulder blades.

"You're looking chipper this morning," he chirps, barely winded despite pounding the treadmill with his top-of-the-range sneakers created for premium comfort. "Did someone die?"

"It was Hell Fire Night last night. Lots of people died."

Sinclair presses a few buttons and the treadmill slows to a walk. Reaching for his sports bottle, he squirts water straight onto his face like an uncultivated prison inmate. I swear the man was raised by wild coyotes.

"Fair point." He takes a sip, then tosses the empty bottle aside. "Good times. Shame we have to wait another five years for the next party."

I remove the towel around my shoulders and place it on a bench before joining him on one of the other treadmills. "It disappoints me sometimes how much of a simpleton you are, Nathaniel."

"Says you, the man who defied the Exiled and forced a chick into marriage like a caveman."

"I didn't force her. I merely bargained."

Sinclair laughs. "It was a hostile takeover, if I've ever seen one. How is the stunning bride this morning?"

"Call my wife stunning again, and I'll remove your crown jewels and personally return them to the King of England."

"Where's my friend, and what have you done to him?" He chucks me on the shoulder, but I'm not impressed. "Seriously, how did it go last night?"

I turn up the speed. "Well, I had to strong-arm her home, and then she spent the next hour ripping out the brand new clothes and accessories I had express delivered to our home and tossing them on the floor. I'm sure she stomped on them too. Ungrateful, if you ask me, after the staff hauled ass out of hours to hand deliver *everything* in her size."

"Wow." He snickers, covered in sweat. "You sure have a way with the ladies."

"What I have," I pause to correct, "is leverage. Mrs. Delacroix cares awfully much about her friend."

"Blackmail. I dig it."

I roll my eyes, jogging now. My heart remains steady. I'm bored, so I check the time on the machine. Another twelve minutes and twenty-two seconds until I can move on to my strict weight routine.

"Is this your revenge plan, then? Imprison Mr. van der

Meer's daughter against her will and keep her identity a secret from the Exiled?"

"Amongst other things."

"Such as?" He swipes for his towel and wipes his sweaty face, then throws it at me.

It slaps me on the side of the face and then falls to the floor with a wet plop. If I could get away with killing my best friend, now would be the time. I glare at him, but he's unfazed, whacking the treadmill up to dangerous speeds.

If he's not careful, he'll shoot off into space like a comet, and I imagine the machine falling to pieces beneath his heavy weight, like the car in *The Mask*.

"By the time I'm done with Mr. van der Meer," I respond, "there will be nothing left for him to salvage if he ever sees daylight again—which he won't, by the way."

Sinclair's face falls, and he sprints until sweat drips from his pores before switching off the treadmill and heading to the weights. I'm still jogging. Another six minutes and thirteen seconds.

*What is Cecilia doing now?* The last time I checked the surveillance camera, she was searching every inch of her new cage—her luxurious bedroom—for weapons or something to break down the door. God only knows what goes through her pretty head, but I'm not stupid enough to let her into my own space. She'll kill me the moment I close my eyes.

"Word of advice now that you're a pussy-whipped man," Sinclair says as he flexes his muscles in the floor-to-ceiling mirror. "We need to discuss her father."

"I'm not pussy-whipped," I reply with a heavy sigh.

"Yeah, keep lying to yourself."

When I speed up the treadmill to drown him out, he says, "You know I'm right. We need to have this discussion. You can't avoid it forever. She'll kill you if she finds out."

"She won't find out. And she'll kill me anyway."

"I like her already," he says, his shoulders shaking with suppressed laughter. He selects dumbbells while I sprint like I can outrun my new obsession, a feisty heiress with a Venus trap for a pussy. When the machine finally slows down, Sinclair eyes me through the mirror. "While I'm worried about the potential fallout, I think she could be good for you."

"Not only are you simpleton, but you're delusional too." I step off the treadmill and wipe my face with my towel. "It's a business transaction. I give her my name. She gives me her family fortune and legacy for me to burn to the ground."

Focusing on his bulging biceps, he lifts the weights, and I curl my lip. "Why do you always have to sound like you fuck when you work out."

"Unless your prude ass hasn't noticed," he says, grunting, "fucking is a form of cardio."

I select my own dumbbells. "Why do you think she could be good for me?"

Why am I even asking? I plan on spending as little time with her as possible. I'm certainly not curious about Nathaniel Sinclair's opinion.

"You know why," he replies in between counting the reps. "You need someone to shake up your life."

"I'm not a fucking snow globe."

"Dashing through the snow," he sings, then places the dumbbells back down, "on a one-horse open sleigh—"

"Shut up!" I growl, contemplating hurling the dumbbell at his head.

"Mr. Delacroix," a voice comes from the entrance. "Phone call. They say it's urgent."

I eye Sinclair, who's still laughing, and then I place the dumbbells down. "Did they say what the matter pertains to?" I ask the nervous-looking staff member.

"Your wife, sir. She escaped her bedroom, and now she's throwing your art collection over the banister."

Sinclair grabs my head with his sweaty hands and shakes it while singing the lyrics to "Let It Snow! Let It Snow! Let It Snow!" I swat him away and flip him off as I stride out of the room, thoroughly pissed but also strangely exhilarated that my newest acquisition decided to wreck my home.

---

THE FEELING DOESN'T last long. The moment I enter the foyer, I hear it—the sound of six-figure-dollar art pieces, some hundreds of years old, crashing and splintering against the marble flooring. Still, I walk deeper into the foyer, rolling up my sleeves.

I'm simmering on the inside, but I'd never stoop as low as to show it. I take pride in being in control and refuse to let an angry, vengeful woman—no matter how attractive she looks with that feral glint in her eyes—crack the control I've spent years mastering.

Dressed in a dusky silk nightgown, her hair tumbling over her shoulders in messy waves, and her face free of makeup, she stumbles toward the banister with an original painting.

I arch a brow. "No need to exert yourself, Mrs. Delacroix. If you wanted to rearrange our home, all you had to do was ask. It could do with a womanly touch."

"Oh, look, if it isn't my dearest husband. I see you haven't died in an inferno yet. Such a pity." Driven by rage, she hurls the painting over the banister, and a maid beside me squeaks and jumps back. I stay where I am, hands in my pockets, an unmoving mountain in the wake of a typhoon. "I sure hope our children don't inherit your temper."

"Our children?" she all but shrieks, glaring down at me. "You think I'll go near you with a barge pole?"

The sight of her wild eyes and even wilder hair does funny things to my body, but I chose to ignore that for the moment. "You already did. Twice." I wave her off, done with her dramatics. "How about we talk about this? While it's a little soon for marriage counseling, I'm pretty certain we would be advised to use our words."

"Oh, yeah, because talking worked so well the other night when you had my friends murdered."

There goes another painting. I was particularly fond of that one.

I check the time on my watch. Twenty minutes until my next meeting. My wife looks nowhere near ready to calm down. Not until she has wrecked our house.

I address the maid. "Tell Miss Sanders to cancel my next meeting."

She bows and scurries away, glad to escape the raging volcano on the second floor.

"What a beautiful antique vase," Cecilia sneers. "Looks expensive." She throws it inches from my Oxfords, and I stare down at the mess.

A spark of annoyance flares inside me, and I take the stairs two at a time, but when I reach the top, my delightful wife scampers off, escaping down the hallway like a runaway bride.

It's a little too late for that. I allow myself two seconds to enjoy the sight of her blonde hair flying behind her before I dart forward, determined to teach her a lesson for being such an ungrateful brat. I could have killed her last night, but instead, I gave her one of the most sought-after things this side of the world—my surname. She should show me her appreciation, preferably on her knees, but I don't mind a good chase.

She takes one look behind her, sees me close on her heels, and lets out a scream before slipping into the library and slamming the door shut in my face.

The lock clicks into place, and I ram my shoulder against the wood. "You think you're safe in there, baby? Think again."

It turns out these sturdy doors are harder to break than they are in the movies. Five minutes later, I'm still trying to break in, convinced I've dislocated my shoulder.

"Your book collection is as unimpressive as your art collection," she shouts from the inside. "I'm falling asleep reading these titles."

"I'm impressed you're literate," I growl, ramming my foot into the door once again, and Cecilia squeaks, causing my dick to jerk behind my zipper.

"What's wrong, sweetheart?" I coo. "Are you scared Daddy will hurt you?" Straightening up, I roll my shoulders, jaw setting. "Damn right, I will. Once this door is down, I'm going to smack that little pussy raw. You won't be able to sit for a week."

"I'm *sooo* scared, Daddy," she taunts close to the door. "You're such a bad, bad man."

I tear myself away from the door, stomp across the landing to the banister, and bark to the Commoners in charge of making sure my wife doesn't try to flee the premises. "Grab her if she tries to leave."

They blink up at me from the bottom floor, no doubt surprised to see me this ruffled. There's usually not a hair out of place, but now I'm drenched in sweat, and I'm sure my left eye is twitching, too.

When I raise a single brow, they scurry into action,

ascending the stairs like they worry I'll shoot them on the spot.

It's a possibility.

They salute me, out of breath, and I shoulder past. If my wife thinks she can outsmart me, she's got another thing coming. No one wins over me. Cecilia will soon learn who holds all the cards in this marriage.

I return minutes later, clutching an axe, and when I barge through the Commoners, they stare at me like I have three heads.

"Last chance to say sorry to your husband, Mrs. Delacroix."

Something hard hits the door with a loud thud. "Burn in hell!"

The guards shift, uncomfortable, exchanging glances.

"Have I told you how much I love your pillow talk?"

"Have I told you how much I dream about killing you?"

"You're making me hard, baby. Tell me more." I swing the axe into the door, and she releases a scream on the other end.

"You're fucking crazy!"

"What's that, baby? You want to choke on my cock?" Yanking the axe out of the wood, I slam it back in, lodging the blade deep. "I've told you already, good girls get to choke on my dick. My wife, on the other hand…" I pull the blade back out, leaning my shoulder against the door, ignoring the curious guards. "She's an ungrateful bitch."

She appears in the splintered gap in the wood, tilting her head and showing me her bared teeth. "Oh, your wife is a bitch, alright. She serviced your guards on her knees when you were at work."

I swivel my head toward the alarmed Commoners, who

back up a step, pale as ghosts, hands raised. "Boss, we never…"

My wife is messing with me to prove that she can slither beneath my skin, but my fury is unleashed, and I turn back around before I decapitate them both. "Nice try, baby. We both know they wouldn't dare touch what's mine."

"Aww," she drawls, sticking her finger through the hole and poking me in the eye. "You love me."

"Ouch, fuck!" My eyes are watering. I blink once, twice. "A hernia is more lovable than you."

Cecilia cries out with fear when I set upon the door with the axe.

This time, I don't hold back. Whatever monster crawls out from the darkest corners of my soul is an ancient beast. Something born from evil.

Trust my insufferable wife to be the one who finally succeeds in making me lose control.

With a final roar, I kick the door open and block the doorway with my heaving, sweat-soaked body. "Oh, honey, did you miss me?"

I scan the room, the axe resting on my shoulder. Now, where's my beautiful wife hiding?

"Baby, don't be angry with Daddy." My shoes clap on the shiny marble flooring as sunlight pours through the windows to my left, casting streaks of light across the open space.

It's quiet. Too quiet.

Out of seemingly nowhere, a book comes flying at me, hitting me square in the shoulder, and I stumble back, almost tripping.

Cecilia throws another book, but I'm prepared for her poor aim this time and duck before the hardback can smack me square in the face and ruin my perfect nose.

"Don't you think you're overreacting?"

She pops her head out from behind a pillar, a book at the ready, and even I can admit she looks a bit scary.

"Overreacting? Oh, my dearest husband." Airy laughter bubbles from her chest as she steps out from behind the pillar. "Buckle in, because you haven't seen anything yet."

The book goes sailing, bouncing off my other shoulder. She flips me off and screams when I hurl the axe in her direction.

It lodges deep in the bookshelf beside her, and she stares at it while I run a hand through my ruffled hair.

"You threw an axe at me."

"There you go, overreacting again. I threw it in your direction. Not at you."

"An axe? You threw a fucking axe."

"Would you prefer if my choice of weapon were books?"

Her face turns blotchy red, and I swear she's two seconds away from stomping her foot like a petulant child. Why I'm entertaining her mood swings is beyond me. No one else would get away with such unruly behavior, but I like her fiery spirit for some mysterious reason. People are too quick to kiss my ass in this world. With a snap of my fingers, I get what I want. Power has its quirks, but it gets boring fast, and my wife is the only woman I've met who has a spine.

"Now," I say, loosening my tie, "if you're done with your temper tantrum, it's time for your punishment."

Her eyes blow wide. "You can't be serious?"

I step toward her, and she inches back. "You've destroyed hundreds of thousands of dollars' worth of art pieces, thrown books, and damaged a door. A pussy spanking is the least you deserve."

"I didn't take an axe to the door. You did."

"I wouldn't have had to if you'd let me in like a civilized

citizen." Another step. Cecilia looks around, nervous. "Are you coming to me willingly, or will I have to capture you?"

The sentence has barely left my lips when she pivots and runs deeper into the library, disappearing into the countless rows of books.

I gesture for the Commoners to block the entrance, and they take up position.

"There's nowhere to hide, wifey," I call out as I move forward on light feet. "I'm starting to believe you enjoy being chased." Kicking a book out of the way, I scan the rows of shelves, then take a left. "Running is what you're good at, after all. You've done it for the last ten years. Did you really think the Exiled wouldn't find you eventually?" I'm goading her on purpose, hoping she'll give away her location.

I pass another two rows, hands clasped behind my back. "You're lucky it was me and not one of the other Dukes. With a family fortune like yours and such a powerful bloodline..." I whistle. "You were already promised to the highest bidder."

My shoes are now silent on the marble flooring as I enter the next row, walking on light feet along countless leather spines. "I would have paid triple the price of the highest bidder."

Cecilia will never know her true value to a broken man like me. She's priceless.

The moment I laid eyes on her, I knew I would burn down the world to make her mine. Mr. van der Meer's daughter was always destined to end up in my clutches. He made sure of that.

I turn slowly, pushing a book forward with a single finger to reveal a startled Cecilia on the other end, and when the book topples to the floor with a loud thud, she yelps.

"Boo!" I say, and she runs away, but I'm faster, catching her as she comes flying from the end of the row.

I slam her up against the bookshelf with such force that a surprised gasp slips from her plump lips.

"Darian?" There's a question in her voice, a hint of fright.

"Shut up!" I yank her dressing gown from her shoulders, tossing the flimsy material onto the floor, her generous breasts nearly spilling out of her low-cut balconette bra. "I caught my prize. Now it's time for my reward and your punishment."

My eyes find hers as I run a finger along the elastic hem of her lace panties, and with a quick flip of my wrist, I tear them off and stuff her mouth.

"I see my wife missed me," I say, palming her cunt and squeezing it.

She's sopping wet.

Her eyes glower as I lean in to suck on her dusky nipple through the sheer lace. I bite and nibble on the hard pebble, looking up at my wife through my lashes while palming her fine ass and dragging my other hand along her needy core.

Cecilia is so responsive, even when she doesn't want to be—or maybe *because* she doesn't want to be. She likes a good fight with an opponent stronger than her, someone who'll hold her down and take what they want. She proves as much when she grabs a book off the shelf and whacks me in the head before kneeing me in the balls. Luckily for her, her aim is off, so she misses my jewels by a hair's breadth.

After she spits the panties from her mouth, she bares her teeth.

Now I'm thoroughly pissed off and horny for her. My engorged dick throbs, and I can barely think straight.

"You want to fight me, huh?" I grab her chin and mash my body against hers, her heat searing through my clothing everywhere we touch. I want more. I want this woman to come undone at my touch. I want to break her like a shiny new toy. "Think you're stronger than me?"

She tries to shove me off, but I force her hands away before I shift my grip on her chin and ram my thumb past her parted lips. Her mouth is warm and delicious and fucking tempting.

A warning flashes in her eyes, and I know what it means.

"You want to bite me?" I taunt, my gaze locked on her mouth. "Do it, baby. Hurt me. Make me feel it."

Her teeth sink into my skin, making me hiss.

She could bite my finger off if she wanted.

I tease her wet slit. "You're such a wildcat."

Her back bows when I smack her pussy hard enough to make my own fingers tingle, and then I'm back, smashing my body against hers, replacing my thumb with my tongue. Our kiss is dirty and frenzied, and Cecilia moans and squirms. I trap her wrists above her head with one hand, then dip down to bite her jaw, determined to leave my mark.

Why does she have to smell so fucking good, like late summer evenings and morning dew? Everything about her is untamed perfection. I should've never taken her as my wife—it was impulsive—but vengeance is a bloodthirsty hellhound.

I rip open my belt to free my massive dick, and Cecilia licks her lips in anticipation as I stroke the length, holding her wrists against the leather-bound books, close enough for our lips to brush.

"Fuck me, Darian," she pleads, and it's not lost on me that she uses my first name.

Pleasure pools low as sweat drips from my temple. Cecilia's chest heaves with her rapid inhales and exhales.

"Beg again," I demand, stroking my length in long pulls and darting my tongue out to lick my top lip. "Let me hear how much you want your pussy filled to the brim with my dick."

She's staring at my hand on my cock with such longing, a shiver travels up my spine. "Please, Darian, fuck me."

I wait until her eyes meet mine. "Look at us getting along. Our hypothetical marriage counselor would be proud." And then I come all over her pussy and stomach.

With a gasp, she looks down at the white ropes of cum squirting from my dick and onto her smooth skin. I lock my jaw, shuddering from the onslaught of my orgasm.

As I catch my ragged breath, I tighten my grip on her wrists, then swipe a finger through my release, drawing battle marks on her cheeks. I like the pink hue of her flushed complexion and the hitch in her breath as I paint the final mark.

Before she can annihilate me with her damn eyes while my guard is down, I step back and tuck my dick away. Collecting her dressing gown, I toss it at her. "I expect you to tidy up the mess you created in the foyer."

She growls at me, but I'm already gone, retrieving the axe on my way out. "Miss Sanders," I shout, and she materializes like a genie when I exit the library. "See to it that this door is replaced."

# CHAPTER EIGHT

## CECILIA

I haven't seen my husband for days. He's kept his distance, holed up in his home office, ever since he chased me into the library and left me unsatisfied and enraged. I should be grateful—I *am* grateful—but I'm also bored, having searched every inch of his house for something to use against him. Some kind of clue about what happened to my father. I haven't seen or heard from Lauren.

"Do I dare ask what you're doing in Mr. Delacroix's bedroom?" his secretary, Miss Sanders, asks from the doorway. "You know it's out of bounds."

I keep dusting itching powder over his branded underwear. "Oh, I almost forgot my life is a *Beauty and the Beast* retelling."

She suppresses a smile. Miss Sanders is actually nice and always immaculately dressed in pencil skirts and matching blouses. "What trouble do you intend to stir today except for making your husband itch?"

Humming, I shut the drawer and spin around in my new Louboutins. "I heard from a fly that he has an important meeting tomorrow about a weapon delivery. According to sources, the King will have everyone's heads if it falls through."

"So not only are you eavesdropping, but you also thought you'd make him itch." She fails to suppress her smile. "You're on a mission to drive him insane."

I roll my eyes. "He trapped me in his gilded cage. What does he expect?" Something occurs to me, and I turn my body toward her, feeling strangely fidgety. "Have you and Mr. Delacroix…?" My cheeks heat, but I can't bring myself to finish the sentence.

"I'm his secretary," she responds, unable to meet my gaze.

Silence speaks louder than words. My chest tightens, so I clear my throat and breeze past her, handing her the itching powder.

Of course, Darian has slept with her. It's not like he's a virgin. At least, that's what I tell myself as my high heels click on the floor, but the unpleasant sensation clings like a cheap perfume.

I need a plan; I can't stay imprisoned in Darian's luxury mansion forever. Why am I even here? He doesn't like me and doesn't strike me as a man who needs my fortune. He's already one of the richest men on the planet. So why marry me? What does he get out of it except for my father's money and a high-maintenance wife who hates him? It doesn't sound like a fair trade when plenty of influential families have unwed daughters he can pick and choose from.

I accepted the marriage because I had no choice if I wanted Lauren to live. I've heard of the initiation games they play at Hell Fire Night. Join or die. If you choose to join, you have to play a game. Sometimes, one that's impossible to win. Delacroix set out his terms. Marry him or die.

What other choice did I have? I want him gone, but I

can't kill him if I'm dead. No, this was a good outcome, even if it's a struggle not to strangle him every time I lay eyes on his indifferent face. Keep your enemies close.

I draw to a halt when voices drift from his office. The door is cracked open to reveal Darian seated behind his desk, looking regal and formidable. He has an air about him that makes grown men quake in their boots. Behind him, two Commoners stand guard.

Scanning the corridor, I inch closer, careful not to let my heels click on the floor. Darian listens to the blabbering man across from him, but his attention is elsewhere. He fingers a gun on the desk, while the men behind him hover like statues.

"Please," Darian's guest pleads, loosening his collar, sweat beading on his shiny forehead. "I'll get you the money by Wednesday. I just need a few days' extension."

"I don't offer second chances, Mr. Gorey. You knew my terms and conditions. You will deliver the money and the thirty percent interest rate by five p.m. tonight, or I'll see to it that your limbless torso is gifted to your wife."

"Thirty percent?" the man chokes out, and from my hiding spot, I see him lean forward in his seat. "The interest rate was twenty percent."

"You inconvenienced me, Mr. Gorey. Now it's thirty." He collects the gun, kicks his feet up on the desk, and inspects the weapon. "You can leave now. We're done here."

"But Mr. Delacroix, with all due respect, I can't possibly… I don't have the money right now."

Darian hums, placing a silencer on the gun. "That's a shame." Extending his arm, he plants a bullet between his guest's eyebrows, and I fall back with a gasp, barely slamming my hand on my mouth in time to silence the sound.

Darian puts the gun on the table, calm and collected. "Did

you seek me out because you miss me, Mrs. Delacroix, or are you here to tell me that you set the kitchen on fire?"

My heart gallops wildly. I'm still breathing hard.

"I don't have all day."

I lower my hand from my mouth and brush my hair out of my eyes, trying to steady my trembling. Darian is waiting for me to enter, so I steel my spine and tip my chin.

The moment the door creaks open, he leans back on his royal throne, hands interlaced, and lets his eyes travel down my body and back.

I've seen dead people before, but I still break out into a cold sweat at the sight of the blood trickling from the bullseye between the slumped dead man's eyebrows. My new husband is ruthless.

"You haven't cooked since you entered my home, so I doubt you set the kitchen on fire. What can I do for you?"

I stop beside the corpse, clenching and unclenching my hands. "I want to see Lauren."

"That's out of the question." He gestures to the Commoners. "Take him away."

"Why won't you let me see her?" I ask when the guards remove the bleeding body.

"Hmm, let me see." He counts on his fingers. "So far, you've trashed most of my very expensive art collection, thrown my books, set fire to the curtains in the ballroom because you wanted to let in the daylight, and hurled more items at me than I can count."

Despite my previous shock, I cross my arms over my chest and pop my hip. "Are we playing tit-for-tat? You murdered my friends, so the least you deserve is a few damaged paintings and maybe a broken nose."

"Not the nose," Sinclair says from the doorway, entering

with an obnoxiously big smile. "Hello, troublemaker." Sauntering past me, he flops onto the chair across the desk.

Darian glares at him, but he pays him no heed. Instead, he flashes another smile at me and says, "Why don't you make yourself useful, sweetheart, and pour us whiskey."

I flip him off. At the same time, Darian says, "Smile at my wife one more time, and I'll rearrange your smug face. She's not the fucking help. Pour your own drink."

Sinclair turns his attention to me and jabs his thumb in Darian's direction. "Please tell me you've fed him the cream, at least."

That's my cue to leave. I lift my chin. "The only cream I'll ever let my dear husband come near is the curdled, out-of-date one in the fridge." I pivot on my heel, my skirt flaring around my thighs, and Sinclair's laughter follows me through the hallways as I stomp to my bedroom.

I need to get hold of Lauren somehow. Make sure she's okay. But how? My husband is as agreeable as a sour lemon. Unfortunately, I can't murder him in his sleep because of his threat about what would happen to my friend. Such a shame. I'd love to put a pillow over his face.

# CHAPTER NINE

DARIAN

*"Darian," Mom's soft voice invades my dreams. "You have to wake up, sweetheart." Soft, trembling fingers shift my hair away from my face.*

*Removing the quilt, she helps me sit up before stroking my hair and cheeks as though she's checking for injuries. "Remember your favorite game, hide-and-seek?"*

*"Huh?" I rub my eyes, confused.*

*A sudden crash from somewhere in the house causes her to jump and squeeze her eyes shut briefly.*

*She inhales a shaky breath and looks at me. "Do you remember?"*

*I'm tired, and Mom makes no sense. "I remember."*

*"Good," she replies with a weak smile as she palms my cheeks. "This will be just like that time." Unclipping her heart-shaped necklace from around her throat, she fastens it around my neck. Tears gather on her lashes, so she quickly wipes them away before rising to her feet and pulling me to mine. We cross the room to the closet, and she guides me inside, crouching down. "No matter what you see or hear,*

*you don't come out, understand? You don't make a sound. No matter how frightened you are."*

*"You're scaring me, Mommy." My heart hammers as my bottom lip begins to wobble. I've never seen her this pale before. Where's Daddy?*

*She cups my cheeks, and her firm touch both soothes and frightens me.*

*"I know you're scared, but you have to be a big boy for me. Can you do that? You need to be brave, okay? Hide in here and don't make a single sound."*

*"Mommy?"*

*"Promise me that you'll hide in here."*

*"I promise..."*

*Heavy footsteps thunder on the stairs as deep, scary voices filter through the walls. Mom slaps a hand over her mouth and whimpers, but then she seems to shake herself off.*

*She quickly pulls me in for a hug before closing the closet doors, and I shrink back into the shadows.*

*"Remember to stay quiet. Don't let them hear you," Mom whispers seconds before the bedroom door flings open.*

*Three men enter, dragging my broken and beaten father by his arms. I surge forward to peer through the slats.*

*"Oh, looky what we have here. Did you think you could hide from us?" one of the men says to my mom, cracking his knuckles while the others toss my groaning father to the floor. Mom backs away and picks up a pair of hair scissors on the dresser.*

*"What are you going to do with those, sweetheart?" Chuckling, the man tightens his grip on his gleaming knife.*

*"Stay away from me," Mom bites out.*

*A fourth man enters the room, wearing a three-piece suit and shiny black shoes. Something about him makes my fear skyrocket. Shadows cling to him as if he's Lucifer himself, and I can't keep my teeth from chattering.*

*His cold, cruel eyes darken even further when he spots my mom.*

*Removing a pair of black latex gloves from his pockets, he snaps them on and says to the other men, "Make Mr. Delacroix watch, but don't kill his wife. Not yet. She's my offering for the night."*

*"It'll be my pleasure, Mr. van der Meer," the man with the knife replies as he leers at Mom.*

*The bad men prop my dad up against the wall. He can barely keep his head upright. His right eye is swollen shut, and blood is trickling from his broken nose.*

*When the man comes for my mom, she lashes out with the scissors, but she's no match for his strength. He drags her over to the bed and tears at her clothes.*

*The urge to run out there and tell him to leave her alone overwhelms me, but I stay hidden because I'm scared. Besides, I promised Mom I would hide and not make a noise.*

*When the screaming starts, I shrink back into the shadows and slide down against the wall with my hands over my ears.*

I wake with a start, drenched in sweat, my heart hammering hard enough to make me briefly worry about an impending heart attack. These nightmares are happening nightly now. I can't shake them.

Rubbing my eyes, I dig my fingers into my eyeballs. Not that it helps when the last remaining reason behind these recurrent nightmares is sleeping in the other wing.

Restless, I throw off the quilt and swing my legs over the side of the bed. I should kill her. Get it over with. Silence these voices once and for all.

With my elbows on my thighs, I drag my hands down my face. Sweat clings to my bare back. I didn't shave this morning, which isn't like me. When life is normal—and I don't have a firecracker living under my roof, making her presence known with her trail of destruction—I live according to a strict schedule. Some say I have OCD. Me? I like to feel in control.

Control over my surroundings and others. But then my new wife barged into my life like a typhoon and turned my home and routine upside down.

Sinclair thinks she's good for me, but what does he know?

My day-old stubble rasps beneath my fingers as I try to silence the echo of my mother's screams that linger like the sweat on my back. Guilt is slowly eating me up from the inside, chewing on my intestines like parasites. I hid in the closet that night because I was scared.

*Weak.*

I'll never forgive myself for not rising above my fear. A strong man acts; he doesn't hug his knees to his chest and cower.

I ball my hands and punch my head. "Shut up, shut up, shut up."

*"Oh, looky what we have here. Did you think you could hide from us?"*

Shooting to my feet, I pace a hole in the carpet.

*"Make Mr. Delacroix watch, but don't kill his wife. Not yet. She's my offering for the night."*

My mother's necklace is in the bedside drawer, so I pull it open and shift random items out of the way until my fingers touch the silver chain.

I lift it out, brushing my thumb over the heart pendant. "I should have done something that night." My voice sounds far away, lost in memories of the past. "I should have stopped them."

I place the necklace back inside the drawer with trembling

hands, and then quickly shower to wash off the lingering nightmare. There's no way I can sleep now; it would only send me back to that day.

Once dressed in joggers and a T-shirt, I leave for the office, or at least that's my intention, until I pause at the top of the grand staircase.

The hallway leading to Cecilia's quarters is dark and terrifyingly inviting. I'm on the move before I even know what's happening, too curious not to inch her door open and peer inside. Just one peek. But of course, her door is locked, and I glower as if it'll magically open if I direct my ire like a solar flare.

No such luck.

Retrieving my phone from my pocket, I do the only logical thing: I wake up Miss Sanders and demand she bring the spare key to my wife's bedroom.

Exactly seven minutes and thirteen seconds later, on the dot, she turns the corner, flustered.

Her hair is a mess and her blouse is buttoned up wrong. I've fired people for less, but I have greater issues at hand than the state of my PA's clothes.

"You're two minutes and thirteen seconds late, Miss Sanders. You know how I feel about tardiness."

"I'm sorry, sir." She holds up the key between us like a peace offering. "In my defense, you woke me up at three in the morning."

I snatch the key. "Don't let it happen again."

"I won't."

When she fails to move, I glare. "You're dismissed."

She turns on her heels and hurries out of my sight, no doubt breathing a relieved sigh on her way.

In the ensuing silence, I stare at the key in my hand like a foreign object from an alien planet, confused by my feelings.

On the one hand, I've dreamed of avenging my parents, but on the other, I'm also curious about the sleeping woman on the other side of the door—curious enough to insert the key and turn until the lock clicks.

I poke my head inside her dark room. She's asleep on her side, facing away from me, so I open the door farther, stepping over the threshold.

Her feminine, flowery scent is everywhere, perfuming the air, and clothes are strewn on the floor. I almost trip over a designer shoe. My wife is messy. That much is clear.

As I near the bed, my steps slow, and I just…stare.

Her blonde hair looks almost white in the moonlight. I gently touch a lock and bring it to my nose, inhaling the scent of tropical coconut and summers on the beach.

A soft breath escapes her as I let go of her hair, and she rolls over onto her back.

How does something so lovely and untainted come from a monster like Mr. van der Meer? A man who didn't think twice about raping and torturing a mother of a young, terrified child in front of her husband.

My father had to watch her scream and cry and beg for her life before they finally put a bullet through his head. And my mom? Well, that was the last time I saw her. Once my father was dead, Mom was dragged out of there, naked, bruised, and bleeding. All in the name of the secret society that raised me.

It's funny how that works. We accept the old traditions blindly. We don't rebel. Not in the traditional sense, anyway.

I hook a finger in the quilt and pull it down to reveal the swell of Cecilia's generous tits inside the silk gown she wears. Mr. van der Meer's daughter soon grew up.

As I trace my thumb over her plump bottom lip, her soft

breath fans my skin. At least she's agreeable when she's asleep, but even so, I miss her smart mouth.

---

THE STEEL DOOR creaks open on rusty hinges, and I descend the spiral stone steps to the cellar, where the cell is located. This small space is cold and damp and smells of mold and rot.

I light the torch on the wall. "Your daughter tastes divine, van der Meer. Quite delectable."

A shadowed figure slowly comes into the light, shuffling on the floor.

Covered from head to toe in grime, Cecilia's emaciated father grabs hold of the bars and presses his face up close. "Touch a hair on her head and—"

"You will what? Kill me?" A bitter laugh echoes off the stone walls. "You did that a long time ago, van der Meer, when you broke into my home and murdered my family. It's only fair that I return the favor. We're family now, after all."

I take great joy in seeing him blanch. Years locked up in my cellar have reduced him to bones and tattered clothes. The seemingly larger-than-life man who destroyed my family is nowhere to be seen.

"That's right," I reply to his unanswered question. "Your daughter is now my wife. Oh, don't look at me like that," I say when he looks like he might throw up. "She was quite the willing participant."

Okay, I'm exaggerating, but he doesn't know that.

"You thought I wouldn't find her. That I thought she was dead." Shaking my head, I crouch down before him. "I'm not that easily fooled. You see, I had you captured, but then your wife disappeared with your daughter before I could find them

—before *anyone* in the Exiled could. Your wife hid her well from the greedy wolves, I'll give you that. I looked for her everywhere without luck, but then one day, your daughter walked into my territory to revenge your name."

My face breaks into a deranged smile. "Like a turkey jumping up onto a Christmas table."

"Please don't hurt her," he pleads.

His sour stench assaults my nostrils, so I waft it away. "How does it feel to rot away in your own feces, van der Meer? Oh, how the mighty have fallen." I rise to stand. "I have no intention of hurting your daughter because, unlike you, I don't touch women unless it's to bring them pleasure; remember that when you're stuck in the dark with nothing but your thoughts to eat you alive. Everything you've ever owned is mine—your precious money, legacy, and even your daughter."

The satisfaction I feel seeing him reduced to nothing is unrivaled. I could feast on the sight for eternity and never grow bored.

"And your daughter's tight pussy?" I stare down at him with a cold smirk. "It looks so fucking pretty after I've stuffed it with cum."

"You're a sick asshole," he sneers weakly, retreating into the shadows.

"Maybe," I agree, then stroll to the door with my hands in my pockets. "Do you think your daughter will hold you in such high regard if she finds out what a sadist you are?"

His eyes seem to gleam in the dark. "You think you're any better? You think she'll love you when she finds out you're keeping her father locked up in your cellar?"

"With all due respect, Mr. van der Meer. I didn't marry your daughter because I wanted a companion. I married her because I knew how much it would torment your mind to know I'm fucking her every chance I get. She's a little slut, you know? Moans like a porn star. Always ready to be bent over the desk and fucked to within an inch of her life."

I haven't actually fucked her yet, but the white lie is worth seeing the rage on her father's face.

"Because I'm feeling generous tonight, I'll leave the torch lit and let you enjoy a few hours of light." Turning on my heel, I leave him to wither away in misery, forgotten and insignificant.

# CHAPTER TEN

CECILIA

Weeks have passed since I became Darian Delacroix's imprisoned wife in his ivory tower of wretchedness. I haven't seen much of him since. He has made himself scarce, always locked in his office or attending meetings, and my feeble attempts at pissing him off seem to go mostly ignored, though I'm not blind to the unfortunate staff that has to clean up after me.

Today, I'm bored.

Bored of having nothing to do.

Bored of being ignored.

I've searched every crook and cranny in the house for clues about what happened to my dad. The only place left to search is Darian's office.

I'm on my way there, when I do a double take outside the kitchen.

I backtrack, a smile creeping onto my lips. "Mrs. Jones?"

She's wiping down the large island, but at the sound of my voice, she looks up. "Cecilia!" Seeming to catch herself, she lowers her voice. "You can't be seen talking to me in public."

I enter the room. "It's so good to see you. The last time—"

"We polished glasses at the cottage before Mr. Delacroix called you into his office." She tuts, resuming her wiping. "You got yourself into a right mess."

It feels so good to see a familiar face in this gilded cage. Throwing myself at her, I squeeze her so tight that she almost wheezes.

She pats me awkwardly. "There. There."

"You have no idea how happy I am to see you."

"Miss… We really can't be seen together."

I release her, my cheeks hurting from smiling. "Darian is out for the day."

"Darian?" She shakes her head with disapproval. "You're on a first-name basis now?"

"Never mind that. How are the others?"

A shadow dims her smile. "Many were lost on Hell Fire Night. Too many." She shakes her head again, scooping breadcrumbs into her palm and discarding them in the trash-can. "It never gets easier."

I wish I knew what to say to make it better.

"Keith was a good man," she continues, staring down at the trash, lost in memories. "Good integrity. Fought a losing battle."

"He was a great man," I agree.

"You shouldn't have entered the lair." She avoids my gaze on her way to the sink. "It was a suicide mission."

"He knew what he was getting into."

She whirls around. "That doesn't make it right. He was driven by hatred and a misplaced desire for revenge. More death isn't the answer to pain. It won't bring his loved ones back." Tears cling to her lashes as her jaw tightens. "And it won't bring yours back either."

A lump has formed in my throat. I swallow it down. "I know…"

Mrs. Jones brushes down her black maid's skirt and then wipes the counter while I worry my lip. She's right. It was my idea to invade the nest. I suggested it, so their deaths are on me.

It's easy to be excited in the moment and feel like there's a purpose behind the mission. We thought we would go out in flames. That our sacrifice would somehow make a difference.

It didn't.

I quickly wipe my tears. "Have you heard from Lauren?"

Mrs. Jones's shoulders stiffen, and she falters, but only momentarily.

Heart stuttering, I march up to her. "You have. Please tell me that she's okay?"

"I must not be seen with you." She hurries to wash the dishcloth and then hangs it over the tap, but I block her way when she tries to move past me.

"How is she? I deserve to know."

Her gaze hardens. "How dare you? Don't speak to me about deserving."

"I just want to know if she's okay. That's all." I'm nearly pleading.

She looks to the side, wiping her wet cheeks, sniffling. "She's alive, thanks to you."

A smile blooms on my lips, but she holds up a palm.

"Sometimes death is a kinder mercy."

"I'm confused," I reply when she walks away. "Are you saying I should've let her die?"

She turns in the doorway, regret written on her face. "I'm saying you shouldn't have involved yourself with this world. Your mother got you out. She protected you and your legacy, so the best thing you can do is keep your head down.

Don't look for answers to questions you don't want the answer to."

This time when she leaves, I slouch, defeated, against the counter.

---

THERE'S no sign of Mrs. Jones when I exit the kitchen. *In fact, there's no sign of anyone.*

I try to look innocent as I hurry to Darian's office. Nothing to see here. I'm just going for a stroll.

Unfortunately, there's no way to avoid the security cameras, which are everywhere, like watchful, beady eyes.

A Commoner walks past, and I pretend to inspect a vase on a console table outside Darian's office. Such intricate detailing but also ugly as hell.

As soon as the nameless Commoner turns the corner, I place the vase down and dash inside Darian's office. The door shuts with a soft click like a gunshot in the quiet house, and I wince, waiting for footsteps to thunder down the hall, though nothing happens. No one comes to find me snooping on my husband.

I scan the large, monstrous mahogany desk and wingback chair, which occupy most of the space. Behind it, rows of bookshelves span the back wall. I've been in here before, watching Darian kill a man like it was nothing, callous and without an ounce of emotion—a true monster—but I was too shocked back then to take in the décor. Now, I miss nothing, but I still can't look at the chair across from the desk without feeling queasy.

When I sliced Keith's throat, it was instinct and mercy. I had no other choice, or he would've suffered a much worse fate. Darian didn't have to kill that man. He could have granted him an extension instead of putting a bullet between his brows.

I rush over to his spotless desk, which gleams in the morning sun, and root through the drawers, finding nothing but bills and paperwork. Useless stuff I have no need for. I discover no information that can be used against Darian.

Slamming it shut with a defeated sigh, I blow a strand of hair away from my lips. He must have sensitive information somewhere hidden. There's no chance he spends all his time in this fancy office without also storing his secrets within reach.

I turn my attention to his shiny laptop and try to suss out the password. What would I use if I was a stuck-up asshole with zero personality?

*Iamamassived1ck*

Nope, not that one.

*asshatismymiddlename*

*Smalld1ckenergy*

Well, that one isn't true. I've seen his cock, and it's huge. Great… Now I'm thinking about his elephant trunk of a dick.

I close his laptop and drum my coffin nails on the desk. I need access to the files on his computer somehow. Maybe I can seduce him and pretend to kiss his neck while he signs in. That could work, but I'm not sure my poker face is that impressive. Not when he makes me want to gouge out his eyeballs with a spoon every time he shows his smug face in my vicinity. My smile alone would look like I'd bitten a slice of a lemon.

I spin around and scan the bookshelves. Nothing looks out of place, but I do notice something unusual. All the spines are perfectly aligned—all except for one. I step closer, tilting my head. The book protrudes—not by much, but enough to stand out, so I pull it out and open it up. The inside is hollow, much to my surprise.

Photographs tumble out. Lots of them. I gasp as pictures of me and the other rebel members flutter to the floor.

Crouching down, I pick one up of me when I first met with Keith and Carlo. We thought we'd been discreet when we met at a local café.

We thought wrong.

Regretful understanding dawns on me as I look through the other photos. Darian has kept a close eye on the Antichrist, mapping our movements. He also seems to have taken a special interest in me. There are more photographs of me than of the other rebels. I pick up one and use it to fan my face as I scan the rest of the room. Darian must have known who I was the moment he saw me on the security camera. Maybe that was why he returned to his office with Sinclair. He wanted a closer look.

I remember how his gaze burned into me while I cleaned the glasses. He knew he'd let the enemy into the secret society's stronghold, so why didn't he have me killed? Why go through all of this?

After collecting the photographs, I put them back where they belong to hide my tracks. It's important to be careful. If Darian notices something is amiss, I'll be in a heap of trouble.

As I return the book to the shelf, a file wedged between the spines catches my attention, so I pull it out, the pages worn and curled at the edges. A photograph is attached to the top, held in place by a paper clip.

A photograph of my dad.

My heart falls to my stomach, but I don't have time to read because voices drift closer outside.

"Shit…" I drop down and scurry under the desk.

My father's photograph must have slipped from the file

because it lies on the floor, so I crawl back out to retrieve it, but on my way back, I knock my head on the hard surface. "Damn it," I curse, rubbing the sore spot.

The door opens the second I'm hidden. "We have our best snipers stationed as a precaution. Everything is assured to go according to plan," says a gruff voice I haven't heard before.

I press a palm over my mouth to keep quiet, and my pulse gallops as sweat trickles between my breasts.

"I expect full discretion." Darian's smooth timbre rolls over me like a forbidden kiss, making me shiver.

Fuck him for making me feel this way. Even now, beneath his desk, annoyance flares inside me.

"You have my word."

Shoes clap on the floor. Darian is closer now, placing something on the desk. I inch back as far as the confined space will allow.

"Your word means little in this world," Darian says as he rounds the desk and removes his phone from his pocket. Next up is his gun from the back of his pants, which he tosses onto the desk.

It's a show of power—*I don't fear you.*

"In case you think to cross me or fail to fulfill your end of the deal..." He moves back enough for me to see him remove a USB stick from his pocket and wiggle it in the air. "I have insurance." With a practiced flick of his wrist, he throws the USB to the man. "Word of advice. Watch it alone."

"What have you done?"

"I have insured my property."

Silence settles in the room, thick and heavy.

"As long as you keep your end of the deal, no one gets hurt," Darian says, undoing his cufflinks. "You see, I know you've met up in secret with Mr. Studdard." He disappears around the desk, and I exhale in relief. That was too close.

Ice cubes clink together. Darian pours himself a glass of whiskey by the sounds of it.

"His housekeeper found him hanging from the rafters this morning. Mr. Studdard, I mean." Darian sounds conversational. Almost friendly. "Shame what happened to him. He had a lot to live for. Did you know"—his shoes sound on the floor—"he murdered his family before hanging himself? Stabbed the kids to death and then drowned his wife. Gruesome, if you ask me."

"You're a sick bastard."

"I'm a businessman," Darian counters.

"I won't let you get away with this."

"You will. You already have. Go home and watch what's on the USB."

More silence. Spine-chilling, suffocating silence. Seconds pass while I imagine the stranger glaring at Darian, who smirks like a movie villain. In my short time here, I've learned how ruthless my new husband truly is.

The door slams shut, and Darian chuckles as the ice in his drink clinks together.

I can picture him swirling the glass.

"You can come out now."

Every muscle in my body goes rigid, and for a precious few seconds, I clutch the file to my chest, hoping he'll go away. Of course, he doesn't. He knows where I'm hiding.

I pop my head up. "What was on the USB?"

Humor sparkles in Darian's frosty eyes as he watches me over the rim. "It's nothing for you to worry about."

I climb out, brushing my hair out of my eyes and straightening my clothes, pretending my dignity isn't still hiding under the desk.

I've given up on it now.

"What have you got there, darling wife?" Darian downs

the last of his whiskey, puts the tumbler down on the nearest surface, and levels his breath-stealing and clit tingling attention on me. My knees almost buckle, but I stay upright by some holy miracle.

Maybe I should start praying for protection against deadly men like Darian. Even better—perhaps smoke pours from his skin, like a barbeque, if I throw holy water on him. I'd love to see him hiss in pain before he is exorcised back to Hell.

"What's in your hand?" he asks again.

I hide the file behind my back. "Nothing."

"Nothing?" He walks closer, unhurried, so I step back, my spine colliding with the bookcase. Darian closes the distance between us, grabs hold of the shelves beside my head, and leans in close.

Why does he have to smell so nice? And why do my insides melt when he looks at me with such heat in his darkening eyes? He's a cold-hearted murderer. A monster.

"Trying to figure out my password was a bad move." His whiskey breath fans my lips. "I get notified if someone tries to gain access."

Damn it. I didn't think. I could have just as well walked into a bank, shot at the roof with a loaded gun, and told everyone to get on the floor. The moment I tried to unlock his laptop, I triggered his alarm.

In a swift move, he snatches the folder and wiggles it in front of my face with a disapproving tut. "You shouldn't be snooping around in my office."

"What do you know about my father?" I bare my teeth. "Did you hurt him?"

He turns artic in a matter of seconds, and shutters come down over his eyes. He tosses the folder on the desk, and I try to snatch it, but he grabs me by the throat and slams me back against the bookshelf.

"Jeez," I wheeze. "You run from hot to cold in seconds. I'm getting whiplash."

"Don't speak about your father in my vicinity."

"Did you hurt him?" I press, eyes narrowed at his strong reaction. "Was it you that killed him?"

"Let me remind you that you haven't seen your father in years. You were a naïve little girl when he disappeared. What do you know of your father's character? What kind of a man he truly was?" Darian pushes away and turns his back on me.

I swallow hard. "And what kind of a man are you, Darian Delacroix?"

When he stays silent, I itch to hurt him in some way, but instead, I ask, "What about that man, Mr. Studdard? You killed his family."

Darian spins around. "I did no such thing. He killed his own family when he was faced with the music of his sins. His double life was about to be exposed—his reputation dragged through the mud. Mrs. Studdard would have left him and took the kids with her. He couldn't face it, so he killed his family." Darian is close now, and I struggle to breathe in his proximity. "I may be cruel, Mrs. Delacroix, but don't for a second think that I would ever lay a hand on an innocent child or woman."

"Why did you let that man think you were behind the murders."

Delacroix fingers a strand of my hair. "To keep him in his lane. He's a snake who wouldn't hesitate to sink a knife into my back if he had the chance."

"So you're a bad man with morals?"

"Is it such a strange concept?" he asks, tucking my hair behind my ear and tracing the swell of my bottom lip with his thumb.

"Yes…"

"Have I ever told you that you have the most delectable lips? Made to be sucked on."

My thighs clench as I ignore his comment meant to distract me.

"What is it about you and bookshelves? This is the second time you have me cornered against one."

He sucks my lip between his teeth, invading and conquering me with his scent and taste. I'm nearly melting. "Literature and sex go hand in hand," he whispers, grabbing hold of my hips and pressing his growing erection against my stomach, "like whiskey and ginger."

"I prefer Coke," I say too breathily.

"Is that so?" he asks, snaking my skirt above my waist.

Cool air licks at my exposed legs in stark contrast to the heat of his hands, his fingers trailing over my skin, starting at my belly button. He circles it, then lets his fingertips trace lower in a featherlight, teasing touch.

By the time he slips a digit inside my panty line, I'm panting, my skin erupting in goosebumps.

I'm burning up.

He pulls the elastic away from my skin and lets it snap back into place. "I should punish you for breaking into my office."

"I didn't break in," I reply. "The door was unlocked."

I've never regretted wearing underwear as much as I do when he trails a finger over my damp slit. How can a flimsy piece of lace fabric create such a barrier?

"You thought you'd let yourself in." He leaves me quivering, two seconds away from hyperventilating, with my skirt bunched around my waist. "Thirsty?" he asks, making his way to the minibar.

He's such a strange man, and I'm still too aroused to

make sense of his words. Tingling all over, my pussy feels empty.

He pours us two tumblers, carries them over, and hands me mine. I greedily accept it, needing something to burn away my embarrassment.

I gulp it down like soda, and Darian raises a brow but stays silent.

When I place the empty tumbler on the shelf behind me, it dawns on me that Darian has yet to take a sip of his.

"Why are you looking at me like that?" I ask.

"You really are quite a wildcat, aren't you?" He counters as he turns to put his drink on the desk, slow and unhurried. The next thing I know, he picks me up by the waist, puts me down beside the tumbler on the desk, and guides me to lie back with his fingers splayed over my sternum. "Sharp claws, a loud hiss, and an even louder purr." He retrieves something from the desk, and I push onto my elbows to get a better look, but he shoots me a warning glare, so I obediently lie back down with a thundering pulse, wondering why I'm so willing to let him play with me like a marionette doll.

My thoughts grind to a halt when I spot the scissors in his hand. "What are you doing?"

It's a stupid question. I know exactly what he's doing—cutting my skirt down the middle. The fabric parts like the Red Sea for Moses as the scissors glide over my stomach and between my breasts. He carefully guides the fabric away before leaning over me to take my left nipple into his mouth, drawing it into a hard bud and eliciting a moan as I arch my back.

His hot tongue swirls over the sensitive peak, and he bites it between his teeth and looks up at me from beneath his dark lashes. It hurts in a good way, and I'm on edge, both anxious and aroused.

As the abused bud slips from between his wet lips, he trails the scissors back down and nudges my panties aside to expose my glistening cunt.

"Perfection," he whispers, burying the flat ends of the scissor blades between my lips and spreading them until my clit peeks out in between. He could snip my clit right off if he wanted to, injure me beyond repair, but I know he won't. His lust-filled eyes drink me up like the finest whiskey.

Speaking of whiskey. Darian keeps me spread open with the scissors as he reaches for the tumbler beside my head. "Do you know why sweet vermouth is one of my favorites to mix with whiskey?"

"I thought you liked ginger the best?" My sensitive nipples ache with anticipation.

With a hum, he dips the glass and pours whiskey over my nipples. "Ginger is nice, too, but sweet vermouth reminds me of you."

Cool whiskey pools in my belly button next.

"Why me?"

He takes a sip, his throat rolling with the movement, and then he pours whiskey straight onto my pussy and sucks it clean. I'm whimpering, almost bucking into his dirty mouth, but I don't dare move with the scissors spreading my pussy lips like the curtain on a stage.

"Vermouth, like you, is very complex." This time, he pours a generous amount of whiskey, and I feel it pour between my ass cheeks, cold and wet. "And delicate, with notes of vanilla, orange, and clove."

"Aah," I moan as he slurps it up and sucks on my clit. The sensation of the scissors and the threat of pain excites me more.

Darian sucks on my pussy lips, then drags the flat end of his tongue through my slit, lapping at my slick desire. "Can you see now why sweet vermouth goes so well with whiskey, Mrs. Delacroix?"

He peppers kisses across my stomach and then laps at the whiskey pooling in my belly button. It's sinfully hot. His lips continue upward, latching onto my aching nipples. First, my left and then my right while he nibbles and licks and sucks. I'm so sensitive that I nearly come from nipple stimulation alone.

"Answer the question, wife."

"Ye-es."

He chuckles, straightening up, his mouth glistening with whiskey and me. As he guides me to sit, he reaches behind me and hands me the folder. "Read."

Unsure, I look down at the folder in my hands. Is he serious? I'm naked, and at the mercy of my ruthless husband, yet now he waits for me to read about my father. "You said you don't want me to speak about him."

"I changed my mind." He removes his shirt, distracting me with his rippling muscles.

The urge to map them with my tongue pools between my thighs like lava, my pussy clenching and throbbing, but before I can lean in, he unbuckles his belt and tips his chin toward the file. "Read."

Uncertain if this is such a good idea, I open it. Darian downs the last of the whiskey and throws the tumbler behind him without a care in the world that it smashes to pieces on the floor.

I shouldn't have broken in here. I'm in trouble. Darian looks at me like he wants to feast on my soul until every remnant has been consumed by his greedy, black heart.

I gasp when he grabs me by the waist and pulls me closer in a sudden move.

"I'm going to fuck you now, Mrs. Delacroix, and you'll read about what a true monster your father was."

"Darian," I whisper, gulping.

He bunches my panties in his hand and rips them off in one clean slate. "That's 'husband' to you, Mrs. Delacroix."

The folder trembles in my hands as Darian unzips his pants to free his big cock. It's long and thick and perfect, with angry, purple veins and a pearl of precum on the tip.

"Read," he demands once more, spreading me wide by my knees.

"I don't want to read about my father now…" I try to deny him.

"There's no time like the present, Mrs. Delacroix." Grabbing the base of his cock, he rubs the engorged head through my slit. "Read."

"What about protection?" My body suddenly tenses as I worry my lip. "I'm not on birth control."

"I know you're not." His dark eyes lock with mine, and he presses forward, stretching me with the tip. I gasp at the sting, but welcome it all the same. With the folder trembling in my death grip, I do nothing to stop him.

"You're going to take my cum like a good wife, Mrs. Delacroix. Understood? You're mine now, and I'm going to fuck you."

"Fuck me—" The words cut off when he rams his cock inside me, and I yelp, sucking in a sharp breath. "You're too big," I whimper.

He shushes me, releasing one of my legs to clamp his hand over my mouth. "Your tight cunt was tailor-made for me. Feel how it grips me. You're taking my cock so well, Cecilia."

Darian waits for me to adjust, shushing me every time I make a pained sound, his fingers twitching on my cheeks.

The burn soon dulls, and he removes his hand from my mouth to help me open the file, then orders me to read.

I try to get the words past my lips, but it's easier said than done. Darian pulls out to the tip, his dick smeared with my creamy arousal, and then he rams back inside. He fucks me like that—slow, deep, hard.

The words blur on the page, and that's when I realize I'm crying. The folder contains my father's crimes. The families he tore apart. The destruction he left in his wake. All of his shady deals.

"Ah, that one," Darian says as he pulls out and flips me onto my front. "Particularly nasty." With a hand in my hair, he fills me up with his dick and removes a sheet from the file beside me.

He slams a photograph in front of me of a naked woman, beaten and bruised, with countless stab wounds. "Your father snatched her off the street and raped her for days."

"No…" My voice shakes. I don't want to believe it. "You're lying to me."

"Oh, wife," Darian says, patting my head like a dog while rocking his cock deep inside me. "So naïve and innocent in a world of hungry wolves."

I choke out a cry when he fists my hair and slams my cheek against the photograph.

He takes me hard and fast to the soundtrack of slapping skin. "Let's fuck some of that innocence out of you, Mrs. Delacroix."

Tears stream down my cheeks, and my pussy tightens around Darian's massive cock.

A wave of pleasure builds between my legs, and I hold onto the edge of the desk for support, letting out soft moans and whimpers.

*It can't be true. The photograph... No, I refuse to believe it.*

"That's it, Cecilia. Come on my cock. Show me how much you like it."

"Darian, please…" I moan.

"Please, what?"

"More."

He chuckles, fisting my hair so tightly that my scalp prickles. "I'm going to come so hard inside your tight little cunt, Mrs. Delacroix. Think you can take all my cum?"

"Yes, yes!" My own climax washes over me as I quiver in his hold.

"Fuck…" He grunts, slamming into me one final time, and bites down hard on my shoulder, pulsing his release.

I've barely caught my breath when he shifts me over onto my back and stares down at my pussy.

His cum leaks from my gaping hole, thick and milky white, as I look around for wipes, but Darian drops to his knees without hesitation and licks me clean. It's the hottest thing I've ever seen, his tongue swirling over my opening.

Looking up at me, he dips his tongue inside, and when he stands up and grabs my jaw, I part my lips with a gasp.

He invades my mouth with his tongue, smeared with cum—mine and his. The kiss is filthy in the best way possible, and I cling to him as he tastes every inch of my mouth.

Darian grunts as our teeth clash, but then he pulls away, panting hard. "I should punish you for breaking in here."

"This wasn't a punishment?" I smile.

It's strange how I don't hate him, not even a little, and when he kisses me again, I wrap my hands around his neck and my legs around his waist. "Fuck me again, *husband*."

He growls into the kiss and then proceeds to fuck me against every surface in his office.

# CHAPTER ELEVEN

CECILIA

Glitz and glamor aren't all they're jacked up to be. My expensive burgundy dress is slowly suffocating me, and my boobs alone are so pushed up that they threaten to touch my chin. Women mill around in expensive gowns, Venetian eye masks, and high updos. Meanwhile, their narcissistic husbands, dressed in tuxedos, eye up the young waitresses like they're juicy pieces of steak.

The stench of Chanel and greed pricks my nose as Darian steers me deeper into the sparkling ballroom with his hand on my lower back. It's unfair how devilishly handsome he looks, groomed to the nines with his dark hair slicked back and a black eye mask with intricate detailing.

"Try not to glower." His low, seductive voice caresses my ear.

A shiver runs through me, so to distract myself, I turn and grab a champagne flute from a male waiter's tray. I down it in one go, watching his firm ass weave effortlessly through the crowds.

Darian's fingers dance higher up my spine, and then he's gripping the back of my neck firmly enough to make me yelp.

"Look at another man like that again, and I'll see to it that they walk out of here dickless."

He steers me forward, nodding politely to mustached, balding men. I smile at a stranger, discarding my flute on another passing tray. "You can let go of me now."

"And trust you to behave?" he grumbles. "I think not. You'll destroy the nearest artwork if I let you out of sight."

I whirl around. "You're insufferable."

"And you're a pain in my ass."

"Takes one to know one."

Darian's left eye twitches, and he opens his mouth to retort, but Sinclair joins us with another flute of champagne.

As he hands it to me, I happily accept it, and they watch me gulp it down.

"Where did you find her again?" Sinclair asks, amused, sipping his bubbly.

"Either a back alley of some dingey bar or a circus," Darian replies drily, snatching the flute from my hand before I've had time to drink it all.

"Hey!" I protest.

Ignoring me, they scan the room. "Think Beaumont will show his face?" Sinclair asks.

"I know he will." Darian puts the half-full flute on a floating tray. "Now that the news about my mysterious marriage has broken, he'll sniff blood."

"He's harmless." Sinclair smacks Darian on the back the way men do—a little too hard. Darian grunts. "You've dealt with worse sharks."

"Who's Beaumont?" I ask, pretending to be very interested in the scenery.

"Oh, no one special." Sinclair sounds conversational, but there's a bite to his tone.

"I sense a story." I inch closer and trail my tongue over

my lip, if only to evoke a reaction from my husband, who looks mildly annoyed by the inconvenience of attending such a *tedious event.*

Those were his words. Not mine.

Sinclair smirks around the rim of his flute when I place my hand on his arm.

"I love a good story."

"Is that so?"

I make an agreeing sound, but it turns into a very unladylike squeak when Darian rips me away from Sinclair by the neck.

"That's enough flirting with Mr. Sinclair," he says tersely, disposing me unceremoniously by his side.

Sinclair chuckles as he pushes his circular glasses up his nose, having forgone an eye mask. "Are you sure you have a handle on your wife? She's a wild one."

"About that story—"

Darian shuts me up with a single glare.

Sinclair's amused gaze bounces between us. He drinks the last of his champagne and hands it to a man in a tux who is certainly not a waiter, and then he interrupts mine and Darian's stare-off with another one of his smooth laughs. "I see you've met your match, Delacroix. She's a keeper."

Darian snorts, and I narrow my eyes.

Sinclair focuses on me. "Beaumont is your husband's archenemy."

"Archenemy?" I deadpan. "Seriously?"

"Oh yes, quite. Beaumont is a… What's the word?" He pretends to think and then clicks his fingers. "Asshole."

"Oookay." I give him a 'you're weird' look.

Sinclair humors me. "Your husband is such a friendly gentleman. Last year, in fact, he took immense pleasure in sabotaging Mr. Beaumont's weapon trade, which ruined his career."

My mouth falls open, and I look at Darian. "You did what?"

He rolls his eyes and then surveys the crowd.

"In his defense..." Sinclair continues. "Their feud goes way back. The Beaumonts have tried to destroy his family's business and reputation for generations."

"I don't see how that justifies ruining a man. Shouldn't you turn the other cheek or something?"

Darian laughs—actually laughs, but then he stops just as fast and knocks on my head. "Hello? Anybody home?"

I bat him off. "Jerk."

"Oh, honey, wasn't two orgasms this morning enough for you? Do I have to remind you that we're at a fundraiser event for orphaned kittens? This isn't the place for dirty talk."

Sinclair steals another flute of champagne, shoulders shaking with stifled laughter.

"This isn't a fucking fundraiser for orphaned kittens." I arch a brow, my hand already on my cocked hip. Next, I'll stomp my foot or smack his annoyingly handsome face.

"No?" he asks, turning his whole body to face me. "What is this fundraiser for if not to raise money for fluffy animals needing rescuing?"

"You tell me," I challenge. "You're a Duke of a secret society. Whatever this is"—I wave a hand around the milling billionaires and their dolled-up wives—"it's a front for what's *actually* going on here."

"It's not a very secret society if you know about it." His blue eyes sparkle, challenging me to more than a verbal duel.

We stare at each other, and Darian smirks in that infuriating way he has.

Sinclair clears his throat. "Only two orgasms? Should

have gone for a third, Delacroix. I thought I taught you better."

"We didn't fuck this morning," I clarify. "To fuck, he would need to know how to get hard." I break away from Darian's ocean eyes, wetting my lips, surveying the crowd. "They sell pills for that now."

Sinclair throws his head back and laughs.

I bow at the knees and then smile sweetly at my husband, who looks like he might explode any moment now. Even the tips of his ears are red. "I'm going to powder my nose."

"You didn't complain yesterday when I fucked you three times in the office!" he shouts as I walk away.

Shocked gasps ring out around us, and the ladies in the room clutch their pearl necklaces while their husbands twitch their mustaches in disapproval, as if they weren't hacking humans to pieces or watching orgies mere weeks ago during Hell Fire Night. But *this* ruffles their feathers? Hypocrites.

I make a beeline for the bathroom, furious and humiliated.

How dare Darian tell everyone present that I suffered a temporary lapse in judgment yesterday. One of many where that infuriating man is concerned.

I should've never slept with him again. I could be pregnant for all I know.

Barging into the bathroom like a derailing train, I nearly barrel through a gray-haired woman, who stumbles back with a mortified gasp. What is it with these people? One moment, they spend ten hours killing humans for sport to show the leaders of the world that they're above the law. Then they dress up in expensive clothing and fancy masks and parade around a ballroom like this is a debutante ball for the Upper West Side's elite.

I ignore the woman's disapproving tut as I enter one of the stalls, half expecting someone to wipe my backside for me with dollar bills. The stall alone could classify as a bathroom suite to some.

After I've relieved myself, I wash my hands while avoiding eye contact with anyone entering the bathroom. My mother was a van der Meer; I was born into this world of money and power—secret society royalty. Thanks to my father's inheritance, I'm not short of old money. I've got my own fortune. But I was young when he disappeared on Hell Fire Night. Mom packed our things and moved us somewhere no one would find us. Years passed, and I grew used to a different way of living.

After drying my hands, I exit the bathroom.

The hallway is a quiet reprieve from the busy ballroom, so I lean against the wall while listening to the muted hum of conversation, soft piano music, and the clink of flutes.

A fire exit catches my attention, the door propped open with a brick. How long would it take Darian to realize I'm gone? How long before his Commoners chase after me? How far could I make it? Far enough to jump on a train or a bus?

"Why is such a beautiful woman like yourself hiding out here?" a deep voice asks.

My head shoots up.

A man with short brown hair, thin lips, and sideburns that could rival Mr. Darcy's in the Keira Knightley adaptation of *Pride and Prejudice* waltzes closer.

I back away out of instinct, but stop when my back connects with a Greek statue. "I'm not hiding."

He's close now. Close enough that I can smell the cedarwood and woodsy amber notes of his cologne.

His eyes drift over my shoulder. "You're out here by yourself. Looks to me like you're hiding."

"You are?" I ask, uneasy.

He smiles at me, but there's nothing warm about it.

"Where are my manners? I'm Mr. Beaumont." Taking my hand, he places a kiss on my knuckles.

I try to free my fingers from his steel grip without luck. Aside from the whole 'enemy of my husband' dilemma, something about him sets me on edge. He's undressing me with his eyes in a way that slithers over my skin like slick eels.

His eyes bore into me as he lingers with his lips on my skin, and I try to yank my hand away again.

Releasing me, he straightens. "You look breathtaking tonight, Miss van der Meer."

"Drop the flattery. How do you know my maiden name?"

"I have my ways, but don't worry. Your secret is safe with me."

I try to slide from between him and the Greek statue at my back, but he blocks my path, imposing and large.

"I can help you."

"Help me? I doubt it." I try to sidestep him again.

Beaumont doesn't stop me this time.

My shoulder brushes against his chest, and I try not to sprint.

I hate feeling like I've turned my back on an enemy, but I also refuse to show weakness when I'm unarmed and at a disadvantage to the opposition.

"Don't you want to find out what happened to your father?" he calls out.

I can hear the assured smile in his voice. Beaumont knows he's caught me on his hook, and he humors me by allowing me to walk away because he knows I'll turn around.

"Let me guess. That husband of yours isn't giving you the answers you seek."

I come to a halt. *Don't fall for it. He's baiting you on purpose. Don't turn around.*

As I hold my breath, my frantic pulse pounds in my throat.

"Mr. Delacroix knows more about your father's fate than he lets on."

I'm sure my heart is about to beat out of my chest. I've looked for answers for so long without luck. Everywhere I turned was another dead-end, and I was ready to throw it all out, ready to die if it meant killing as many members of this corrupt secret society as possible. At least then, I would have dented their armor.

I slowly turn around. "What do you know about my father?"

His eyes crease at the corners, reminding me of a cat who caught the canary.

Before I know what's happening, I'm striding up to him like a woman on a mission. "What do you know about my father?" I ask more forcefully this time.

He reaches out to trace my collarbone with his finger, so I swat him away.

"Don't touch me!"

Chuckling, he slides the offending hand into his pocket. "I know your husband is connected to your father's disappearance."

"How do you know that? More importantly, how can I trust you? I know all about your family rivalry." *I don't.* "What if you're making this up? For all I know, *you* murdered my father…" I step closer, baring my teeth. "And I should kill you."

"You can't trust me," he replies with a shrug, ignoring my threat, "but I'm your best shot at finding answers."

"What's in it for you? Money? I heard about your financial woes after Darian sabotaged your weapon run."

His eyes darken, and he looks away, rubbing his ticking

jaw. When he returns his focus to me, my insides shrivel. If hatred had a face, it's staring back at me now. "Your money is no good to me, Mrs. Delacroix."

"Then what do you want?"

"Information about your husband."

"You want me to be your spy?"

"*Informant.* But we can go with the word 'spy' if that makes you happy."

"And why would I help you?"

"Because I can give you answers about your father."

"You said that already, and somehow, I don't believe you."

A man walks past, nodding a greeting to Mr. Beaumont. I dip my head.

"How about I sweeten the deal with a sign of goodwill," he continues, watching the man enter the men's bathroom. He waits until we're alone and safe from prying ears before fishing a creased, unopened letter from his inside pocket. "Lauren sends her regards."

My eyes widen with surprise as he holds it out of reach.

"Provide me with sensitive information about your husband, and I will investigate your father's disappearance *and* let you have Lauren's letter."

"How do I know it's a letter from her? What if you're bluffing?"

He angles it. "Recognize the handwriting?"

I feel an ache spread through my chest. *Lauren wrote me.* Suddenly, I want to be alone so I can read her words in private. I need to know that she's okay. "How is it a sign of goodwill if you won't let me read it now?"

"Let's call it more of an incentive to give me what I want. I'll see you around soon, Mrs. Delacroix." He tucks the letter into his inside pocket before sliding away like a shadow.

I'm too shaken up to rejoin the party, but Darian will grow suspicious if I don't return soon, so I shake out my trembling hands and smooth down my dress.

The first thing I notice when I enter the ballroom is that my husband and Sinclair are not where I left them. I search the crowd until my eyes land on my husband by the tables.

A slender woman with chestnut hair, perfectly curled and arranged into an even more perfect hairdo, hangs off his arm like he's a prized possession she won at a carnival. He looks mildly inconvenienced by her presence but makes no move to peel her off, and when she pushes her generous tits against his arm, he checks his watch.

"Uh-oh, that's the governor's wife." Sinclair's voice slithers into my ear from behind like a serpent's tongue. "She's had a thing for our Delacroix forever."

"I see what you're doing, Sinclair. You're trying to make me jealous."

"Oh, sweetheart," he snickers, flicking my eye mask, towering beside me. "I don't have to try. You look like a wet dick slapped you in the face."

"Are you always so crass?" I ask, now glowering at my husband and the governor's wife.

*Why is he allowing her to rub her tits against his Armani tux?*

Darian spots us, his eyes hardening, though he still lets the parasite cling to him like a leech.

"It's a gift," Sinclair replies, waiting for effect. "Word on the street is that she has better suction than a Dyson." He slinks away, giving the devil on my shoulder enough material to taunt my angel for the next century.

*Does he like her?* She's pretty, with her big breasts threatening to spill out of her dress and legs that go on for miles, judging by the high slit in her skirt.

Because my dignity has left the party with what little common sense I have left, I spin on my heel and all but run for the fire exit. Fuck him and Mrs. Dyson. I refuse to stick around and watch him flirt with someone else.

Before I have a chance to exit the ballroom, Sinclair blocks my path and takes my hand like a gentleman from Tudor times. He presses a kiss to my knuckles. "In a rush somewhere?"

"You're enjoying this, aren't you?" I snatch my hand back with a huff.

"Immensely. You should really do something about that dick imprint on your cheek."

I sneer, trying to move past him, but he takes up more space than a damn tank.

"Can I have this dance?" he asks.

That's when I notice the waltz music.

"I don't think that's a—"

"I wasn't asking." He guides me to the middle of the room, where men and women twirl and dip.

"I've never waltzed in my life."

"Good thing I'm an expert."

I give him a critical look before eyeing the hallway longingly. If only he wouldn't insist on dancing. I could escape this wretched place and forget about Darian and the conflicting emotions he stirs. I could live the rest of my life on the run. It's what I've done for years.

My lips part when Sinclair puts his big hand on my lower back and pulls me close. What is it about men smelling like sex gods in this corrupt world? Why can't they be gentle on women's hearts by smelling of sweat and bad oral hygiene?

Taking my other hand, he begins to lead the dance. I stumble over my feet like a newborn lamb. My mom did everything in her power to shield me from the wolves, yet here I am, dancing in the forest beneath a full moon. If she saw me now, she'd squirm in her grave.

"You'll never survive this world if you run," Sinclair says, keeping his voice low. "You were born and bred by Exiled royalty. Act like it."

My pride prickles. "I never asked for this."

"What *did* you ask for, Mrs. Delacroix? To be murdered in cold blood by monsters? Did you think your little stunt on Hell Fire Night would have made a difference? That your mother would be proud? Your father avenged by your act of rebellion? You're smarter than this."

"Fuck you," I hiss, meeting his hard eyes. "You know nothing."

"I know you're married to one of the most powerful men in this room. You need to toughen up, or you'll become chum to the sharks. Look around you, Mrs. Delacroix. They're foaming at the mouth. Whether you like it or not, you've been dragged back into this world."

"And whose fault is that?" I glare up at him. "I never asked to marry your friend."

"That may be so, but you looked like a wounded puppy when you watched him with the governor's wife."

"I did not—" I stop myself from saying more. Why am I justifying myself to this man? I don't owe him an explanation.

"Darian is a lot of things," Sinclair says conversationally, twirling me like a pirouetting ballerina, "but he's not a cheater."

"No?" I slam into his chest again, winded and dizzy. "Why did he let that woman paw him?"

"You offended his sexual prowess. Pride has always been your husband's biggest downfall. While he can murder in cold blood without batting an eye, he doesn't know how to handle emotions. You're uncharted territory, Mrs. Delacroix." He dips me so low my hair touches the floor. "His mission with that little stunt was a success."

"What mission?" I ask, clinging to his shoulders for dear life so I don't fall.

He finally straightens. "To make you jealous."

As we dance by a couple, I catch sight of Darian. The woman is gone, and my husband is staring at me like he wants to douse me with gasoline and set me on fire.

"And now *he's* jealous," Sinclair drawls, then spins me again and pulls me back into his arms. "Do me a favor and fuck the rage out of him after this."

I roll my eyes, finally learning the sequence of steps to this dance. "Should you encourage such toxicity?"

"With all due respect, it's the best recipe for amazing sex."

Darian is on his way over within the next second, tense and on edge, as Sinclair dips me again.

"I charge by the minute. You can write me a check."

"Sorry? A check?"

He straightens and pulls me up. "Marriage counseling. You're welcome, by the way." Stepping back, he hands me over to Darian, who glares at him like he's two seconds away from ripping his head off. "Thank you for letting me take her for a spin."

He's gone before Darian has a chance to open his mouth, though I doubt he could if he wanted to. His jaw is screwed shut, a muscle ticking madly in his cheek.

Without a word, he aggressively pulls me to him and begins to dance, causing a surprised squeak to tumble from my lips as I crash into his hard chest.

"You seem awfully interested in my friend. Do I need to remind you whose wife you are?"

"Like you're one to speak," I snap. "You looked very cozy with that woman."

"Mrs. Auclair?"

Just her name on his lips makes me see red.

*Don't march over to her table and claw her eyes out.*

Darian twirls me once, then twice. "You're ready to run at the first sight of a woman flirting with me? I'm disappointed. I thought you had more backbone than that. What happened to the beautiful, fiery woman who crashed the Hell Fire Night party, ready to die for a taste of revenge?"

I refuse to reply. He can take his smug face and kindly fuck off to Mars. Or better yet, the farthest distant planet in the galaxy. Scrap that, make it the goddamn universe.

Darian flicks my nose. "You flare your nostrils when you're angry."

"And you clench your jaw when you're mad. I think we've established that we have equally good observational skills."

"Your smart mouth makes me hard," he states, like we're discussing the latest affairs in Congress. How he can remain calm when he's vibrating with repressed anger and testosterone is impressive. Meanwhile, I'm barely keeping the snarl off my face.

"Your smart mouth doesn't make me wet."

He spins me so fast that I swear I'm on a Graviton ride. Nausea clenches my stomach when he finally pulls me against his chest. "Don't mistake me for a gentleman, Mrs. Delacroix. We both know you're soaking your panties, and I won't hesitate to finger your tight pussy in front of everyone to prove my point." Quick as a flash, his hand finds the slit in my dress, and he hikes it up my thigh with a possessive look in his cobalt eyes, ready to devour me.

I grab his wrist to stop him, aware of the dancing couples

around us. We must look weird, standing in the middle of the dance floor. "Please, don't do this here."

He has the decency not to flaunt his triumph as we resume dancing. Darian drinks me in, and I know for certain, no man has ever looked at me with such hunger.

It's impossible not to flush beneath the weight of his full attention.

"I must admit," he says, "I wanted to flay him alive when I saw you two dancing."

"He's a good dancer. Smells nice, too."

Why am I antagonizing him? Not only is it cruel, but it's also immature. I'm better than that. Better than my petty jealousy. Even so, I can't get the image of Mrs. Auclair all over him out of my mind, which is messing with my head.

In a swift move, Darian flips me around so that his chest is against my back. Goosebumps litter my arms as he curls his fingers around my throat and brushes his warm lips over the shell of my ear. "You're begging for a hard spanking, *wife*."

"Give me your worst," I spit, sounding braver than I am while quivering on the inside.

His chuckle dances over the curve of my neck, low and husky—a nefarious, delicious threat.

He takes my hand and drags me off the dance floor, past a smirking Sinclair, who raises his glass and winks, but I don't have time to flip him off before we stumble into the hallway.

Two Commoners guard the grand staircase, their faces hidden behind animal masks, but they part like a curtain upon seeing us.

"You two, upstairs now," Darian demands, then pulls me along, giving me no choice but to follow.

His grip on my hand is so tight that I wouldn't be surprised if he cuts off my blood supply.

The Commoners exchange glances, but they don't object, and I get it. No one says no to Darian Delacroix.

We reach the landing. Gold-framed paintings larger than me line the walls, and a glass dome overhead overlooks the foyer downstairs and the second-floor balcony.

I stay clear of the banister in case my husband decides he's had enough of my attitude.

"Where are you taking me?" I ask nervously, aware of the Commoners behind us.

Darian opens a door to a spare bedroom and shoves me unceremoniously inside. I stumble onto the gleaming marble floor, surprised by the dark energy emanating from Darian as he removes his suit jacket.

The Commoners close the door, hovering awkwardly, waiting for my husband to give them orders.

I try to stand up, but Darian bites out, "Stay."

On his way to the bar in the far corner of the room, he loosens his bowtie and uncorks a whiskey bottle. He grabs a tumbler and fills it with ice.

My heart thuds harder as I glance behind me at the Commoners blocking the only escape route with their hulking builds.

Darian pours a thumb of whiskey and takes a large sip, the ice clinking as I watch him warily, feeling cornered by a vicious, masked serpent.

His throat rolls as he swallows it down. "Cat got your tongue, Cecilia?"

When I remain silent, he takes slow, calculated steps toward me. "Has that fuckable mouth no snarky comeback?"

I glance behind me again at the Commoners, but Darian tsks.

"They're not going to help you, honey. You've been a very bad girl."

# CHAPTER TWELVE

## CECILIA

My head whips back around. He's closer now. So close, panic sets in.

I scramble away, crawling like a [illegible] injured animal, and Darian follows behind, his shoes [illegible] on the marble.

The dress gets caught beneath my knees, and I fall forward.

"There's nowhere to go, Mrs. Delacroix."

Masculine laughter bounces off the walls as I slide beneath the bed to escape Darian's sinister mood. Still, he's faster, grabbing me by the ankle and dragging me back out, my skirt riding up in the process to expose my silk panties.

I try to crawl away again, but Darian fists my hair and pulls me farther into the room before dropping me onto the floor.

"Sinclair smells nice, does he?" He downs the last whiskey, then throws the tumbler at the wall, and I yelp when it explodes into countless shards that spray everywhere.

"He's a good dancer?" Swiping the whiskey bottle from the bar, he storms over to me.

I try to crawl away again, but he flips me over onto my back and puts the sole of his shoe on my chest to keep me down. I can barely breathe; the look in his eyes is unlike any I've seen. Unhinged.

He tips the bottle and pours whiskey on my face, waterboarding me to his heart's content. I splutter and cough, eyes squeezing closed.

My thighs snap together as panic fills my veins. I thrash, terrified and aroused. Fucked up beyond saving and in need of more of his toxic jealousy.

*I* make him this way. *I* make him feel possessive, deranged, and out of control.

"Are you ready to apologize yet, baby?" Offering me a reprieve, he lifts the bottle.

I gasp for breath, my lungs burning. "Fuck you!"

He takes a swig of alcohol, then tips the bottleneck again. "Suit yourself."

Whiskey splashes over my face and eye mask. I buck and squirm on the floor to get away, but his boot digs into my chest. It goes on forever. Or so it feels. When the bottle is empty, one of the Commoners hands him another.

Just as I think I might pass out, he stops again and stares down at me with a wicked smirk. His pants are tenting, and his long, thick cock looks delicious. Unfortunately, I'm too busy coughing up a lung to appreciate the view.

Before my coughing has subsided, he grabs me by the arm and hauls me toward the four-poster bed. He lifts me effortlessly, as if I weigh nothing, holding me upright with one hand on my arm. With an impatient flick of his wrist, he gestures to one of the Commoners, asking them to hand over a set of handcuffs attached to their belt.

"What are you doing?" I ask croakily, my nerves ratcheting another level.

He secures me to the pole and slowly slides down the zipper of my dress. A cool breeze from an open window brushes against my back as I attempt to glance behind me, but I can't see him or the Commoners. With a sharp tug, he tears the dress the rest of the way, leaving it hanging in tatters around me, and then he removes my panties, so I'm left in just my bra and heels.

Whimpering, I yank on the handcuffs.

"Do you like what you see, gentlemen?" Darian asks the Commoners from somewhere behind me.

"She's beautiful, sir."

Darian strokes his big hand over my hair, and when I plead with him to let me go, he shushes me before addressing the Commoners. "Spank her raw."

Fear latches onto my heart, and I rattle the handcuffs again. "No, Darian, no. Please, don't let them do this. I'm sorry."

Agonizingly long seconds pass until heavy footsteps drown out my frenzied panic, and I tug hard on the handcuffs. It hurts, but I'm too high on adrenaline to truly feel it.

One of the men grabs my hair and stares at me through a creepy beaked duck mask.

A hard slap lands on my ass, causing me to cry out, and laughter whips my skin as I try to find Darian in the room. He's leaning against a wardrobe, hands in his pockets, his intense gaze on me.

Another hard smack connects with my burning ass cheek, and I fall forward against the pole. More slaps follow, brutal and degrading, as I drown in Darian's eyes.

Behind me, the men laugh, alternating between squeezing my ass cheeks and smacking them hard enough to cause my knees to buckle.

Darian smirks, and my nipples ache from that hungry

look alone, but then another brutal slap steals my breath, the insides of my thighs sticky with arousal. I throb all over, yearning for Darian to unleash the restrained monster lurking in his gaze.

As I watch, he unzips his pants and shoves his hand inside his briefs to stroke his hard erection.

I don't feel the smacks anymore, and my ass is no longer burning; it's ice cold with pain instead and a roadmap of handprints. Yet they keep spanking me and degrading me with their cruel laughter.

A deprived part of me loves every second because it has set something sinister loose in Darian's eyes. Something that's circling and preying on us.

My inner walls clench as his hand moves inside his briefs. He wets his lips, his heavy-lidded gaze intense, before reaching into the back of his pants to pull out a gun. I can barely process what's happening when he fires two shots, blood spraying over my bare back, warm and coppery.

The men drop to the floor.

I tremble, staring down at them over my shoulder.

Darian palms my numb ass. "Such perfection," he whispers, sliding his thumb between my cheeks, chuckling softly when I tense up. He then presses the barrel against my temple before trailing bites and licks across my shoulder, his breath brushing against the curve of my neck. "Are you ready to apologize now, or do more people have to die first?"

"I'm sorry…" My voice shakes as much as my body.

"There's a good girl. It isn't so hard to keep that pretty mouth in check, is it?"

One of the men is still alive, groaning on the floor and clutching his bleeding chest. The bullet went straight through him.

Darian picks up my panties off the floor, walks over to the

dying man, and stuffs his windpipe with the silk fabric. He straightens up and watches me observe the Commoner. I've never witnessed such a prolonged death before.

The Commoner's wide, terrified eyes lock on mine, and I pulse in forbidden places as I watch the life drain from him.

I'm sick for liking this.

Darian slides a pocketknife from his pants and then proceeds to strip the men naked and remove their genitalia. It's gory and gruesome and utterly fascinating.

When he's done, he puts the severed cocks on the bed for me to see, but I'm more turned on by his blood-soaked, veiny hands.

"Don't say I don't bring you trophies. You better enjoy this moment, because it's the closest you'll ever get to other dicks."

"You're sick."

Stalking up behind me, he yanks my head back by my hair, smiling like a villainous monster from my worst night-mare. "Don't you think I can see the lust in your eyes? How horny you are?"

Before I can respond, he rams three slick fingers into my mouth, assaulting me with the coppery taste of blood and gore, and a moan escapes my lips as liquid heat pools between my legs.

"That's it. Good girl," he praises. "Suck them clean. Show me what a depraved little thing you are." Biting my earlobe hard enough to make me yelp, he whispers darkly, "That smart mouth is good for more things than talking back, isn't it?"

I'm desperate for friction, so I rub my ass against his straining erection, begging wordlessly for more. The severed cocks on the bloodied mattress have tingles dancing over my bare skin. It scares me how far he's willing to go where his darkness is concerned, but it also excites me.

As he removes his fingers from my mouth, I chase them for another taste. "Please," I beg. "I need you inside me."

With his big hands on my hips, he fucks himself on me, his fingers twitching as he teases me with his hardness.

"Please put it in me," I plead, shivering with desire when he rolls his hips and grinds his erection against my soaked pussy.

*Why does he have to torture us like this?*

"Do you enjoy looking at the cocks?" he asks, releasing my hip and circling my throbbing clit. "Do you imagine them inside you?"

I bite down on my bottom lip as an orgasm washes over me, and then I rock back against him, moaning loud enough to wake the dead corpses on the floor. Darian's touch turns rough, and I come again with a scream.

"Do you want to suck on dead men's cocks?"

I shake my head, clinging to the pole the best I can while he continues rubbing my too-sensitive clit. "Why are you torturing me like this?"

"Answer the question, Mrs. Delacroix."

"No," I choke out between gasps. "The only cock I want to suck is yours."

"Good answer." He shifts behind me, and I feel his bulbous crown press against me. "Hold on to the pole."

I do as instructed, and then he impales me on his big cock.

My lips part in surprise. Darian is large and powerful—overwhelming. His hips rock against me at a relentless pace, the sound of his belt clinking. I moan softly, my nails digging into the pole. Fuck, I've never felt anything this good. Never been this cock drunk before.

"Harder, Darian," I beg, my pussy rippling around him. "Aah, yes!"

"You like it hard, huh?" He slams into me, and I fall forward. "You like being my little cum bucket, baby? A warm hole for me to sink my dick into?"

"Yes!" I admit, moaning, my aching tits straining against my bra, and he palms one, squeezing it hard enough to hurt.

"You should see your red ass. I love pounding it while it has other men's handprints on it, but don't ask me why. It's fucking insane how mad you drive me." He bites my neck like a feral animal, his cock pulsing inside me.

His groans of pleasure trigger another climax, and I moan his name as I tighten around him. Darian's thrusts slow, and he grinds his cock deep, holding me tightly, as if he never wants to let me go.

As soon as he pulls out and steps away, his cum trickles out of me.

I attempt to catch my breath while he makes a quick call to a cleanup crew, but I feel too weak to stand, so I cling to the pole for support. My fingertips tingle from the tight cuffs, which isn't a good sign, but I don't mind. Exhaustion washes over me with my next breath, and my head feels heavy.

I'm vaguely aware of Darian removing my handcuffs and scooping me into his arms.

I'd open my eyes and say something if I could, but my body won't obey. I'm floating in a sea of cardamom and tonka bean.

Warm lips press against my damp forehead. "Sleep, baby. I've got you."

## CHAPTER THIRTEEN

DARIAN

*I rock in the corner of the dark wardrobe with my hands over my ears. I rock and rock, begging for the screaming and crying to stop.*

*Salty tears stream down my cheeks, but it doesn't matter how hard I press on my ears, I still hear Mom's cries. She won't stop.*

*When I can't take it anymore, I lower my hands and crawl forward, careful not to knock over shoeboxes. She made me promise to stay in here—and I will—but I just want to peek.*

*As I peer through the slats, I hold my breath in case they can hear my shaky exhale. I spot my sobbing dad first, a gun digging into his temple, forcing him to watch the bad man on top of Mommy.*

*I bring my trembling, clammy palms to my mouth. Mommy is naked and hurt, and a big monster holds her down on the bloodied bed.*

*With his pants and underwear halfway down his hairy legs, he grunts and makes noises like a big bear.*

*A scary bear.*

*Daddy roars, and the man next to him whips him with the*

*gun. I muffle a scream and scamper back into the shadows before slowly creeping forward again. Blood is pouring from Daddy's eyebrow.*

*Mommy made me promise to hide, but Daddy needs me. I look at the bad men. They're all big and scary and carry weapons.*

*Daddy owns a collection. I'm not allowed in his office, but I've caught glimpses.*

*The men who come to our house remind me of these big, scary men with cold eyes and scars. Some wear expensive suits like Daddy, and those men are the scariest.*

*Why is Mommy bleeding? I don't like to see her hurt.*

*I shake all over as fear ripples through me, and my teeth chatter violently.*

*The bad man climbs off Mommy and pulls his pants up. "Your wife's cunt felt amazing, Delacroix. Tight and warm, like a high-end whore's. I appreciate your hospitality. You don't mind if my men have fun, too, right? It's Hell Fire Night, after all." He gestures with his gun for one of his masked friends to step forward. Mommy soon stops crying and stares at the ceiling while the man does to her what the other man did.*

*Bad, bad things.*

*The scary man turns to Daddy. "I'm disappointed. I expected more from 'the mighty Delacroix.'" He extends his arm and fires his gun.*

*Mommy panics again. She screams and fights, slapping and kicking. But the man is stronger, and so is the other one who joins in.*

*Daddy stares right at me as blood trickles from a big hole in his forehead.*

I wake with a gasp, drenched in sweat.

What the fuck is happening to me? The nightmares are

growing more intense and vivid by the day, transporting me back to the worst night of my life.

I swipe my arm over my sweaty forehead and check the time on the nightstand before throwing off the quilt and placing my feet on the floor.

My mind races, and I dig my fingers into my eyeballs in a feeble attempt to erase the memories. Nothing works; the echo of my mother's fearful screams ripples through my tormented mind.

If only I could take a pickaxe to my skull and chip away at the sound.

Bunching my fist, I whack my head. "Shut up!"

What will it take to forget? What the fuck do I need to do to move on? I went to extreme lengths to get my revenge—kidnapped the man responsible for my parents' demise, locked him up, and left him to rot while I searched for his wife and daughter. Now that I have his daughter in my clutches, the dreams should stop, but they're intensifying instead.

Pulling open the bedside drawer, I remove my mother's necklace, cinching it in my palm. Why am I not feeling better? Why is nothing working?

After carefully placing the necklace back inside the drawer and sliding on a pair of joggers, I grab my gun from the bedside table and leave the room.

The old house groans in the night breeze outside as I make a beeline for the cellar.

Cecilia's father should be left to wither away in the dark, but I can't rest until I get answers. All these years, I've bided my time while waiting for him to confess, but it ends now. I'm done waiting.

As I enter the cellar, a familiar scent of decay settles in my nose. The temperature drops and the air becomes humid. I doubt I'll ever get used to how chilly and damp it is here.

Descending the spiral stone steps, I focus on the feel of the gun in my hand. I should shoot him in the head like he shot my father, have him put down like a rabid dog, or line him up against the wall and taunt him with execution until he pisses himself. Though after so many years locked up in a dank cell, death would be a mercy, and he is the last person deserving of forgiveness.

"Let's cut the crap," I say as I walk up to this cell and slam the gun against the rusty metal bars. "I'm done playing your games."

It's too dark to see, so I light up the torch on the wall with the tools I leave down here for such occasions.

His grimy cheeks and weathered, wrinkled skin come into view, and he watches me wearily from the corner of his cell, legs drawn up close to his body, his bare feet so dirty they almost look black. Shadows from the dancing flame flicker over his features while he watches me pace in circles and restlessly tap the gun against my thigh.

"I can't sleep," I say after what feels like an eternity. "I dream of that night over and over and over again."

He remains silent, which pisses me off more.

I hate that even now, locked in a tiny cell, he remains calm and in control. Meanwhile, I'm falling apart on the inside.

I aim the gun at him. "The memories haunt me. They fucking haunt me, and it's your fault. I should finally kill you."

"You should," he agrees in his croaky, unused voice. "You should set me free."

The gun trembles in my hand. "Set you free? You would love that, wouldn't you?" I shake my head, and a bitter chuckle cuts through the thick silence, my lip curling over my teeth in a sneer as I tighten my grip on the gun. "You don't deserve freedom."

We watch each other in the ensuing silence, the lone torch casting elongating shadows on the stone walls. It would be so easy to kill him. One bullet is all it would take to end this nightmare, but his death won't bring me answers.

I lower the gun. "What happened to my mother that night? How did she die? Who killed her?"

"Your mother is gone, and she's not coming back—"

"Shut up!" I roar, surging forward and slamming the weapon against the bars. Van der Meer watches me calmly as I unravel before him, layer by layer, until nothing remains but fury.

I point the gun at him again, clutching it like I might disappear if I don't end him right here and now. "What did you do to my mother after you dragged her out of the house? Where did you take her?"

"You already know the answer."

*The Exiled party.*

"How did she die?"

He doesn't grace me with an answer, so I tighten my grip on the gun, determined to pull the trigger. "Answer the fucking question."

"Pull the trigger, son."

"I'm not your son. You murdered my father in cold blood."

"End this."

"No," I bite out, pulling back on the hammer. "You don't deserve to die."

"Kill me."

My eyes burn with unshed tears as he shuffles forward on the dirty stone floor. An ugly feeling sits on my chest, heavy and suffocating, and I bare my teeth as he presses his grimy face against the bars.

"Kill me, Delacroix. Don't you want revenge?" His lips peel back to reveal yellowed, rotten teeth that haven't seen a toothbrush in ten years. His gums have receded, and now the roots are visible. "Can't you taste it in the stale air?" Pretending to taste the air, he then levels his eyes on me. "Shoot me."

"Fuck you," I sneer, and he rolls his forehead over the bars as he snickers under his breath.

"You can't do it, can you, Delacroix? You're pathetic." His smile turns cruel. "Just like your father. He was weak, too. He didn't even try to save your mom, did he?"

"He had a gun to his head."

"So instead, he slumped in defeat while we took turns with his wife." He tuts, pressing his mouth through the rusty bars. "A real man fights back."

"You were four against one. He was injured."

"Weak," he taunts, then retreats back into the shadows. "You're just as weak as your father. You were too scared to save your mom then, and you're still scared."

My finger itches on the trigger, but I lower the weapon. I won't kill him. Not today. Not until I have my answers.

"You want to die?" I ask, stepping closer to the bars.

The stench of ammonia thickens the air the closer I get to his cell.

"You want me to set you free, van der Meer?" Removing the bullets from the chamber, I make a show of dropping them to the floor, one by one.

*You won't get to escape your prison any time soon.*

"You're not deserving of death."

# CHAPTER FOURTEEN

CECILIA

Unable to sleep, I scoot up on the bed with my father's file on my lap and lean against the headboard.

Rain lashes against the window, and the blustery wind howls as a streak of lightning illuminates the room. The eerie sounds fade into muted background noise when I open the file. The man I thought was my father—who I looked up to and who kissed me goodnight—was a monster.

Yes, I was born into a dark world, but my father didn't stop at killing traitors or enemies. He murdered and tortured women and children, too. Entire families. Anyone who crossed his path or happened to be in the wrong place at the wrong time.

I study a grainy photograph of my father leaving an apartment complex on a late winter's night. Snow flurries are visible in the glow of a nearby streetlamp. It looks peaceful, like the impenetrable silence that follows three gruesome homicides.

The next morning, I asked him about the scratch marks on

his face at breakfast, and he blamed it on a cat. Mom fussed over him like she always did when he sustained injuries.

How could she be so blind to who he was beneath the charming smiles? She worshipped him like he was a hero, and never saw through the façade. My father was like a lot of the members of the Exiled: greedy and hungry for power, but it didn't stop there. My father was a sadist who murdered and raped women because he could.

The evidence is all here, in my hands, so what do I do with it? I've spent the last ten years stewing in my own anger and need for revenge.

Revenge for what? The man who called me his little princess and kissed my nose after returning home and washing off the blood of whatever family he had spent hours torturing? My childhood was a lie. Dad wasn't my hero, and I wasn't his princess.

I close the folder, tossing it to the side, then stare unseeingly at the window. Whatever happened to my father on that Hell Fire Night ten years ago, he had it coming, and now I have to decide how much I care about the truth and what lengths I'm willing to go to find out. I already let my hatred lead my friends to their death. Yes, they would have still fought on Hell Fire Night, but it was my suggestion to strike Exiled's stronghold. *I* brought them there. For what?

I need a drink.

After sliding on my silk gown, I head to the kitchen to pour a glass of water, but before I get there, I stop short outside the living room. The door is ajar, and the fire is lit. I've only been here the one time when I stuck my head inside out of curiosity.

A stone fireplace provides the sole illumination in the vast room, crackling in the heavy silence. Luxurious leather armchairs are arranged around a glass coffee table, with cream cushions scattered on each.

I pause when I spot Darian on the couch, facing away from me. "Darian?"

He turns his head slightly sideways and drinks straight from a bottle of whiskey.

Frowning, I open the door farther and enter the room. "It's the middle of the night."

He takes another swig and rests his head against the back of the couch, slurring, "Go back to sleep, Cecilia."

Is he drunk? I cross the room, coming to stand beside him. Darian stares straight ahead at the fireplace, shadows dancing across his tired face, pronounced collarbones, and ridged muscles on his bare chest.

My gaze slides down his carved body and lingers on the trail of dark hair leading into his pants. Dressed in only a pair of joggers, he looks nothing like his usually put-together self.

When he lifts the whiskey bottle to his lips again, I wrench it out of his grip and place it on the coffee table. "You've had enough."

Darian shoots forward and tries to grab it, but I knock it over, and whiskey spills from the bottle and pools on the table before pouring over the side.

I cross my arms as Darian slumps back against the couch. We stare at each other for a while until he leans forward and hardens his gaze. "Go back to bed, Cecilia."

"What's all this?" I ask, gesturing to the whiskey bottle on its side. The state of Darian. "You're drunk."

"You're not my mother." He tears his pained gaze away and flops back, covering his face with his arm.

Something softens inside me when his chest inflates with a pained, ragged breath.

From the first moment I met Darian, he was an immovable fortress and larger than life, so what happened to reduce him to this shadow of himself?

Struck by the urge to comfort him, I reach out to place my hand on his shoulder, but he's faster, grabbing my wrist. "Don't touch me."

An ache blooms in my chest at the hard look in his eyes, and he drops my hand like touching me disgusts him. "Just… Go away."

His rejection stings more than it has any right to. Blinking away tears, I turn my back to him so that he doesn't see me cry.

Sparks from the fire shoot into the air as I leave the room. Minutes later, I return with a towel to wipe up the spillage.

Darian remains silent while I mop up the whiskey, but I feel his eyes on me.

"Leave it to the cleaners." His honeyed voice warms my back.

I ignore him as I continue cleaning, maybe because if I stop, I have no reason to stay here with him. He wants me to leave, but I can't bring myself to walk away when he's like this. I want to stay.

"Leave it," he snaps, sitting forward and wrenching me back by my arm. I fall against the couch, trapped between his legs as his fingers dig into my skin.

He presses his lips to my temple and whispers, "Why won't you just leave?"

The scent of whiskey on his breath makes me want to lift my chin and taste it on his lips. To feel his prickly stubble against my skin.

I wet my lips instead, savoring the feel of him this close. "I don't want to."

"I'm not good for you," he replies as my pulse pounds beneath his fingertips on my wrist.

My first instinct is to argue and tell him that only I know who and what is good for me, but I bite my tongue, a little concerned about my reaction. Although I want to keep my guard raised, I can feel it lowering in his presence.

"Darian?" I ask instead as he releases me.

He rests against the couch, his eyes closed. "Hmm?"

"Why did you make the deal?"

"What deal?" he slurs.

"The marriage deal."

His brows pull together, as if in pain. "I wanted him to suf…" He drifts off midsentence.

"You wanted what?" I sit up straighter. "What did you want?"

"It doesn't matter." His dejection has me moving closer.

I climb onto the couch, settling beside him, and study his face now that he's half asleep and barely aware of my presence. He's devastatingly handsome, with dark lashes fanning his cheeks and thin yet full lips that look far too tempting.

I stare at them for too long, imagining leaning in and tracing the seam with my tongue.

It doesn't help that I know the sounds he makes when he's aroused. Besides, it wasn't that long ago I wanted to kill him and see the life drain from his eyes.

His gun rests beside him on the couch, so I pick it up, feeling its weight in my hand, and press it to his temple. How easy it would be to pull the trigger and end him.

His heavy-lidded blue eyes open, and he sweeps them over my face. I hold my breath as he reaches out to brush my hair away from my brow.

"I'm sorry for everything. It was wrong of me to bring you into my world for my own selfish reasons."

"I was going to attack the party."

He drops his hand, his eyes falling shut. "I know."

"Kill you and your friends."

"Yes…" Trailing off, his frown smooths. He looks younger and less troubled, the sight twisting my stomach, as I have the impulse to lay in his arms.

Conflicted, I stare at his sleeping form as the gun trembles in my hand. This is the same man who let my friends die in cold blood, who didn't bat an eyelid. I can't let myself forget, but I struggle to see how that man is the same man asleep before me now. He seems so…broken.

This is my chance to get out of here. Maybe even my only chance, so why can't I bring myself to pull the trigger?

Placing the gun back down, I climb off the couch to grab him a blanket.

# CHAPTER FIFTEEN

DARIAN

I pride myself on staying in control at all times and have worked hard over the years to stay on top.

To be the best.

Brutal.

Ruthless.

Yet Cecilia van der Meer waltzes into my life with her long, shapely legs and fiery attitude and turns it upside down without trying.

At first, I sense a dull ache behind my temples, and then a bright sunbeam streams through a gap in the curtains and hits me straight in the face. I groan as I shield my eyes with my hand. How much did I have to drink last night? Enough to sink a ship of sailors, it would seem.

Jeez. I lower my hand but immediately regret it when I'm blinded by the morning sun.

Great, I never made it to bed last night. When was the last time I slept on the couch? It was so long ago that I can't recall.

I rub my eyes, wincing at the insistent throb in my skull.

I can barely remember the previous night. A nightmare woke me, and I went to see Cecilia's father before deciding to dull the pain with enough whiskey to shut down my kidneys.

My thoughts grind to a halt when I become aware of soft breaths against the crook of my neck, and I lower my hand.

What the hell? Cecilia is curled up beside me with her head on my shoulder and her fingers on my chest, above my heart.

I swallow around a thick lump in my throat, not daring to move as my heart begins to pound. What is she doing here? More importantly, why is she cuddled up with me?

My first instinct is to extract myself from her, but something stops me. Maybe it's the sensation of her breaths against my skin or the way my heart hammers beneath her fingers, almost as if it's chasing her touch.

I wet my lips nervously and shift my head to look at her.

A tendril of blonde hair threatens to escape from behind her ear, and dark lashes fan her cheeks. She looks peaceful. Or maybe I like to believe she feels safe beside me.

My gaze shifts between her long lashes and slightly parted plump lips. I've kissed her before, but those kisses were aggressive and dominant. Now, as her eyes move beneath her lids, I wonder how it would feel to savor her kiss and those pillowy lips that look so soft.

To taste her shaky breaths and make her fall apart with a kiss alone.

I lean in slowly to avoid waking her, wetting my lips in anticipation. Just as I'm about to taste her, her eyes flutter open and widen. She shoves away from me like her ass is on fire, tumbling off the couch with a loud thud and a startled yelp.

Flustered, she pops back up, brushing hair away from her face. "Good morning," she says, standing and looking around as if she can't remember falling asleep on the couch. Her gaze returns to me, and she attempts an awkward smile. "I, uh…" She glances past me to the door. "I should go."

I turn my head as she scurries away, eager to escape, and just before she exits the room, I call her name, causing her to skid to a stop. I choose to ignore the pounding headache for now as I rise from the couch, and Cecilia stiffens when I approach her from behind.

Although she has always been careful to keep her guard raised around me, this is different—almost as if I caught her with it lowered, and something about that pulls me forward.

"Did I say something last night?" I ask as she touches her chin to her shoulder to gauge where I am. I'm close enough to cloak her in my heat without us touching.

"Say something?"

*Did I confess to keeping your father locked up in the cellar?*

No, I couldn't have told her. Cecilia would have murdered me in my sleep if I'd revealed that tidbit of information.

"You don't remember," she states as I slowly inch her gown down her shoulder to reveal her creamy skin.

"Pointing out the obvious."

She jerks away and spins around. "You were drunk, so I got you a blanket."

"And then decided to crawl up beside me?"

Her cheeks redden, and she turns to leave again, but I grab her hair and yank her flush against my chest. She gasps, breathing hard, tits straining against the silk fabric of her flimsy gown.

"How come you didn't kill me?" I ask, tweaking one of her nipples into a hard bud. "The gun was right there."

Panting, she tries to elbow me, but her attempts are half-assed. "I didn't know it was there."

"Bullshit, and you know it. Are you feeling sentimental, wife?"

"Don't be delusional. I hate you with every atom in my body."

I chuckle, nipping at her ear. "Such foreplay. You had your chance, and you blew it."

Cecilia wrestles free, throwing me up against the wall, and then her lips are on mine and her hands are in my hair, tugging and pulling. She climbs me like a tree while I tear her robe open to palm her full breasts and squeeze her ass.

*Fuck me; she's perfection.*

I growl into her mouth as I spin us around. "You should have killed me."

She breaks away, her pretty green eyes falling to my lips, and a smirk crosses her face as she lowers my joggers. "It's not too late."

My cock springs free, pulsing in her grip, and when she tugs, my knees nearly buckle.

"Fuck," I whisper, kissing her hard and deep, my hands in her long hair.

"It would be a waste of a perfectly fine cock if I killed you," she says, humming into my mouth, stroking me in long, maddening pulls while an erotic smile plays on her lips.

Grabbing her perfect perky ass, I grind against her. Why does she have to be my weakness and hold so much power over me? I love and hate it in equal measure.

In a few short weeks, she has burrowed so deep beneath my skin that there's no chance of redemption. I'm a lost cause and a fucking glutton for her.

"I should've known you only wanted me for my body," I tease, fucking her hand.

"You could benefit from a personality transplant."

"Is that so?"

Cecilia traps her lip between her teeth while running her thumb over the weeping crown and pulls me closer with a firm grip. I nearly come on the spot when she flashes a flirty smile that's all sex and debauchery, and then she says, "You're intolerable at the best of times."

"I love your aggression."

"You do, huh?" Palming my balls with her free hand, she digs her long nails into the sensitive skin.

Turned on beyond belief and a little afraid by this crazy, unpredictable vixen, I suck in a breath and grab hold of the bookshelf behind her. "You're a feisty little thing, aren't you?"

"And you're an asshole. Don't we make the perfect couple?"

"The fucking best." I slam my lips to her soft ones and flatten her against the shelf. Fuck. I could taste her all day long. Stay here and kiss until my lungs shrivel up. "You were right about one thing," I say as books tumble to the floor.

"Yeah?" she pants between hungry kisses, hiking her thigh around my hip and guiding me to her slick entrance.

Shivers race along my skin as I trail kisses down her neck. "We do have a thing for bookshelves." I bite her pulse point, reveling in her whimper.

"Isn't that romantic?" a different voice asks, and Cecilia gasps. The next few seconds pass in a manic blur as I spin around to hide Cecilia behind me then pull my pants up.

Sinclair looks far too fucking amused, leaning against the doorframe with one ankle crossed over the other. He blows on his glasses and rubs the surface with his sleeve. "Sorry to interrupt your little book club, but we have a meeting with the other Dukes and the King."

Cecilia tries to peer over my shoulder, but she soon

shrinks back when I growl like a caveman. With a smirk, Sinclair puts his glasses back on.

"You better bleach your eyes," I warn. "I swear if you—"

"Relax," he says, stifling laughter. "I have no interest in your wife."

I should receive an award for staying put and not slaughtering my best friend. Just the thought of another man laying eyes on my woman, my wife, makes me want to spill blood. And a lot of it. Paint the room red and decorate the curtain poles with his innards like tinsel.

Sinclair exits the room, unbothered by my unhinged, murderous glare. "They're waiting for you in the office."

Cecilia crouches down to collect her gown. She dresses in silence and then tries to sneak past me, but I grab her neck and crush my lips to hers before she can escape my clutches.

This kiss is a claiming. A feral need to own and possess her after she was naked in another man's proximity—it doesn't matter that she was in my arms. My mind doesn't make the connection. My mind wants to conquer. To show her who she belongs to.

I release her just as fast and stride out, leaving her to reel in the aftermath of whatever fucked-up collision that was of sexual tension and crumbling walls.

---

I SPEND the meeting listening to the King with half an ear while doodling on a sketch pad.

Fucking doodling.

I've never doodled in my life.

Seated beside me in a crisp suit and a Patek Philippe watch strapped to his wrist, Sinclair gives me funny looks. I ignore him, too preoccupied with thoughts of my new wife, which should be my first warning that something is seriously wrong. I never spend the night on the couch like some rough sleeper in a dank corner of the city center, and I don't doodle or let my thoughts drift to the female gender. Yet I'm guilty of all those things in the last twenty-four hours. Cecilia is a plague. Admittedly, she's a very nice one, with plump lips, a breathtaking smile, and tits I want to suck on. But a plague, nonetheless. I need to rid myself of this disease.

Once the meeting is over, Sinclair pulls me aside while the others filter out. We smile politely at them, nodding a few goodbyes.

Sinclair waits for them to leave before he turns back to me. "I'm worried about you."

"Wow. I see you're not skirting around the subject."

"You're not acting yourself."

"You don't need to concern yourself with my business, Sinclair—"

"The hell I do," he growls, losing his temper briefly before he clears his throat and composes himself. "I'm your friend, probably your only friend. Believe it or not, I care about you."

I walk past him. "That's enough of the sentimental bullshit. We have more important issues at hand—"

He strides around me, blocks the exit, and puffs out his cheeks like he's done with my crap. When he finally speaks, his voice is lacking its usual amused lilt. He sounds…tired. "Look… Miss van der Meer, she—"

"Mrs. Delacroix," I correct.

"Mrs. Delacroix." His throat rolls with his next swallow. "She could either be the best thing that happened to you or the worst."

He lets his words settle for brief moments before he runs

his hand over his mouth and says, "I've known you since we were kids. I was there when—"

"Don't!" I snap. "Don't say it."

"It needs to be said. You've buried the past like it never happened, Darian. It's eating you up from the inside. I hate to say it, but you're not the guy you used to be. You're this…" He gestures at me. "…this shell. An emotionless robot."

"Jeez, thanks." I try to move past him again, but he takes up more room than a tank.

"Step aside," I warn. "You don't want to mess with me today."

"Dammit. Listen to me."

I cross my arms, waiting him out with a raised brow.

"She's the first person to knock down your walls, which is great. But you built them so damn high in the first place that there's bound to be collateral damage when they collapse. I just need you not to be buried beneath the rubble when all is said and done."

"What's next, Sinclair? Poetry club?"

"This is what you do," he says, exasperated. "You push people away. You keep your distance from everything and everyone. "What about her father? Have you talked to your wife?"

Hardening my jaw, I look away as my stomach coils.

"It's not her I worry about. It's you. You're pale as fuck because you barely sleep anymore, and you reek of a distillery."

"You don't need to worry about me, okay? I'm fine. I'm always fucking fine."

"Sure," he bites out with a glare. "You're so fucking fine."

"What's that supposed to mean?"

The fight leaves him as he blows out a breath. "Nothing.

Just, uh, be careful, okay? I don't want to see you so broken again."

"Fine…"

He lets me pass this time, but before I exit the room, he pleads, "Don't enter the cellar again. Please."

I walk out, tossing him one final confused look over my shoulder.

# CHAPTER SIXTEEN

CECILIA

Darian's assistant pops her head through the door after lunch to announce that Darian is taking me out for the afternoon.

It marks one of the few rare occasions I've been let out of my gilded cage since this nightmare began. Darian keeps a short leash.

Is it even a nightmare anymore? The truth is, I'm not excited because I get to leave the house; I'm excited because Darian wants to spend time with me.

I squash those traitorous thoughts. I can't let myself forget that Darian Delacroix forced me to marry him against my will after he had my friends murdered.

After applying mascara to my lashes and my favorite raspberry-scented lip gloss, I put on a yellow knee-length sundress and leave my hair loose. Lucious blonde curls cascade down my back, and my skirt swishes around my knees.

I wonder briefly what type of women Delacroix likes as I lift my hair from my neck. Is he a leg or a boob man? Does he prefer blondes or brunettes? The man is a mystery.

A sinfully hot mystery.

There's a knock on my door, and I turn just as it creaks open to reveal Darian standing in the doorway. I lean against the vanity table, taking in his crisp white shirt, slim tie, and black pants. His enticing cologne fills the air as he steps into my room and glances around, looking out of place, like one of Satan's hellhounds in a Barbie house. When his eyes meet mine, they darken, and as he remains silent, my heart begins to thud.

"Miss Sanders didn't tell me where we're going, so I wasn't sure what to wear," I say.

"What you're wearing is fine."

Okay then.

I push off the desk and waltz up to him, painfully aware of my tingling nipples. Darian watches me like I'm a dangerous predator—one that makes him wary but intrigued.

"So," I say when I'm within touching distance, "where are you taking me, Mr. Delacroix?"

His eyes narrow as I smooth his slim tie. "What are you doing?"

"What do you mean?" I ask, much too innocently.

"You're playing nice. I expected to walk in here and find you cutting up your clothes or planning your great escape."

"Can a wife not treat her husband nicely."

"You? No."

A smile creeps onto my lips as I walk past him to retrieve my purse from the chair. Darian follows me like a hawk, his eyes warming my back and the curve of my ass.

Whatever sizzles between us is too poignant to ignore. Do I even want to? Sure, he's a controlling asshole and a member of the organization I set out to destroy, but he's also hot as hell, and it would be a shame not to fuck him out of my system before killing him like I should have done the moment I first entered the Exiled party.

Besides, if I'm going to find out what happened to my dad, Darian is my best lead, and I can't get him to trust me if I don't try to seduce him first.

Straightening up, I clutch my purse as I turn around. Darian clears his throat and looks away, but his eyes soon trail back, almost as if he can't help himself.

"Tell me," I say as I saunter up to him, "is there perhaps a library where we're going?"

Darian holds his breath while I remove invisible lint from his shirt.

My gaze lifts to his. "I have an affinity for literature."

"Yeah?" he croaks.

I almost laugh. *Almost.* I'm not unaffected by his presence and sheer size as he towers over me with his broad shoulders and tall height. I have to crane my neck to look him in the eye, which my clit likes, judging by the throbbing heartbeat between my thighs.

"What type of literature specifically? Thrillers? Women's fiction?"

"Try erotica."

He chokes on his breath before he spins around and walks out. "We're setting off in five minutes."

Pressing a palm over my mouth, I suppress a bout of giggles. The man is too easy to rile up.

---

THE CAR RIDE IS TENSE.

I don't know where we're going because the man beside me won't engage in conversation. I've tried, but he's a locked vault, and all my questions are met with one-word answers. I get the distinct feeling he's nervous about something, which makes me nervous. The anticipation messes with my head.

Darian sits with his legs spread, his thigh pressing against mine. Every time he shifts, his cologne thickens in the air, making it even harder to breathe in this confined space.

I straighten when the car rolls through a set of large iron gates with greater security than the White House. "Where are we?"

Darian checks his Rolex. "This estate belongs to Mr. Visage."

My eyes widen, and I swing my head around to look at him. "He's the man who purchased Lauren."

We come to a stop in a circular driveway next to a set of steps, and Darian exits the car without another word.

I stare out at the large estate, admiring the elegant architecture and impressive columns. Large windows reflect the manicured gardens, the sun glinting on the shiny surface.

Warmth unfurls in my chest as I gaze at Darian, who greets Mr. Visage with a firm handshake. Something tells me we weren't invited here; Darian arranged this dinner because he wanted to please me.

The driver opens my door, and I take his outstretched hand as he helps me out of the car. After I thank him, he tips his hat in acknowledgment. My eyes shift to Darian, who is already looking at me while his friend continues to talk.

A blush creeps up my neck from the intensity of Darian's frosty gaze as I walk closer, ignoring the other man's dismissive glance in my direction. Darian seems focused solely on me, but then my attention slides past him to the woman waiting by the door. A smile spreads across my face so wide that my cheeks begin to hurt.

I slam my purse against Darian's chest and then take off running. Lauren is here; she's really here, and she's okay.

I swoop her up in a bear hug. "You're okay."

"I'm okay."

"Let me look at you." Releasing her, I grab her shoulders, unable to believe my eyes. It's only been weeks, but it feels like an eternity. Laurens's wild auburn hair tumbles over her shoulders. She's makeup-free, with freckles smattered across her sun-kissed cheeks. Dressed in a simple dress and sandals, she looks effortlessly beautiful.

"Are you sure you're okay? I've been so worried."

She looks past me at the men, and the light in her eyes dims before she smiles again. "I'm fine. I promise. Let's go inside. I'll give you a tour."

Lauren shows me around the grand estate while the men barricade themselves in the office to discuss business. Maids make themselves scarce when we enter rooms. It's a beautiful home without much heart.

"What's it like being a Commoner?" I ask as we walk through the rose garden out the back.

Deep in thought, she lets her fingers drift over the fragile petals of a flower. "It could be worse."

"Worse?"

She shrugs, not looking at me, and then she starts to say something, but my eyes snag on a bruise peeking out from her collar. I shift it aside, horrified when I see the yellow and purple blotches.

"He did this to you?"

Pushing my hand away, she rights her collar to hide it. "It's nothing."

"Nothing?"

"That's what I said."

"Lauren, he beats you."

She glances at the windows behind us, her throat jumping on a swallow. "Just…let's talk about something else."

"No, we're talking about this."

Her eyes take on a hard edge. "What did you think would happen, huh? He purchased me on Hell Fire Night, like an item to be owned. I'm a Commoner, Cecilia. We're the lowest of the low. Maybe some Commoners are treated with respect, but I'm a whore and an object for his vile sexual perversions."

Tears swim in my vision as I glance at the estate behind me, but there's no sign of anyone else. Lauren struggles to meet my gaze, so I pull her to me and hold her tight. "We'll get you out of this. I promise."

"I'm in contact with the Antichrist."

I gasp, releasing her. "You've spoken to them?"

She nods and lowers her voice. "They're planning a rescue mission."

"They are?"

"Yes. Not just for me, but for you, too."

My chest tightens when she smiles at me with such hope that I want to look away in shame for feeling these mixed emotions. I should jump for joy at the prospect of being taken away from Darian's clutches.

"Did they say when?"

"No," she replies with a shake of her head. "But soon."

"I don't know…"

"What don't you know?" she asks, frowning.

I look away, but she cups my cheeks and says, "Hey, this is good news. They'll set us free. It's what we want, right?"

When I fail to respond, the crease between her brows deepens as she presses, "Right?"

Inhaling a shaky breath, I finally nod and take her hand. "Of course."

But it's not 'of course.'

Nothing about this feels right.

"I just don't want anyone to get hurt," I explain.

It's a poor excuse, but the idea of Darian coming to harm makes my stomach queasy.

Lauren frowns and begins to respond, but masculine voices interrupt her. Darian looks between us, a question in his eyes as Mr. Visage walks up to Lauren and guides her back to the house with a possessive hand on her lower back. "Dinner is served."

---

I BREAK open the clam's shell, poking at the orange flesh inside. I've never liked seafood, but I'm not about to complain in the presence of a man as scary as Mr. Visage. He has an air about him that sets me on edge. Maybe it's the cold way he observes Lauren while she eats or the clipped tone he uses with the servers, but he makes my skin crawl.

Meanwhile, Darian indulges him in conversation, and I watch curiously as he sets down his cutlery and rests his arm on the back of my chair.

With his calm demeanor, Darian makes socializing seem effortless, but I know it's just a game for him.

My husband, who is now toying with the tendrils of my hair, is a master manipulator and strategist, yet I can't quite grasp what he's set out to conquer.

Is it business with Mr. Visage?

Or my heart?

He removes his hand from the back of my chair and rests his big palm on my thigh while discussing a shipment from another state. It's unnerving how unaffected he sounds as his hand inches higher up my leg.

He already has me wet, and I try my hardest not to squirm

as I lift my wineglass to my lips, but I'm trembling so much that I place it back on the table.

As his pinky brushes up against my panties, my mouth falls open with a silent gasp.

His smooth baritone swims around me like a warm, exotic evening breeze. I spread my thighs, struggling to regulate my panting breaths. How a man can reduce me to pure need is scary and exciting.

He dips his pinky inside my panties and runs it up and down my slit. I glance at Mr. Visage, who breaks open another clam and then reaches for his tumbler of pure vodka.

Delacroix slides his pinky inside me. "You seemed hesitant about my offer earlier. I'm willing to double my offer to ensure the sale."

Vodka spills everywhere as Mr. Visage chokes on his drink. "Excuse me?" he says, placing the drink back down and mopping at the wet stains on his shirt and lap with a tissue. "Double the price?"

"It's a good deal. No one else will offer you that kind of money for a Commoner. You'd be foolish not to accept my offer."

*A Commoner? Who is he talking about?*

"While it's a tempting offer," he replies, placing the tissue on his plate and easing back, "I don't see what's in it for you. She's no different from the other Commoners."

"I have my reasons." He slides his pinky out and circles my clit with his fingers. "Do we have a deal or not?"

Mr. Visage studies Delacroix with an unveiled interest, almost like he can't figure him out, then chuckles and shakes his head. "Like you said, only a fool would say no to such a lucrative deal. She's all yours. Though be warned, she's spoiled goods now."

"Duly noted." Delacroix removes his hand from my

panties and holds it out for the man to shake, and my cheeks heat at seeing my arousal glisten on his long fingers. What is he doing? I'm not a professional at reading the energy in a room, but the dark shadows clinging to my husband bode badly for Mr. Visage.

Darian smirks while they shake on whatever business deal transpired, neither man willing to let go first. Is it another power play?

They finally separate, and my husband stands up, smooths down his tie, and thanks Mr. Visage for his hospitality. Then he turns to Lauren, smiling politely. "Kindly pack your bags. We're leaving in ten minutes."

I gawk at Darian. Did he buy Lauren from Mr. Visage for me? How much money did he offer? He said double his original bid. How much was that? And why?

A small voice whispers that he did it for me, but I brush it away. Why would he go to such lengths? What has he got to gain? *You,* you idiot. Your heart is the prize. Delacroix is playing to win.

But why? Why does he want to win my affections? My trust? Why does he care? What's in it for him?

My heart swells two sizes, and tears prick my eyes at the thought of him bringing me here to see Lauren. But not only that, he also went to great lengths to get her back…for me.

Averting my gaze, I blink rapidly.

Maybe I underestimated Darian Delacroix? Perhaps he's not as bad as he leads the world to believe?

# CHAPTER SEVENTEEN

CECILIA

By the time we return to the house, it's past midnight, and I find myself leaning against the doorway, watching Lauren as she studies her new surroundings. Darian offered her one of the spare rooms in the same wing as mine so we could be close. The sentiment makes me feel things I shouldn't, and I can almost hear the ice cracking as it melts around my heart.

Lauren stares at the countless scattered cushions on the queen-sized bed for long moments before she hauls her suitcase onto the sheet and zips it open with her back to me, carefully folding and arranging her meager belongings in a pile. "Mr. Visage let me keep a few things he bought for me while I was his Commoner. It's not much but…"

She's right. It's not. I make a mental note to take her shopping first thing in the morning if I can sweet talk Darian into letting us leave the property.

"I hope you will be comfortable here," I say. "Darian is… Well, he's not bad."

She looks at me over her shoulder with a raised brow,

then turns back around and continues unpacking the suitcase. "I exchanged one cage for another."

I frown, pushing off the doorframe. "It's not ideal, I know, but at least he won't hurt you like that asshole—"

She slams the lid shut. "Why are you defending him? We're prisoners, Cecilia. This situation isn't normal." Her shoulders slump, and she looks at me with frustration as I come to stand beside her. "Out there in the real world, people don't get a green card to murder and commit crimes every five years. They don't get away with human trafficking."

"This isn't the real world." It's a sobering thought but doesn't make it any less true.

"Is it true?" she asks, busying herself by folding a top.

"Is what true?" I reach for an item and help her fold it.

"You were born into this world? The daughter of a Duke?"

I don't like the way she sneers when she says Duke. My father may have been a monster, but my mother was a good person. And no matter how despicable my father was, I can't erase all the good childhood memories I have of him.

"Yes," I reply, refraining from elaborating. "It's true."

"What happened?"

"The Exiled happened. Hell Fire Night."

I feel her watching me, but I focus on folding the clothes. Lauren would never understand even if I tried to explain my reasons for joining the Antichrist. Unlike me, she was born a regular member of society. Her mother was an accountant, and her father worked as an electrician.

Then one night, they happened to be at the wrong place at the wrong time and were spotted by a group of Commoners as they walked home after a meal at a friend's house on Hell Fire Night.

Lauren, orphaned at the tender age of nine, moved in

with her grandmother, who was going through chemotherapy. After her passing, Lauren found herself without a legal guardian when she was fifteen, and that's how she stumbled upon the Antichrist. An angry teen with nothing left to lose.

I place the folded pants on top of the pile nearest to me. "I joined Antichrist for the same reasons as you."

Lauren remains silent, waiting for me to continue as she takes a seat on the mattress.

"We've both lost people we love."

Her eyes meet mine, glassy with pain. I wish a magic eraser could make it all go away. That we could be kids again in a world where our parents weren't murdered for shits and giggles. It's all so fucking pointless.

Our parents, Keith, and Carlo.

They all died for nothing.

"I was orphaned, too, by the Exiled. My father disappeared on Hell Fire Night, and my mother died in a car crash years later. I didn't lie. I just…" I pinch the bridge of my nose and shake my head, trying to swallow down the thick lump congesting my throat. When I speak, my voice is choked with suppressed emotion. "I didn't know how to tell anyone who my father was."

"Would it have made a difference?"

I lower my hand. "You tell me. Would you have welcomed me if you knew I was born into the secret society responsible for the death of your parents?"

She observes me for a moment, then stands up and pulls me in for a hug. I cling to her while breathing in her clean floral scent, grateful she's here. "We'll be okay," she says, and I squeeze her tighter. "I know."

"What happens now?"

If only I knew the answer.

An ache starts up in my heart as my thoughts drift to the man in the other wing. What is he doing now? Is he asleep?

Struck by the urge to see him, I disentangle myself. "You should get some sleep. We'll talk more tomorrow."

Lauren wipes tears from her cheeks, then glances behind her at the bed. She turns back and gestures to the room. "Thank you for this. I'm really grateful."

"It was all Darian." I squeeze her hand. "Try to get some rest."

"Goodnight," she says as I exit the room and hurry toward Darian's wing.

It's a quiet night, with no wind whistling through the windows or trees tapping insistently against the glass. I turn left and pad softly on bare feet down the hallway until I reach his room. A muted light spills onto the floor through the gap in the door, suggesting he's either awake or sleeping with the light on.

I carefully push down on the handle and peek inside. Anyone else would knock, but I still haven't decided if I'm brave enough to talk to him or if I simply want to spy on him without his knowledge.

He's not in bed, and the room is empty.

Curious, I inch inside, sweeping my gaze over every piece of furniture. Although I've been in his room before, something feels different tonight.

The *air* is different and smells of him, heady and warm—an alluring scent that settles in my nostrils like a seductive trail of kisses on the curve of my neck. I shiver as I glance at his unmade bed, the sheets creased and inviting.

I take a step forward, but I gasp when a hand clamps over my mouth from behind, pulling me against a firm chest. Darian's low voice reaches my ear. "Did you think you could sneak in and kill me?"

A shiver runs through me as I feel his hard length press against my lower back.

His fingers trail a teasing path up the inside of my thigh, lifting my skirt as his other hand covers my mouth to muffle my whimpers.

"How were you going to do it? Shoot me?"

My knees nearly buckle when his fingers drag over my panties in a slow tease with enough pressure to make my clit pulse, yet it's not enough.

"Stab me in my sleep?"

He smacks my clit, and my muffled cry fills the room.

"With what weapon, Mrs. Delacroix? You're not very prepared." Shifting my panties aside, he palms my pussy while chuckling in my ear. "So wet for me already."

In a swift move, he spins me around and grips my throat, backing me toward the bed. I claw at his wrist, desperate for a sliver of breath, but he remains an unmovable mountain.

When my calves connect with the bed, he shoves me, and I topple back, bouncing on the mattress. Before I can catch my breath or sit up, he kneels over me and presses a pillow over my face.

"Maybe you planned to smother me to death? Like this?"

Panicked, I kick out with my feet and buck my hips, but I can't shift him no matter how hard I thrash. I can't breathe. I can't…

Darian growls as he bats off my grappling hands, then smacks my thighs apart to squeeze my pussy. "Such a wet little cunt. You like this, don't you, Mrs. Delacroix? You like a firm hand." He slaps my cunt hard, and I freeze for a moment before my fight renews.

As his grip on the pillow loosens, I inhale greedily, but he immediately covers my face with his large hand. I bite down on the fabric, but the cushion is too thick.

Darian laughs coldly and slides his middle finger inside my cunt. "Fuck, baby. You're worked up, huh."

A shameful moan slips from my lips because he's right, and I bite down on my tongue to stop it, but it's too late. My fight has ceased, and now I'm squirming instead—squirming for more.

Darian removes the pillow and pats me on the cheek. "Good little wife."

"Fuck you!" I sneer, angling my hips to take his pumping finger deeper. "Dammit, why do you have to be such an asshole?"

"Would you love this so much if I weren't?" he asks, stretching me with a second finger. "Look at what a mess you're making of my hand. Such a dirty little slut."

I push up on my elbow and reach for him, but he smacks my hand away and grabs my chin. When pain erupts where his fingers dig in, I find myself moaning.

I'll sport bruises tomorrow, but it'll be worth it. So fucking worth it.

"Listen to that greedy cunt. It missed me."

"I don't fucking think so," I reply, the words muffled in his ruthless grip. "You could be anyone."

His eyes turn a lethal shade of cobalt. "Shut your mouth. I'm not just anyone. I'm your husband." He releases me, pushing up on his knees and shoving his briefs down to reveal his engorged dick, and then strokes it in front of me. "And this is the only cock you get to worship."

I wet my lips in anticipation. Everything about him is perfect, from his chiseled chest to his defined V and veiny dick. It's unfair how attractive he is.

He tangles his fingers in my hair and guides me closer to his balls. "Let me see you suck on them."

"And what if I don't want to."

"Do you always have to fight me on everything?"

"Would you like me as much if I didn't?"

His lips pull up in a wicked side smirk. "Suck on my balls like an eager wife, or I'll suffocate you with the pillow again. Maybe I'll even kill you this time."

"You won't kill me." I make a show of dragging my tongue over his balls, humming low in my throat. "You like me too much."

"I like the tears in your eyes when panic sets in," he snaps. "Now shut that mouth and do as you're told."

"If you wanted a pliant wife, you really made a mistake when you forced me to marry you."

A growl rumbles in his chest, and he shoves his dick into my mouth, clearly fed up with my attitude, unbothered that my teeth graze along his shaft. If anything, I think he likes a lick of pain with his pleasure.

My hands fly up to his muscular thighs, and I try to push him away, but he holds my head in place with both hands and fucks my face like I'm nothing more than an object—a hole for his cock.

Every time his dick hits the back of my throat, I gag, and he praises me.

*"That's it, baby. Such a good girl."*

*"Open that throat for me. Your mouth was made to be fucked."*

*"I'm going to come so damn hard down your throat, you'll choke to death on my cum. The coroner will class it as an accidental drowning."*

The last part made my pussy flutter something fierce, and I tremble, barely able to cling to his thighs while he pistons his hips.

His pubes tickle my nose as I look up at him with teary eyes, saliva dripping down my chin. With one final grunt, he shoves my face against his groin, his cock buried so deep down my throat that I can feel it pulsing his release. He stares at me with intense heat and desire in his darkened gaze, and I feel myself melt against him as he strokes my damp hair away from my forehead. "You're a vision with your husband's cock down your throat, Mrs. Delacroix."

I swallow around Darian's length, and a wave of nausea cramps my stomach. Gagging, I dig my nails into his thighs again as he holds me in place with his hand behind my head. "Suck it."

*But you've already come...*

He lifts his brow and smirks, as if he can hear my thoughts. "What are you waiting for?"

As his grip lightens, I greedily suck his softening cock, and it doesn't take long for it to swell again and grow even harder than before. I trail my tongue over each angry vein, then flick the tip through a bead of precum on his crown.

"Take it deep and hollow your cheeks."

I look up at Darian, sucking on his cock like it's a damn lollipop, and then swirl my tongue over his crown.

"Fuck yourself," he instructs, brushing my hair away from my cheeks as I suck him deep. "I want to hear how wet your pussy is."

Dipping my hand beneath my skirt, I moan around his length, easing my fingers inside me. My pussy is drenched, so it's no surprise I meet zero resistance.

"There's a good girl," he praises as my head bobs in his hands. "Fuck yourself on your fingers."

I grind my hips, lost in a heady sea of pleasure, where Darian's every praise is a siren's song. I want to please him. To be good for him.

"That's it, beautiful. Fuck. That feels amazing."

He wraps my hair around his hand, his tight grip causing

my scalp to prickle as he guides my mouth over his cock, setting a steady, ruthless pace. I'm a fuck toy to him—a tool to get him off.

It gets me off, too, when he's rough like this.

"Look how cock drunk you are. Eyes on me, baby. Let me see how much you like it."

His cock pops out of my mouth with a wet sound, a string of saliva connecting my lips to his crown, and he juts his chin to my grinding hips. "How many fingers are you riding?"

"Four."

"Let me see." He unwinds my hair from his hand and shoves me back onto the bed with his full palm on my face, then spreads my legs obnoxiously wide and stares down at my puffy cunt.

Kneeling like a savage monster, he hikes a finger in my panties and pulls them aside so he can get a better vision.

"Use your other hand to tease your clit."

A moan fills the room as I strum my bud while curling my fingers inside me. My walls ripple rhythmically and heat swirls low in my core. "I'm about to come," I pant, biting down on my swollen lip.

Darian strokes his cock while watching me fuck myself like it's the most erotic sight he's ever seen. "I want to make such a fucking mess of you."

"Yeah?" I goad as my pussy clamps down on my fingers. "What do you want to do to me?"

"Come all over you, for starters, and then stretch your cunt with the biggest fucking object I can find."

"Should I be scared?"

"Of me? Always." A shudder runs through him as he thrusts forward, letting out a deep groan. Warm ropes of cum rain over my face and body like a reward and drips down my cheeks.

He milks his cock until his balls are emptied, and the last squirt hits my throat and chin. Afterward, he tucks his dick away and smacks my hands away as he positions himself between my legs.

When his warm mouth descends to ravage me, my hips buck off the mattress, and I gasp at the sensation of his wet tongue. Darian brings me to the edge, holding me tightly while he licks and sucks. As his tongue swirls over my clit, I grip the sheets as if I might float away.

"Fuck," I whimper, grinding against his face.

I'm just about to come when he pulls away and climbs off the bed.

I push up onto my elbows, my pussy pulsing painfully in need of relief. "Where are you going?"

Darian walks over to his dresser and removes a pair of handcuffs and what looks like a monster dildo.

I lift my head. "What the fuck is that?"

As he nears, he studies it. "I'm not entirely sure. I think it's a dragon cock?"

"A dragon cock?"

"It could possibly be a dinosaur dick."

"What—"

The words die on my tongue when he tosses the dildo on the bed before kneeling over me and securing my wrists to the headboard. I try to fight his hold on me, but it's useless, and in no time at all, I'm yanking on the cuffs around my wrists.

"What the hell, Darian?"

"I looked at the other cocks, but they were so lifelike, and I thought to myself: my wife looks like she'd enjoy a dragon cock with scales."

"Well"—I rattle the cuffs again—"you thought wrong. Next time you want to shop for sex toys to spice up our sex life—don't. You've already proven you shouldn't be let loose in a sex shop."

He presses a button and his face lights up. "Look at that; it vibrates."

"Wow. You deserve a gold star for your observational skills—" My words end in a choking sound when he presses the vibrator against my clit.

"You were saying?"

My wrists pull on the cuffs as I squirm on the bed, fighting off the pleasure. This is now a matter of pride. While a dragon cock could be fun with anyone but my infuriating, intolerable husband, there's no way in fucking hell I'll let him get me off.

"Oh, look, you're making a mess of the scales." He chuckles as he circles my sensitive clit. "I bet it would feel amazing inside you. What do you say, wife? You love literature, right? What do they call it? Romantasy."

"Asshole!" I groan, but my hips jut closer as if my body's working against me.

"You want the dragon cock in your ass? Easy there, tiger. I know you're eager—"

With a growl, I try to kick at him, but he easily overpowers me and asks, "Do you know what makes the dragon cock special?" He slides it through my slit until it rests against my slick entrance. "It's bigger than the others. It's even bigger than the King Cock. Think you can fit it?"

"You have a thing for size, you pervert?" A moan strangles my vocal cords when he inches it inside me. Fuck. It's big. So fucking big I'm panting by the time the tip is in.

"You're going cross-eyed," he says with another maddening chuckle.

"You know," I reply, fighting back another choked moan,

"if I weren't shackled to the bed, I would slap your smug face."

He pulses the dildo inside me, sliding it a little bit deeper with each thrust. "I have to say, Mrs. Delacroix, you look a mess, with a dragon dildo in your cunt while covered in cum like a Picasso painting."

"What are you doing now?" I ask as he bends me in half and whacks the speed up to max on the vibrator. It's too much too soon, and I quiver as he works the dildo deep, thrusting harder and faster, until the only sound louder than my moans are the traitorous, obscene wet sounds my pussy makes.

With the dildo fully inside me, he shifts his briefs out of the way with one hand while he traps my ankles with the other.

I'm impressed by my own acrobatic skills. No man has ever held me bent in half like this before. Not that I have a lot of experience with sex, but this is new.

Darian retrieves a bottle of lube from the nightstand, and I crane my neck to see what he's up to, not wanting him to stop.

Then I feel it.

Pressure against my asshole.

"Relax," he says when I tense up. "Keep your legs there." He lets go of my ankles, then thrusts the dildo deeper when it threatens to pop out because I stiffen. "Good girl. It was one of the biggest dildos in the store, and you take it like a fucking champ. Think you can handle your husband's cock, too?"

I nod as pain burns in my ass. "Y-yes."

"You want to please your husband, don't you, baby?"

Another nod as I answer without hesitation. "Very much, but I haven't done this before."

A bright smile spreads across his lips. "That's okay. Relax. Deep breaths, baby."

I inhale as he thrusts forward. It hurts, but the intoxicating swirling shadows in his eyes make it worth every moment of discomfort.

I never realized before how much I want to please Darian Delacroix. How much I want to make him feel good, or how much I love it when his hair falls over his damp brow and how his lips part with pleasure.

Once his cock is halfway inside my ass, he drags his big hand over my face, smearing the cum, and then he pushes two fingers past my lips, watching me suck on them. "I knew from the very first moment I saw you that you would be this pliant for me. My own fuck toy to use however I want." His cock twitches in my ass, and I clench around it. "I wanted to break you." He presses down on my tongue, making me gag as tears spill from my eyes. "Humiliate you, like your father humiliated my mother."

Before his words can fully register in my hazy mind, he slams his hand over my mouth and buries himself in my ass. The full sensation overwhelms me as the vibrator hits some magical spot within, making me tremble.

He pulls out to the tip before ramming inside me again, and again, and again.

"But then I realized that you get off on humiliation. That you're as fucked up as I am. And guess what?" Balanced on his forearm, he drags his tongue through the cum on my face and then whispers, "I like it."

As he straightens up, he removes his hand from my mouth and grips the dildo, thrusting it in sync with his pumping hips. We move together like waves in a clashing of tides, and when an orgasm barrels through me, I yank on the cuffs.

"That's it, baby. Come for me."

Darian fucks me so hard the headboard bangs against the wall, and then he pulls the dildo out before thrusting his dick inside my pussy. I'm stretched from the huge toy and can barely feel him, but that seems to be the point.

He grabs me by the throat, gazing into my eyes, and then he crushes his lips against mine as his hot semen fills me up.

"Fuck me, you're beautiful." His strangled whisper drips with admiration, his body shuddering.

I lower my legs and wrap them around his waist as he settles on top of me, his prickly cheek resting against my chest.

"Why did you come here tonight?" he asks after a while.

"I wanted to see you."

His chest lifts and falls with a content sigh. We might be enemies, but this feels like a truce. I'm tired of fighting my desire for this man, even if it's wrong, even if he turns out to be the man behind my father's death. The question tastes bitter on my tongue. Would he tell me the truth if I asked him now? Not that it matters because I can't bring myself to form the words. Instead, I ask, "Why did you make the deal with Mr. Visage?"

Darian rests his chin on my chest, studying my face in dim light. "You care about Lauren."

My heart gallops at the intensity of his gaze. He's watching me carefully for my reaction, and when I break eye contact, he crawls up my body.

"She's your family." He removes my handcuffs and places them on the nightstand.

I swallow hard as his attention returns to me. "You're supposed to be a coldhearted monster."

"Would it be easier to hate me?"

I trail my fingers through his stubbly beard, pausing when he dips his lips to mine.

It's a tender kiss, soft and gentle, and a promise of more.

He sucks on my bottom lip, then whispers, "I am a monster, but not with you."

"Will you set Lauren free?"

A crease forms between his brows as he lifts his head. "She belongs to the Exiled now. There's no out once you're in."

"I don't believe you."

"You have no other choice."

I try to push him away, upset with his response, but he secures my wrists on the pillow beneath my head and uses his free hand to keep my gaze on his. There's no escaping Delacroix. He plunders and leaves no one left alive. My soul is no different.

"There's only one way out of the Exiled."

I try to yank free of his grip on my jaw, but it's as solid as concrete.

Darian drags his nose down the bridge of mine. "And it's in a body bag. At least your friend will be safe under my roof."

"He beat her." My voice is a mere whisper as a tear slides from the corner of my eye.

Darian kisses it away. "I know."

"He's a monster."

"He is."

"How are you any different?"

"I'm not," he replies, placing kisses on my lids, nose, and mouth. "I won't ever set you free because I'm a selfish man with selfish desires where you're concerned." He gets out of bed, enters the ensuite bathroom, and returns with a bowl of soapy water and a cloth.

My chest warms as he spends long moments stroking the damp cloth through my tender folds until he's satisfied I'm clean, and then he wipes my face, his eyes on the task as he says, "While I'm a villain in my own right, I promise I'll never lay a hand on you unless you beg me to."

I duck my head to hide my blushing cheeks. His words shouldn't make me want to smile, but they do. "What will Lauren do while she's here?"

"Anything she wants." The wet cloth trails down the curve of my chin and throat. "Maybe she wants to spend her days sunbathing in front of the pool or take up pottery."

I smile despite myself. "I don't think she's into pottery."

After placing the bowl on the floor, he crawls beside me and pulls me into his arms. "I don't care what she does, as long as you're happy."

*Dammit. Why does he have to be so sweet when he wants to be?*

I snuggle closer, breathing in his earthy scent, and release a content sigh.

My pulse soon slows to a gentle thud, and I kiss the space above his heart, feeling it pound beneath my lips. "Thank you for what you did today."

His muscles seem to relax, and he holds me tighter. "Sleep, or you'll be too tired to take my cock tomorrow."

# CHAPTER EIGHTEEN

CECILIA

A week passes. Lauren settles into her new environment. Darian lets us go shopping for new clothes without a fight much to my surprise and orders his driver to take us for days out to various places as if we're dogs in need of walks. I almost feel sorry for him for getting stuck with us when he's used to being Darian's shadow, but then I remember that every move I make gets reported to his boss. I'm not used to looser reigns, but Darian seems more relaxed lately. He stays out of my way for most of the time, except when we fuck. He seeks me out at least once a day to eat me out between meetings or whatever planned shady business is on the agenda.

At night, he sneaks into my room and spends hours fucking me into oblivion before he leaves again, like a shadow. I always wake up alone, sore, and with an uncharacteristic heartache, wishing I could separate my feelings for him from the reason I'm here, which is my father's disappearance. I can't let myself forget my reasons, but it's becoming harder and harder to remember why it matters.

Does it even matter? Yes. It does. The Exiled is behind my family's torment.

"So, what do you think of this dress?" Lauren asks, parting the curtain in the changing room to show me the ball-gown she has tried on.

The King is holding a masked fundraiser over the week-end. Another posh affair with flowing alcohol and bursting wallets. Darian handed me a black card and told me to have fun.

Fun?

I don't even know the meaning of the word anymore.

"Is it too much?"

Torn from my thoughts, I shake my head, gesturing to the wine-red bodice. "It's nice."

"Nice?" Lauren flicks her hair off her shoulder. "I don't want nice. I want chin-on-the-floor breathtaking. Since I'm in this position, I might as well make the most of it and milk your husband's bank account."

I think the look on my face says it all, because she laughs and escapes behind the curtain. The sound of the zipper fills the room. "Can you ask them to get me the forest green dress? The one near the window display?"

"Sure." I stand from the bench and exit the changing area.

After asking the assistant to help Lauren with the green dress, I browse the racks for a dress for myself. I don't need a new one since Darian had his Commoners fill my wardrobe with everything I could possibly need the night I entered his home.

"That's not weird at all," I mutter to myself as I pause in front of a golden dress with a bejeweled bodice.

"You're hard to catch alone," a deep voice breathes near my ear, and I spin around, my heart pounding at the sight of Mr. Beaumont.

He towers over me in freshly pressed blue pants and a white shirt. The two top buttons are undone to reveal a smattering of dark chest hair, and his chestnut hair has been swept back.

"Mr. Beaumont. What are you doing here?"

"I've been trying to get a moment of your time, but that husband of yours always has a tail on your end." He looks over my shoulder toward the changing area. "But not for now." When his eyes return to me, they flicker with something cold and cruel.

I step back against the dress rail. "You should leave."

"I think we made a deal."

"There's no deal. I don't want anything to do with you."

He moves closer, and his imposing figure looms over me. With nowhere left to escape, I feel trapped as his sickly cologne swirls around me while he grabs the rail and leans in close to my face. "I was polite last time, but even my patience has limits, Mrs. Delacroix."

When I try to look toward the changing rooms, he tuts and grabs my jaw in a punishing grip.

"Your friend won't come to the rescue. She's busy."

With a frown, I jerk free, only to gasp when he fists a handful of my hair and yanks my head back. "What did you do?"

"I might have paid the assistant a hefty sum of money to keep your friend occupied while we chat."

"What do you want from me?"

"It's easy," he drawls. "Delacroix has sensitive information on his hard drive. I want you to find it for me."

"Are you crazy? What information?"

He pulls my hair, making my scalp ignite in uncomfortable prickles. "Do as I say, or you won't like the consequences."

"W-what consequences?"

Beaumont shifts closer, pressing up against me, and grabs my ass with his free hand. "There are other ways to ruin Delacroix. You see, he has a weakness. I can always hand you back to the King."

Ice runs through my veins. "You wouldn't do that."

"No?"

"You'd be left with no blackmail to use against my husband."

Beaumont is aroused, and I feel his hard cock against my stomach as he leans down to brush his lips against my ear. I try to push him away, but I'm trapped between him and the dresses.

His wet breath fans my neck, and he pulls harder on my hair. "I wonder if he would touch you again after I take you for a spin."

"No." My fight turns desperate as my stomach drops to my feet. I try to scream, but he muffles the sound with his calloused hand, which smells of tobacco, as he shushes me.

"Calm down, Mrs. Delacroix. Give me what I want, and I promise not to touch you."

I clamp my eyes shut while he makes a show of squeezing my breasts through my top.

His rough touch has my skin crawling in the worst way possible.

"I would lie if I said I'm not tempted," he whispers. "You're a fine woman."

As he yanks up my top before shoving down my bra to smack my left breast, my eyes brim with tears, but I refuse to let them fall.

The creep tugs on my tender nipple until fiery pain throbs in the wake of his touch and says, "Consider this payment for testing my patience. A little taste. You have one more chance to give me what I want, or I'll return for more." He releases me and walks away, the bell dinging above the door as he exits without another word.

I slump, forcing down a wretched sob, and then straighten up to right my clothes. Lauren calls out my name from the changing area, so I wipe the tears from my cheeks and plaster on my best fake smile.

I can do this.

I can pretend everything is fine.

---

THE FOLLOWING DAY, I try to look as innocent as I possibly can when I open the door to my husband's office.

He's seated behind his desk, his gun in his hand, like a dark mafia lord. Across from him, appearing far more relaxed in a navy suit, is Sinclair.

Hesitating in the doorway, I look between them. "I didn't mean to interrupt."

Sinclair smirks at Delacroix, who hasn't taken his eyes off me since I opened the door.

"I hope you're not planning to kill your best friend with that weapon." I wave a hand at the gun.

Sinclair swings his head around and treats me to his best smile. "Not at all. We're planning our next sleepover, where we dress in silk pajamas and paint each other's toenails." He looks back at my far-too-intense husband. "Remember the ones you used to wear when we were kids? The ones with the bunnies."

"You had sleepovers?" I ask skeptically.

"Mhm," Sinclair hums, kicking his Oxfords up on Darian's desk and interlinking his fingers on his stomach. "Darian loved a good pillow fight. Feathers flew everywhere, which used to drive his mom insane."

Darian slides his eyes in Sinclair's direction so slowly, I'm surprised the sun hasn't swallowed the earth whole by the time he finally raises a brow. "Pillow fights? Really?"

Sinclair throws his head back and laughs.

Rolling his eyes, Darian turns his attention to me, and his mood darkens like a storm cloud. "What the fuck are you wearing?"

I glance down at my checkered mini skirt and matching black top.

"I can see your cunt from here."

My mouth falls open as Sinclair's shoulders shake with silent laughter.

*Did he just...? I'm at a loss for words. The fucking audacity!*

"Did you leave the fucking house like that?"

"What if I did?" I ask as I cross my arms, trying not to fidget.

At this rate, I'll have steam coming out of my ears soon, like a damn cartoon, if he keeps infuriating me like this with his caveman act.

One of Darian's dark brows quirks. Sliding his phone closer, he unlocks the screen and makes a phone call.

Miss Sanders answers on the first ring. "Sir?"

"Fire all the male staff who've laid eyes on my wife today."

"But sir—"

"Come to think of it, fire the women, too. You included. I'm not taking any chances." He hangs up and hooks me with those blue, ominous eyes. "Why are you walking around half-naked?"

*Did he just fire his staff? Is he nuts?*

"I like this skirt."

"It's lingerie."

Sinclair is turning red, and I'm pretty sure he'll die soon if he doesn't inhale a full breath. It must hurt to try not to laugh.

On my way past, I smack the back of his head, and his suppressed laughter escapes.

Darian stares at him then, as if he only just remembers his existence. Sinclair is in stitches, clutching his stomach.

"Something funny to you?" Darian asks him.

I cross my arms. "No shit, Sherlock. Stating the obvious."

"Shut your mouth!" he snaps at me.

*Oh, he didn't just fucking say that to me.*

We glare at each other, spitting venom in a silent battle of wills.

Sinclair tries to stand up but falls back down, still chuckling like this is the funniest thing he has witnessed all year. He points at Darian. "You're so damn pussy whipped. What's next? Are you going to beat your chest before tossing her over your shoulder and smacking her ass as you carry her to your bed like a caveman?"

Darian looks at me, so I steel my jaw, warning him, "Don't you fucking dare!"

"Okay, lovebirds." Sinclair slaps the armrests, then rises. "It's been fun, but I think I'll leave you to your little…" He waves a hand around the room. "Book club." On his way out, he squeezes my shoulder, and I swear Darian growls.

The moment the door shuts, silence creeps in from every corner to suck the oxygen out of the air. Darian eases back into his chair, legs spread wide, as he scratches his beard with his gun. The short stubble rasps.

Resisting the urge to pull my skirt down, I shift on my feet, knowing the worst thing I can do now is to show weakness. The best approach is to hold my chin high and pretend I'm not quaking when he's staring at me like this.

"Is there a reason you're flaunting my pussy to every man with a swinging dick in the vicinity?"

"It's not that short—"

"Shut up." His voice is eerily quiet and controlled — deep like the uncharted trenches of the ocean and hiding just as many dangers, too. "Don't argue. Answer the question."

"You can't see my pussy."

"No?" He waves the gun at me. "Turn around."

I hesitate.

What is he doing? His unreadable mood makes me nervous.

"What are you waiting for, Mrs. Delacroix?" he asks, spinning the gun. "Turn around."

With a gulp, I slowly do as I'm told.

He waits until I'm facing away from him. "Bend over."

Bend over? He can't be serious.

The chair rolls across the floor as he stands. "Touch your toes."

"I don't know how bendy you think I am—"

His shoes clap on the floor. "Don't fucking argue with me now. Do as you're told."

"You could ask nicely—"

Before I can finish that sentence, he grabs my nape in a steel grip and shoves me down until my ass is in the air and my hair touches the floor.

I yelp with surprise, and if it weren't for his hold on me, I'd topple over.

"Grab the back of your ankles."

This time, I don't argue. The sharp tone of his voice leaves no room for it.

Behind us, the door opens again, and one of the maids stares at the scene, wide-eyed. "You called, sir?"

"Come here," he says, his fingers digging into my neck. "Can you see my wife's cunt?"

"Darian," I gasp, but he smacks my ass hard, making me squeal.

The maid shifts an uneasy glance my way before her silent steps move closer, and heat burns my cheeks when she clears her throat.

"Yes, sir."

"Hear that, wife? She can see your cunt." Then he dismisses the maid, who scurries out of the room like her ankles are on fire, but they're nowhere near as warm as my cheeks. If only the ground would open and swallow me whole.

"You embarrassed her," I growl at him.

"You did that all on your fucking own," he says, still holding me bent in half by the nape like he's not sure what to do with me. "Are you trying to piss me off? Is that it?"

"I wasn't trying to—"

My words are cut off abruptly when he jostles me. "I'm trying not to snap your neck like a fucking twig. If you know what's good for you, shut your mouth." Releasing me, he unzips his pants. I'm still holding on to my ankles, not daring to move until he gives me permission. Darian is pissed off, and while I love the unpredictable nature of him when he's like this, I'm smart enough to be obedient.

He bunches my panties in his grip and pulls them taut against my sensitive clit. A sharp bite of pain follows, and my loud gasp echoes in the room. With a hard yank, he rips them clean off, then bends over me and forces the damp fabric into my mouth. "You like to piss me off, wife?"

I feel him straighten behind me and line his cock up with

my entrance as the blood in my veins rushes with anticipation and heat swirls between my legs.

"Let me remind you what happens when you flaunt what's mine to other men." Impaling me on his massive cock, he buries himself balls deep as my muffled scream bounces off the walls.

He's too big, and his cock feels like it's splitting me in two. Panting breaths rush through my nostrils, and white-hot pain, mixed with liquid pleasure, pulsates between my legs.

I love how cruel he is. I love that he cares little for my pleasure when he's angry, and I love it even more when he uses me to get off.

As he fucks me on his cock, bruising my hips with his fingers, my pussy ripples around his veiny length while the sound of slapping skin mixes with his grunts and my whimpering moans. I desperately hold on to my ankles, my hair swishing on the floor. Everything tightens, from my pussy to my lower belly, and I dig my nails into my ankles as he releases my hip to press his thumb against my ring of muscle.

"Is this hole feeling left out of the fun, Mrs. Delacroix?" He spits on my ass, massaging my exit, and pushes his thumb into my back hole.

My moans grow louder around the soaked panties in my mouth, and Darian thrusts harder and deeper, hitting that perfect spot inside me that has me needy for more.

A rush of pleasure starts at my toes and rushes through me until I'm coming so hard, I don't know if I'm screaming or sobbing.

Darian fucks me through it until the last violent wave has receded then guides me to my knees and pulls my hair into a ponytail. With his big cock gripped in his other hand, shiny in my arousal, he removes the panties and dips the engorged crown into my mouth while his hooded eyes drink their fill of me, ruined, on my knees.

"Let's see if we can smudge that lipstick some more." He rubs his leaking cock all over my lips before sliding back inside my mouth, all the way to the back of my throat.

I gag, and he pulls out, but not before he rams himself down my narrow throat, forcing me to swallow around his thick length or choke. My stomach spasms before I can get a grip of my initial panic, so I focus on breathing through my nose until my throat molds around his dick.

"Such a good wife," Darian praises, stroking my hair soothingly.

When he pulls out this time, I inhale greedy breaths, and he cups my cheek, trailing his thumb through the mascara streaks. "Do you understand now why I have to punish you?"

I nod around a sob as tears roll down my cheeks. My body already craves another release.

"Sshh," he soothes, cupping my chin. "Don't cry, baby. You know it turns me feral."

I sob harder, my knees trembling on the hard floor.

"Fuck," he breathes and drops his chin to his chest. "You make me want to hurt you, Mrs. Delacroix. You've never looked more perfect than you do now, crying on your knees for your husband." His eyes gleam with approval, and he strokes his cock while tangling his fingers in my hair as though I'm the most precious thing he's ever seen.

He cups my chin again and brings my teary eyes to his, the muscles tensing and shifting in his arms beneath the straining fabric as he pleasures himself with a hungry, primal need that has my heart pounding out of rhythm. "Tongue out, Mrs. Delacroix."

I stick it out to please him, and he circles the pad of his thumb over it before he straightens up and jacks his dick in long, firm strokes that border on frenzied. The heat in his eyes burns brighter, and he tips his head back, his neck elongating, as a carnal growl reverberates through his muscled chest. I gaze up at him in awe, desperate for a taste of him, but he makes no move to use me to get off.

Darian is a force of nature. Every woman's wet dream and worst nightmare. The kind of man we think we can handle, but there's always a tinge of fear laced with the wanting.

His jaw tightens, and our eyes clash in a collision of chaos and primitive desires. Strings of salty cum squirt on my tongue, causing me to flinch, but he grips my hair to keep me in place.

I stare up at him with hazy eyes, goading him to show me his true self, the darkness that rears its head when he lowers his guard.

Another squirt of creamy cum lands on my nose, followed by a third one on my cheek, and Darian grunts, his fingers twitching in my hair. He's breathing like a bull. We gaze at each other for long moments—me on my knees with his semen dripping down my face like a branding, and him with his hand in my hair.

He releases me and steps back. "Get changed into something more appropriate."

I blink in surprise at the sharp tone of his voice, tasting him on my tongue. Darian walks back to his desk, takes a seat, and stares down at me.

Fine. I'll let him win this round. I have no other choice if I want to get access to his password so I can find the folder Beaumont wants.

I stand up on wobbly legs. My skirt has ridden halfway up my ass, and my pussy is exposed, but I refuse to give in to his demands, so I saunter closer, putting extra sway into my hips, and smile sweetly.

Darian narrows his eyes as I walk around his desk to straddle his lap.

His dark hair is soft beneath my fingers as I begin to ride him on the chair, grinding my bare, swollen pussy against his pressed pants. If anyone walks in now, they'll get a full view of my naked ass, but I'll be the first one to admit I like the thrill. "Do you still have the footage of the night we first met?"

"Hell Fire Night?"

"No."

His voice takes on a tantalizing edge. "The day at the cottage when I pulled you from cleaning duties and ate you out on the desk?"

With a hum, I glance down to see a slick patch on his pants. I roll my hips again and bite my lip as heat swirls in my core. "I'd like to see it."

Darian seems unaffected by my out-of-character behavior as he peruses me, but I know him. He's not stupid. Even so, I enjoy his rough swallow when I toss my head back and moan.

"Can I see the footage?" I ask, circling my arms around his neck.

"Why the sudden interest?"

I pull on the short hair at his nape, dry humping his lap. "Do you care?"

"Not particularly. Maybe you like to watch yourself come, or maybe you've got a devious plan up your sleeve. It doesn't matter. If I find out you're scheming against me, I'll put a bullet in your brain." He says the words so casually, a shiver crawls down my back as he picks up the gun on the desk.

He taps my lips with a knowing, cold smirk, but then he pauses when I dart my tongue out to lick the barrel enthusiastically, swirling my tongue around the end. Darian is mesmerized, his lips slightly parted as I get myself off on his growing bulge.

"Anything for my wife," he says.

I sit sideways on his lap, pretending I'm not watching like a hawk as he types in the password. A few clicks later, the footage plays on the screen. Darian slides his big hand between my legs, so I part them to give him better access.

I have to admit, watching Darian feast on me on his desk makes me tingle, and when my husband sinks his middle and ring finger inside me, sparks erupt.

"Maybe I should make you come on my fingers while you watch yourself come on my tongue?"

I tilt my hips into his touch, wanting just that. On the screen, Darian gazes at me from his vantage point between my legs as he tweaks my nipples. We look hot together.

"You're an insatiable little slut, aren't you, Mrs. Delacroix?"

"You're an ass."

With a chuckle, he spins me around on his lap so that I'm straddling him as he frees his dick. My mind spins while he massages my ass cheeks. He's rough, touching me in a way that leaves no room for doubt; I belong to him. I'm his property.

His thick cock glides against my clit as it slides between my folds, and I wet my lips, no longer pretending I'm in control. I rock and grind, rolling my hips up and down his thick shaft.

A deliciously dark smirk plays on his mouth as he lifts me by the hips and spears me on his dick, filling me to the brim. "Keep those cock drunk eyes on me, wife."

# CHAPTER NINETEEN

DARIAN

*I don't know when silence settles like a heavy, suffocating blanket. I've stopped rocking, and now I'm seated in the corner of the wardrobe with my arms around my knees, staring at nothing.*

*Time moves slowly, or maybe fast? I don't even know. I'm too scared to move or make a noise. Even my breathing seems loud. The only time I remember silence this thick was when my daddy got a visit from some friends. At least, that's what he called the tall men in front of me as I peered out from behind my daddy's long legs.*

*"Darian, be a good boy and play in your room while Daddy talks to his friends."*

*The way they looked at Daddy didn't seem very friendly.*

*Before I had a chance to leave, one of the men walked his fingers in the air and said, "Run along now, kid."*

*Mommy called them Commoners. Whatever that means. Commoners who were doing their leader's "dirty work."*

*Building up my courage, I unfold and slowly crawl forward to peek through the slats. Orange streaks of the morning sun stream through the blinds, casting stripes on the wall where Daddy slumps.*

*He's still staring at me.*

*"Mommy? Where are you?" I whisper as I push the wardrobe door open, careful not to make a noise in case one of the bad men is still here.*

*No one is around, so I crawl into the room. "Daddy?"*

*He doesn't move a muscle.*

*I step over to him, settling on my knees in the pool of blood around him. My pajama pants soon soak through at the knees as I wave a hand in front of his face. "Daddy? Are you awake? Where does it hurt, Daddy?"*

*He still doesn't move. Is this like the movie Bambi? His mommy never moved again, and neither did Littlefoot's mommy.*

*I choke on a pitiful sob and shake my daddy's shoulder. He's cold to the touch. Cold and stiff. "Daddy!" My voice is louder this time. "Please, wake up." I stroke his shirt, my eyes blurry with tears. "This isn't funny anymore. Please, wake up." Staring at the spot where I'm repeatedly stroking his shoulder so I don't have to look at the hole in his forehead, my tears spill over.*

*A heavy ache presses on my chest, and I clutch the fabric before releasing it again."I don't know where Mommy is, Daddy." My voice breaks. "The bad men took her."*

*I lift my gaze to Daddy's face. His glazed eyes are milky, and his skin is paler than usual, which makes the streak of blood between his brows look like red paint, only darker.*

*I'm scared. I promised Mommy I would be brave, but I don't feel it at all. I'm weak, and I hate being weak. Daddy says the weak disappear in our world.*

*"Daddy!" I shout, shaking him hard.*

*Why won't he wake up? He can't leave me here. I'm alone. I don't know where Mommy is.*

*Daddy slides down the wall and topples to the side. I scramble back, my hands slipping in the cold blood beneath my fingers. Breathing hard, I struggle to see Daddy through my stinging tears.*

*"Daddy... Please..."*

Seated on the hard concrete floor in the cellar, staring at the gun in my hand, the haunted voice of my younger self echoes through my mind. Even now, the hopelessness that clawed at me as I sat in a pool of my father's congealing blood crawls back in from the blackened corners of my soul. The young boy is still alive inside me, but I don't know if I have enough left to be strong for both of us.

A shadow shifting in my periphery tears me from my thoughts.

Cecilia's father watches me from behind the bars, where he rests against the back wall with his grimy hands dangling off his knees.

A torch flickers on the wall as I take solace in the weapon in my hand. It's the only semblance of control I have left. I could lift my arm, aim it at his head, pull back on the hammer, and end this nightmare once and for all.

So what's stopping me?

I feel my chin wobble as the burn behind my eyes intensifies, so I swipe the vodka bottle off the floor and press it to my lips.

"You're lost." His gravelly, unused voice draws me out of my haze of pity.

"Whose fault is that?"

He remains silent. Forever my tormentor.

A violent wave of anger rips through me, and I throw the vodka bottle at the wall, watching glass shatter everywhere as

I remain seated in a sea of jagged shards, broken and alone. "I thought revenge would feel good." My voice barely carries.

His dirty feet slide over the floor as he lowers his legs and crawls closer to the rusty bars. I sense him studying me, but I keep my attention on the gun in my hand, the only thing tethering me to reality.

"I locked you up and took away your freedom. I punished you the only way I knew how." The broken organ in my chest clenches, but I resist rubbing it better. "And then, I found the only thing you care about in this world and entrapped her, too." I look at him, observing the deep wrinkles on his gaunt, sunken face. The years haven't been kind to him. "If anything, I feel worse. It's like…" My chin begins to wobble, so I break eye contact and tighten my jaw to wrangle the onslaught of unwelcome, painful emotions.

Why the fuck does the past have to hurt? Even now, the memories slice at me like countless knives.

I skate my eyes to him again. "So tell me, what do I do now?"

He drops his gaze to the gun in my hand, and I feel its weight. "You let go of the past."

"I can't. Not until I find out the truth about what happened to my mother that night. Every detail."

"You're killing yourself, Darian."

"WHY WON'T YOU TELL ME THE TRUTH?" I roar, overcome with anger, desperation, and grief.

Ragged, heavy breaths tear at my chest like daggers while we stare at each other in the flickering torchlight. When he stays silent, I stand on shaky legs.

Unfortunately, I can't make him talk no matter how hard I press, beg, or rage. The truth remains sealed behind his cracked lips, and one day soon, it'll follow him into the grave.

Broken glass crunches underfoot as I walk back out with slumped shoulders.

His voice reaches my ears. "Do you think the truth will help you heal? That it will somehow patch you together and make you feel better?"

Stiffening, I pause in the doorway.

"Wake up, Darian. Wake the hell up!"

I reach into my pocket and slide out my mom's heart pendant necklace, the tarnished silver adding to its aged beauty.

*"I know you're scared, but you have to be a big boy for me. Can you do that? You need to be brave, okay?"*

"I know you want to hurt my daughter to get back at me. To take the most precious thing from me, like I took your family. But all you're doing is hurting yourself."

As I palm the heart pendant in my fist, the ache behind my ribs intensifies until I'm forced to inhale or drown in this sea of sorrow.

"End this, Darian. Before it's too late."

I swiftly exit the cellar, jaw clenched, taking the steps two at a time before entering the kitchen, evading his toxic-laced knives that threaten to cut me wide open.

My conflicted thoughts battle it out as I place the gun on the island and rest my hands against the edge.

*What will it take to make the memories of that night cease?* Every time I let Cecilia beneath my skin, she unwittingly chips away at my carefully erected walls.

As a result of her gentle touches and even sweeter addictive kisses, the nightmares find cracks to seep through. How can she peel away my layers with so little effort? And why am I powerless and unwilling to stop her? A part of me is curious about the ease at which she unravels me.

This wasn't part of the plan.

It was supposed to be easy.

Find her. Trap her. Break her.

Make her bend to my will.

Dropping my chin to my chest, I whisper a shaky "fuck."

"Hey…" A hand lands on my back, sliding up between my shoulder blades, and I stiffen as Cecilia's concerned voice creates irreparable fissures in my heart. "Are you okay?"

The pressing urge to shrug her off shouts loudly, but not as loud as the need to feel more of her touch, which burns through my T-shirt.

As I glance at her over my shoulder, I hold my breath.

"You've been drinking again."

I say nothing, watching her eyes, her lips. Everything about her.

With a soft expression, she takes hold of my arms and guides me around so the island is at my back. Her hands slide a slow path up my chest, starting at my abs, then higher across the planes of my pectorals and shoulders, and then back down my arms. She interlaces her fingers with mine and cranes her neck to look me in the eye. "Sleep with me, Darian."

"Sleep with you?"

Her gaze holds mine, vulnerable yet determined, as she leads me out of the kitchen and through the house, until we reach the entrance of her bedroom.

"Humor me," she says, turning the handle behind her and backing into the room.

I willingly follow, our fingers interlaced. When she lets go of my hand to crawl into my bed, it dawns on me that I would go to war for the look in her eyes. No one has ever watched me like she is now, with her heart wide open for attack.

I sheath my sword and let her lead me into her trap.

Crawling into bed, I settle beside her, and she snuggles against me.

"Will you promise me something?" she asks, hiking her smooth thigh over my leg and hugging me close.

I'm stiff, my heart pounding out of my chest.

"Maybe," I croak.

The truth is, I would promise her anything right now. And if she asked me to rip the beating organ from my chest and die a bloody, agonizing death in the process, I would do it in a heartbeat.

"Stay with me," she begs as she traces my nipple with a soft touch, making my throat jump on a swallow. "I want to wake up next to you, Darian Delacroix."

Have I forgotten how to breathe? Yes, I have.

"Okay," I whisper shakily.

She hugs me closer, and within minutes, she's asleep. Me? I'm still holding my breath, worried I'll crack open with my next inhale and bleed out onto her silk sheets.

It dawns on me that I'm scared, as I tentatively trace my fingertips over her smooth shoulder. Scared of what might crawl out of the wardrobe along with my memories if I let myself feel.

For years, I've entertained nothing less than exerting full control in all areas of my life, yet since Cecilia appeared, my control has seeped through the cracks left in her wake.

She's an angel, and I'm her tarnished demon. She's the blinding light to my dark, the only person with the power to break me, and I'm starting to think that maybe—just maybe—I want her to take a sledgehammer to my polished shell and crack it wide open. Maybe I want to give her the power to bring my ghosts to the surface.

Or maybe I'm weak.

*Weak for her.*

# CHAPTER TWENTY

## CECILIA

I slowly drift awake when sunlight pours through the gap in the curtains, and warmth covers my back like a soothing blanket. A heavy weight is draped around me, holding me close to a warm, hard chest.

Memories of the previous night coax me to blink my eyes open. I'm in my bedroom.

Shifting onto my back beneath Darian's heavy arm, I roll my head on the pillow and suck in a breath at how peaceful he looks when he sleeps. Peaceful and boyish.

His lips are slightly parted, and his dark hair stands in all directions. Something about this less-than-perfect version of Darian tugs on my heartstrings.

I slowly roll onto my side and rest my cheek on my palm as I gaze at his handsome face. With my bottom lip trapped between my teeth, I drift my fingers over his cheek, feeling the scrape of his stubble.

If anything, this rugged version of Darian is even more heartbreakingly beautiful. He doesn't need the crisp shirts, expensive watches, and styled hair to steal my resolve to stay away from him. No, my undoing is the air of vulnerability behind those moving eyelids and the wisps of hair falling over his brow.

He stirs, so I pause, waiting until his breathing deepens again. A part of me wants him to wake up and cover me with his big body, but another part of me wants to stay in this moment—a moment where he's not the guarded version of Darian who exists in the daylight, but this softer, boyish man with hopes, dreams, and fears.

I shift closer until my lips hover a hair's breadth from his and then I peer at him to ensure his eyes are closed before I press my lips to his soft ones.

The moment his mouth brushes up against mine, my heart stutters, fragile and trembling, like a leaf in the wind. How can I feel so much all at once for a man I've sworn to hate? When did it happen? I haven't lived with Darian that long. Yet somehow, he disarmed me the moment I laid eyes on him, and I still recall how his gaze seared a path over my skin as I polished glasses.

A trembling breath escapes me as I kiss his upper lip, then his lower.

If I don't guard my heart, I'll fall in love with Darian Delacroix, which would be a very, very bad idea. But maybe I was born with a rebellious heart.

My thoughts evaporate into fine mist when firm but gentle fingers skim my cheek. Darian traces the seam of my lips with his tongue, and a full-body shiver raises the hairs on my bare arms. He takes the opportunity when I gasp to slide his hand around my nape and deepen the kiss, his tongue exploring my mouth, imprisoning my every shaky breath.

I moan and press up against him, running my hands over the rippling muscles in his back. He quivers with restrained desire, and I can't help but wonder what it'd take for him to open his cage and let his leashed power rush out to crush me beneath his weight.

"Darian," I whisper as he trails kisses down my neck and back up to my abused lips, silencing his name on my panted breath with his tongue, his hands in my hair as he angles my head to kiss me deeper.

Who knew Darian's mouth on mine could be so addictive and that the feel of his weight could be so delicious? He settles on top of me, careful not to suffocate me with his big body.

My mind is afloat in a sea of heady desire while I explore the shifting muscles in his broad back. Darian whispers my name between nipping kisses, his large hands roaming every inch of my body and pulling on my hair. We make out like teenagers.

We kiss like there's no tomorrow.

As though yesterday never existed and *now* is all there is.

This moment.

*Us.*

I've never experienced a kiss like this, never felt it burn away my defenses like wildfire, but here we are—aflame in an inferno of desire.

Darian breaks the carnal kiss to trail the bridge of his nose over mine, a softened look entering his eyes.

While Darian's default expression is one of complete boredom, the way he's looking at me now is unlike anything I've seen in the short time I've been chased and tormented by his demons. For once, Darian isn't hiding behind a mask. What stares back at me is the boy behind the hardened exterior.

His throat rolls as he flicks his gaze between mine, but before I can recover from the emotions in those blue depths, he slams his lips back onto mine and hooks my soul with an iron fist. The truth stares me in the face as he rips it from my chest—no other man will ever hold a candle to this broken monster.

This is damnation.

Maybe I'm already in love? Is it possible? Could I love a man so deeply involved with the Exiled?

I don't find an answer to my question because his lips descend on mine with unyielding passion, making me lose all train of thought as I clutch his T-shirt.

Every man I've kissed has tried to remove my clothes and take advantage, but Darian is content moving on top of me in his T-shirt and briefs like a wave lapping at a shore. His hands touch and squeeze, driving me insane with need, but he never tries to take it further. Not this time. I'm truly screwed.

He has my heart surrounded on all fronts, and no deep trenches or reinforced forts can protect me against this moment. So I do something I've never let myself do—I throw my weapons down in surrender and let Darian Delacroix invade and conquer.

Defeat has never tasted so sweet as it does when he whispers my name into the kiss and tangles his fingers in my hair.

Maybe I can take up arms tomorrow when the enemy lies asleep, sated and defenseless. Or maybe I'm lying to myself.

---

After lunch, Darian leaves the house to attend whatever shady business he's involved in. I shudder just thinking about it. For all I know, he could be involved in human trafficking side of Exiled.

Wait. What if he is? No, he wouldn't. But the doubt lingers.

While he's a damn good kisser and hung like a horse, the

truth remains that I don't know anything about Darian or his involvement in the Exiled and my father's disappearance. These thoughts have gone through my head a lot lately. My head and my heart are at war.

My lips still tingle from his heated kisses earlier, and my bruised heart thumps harder every time I recall how he felt and looked on top of me, how he touched me like he wanted to carve his initials on my soul.

No, dammit. Now is not the time to think about my husband and the witch spell he has cast on my withering resolve to avenge my father's murder.

"You better know what you're looking for," Lauren says, taking up her stationed position behind the door to listen out for sounds.

Once Darian left the house, I hightailed it to his office with his password memorized and a heavy weight of self-doubt on my chest. I shake that feeling off now as I settle in his desk chair and exhale a nervous breath. I can do this. I can find the kind of information Beaumont needs.

But why? Why does he want it?

*You know why. Don't be naïve.* He wants to blackmail Darian. Whatever he hopes to find on my husband's laptop is bad enough to ruin him. So the question is, do I hand it over to Beaumont, or use it against Darian myself?

Flashbacks of when Beaumont cornered me in the dress shop and tweaked my nipples invade my head, making my skin crawl at the sensation of his phantom fingers.

I rest my elbows on the desk and massage my temples. If I don't find compromising information, Beaumont will make true to his promise and do what? Rape me? Kill me? He's wrong, though. I'm not Darian's weakness. Given the choice, Darian wouldn't hesitate to put a bullet in my skull. I'm not special to him. A couple of kisses and a fumble in bed don't change the fact that he forced me into marriage because of my last name and the family fortune attached to it. I'm not foolish enough to think that he cares about me.

So why does this feel inherently wrong? Why do I feel like I'm betraying Darian?

Fuck it.

I type in his password, chewing my lip as the computer loads the home screen. Beaumont didn't give me much to go on; he said he wanted sensitive information, something to use against Darian.

"Great help," I mutter as I begin my search.

"What the hell is that?" Lauren says, blinking at a plant on a console table near the door.

I glance at it. "It's a bat flower."

"A bat flower?"

"Yes. I found it in a sale online the other day. It looked like an alien from Mars that could potentially come alive at night and beam my insufferable husband up to the mothership. So I thought: what a great way to spend my husband's blood money. Unfortunately, he's still here. Those teeth, whiskers, and the weird little eyes seem just for aesthetics. The thing can't even catch flies like a Venus trap, but I liked burning his money, so I sent another hundred to his friend Sinclair and his son Elijah."

"You sent a hundred of them to Sinclair and his son?"

"No, I sent a hundred of them to Sinclair and a further hundred to his son."

"Two hundred of them ugly things? You'll give them nightmares."

I open a folder and skim the information. "Careful, or you'll hurt the plant's feelings."

Lauren snorts a laugh.

I continue. "Word on the street is that Sinclair's son is a

psychopath who gets off on torturing women. I doubt a bat flower with whiskers and teeth will break his unfeeling shell."

She bends and stares at it intently. "It's kind of cute in a weird way, don't you think?"

Clicking out of the folder, I open the next one. "I think you should keep a lookout."

She returns to the door and presses her ear to the wood. Silence settles in the room while I read through files. It doesn't take long to confirm that my husband is involved in an illegal weapon trade. No surprise there. He also owns an underground fighting ring. Interesting. Maybe it's a lucrative business? The Darian I know likes to stay in complete control, except at midnight when his ghosts come out to haunt him. He'd never lower himself to fist fights for entertainment.

I'm insanely curious about why he stays up drinking at night. It seems at odds with the Darian I first met—a man who would line up the items on his desk until they were perfectly symmetrical. That man would never reach for the bottle and drink himself into a stupor.

But they *are* the same man. And he *does* drink himself into a stupor.

Besides, I haven't missed the concerned glances Sinclair slides in his direction when my husband isn't looking. While Sinclair is all smiles and jokes, he has a more serious side, which I've only caught glimpses of in Darian's presence.

"Cecilia?" Lauren asks, interrupting my thoughts with the careful tone in her voice.

I open another folder before giving her a raised brow to indicate that I'm waiting for her to continue. With a sigh, she leans back against the door. "Don't you think you're too involved with Darian?"

My hackles immediately rise, but I keep my face blank. "Involved? Why?"

"I hear you two fucking at night." She gives me a pointed look, then enunciates, "Every. Night."

"It's just sex, Lauren." I'm losing patience. Maybe there's no file here with sensitive information like Beaumont seems to think. He said I would know which file it is when I find it, but nothing has stood out to me so far.

"I see how you look at him."

"I don't look at him in any way," I quickly dismiss her.

When she stays silent, I lift my gaze with a frown to find her crossing her arms, hip cocked.

"How about the way he looks at you when he thinks you're not looking?"

"You're delusional."

My stupid fucking heart is beating harder at her words. Can it be true? Is he looking at me?

No. Lauren is wrong.

She turns around and carefully opens the door a smidge then peers through the small gap. "You should break it off before you get hurt."

Frowning, I stop typing as a flare of annoyance flashes through me. "Before I get hurt? Are you serious? Lauren, you don't know anything about me."

I say these words, though deep down, I know the truth. I'm not annoyed at her for pointing out the obvious. Darian will hurt me. My heart isn't safe with a man like him.

He's a Duke. One of the higher-ups in the Exiled.

*Now repeat that until your heart stops skipping a beat every time Darian enters a room.*

I'm annoyed because she wants me to end my dalliance with Darian and pull the plug before it's too late to walk away, but I'm beginning to realize that I don't want to.

I'm about to say something else when my thoughts crash to a halt as I click on another file. "What the hell?" I whisper, gulping hard.

"What's wrong?" Lauren looks at me over her shoulder.

This is it. This is what Beaumont wants to dangle over Darian's head like a noose.

"Nothing," I reply, quickly copying the information onto a USB stick with shaky hands. Lauren looks unconvinced as she watches me switch everything off.

I fidget with the items on the desk to ensure nothing is out of place and no evidence is left behind. My husband has hawk eyes and a special knack for sniffing betrayal from a mile away. I'm actually surprised he hasn't barged in here already.

The USB burns a hole in my pocket as I exit the room with Lauren, but instead of feeling triumphant, guilt gnaws at me.

Can I do this? Can I betray my husband?

*You don't have a choice.*

# CHAPTER TWENTY-ONE

## CECILIA

Tonight is the fundraiser, yet another extravagant affair like the previous one.

Lauren carefully applies her peach lipstick in the mirror, looking nothing short of a goddess [illegible] green cocktail dress, which hugs her every curve.

Curled tendrils of hair frame her heart-shaped face when she peers at me in the mirror. “I think some of the rebels will attend tonight.”

I pause, the perfume bottle inches from my pulse point in my neck, fresh notes of magnolia and lotus flowers saturating my nostrils. “The rebels?”

She zips away the lipstick in the makeup bag and spins around. “It’s a possibility. This is a big event. All the major players will be in attendance.”

I turn away from Lauren to hide my expression, my movements stiff as I spray perfume. While it wouldn’t be the first time the Antichrist has infiltrated an event to spy, it’s the first time the thought of it makes me feel this level of unease. The last thing I want is to place Darian and Sinclair in harm’s way.

"I can't believe it. You've been compromised," Lauren says, stating the obvious. When I fail to turn around, her heels click on the floor. "The Exiled killed your father, or have you forgotten?"

"I haven't forgotten," I bite out as I feel her behind me.

"Darian is no better than them."

Her concern is palpable in the air, and I hate how it stirs the guilt I've festered over the last decade. I couldn't have stopped the events, but I still feel the weight of it.

"He's a Duke, Cecilia. Do you know what that means?"

Steeling my jaw, I turn around to face her. "I'm fully aware he's a Duke."

"Are you?" She shakes her head, and notes of bitterness bleed into her voice. "He *knows* what happened to your father. They *all* do. Yet here you are, spreading your legs for him."

"First of all," I say, pointing a finger at her, "careful! You're my friend, but I won't let you speak to me like that. Secondly, look around you. We're trapped. Our options are very limited. I may not be a Commoner, but I'm still a pawn in this cruel world, the same as you."

Lauren watches me swipe my clutch bag from the bed and inspect my red dress in the mirror. When I'm satisfied my hair hasn't escaped my updo and my boobs are contained in the corset, I breeze past her.

She calls out, "I'm sorry for what I said."

"No, you're not," I reply, smiling at her sadly. "You were right; I've been compromised. But that doesn't mean I won't play my part when it comes down to it."

"Really?" She sounds skeptical as she walks closer. "You would betray Darian if you had to?"

I raise my chin. "I want revenge like you."

My thoughts are a jumbled mess. I'm not lying to Lauren,

but maybe I'm lying to myself. One moment, I thirst for revenge; the next, I question what I'm fighting for. My father is gone, and he's not coming back. The Antichrist and other rebel groups have fought the Exiled since the first Hell Fire Night in an ongoing, never-ending war. All I've seen so far are casualties in the name of revenge. Does anyone ever achieve it? Does anyone actually feel like justice has been served?

Despite these doubts, I still look Lauren in the eye and say, "Believe what you want, but we're fighting on the same side."

As I leave the room, a spike of adrenaline rushes through my veins.

Darian is waiting for us downstairs in a pressed tux, a bowtie, and slicked-back hair, accentuating his sharp cheekbones and jaw.

I draw to a halt, admiring his masculine beauty and effortless ease with which his commanding presence fills a room. Maybe it's an ancient curse to lure women to their deaths.

He finally senses my presence, and my heart thuds harder, called forward by his lure. I hold on to the railing as I descend the stairs.

Darian does a double take, his eyes widening, and he loosens his bowtie as he swallows hard.

I pause on the last step when he clears his throat, blind to the woman behind me. "You look…"

Before he can reply, Lauren breezes past us and disappears outside with an air of silent disapproval.

As the door shuts, Darian clears his throat. "You look beautiful."

I roll my eyes, about to say something snarky in response, but then my cheeks heat, and I dip my chin, relishing his compliment. "Thank you."

His touch on my hand deepens my blush. He lifts it to his lips and softly kisses my knuckles. "I mean it. You look like a dream."

I nervously chew my lip, then stop when I remember my red lipstick. Darian steps closer and invades my senses with his woodsy cologne and consuming presence, which demands my full attention. He lifts my chin with his fingers, and my lips part as he stares at my mouth with so much longing that I'm growing dizzy.

His thumb brushes over my lips in a gentle, barely-there touch so as not to smudge my shade of red. "I would donate my fortune tonight to see these succulent lips wrapped around my cock."

My breath stutters because of the assured, possessive way he handles me, and he smirks knowingly, still bewitched by my mouth. "There's no price I wouldn't pay."

When he holds out his elbow expectantly, I circle my arm through his, barely able to stand upright because of my jelly legs.

"I'm not an escort, Mr. Delacroix," I reply. "Besides, you couldn't afford me."

His chuckle drifts over me like a warm late-night breeze.

As we exit the house, his driver tips his hat and opens the passenger door.

I glance around. "Where's Lauren?"

"She left in a different car."

"Oh."

Darian's touch burns hotter than the sun, despite the silk layer separating us as he guides me inside the vehicle with his hand on my lower back. It sears through me for long moments after he has settled beside me.

The car rocks gently as we leave the premises. Darian stares out the window, seemingly lost in thought. I study his profile, acutely aware of the content on the USB in my bodice. It's like I'm seeing him in a new light, and it's on the tip of my tongue to ask questions. As his wife, I want him to indulge more of himself from a place of trust, which is ironic, considering how I came about this information.

The squeal of leather sends my heart racing down a hill when he turns to look at me, and my chest heaves as I try to control my body's reaction to the hungry yet cautious look in his eyes. He parts the slit in my dress to reveal my bare thighs, and I glance at the partition.

"It's closed. No one can see. Spread your legs."

My dress is too tight, so I lift my ass and pull the silk fabric higher until I have enough room to follow his order. Darian hums and slaps his big palm down on my thigh, reddening my skin.

I ease back against the seat, feeling the cool air on my core as his hand kneads my skin, soothing the burn from his smack.

"I love my mark on you, Mrs. Delacroix." He dips his fingers beneath my panties with practiced ease and slides them aside to reveal my pussy then hums as he slaps his big hand down on my thigh again, squeezing my muscle to the point of pain. "Fuck yourself, wife. Get yourself off."

I gasp as I squirm beneath his possessive, lascivious gaze.

Something about how he looks at me with such total devotion and admiration makes me want to please him. Instead, I say, "We're almost there."

What if he asks to see my breasts? What then? I can't let him discover the USB.

"We won't exit the car until you're done. Either way, we're not leaving until I've watched you come on your delicate fingers."

"Why are you doing this?" I ask as he reaches out to grab me by the side of my neck in a possessive hold.

Staring at my pussy and licking his lips, he watches me circle my clit. "I like to practice self-control in all areas of my life, Mrs. Delacroix. You're proving to be my biggest weakness." His flexing fingers on my neck betray his urge to touch me, which emboldens me to slide my middle finger inside me.

My toes curl with pleasure, and my thighs quiver while Darian runs his thumb over my pulse point and whispers, "So beautiful."

I notice the growing bulge behind his zipper, and my insides clench in response, but when I reach out to touch him, he grabs my hand and shoves it away.

His rejection stings, but I don't have time to give it further thought because my walls flutter around my finger, and I bite down hard on my lip and let out a moan, lipstick be damned.

Darian settles back against the door and squeezes his thick bulge but makes no move to free himself. If anything, he looks mildly disinterested in my disheveled state, though the heat in his gaze betrays him.

Rolling my head on the headrest, I study him while rubbing my throbbing clit. My muscles tremble. I feel so empty, and it's all his fault. If only he would let go of his control and fuck me hard until we're both satiated and breathing harshly, in a tangle of limbs and sweat.

"Don't you want to touch me?" I ask, panting. "Don't you want to forget about the fundraiser and take me somewhere?"

"Do you know what the fundraiser is?" he asks as he tips his head sideways, watching me curiously.

I plunge two fingers inside me and imagine they're his.

"A boring event with boring people raising money for shady, boring business deals."

"It's a battleground," he states as I squirm with need, the insides of my thighs sticky with arousal.

"If you say so." I'm barely able to comprehend his nonsensical talk while my pussy grips my fingers so tight I'm seeing stars. He could discuss the apocalypse in great detail and I'd think he's discussing yesterday's weather.

*Overcast with occasional showers.*

"Fuck," I moan as I curl my fingers, hitting that spot Darian likes to rub.

Darian crawls forward like a prowling lion, manoeuvres me around so that I'm leaning against the door opposite, and spreads my legs wide. When he stares at my pussy with unabashed hunger, a blush creeps up my neck.

"The fundraisers are a show of power."

I'm panting hard, transfixed by the outline of his cock inside his pressed pants. Why won't he stop talking and pull it out instead?

"Only the strongest come out on top." Taking hold of my wrist, he pulls my fingers out of my pussy before guiding them to my mouth and ordering me to suck them clean. "Do you know what happens to the weak?"

My tongue swirls around my slick digits, and I shake my head, listening with half an ear. Maybe I should bite back with a snarky response, but it's in my best interest for once to act pliant and keep him distracted. There's a time and place to show my fire. Not now when I have the USB on me.

*Why did I even bring it?*

In a swift move, he grabs my ankle and yanks me down on the seat until I'm flat on my back.

He keeps his weight off me as he stares down at my flushed face. "They disappear."

My pussy pulses around my fingers as I sink them into my heat, drunk at the sight of him above me.

*Is that what happened to my father?*

*He disappeared?*

"You've ruined your hair." Balanced on one hand, he drags his thumb through my lipstick. "And your makeup."

"Whose fault is that?" I don't recognize my voice or the desire running through each note.

*What happened to my father, Darian?*

*Tell me the truth.*

"Such a mess," he whispers, forcing his thumb between my lips. "I need you to be stronger than this, Mrs. Delacroix."

I bite him, and a muscle jumps in his jaw, but he doesn't remove his finger or ease up on his grip. "I know you want to fuck me. I can see it in your eyes."

"Trust me, I want nothing more than to tear this flimsy dress off your body and bury my cock so deep in your tight little cunt that you scream so loud, my driver thinks I'm hurting you. But if I can't control myself around you now, *my biggest weakness,* I can't win on the battlefield in there." He tips his head toward the window behind him, and it's only now I realize the car has stopped.

When he leans in, his heated breath drifts across my ear. "Now make yourself come, Mrs. Delacroix. Moan my name as your cunt squeezes your fingers."

His dark words are my undoing, and when he whispers, *"My filthy slut,"* an orgasm sweeps through me.

Darian chuckles in my ear, his breath wafting over the side of my face as I tremble beneath him.

With a self-control that could rival a monk's, he sits back to adjust his bowtie and waits for me to wrangle my ruined hair into submission with my compact mirror. Nothing can be done about my slick fingers. I wipe them on the leather seat, but sex is now my perfume of choice.

"Now that your primal urges are taken care of, wife. Are you ready to mingle with the wolves?"

I snap the mirror shut. "Who said my *urges* have been taken care of? I'm a woman, Delacroix. You've merely wet my appetite." I smile sweetly. "I would love to mingle with the wolves."

His eyes narrow and burn into my back as I exit the car.

What did he think would happen? That I would roll over and expose my belly? I don't know what power game he played earlier, but he's sorely mistaken if he thinks he can weaponize my sexuality against me or use it as some weird way to keep his control.

Of course, I can handle a couple of wolves. After all, the Exiled runs through my blood.

# CHAPTER TWENTY-TWO

## CECILIA

Darian resembles an unsmiling stone statue in his eye mask as he guides me inside the grand hall. The man can't look approachable to save his life.

I scan the crowds of overdressed men and women mingling beneath the fancy chandeliers for signs of Lauren. She's by a pillar, laughing at Sinclair.

"I'm gonna kill him," I say, and Darian looks confused as he follows my line of sight, but before he can comment, I disentangle my arm from his.

Sinclair smirks when I stride across the floor, swiping a champagne glass off a floating tray.

My smile could melt butter as I sidle up beside him and give his son, Elijah, a cursory glance. "It's good to see you again, Sinclair."

He hums, stealing the flute from my hand and downing it in one go. "I was just telling your beautiful friend here how much I loved the flowers you sent me. All one hundred of them."

*Beautiful friend?* I narrow my eyes. Sinclair is a dangerous man. Although he has an easy smile and cracks more jokes than the Joker, I wouldn't trust him near my friend. It doesn't matter that he has grown on me since the first time I met him; I won't hesitate to serve his balls on a cheese platter if he touches Lauren.

"And how about you?" I ask Elijah, ignoring his father. "Did you like your flowers?"

If I thought my husband—who is striding toward us after getting hassled by an elderly lady in a gold eye mask insistent on kissing his cheeks—had a stony exterior, I was wrong. Sinclair's son doesn't acknowledge my existence as he scans the crowds with a bored, inferior expression.

"You know," I say, ignoring Sinclair's snicker, "I've heard stories about you."

Elijah slides his gaze in my direction and inspects me like I'm an insect.

I feel the moment Darian's shadow falls over me from behind, not because Elijah lifts his gaze or the bored, dismissive way he scans the crowds. No, none of those things hold a candle to how my core warms at the sensation of my husband's broad chest against my back. He's stiff and uncomfortable around Elijah, which sparks unwelcome excitement.

"If those stories are true," I say casually as a waiter appears with a tray of flutes, "I won't hesitate to kill you in your sleep if you attempt to flirt with my friend." I help myself to champagne and take a sip.

Behind me, Darian turns to stone.

Sinclair chokes on his drink.

Elijah assesses me with lazy intrigue, but I can't be amusing enough for him because he turns on his heel and walks away.

"A simple thank you for the flowers would have sufficed." As I turn back, Lauren stares at me, wide-eyed. Sinclair is laughing so hard, he's almost doubled over, and

Darian is about two seconds away from exploding like a spectacular supernova. I look between them all. "What's up?"

"What's up?" Lauren asks as she gives my husband a concerned glance over my head. "You antagonized that guy on purpose."

"So?"

"So?" It's Sinclair who speaks this time. "You don't want my son's attention."

A big hand lands on my hip, which doesn't go unnoticed by Sinclair. He sips his champagne. "A possessive husband won't stop my son when he sets his eye on something."

I didn't think it was possible for Darian to grow any stiffer, but I was wrong. There's a possibility he's now cemented to the floor. "Stop with the drama. I was letting you both know my friend is off-limits."

"Son or no son of yours," Darian growls, digging his fingers into my flesh. "If he comes near my wife, I'll skin and quarter him."

Lauren pales.

I turn to face my husband, who stares at his best friend with silent murder in his eyes. Sometimes, I wonder how they've maintained this close friendship over the years. My husband seems intent on killing Sinclair most of the time, and Sinclair? Well, he takes it all in his stride with a chuckle and a hard slap on Darian's shoulder.

"Don't worry," Sinclair tells me as he jostles my husband. "He's bark and no bite. Mostly anyway." Turning to Lauren, he offers her the crook of his arm. "Care for a dance?"

"Care for a dance," I mimic in his posh accent as I pull my friend to my side. "I swear to everything holy, if you thought the bat flower delivery was bad, you haven't seen anything yet. Did you know the corpse flower is considered the ugliest plant in the world? Careful with your flirtatious smiles in my friend's proximity, or I'll ensure your house resembles a damn jungle next time you bring a conquest over. By the time I'm done playing Monopoly with my husband's black card, you'll require a machete to fight back the shrubbery just to reach the damn bed—"

A big palm clamps down over my mouth as warm lips brush against my ear. "Careful, wife. If you don't shut up, I might believe you're jealous. And you don't want to find out what happens if I think you harbor feelings toward my friend."

I bat my husband off and spin around, whisper-hissing, "I'm not jealous! I'm worried about Lauren. If he hurts her, I'll kill him."

"And I'll let you."

I slam my lips shut, surprised by the glint of humor in his eyes. Behind me, Sinclair's infectious chuckle mixes with the muted conversations in the room.

"Relax, baby," he says, pausing beside me. "It's only a dance."

Then they're gone, and I chew on my lip as I scan the room for rebels. Unease trickles down my spine. I'm on edge, and I don't know why.

My mind drifts as I glance at Lauren and Sinclair. He's a Duke. A brutal, deadly Duke with a smile that acts as a camouflage for what truly lurks beneath. By the time you sense danger, it's too late. After Lauren's lecturing earlier, she can't be that easily swayed by his charms, right?

Even as I try to convince myself it's all an act on her part, I know it's a lie. It wasn't that long ago I was hellbent on killing Darian.

I didn't care if he was involved in his disappearance or not. He was a part of the Exiled and, therefore, an accomplice.

Now I'm not so certain anymore. Darian managed to break down my barriers with his non-existent charm, so Sinclair could be downright deadly if he set his mind to it.

Darian gets distracted by an older man with a mustache and bushy, silvery brows, who stares at my cleavage for a solid ten seconds before shaking my husband's hand. Judging by the pained look on his face, Darian's handshake is fierce enough to crush bones and then some. At least we're in public, so he refrains from murdering the man in plain sight.

As I place the empty flute back on a tray, I catch sight of a passing lady's necklace, which is subtle yet undoubtedly an inverted cross. She disappears into the gathered crowds, and I excuse myself from Darian's side, mumbling that I need to freshen up.

Where did she go? My shoulders brush up against expensive suits and gowns. I weave between groups of people, craning my neck for a better view, but she's nowhere in sight.

Fuck. She's gone.

A tall man with sandy hair bumps into me as he passes, placing something in my palm. Bristling at the bold contact, I whip my head around as he walks away. Our eyes meet over his shoulder, and a mysterious smirk graces his full lips. I glance down to see a necklace in my hand—the same one the woman wore. When I look up again, he has disappeared into the crowd.

With trembling hands, I stuff the necklace inside my corset while tossing nervous glances around to ensure no one is paying attention.

Lauren was right. They're here. And they're here in numbers.

A shadow falls over me from behind, and a cold, controlled voice says, "Meet me on the upstairs balcony."

I spin around, spotting Beaumont's retreating back. He's a man I should stay far away from, but I don't have a choice.

I'll meet him upstairs and turn him down in person. Why did I bring the USB? What was I thinking? Trying to save my own skin? Now that I'm here, I can't do it—I can't betray Darian. I don't care for Beaumont's threats. There must be some other way to put him in his place. My hands turn clammy, and the walls feel as if they're closing in. I shouldn't be alone with him, not after his threat to hurt me to get to my husband.

Fuck it. I refuse to let a man make me feel weak. I'm not scared of him or any of the men in this damn secret society. Who is he to try to intimidate me into obedience?

With my mind set, I exit the crowded hall and hurry upstairs. My heart pounds the entire time, and my brain screams at me to turn back. I have minutes until Darian comes looking for me—minutes to get this over with.

Finding the balcony hidden at the back of the library took longer than expected. Beaumont is facing away from me, hands in his pockets. He looks sharp in a tux and gelled hair and exudes an air of danger that makes my skin crawl.

The minute I enter the cold evening air, his beady eyes land on my eye mask, and he slowly turns to face me.

"Mrs. Delacroix," he says suggestively, his gaze traveling down my body. "It's a pleasure to see you again."

"I wish I could say the same." My voice bleeds with toxic venom, and I watch him carefully, feeling like he's about to strike any minute.

He sniffs and takes in the night sky and the streetlights in the distance. "It's a beautiful evening. Very tranquil."

"Why are you here?"

"It's a party, Mrs. Delacroix."

A chilly breeze licks at my skin like a sharp blade, cutting and slicing. Beaumont stalks closer, but I hold my ground, refusing to let the vulture sniff my fear in the air. "Did you get the information I requested?"

"I came here to tell you to leave me alone."

"Leave you alone?" He eats up the short distance and swamps me with his large, imposing body. "I thought I made it clear that you have no choice but to sing to my tune, unless of course…" A chill-inducing, suggestive smile plays on his lips as he reaches out to finger a loose tendril framing my face. "You want a secret little dalliance in a dark corner."

"With you?" I smack his hand away. "I don't fucking think so."

One moment, I'm standing there, and the next, he punches me so hard in the face that I fall back onto the ground. Stars explode behind my eyes, and pain ricochets through my skull, but before I can crawl away, he kicks me in the ribs.

I double over, bleeding from a cut on my lip, and a sharp, stabbing pain guts me when I try to sit up.

He circles me with slow, predatory steps, flexing his fingers as if he's readying to strike me with his fists. "Since I'm a gentleman, we'll try again, Mrs. Delacroix. Did you bring the information?"

I feel blood trickle down my chin as I glare up at him, my skirt pooled around my upper thighs, my dress and hair in disarray. Running my tongue over my bloodied teeth, I sneer at him. "Is this all you've got? You think I'm scared of you because you're a big, bad man?" My smile widens, as cruel as the glint in his eye. "Newsflash. I'm not. You're pathetic—"

With a grunt, he kicks me in the head, and for a moment, everything fades away. When he flips me over onto my back and pulls down my corset, I become vaguely aware of the gritty ground beneath me. The cold air nips at my bare skin like tiny bites, and I feel a warm hand squeeze my breasts, tweaking and kneading.

A deep ache in my skull renders me defenseless against his heated, sour breath on my face as he leans down to drag his tongue through the blood on my chin and says, "Thank you for bringing the USB, sweetheart. You should have told me you like a rough hand."

He gropes between my legs while I whimper uselessly, my head lolling on the hard, unforgiving ground. Overhead, stars twinkle and a gust of breeze sweeps over my bruised body.

I pull at his shirt with shaky hands, fighting him off, but my heavy arms refuse to obey. "No, please," I choke out as searing pain spreads between my legs.

A manic look enters his almost black eyes, and he forces another finger inside me. "Relax, sweetheart, and it'll feel good."

A shadow falls over him from behind, and relief curls inside my chest when Darian's murderous gaze gleams like cat eyes in the dark. The weight on top of me disappears as he hauls Beaumont away and lays into him with brutal fists and a vicious, calm control that does little to cloak the unhinged fury in his eyes. I've never seen Darian like this. He's nothing short of lethal.

Sinclair helps me cover up, but Lauren rushes outside and orders him away, faffing over me while the bloodbath continues in my periphery. "Careful with her. She has a concussion." It's only then I realize I'm bleeding from a cut on my brow, and more blood oozes from my throbbing lip.

"Here," Lauren says, draping Sinclair's suit jacket over my shoulders and helping me button it to hide my breasts from view.

I lift my head to see Beaumont held up by Sinclair and

Elijah. Darian inspects his bloody knuckles with morbid curiosity before punching him so hard, a tooth flies from his mouth. "You thought you could touch what's mine?"

I flinch at the putrid hate in his voice, the dark undertone of deadly violence.

He steps up close, baring his teeth in a snarl. "You thought wrong. Putting your hands on my wife was a big mistake."

Beaumont stares defiantly at my husband, who studies him from head to toe like he's a specimen in a lab experiment.

"I can't wait to skin you alive."

"Fuck you," Beaumont hisses, earning him a punch in the gut.

When he finally stops coughing, he lifts his head and flashes a bloodied, condescending smile. "You think your wife is loyal to you, Delacroix? Open your fucking eyes. She's chomping at the teeth to stab you in the back."

My husband's fist flies, and a hard crack rings out in the evening air. Blood squirts from Beaumont's broken nose, pouring down his lips and chin. He wiggles his jaw like a psychopath begging for another round. "Do you think the King will look at you twice when the truth comes out? You're weak, Delacroix. Fucking weak—"

"Shut your filthy mouth!" Sinclair growls.

Beaumont never takes his eyes off my husband. "There's no room for your kind of weakness in the Exiled."

"Sir," a burly Commoner says as he and another Commoner enter the balcony with a cigar trimmer. "Here's the item you requested."

Darian accepts it without glancing at me, focused on my attacker, and a struggle breaks out as one of the Commoners forcefully inserts Beaumont's middle finger into the trimmer.

Sinclair and Elijah grunt as they buckle down to keep him in place.

Held down by two men, Beaumont can't break free, but he still fights and struggles, wasting his energy as he desperately cries for help.

My husband jerks his chin in silent command, and the other Commoner steps up behind Beaumont and chokes him with his arm around his neck, effectively putting a sudden stop to his screaming.

"You don't want to watch this," Lauren says beside me.

She's wrong. I do want to watch.

I can't take my eyes off my husband and the darkness that pours from him in uncontrolled waves. He's magnetic and utterly mesmerizing in his lethality.

"What made you think you could touch my wife?"

Turning red from the brutal chokehold on his neck, Beaumont looks over at me, but Darian blocks his view and says, "Don't you fucking dare look at her."

I hear Beaumont, hidden behind my husband, spit on his tux.

"Answer the question," Darian says in an eerily controlled voice. "What made you think you could touch my wife?"

"I don't answer to you."

My husband sighs, disappointed, nudging his chin for the Commoner to step away and let him take the cigar trimmer. Beaumont breathes hard, cursing and wrestling against Sinclair and Elijah, and the latter smirks at me as hoarse, blood-curdling screams send sleeping birds flying from a nearby tree.

I taste sick at the back of my throat but refuse to look away from the dark sadism in Elijah's cold gaze.

"You thought you could put your filthy fingers inside my wife." Darian turns around, his hands bloodied. "It's only fitting she gets to keep them as a souvenir and a reminder of the consequences of betrayal." Standing before me like an apparition of Lucifer, he holds out my attacker's severed fingers, but I can't move past his words.

"You think I betrayed you?" I ask, flicking my eyes between his.

Darian's gaze burns into me, void of emotion, before he tosses the fingers onto my lap and walks some distance away to toe two items on the ground with his shiny Oxfords. Crouching down, he picks them up and inspects the inverted cross necklace in the dim light streaming through the balcony doors. The same necklace the stranger thrust into my hand back in the main hall. "I have to give it to you, *wife*. You're good." He closes his fist around the cross and looks over at me. "How many times did you evade my security? How did you communicate with the rebels?"

*Evade his security? What is he talking about? I never…*

My heart cracks in two, an ache pressing on my chest as I search for the right words, but what can I possibly say to make things right and bring the warmth back to his eyes? The way he looks at me now… It hurts.

"Isn't it obvious?" Elijah asks. "You have a rat on the inside."

Darian doesn't respond. Instead, he stands and strides over to me, holding out the USB. "You conspired with Beaumont against me?"

Tears spill from my eyes as I shake my head, desperate to make him understand. "No…I came here to tell him I didn't want any involvement—"

In a swift move, he grabs my chin and sneers in my face. "I don't want to hear your fucking excuses."

"Darian, I—" I try to explain around a sob, but he won't even look into my eyes.

He shoves me away, turns to the others, and gives Beaumont a disgusted once over before spinning on his heel and walking out. "Bring him."

As soon as they're gone, I break down.

Lauren pulls me into her gentle arms, whispering soothing words that do little to ease the heartache. If anything, I want to push her away and chase after Darian, but I don't have the energy. My head is dizzy, and I'm trembling all over from the receding adrenaline rush.

"Sshh! You're okay." Lauren strokes my hair behind my ears. "He'll come around."

"He thinks I betrayed him."

"He's angry with Beaumont for hurting you, and he's not thinking straight. He'll come to his senses as soon as he's had time to calm down."

I sniffle pathetically and try to stand, but the lancing pain in my throbbing head is so bad that I wince and press my palm against my brow. I can barely stand upright, never mind walk.

Lauren slides her arm around my waist, taking the brunt of my weight. "Let's find you someplace quiet where you can rest. You shouldn't be up and walking with a concussion."

"What if he doesn't forgive me? After all, I did steal the information from his computer. I can't talk myself out of this one. Regardless of my reasoning, it doesn't look good, especially when I brought the USB with me tonight."

We hobble toward the doorway. "He'll forgive you. He'd be a fool if he didn't."

A fool or not. I've royally screwed up.

# CHAPTER TWENTY-THREE

## DARIAN

After stripping him of his clothes, they secure his wrists and ankles to a bed in one of the spare bedrooms upstairs.

He thrashes with renewed strength, covered in sweat and blood. Sinclair observes me, but I ignore his concern as I scan the room for ways to get creative. A chair sits tucked into a desk beside a mahogany bookshelf.

With a growing smirk, I cross the room, pull the chair out, and kick at the legs until one breaks off, resembling a stake that's ready to inflict damage. The men in the room study me curiously, except for Elijah, who is watching something on his phone with that sadistic glint in his eye—and by something, my guess is torture porn. I might have suggested therapy to his father once or twice when Elijah was a kid. Back then, he enjoyed carving up living things, but Sinclair just shrugged it off and laughed. I used to join in because, let's face it, we're all fucked in the head. The Exiled made sure of it.

"I would start praying if I were you," I say as I walk over to Beaumont.

He really is a pathetic sight, with his tiny dick and retracted balls seeking safety inside his body because he's that scared.

Sweat pours down his temples as he lifts his head to look at the broken chair leg in my hand.

I'll admit I haven't improvised like this before. Usually, I let one of the Commoners do the torturing or simply shoot the motherfucker between the eyes. I rarely feel the urge to inflict damage or kill; such baser instincts are beneath me, but tonight is a completely different ballgame. Violence runs through my veins like a poison, and blood pumps through my arteries at a frightening speed.

As I watch him tremble with rampant terror, throwing furtive glances at the other men in the room, I imagine a million ways to slaughter him slowly.

Did Cecilia meet him in secret?

I swear my eye ticks when I think of him beating her and putting his filthy hands on her body.

"What are you going to do with that broken leg?" His voice cracks with nerves on the last note as he tugs on the restraints.

"What involvement did my wife have in your little plan?" My voice is so calm, even I'm surprised.

Elijah lifts his head in my periphery, mildly curious.

"What do you want me to say?" Beaumont asks, as I toss the wooden leg on the bed and fish out a Swiss Army knife from my pocket.

"The truth. Tell me what I want to know, and I'll make your death swift."

"You won't get away with this. The Exiled will turn against you if you kill one of their members outside of Hell Fire Night."

With a hum, I slip out the blade before pressing it into his thigh and dragging it down his leg, splitting the skin open to reveal sinew and flesh.

No one flinches at the raw, tortured screams bouncing off the walls. No one moves an inch.

"As you can tell, Beaumont, I'm beyond fucking caring about the Exiled or the repercussions of cutting your dick from your body. You should be more concerned about what I'll do to you before I end your miserable life. You see, we have Commoners stationed to ensure no one disturbs us until I'm done with you. And by done, I mean you're unrecognizable and in countless pieces."

Blood bubbles from the deep gash in his thigh, so I order one of the Commoners to put pressure on the wound while I debate my options. I could torture him for hours until he loses consciousness and then wait for him to wake up before doing it again. Alternatively, I could fuck him up now and return to Cecilia. God knows I want to teach her a lesson she won't soon forget for lying to me and meeting up with Beaumont.

The mere thought has me sliding out the corkscrew attachment and ramming it into Beaumont's eyeball. *Violence it is.* His endless wailing drowns out the squelching sound, but it does little to soothe the war inside me. Nothing but complete destruction can touch the madness oozing from my every pore.

I yank the corkscrew out. "What involvement did my wife have in your plan?"

"Nothing."

I jab him in the side with the weapon, driving it deep, and blood rushes to the surface, soaking into the bedspread. I pull it out, and then I do it again and again, stabbing him where I know it'll hurt like a motherfucker but also keep him alive until the beast inside me grows bored. When I finally come up for air, he looks like pale, sweaty Swiss cheese.

As I round the bed, I flip out the scissors. "I want you to start from the beginning and tell me everything."

And he does.

While I snip the skin between each finger and toe, he screams, jumbles his words, and pleads for his life. But he also sings like a lark.

"You don't look so good," I point out as I reach for the wooden stake with my bloodied fingers. "It would be a shame if you passed out on me now. We don't want you to miss all the fun we're yet to have."

He struggles to focus on me with his one good eye, croaking, "Kill me. You promised—"

Feeling the stake's weight in my hand, I tsk. "Looks like we both lie."

The others haven't spoken, silently observing this unhinged, crazed version of myself. It makes me laugh to see blood coating every inch of my hands. My shirt is stained with it, too. Hell, I can smell it smeared on my face.

My smile falls. "You were going to rape my wife after you had finished beating her for your own damn amusement."

"No, that's not—"

"Don't lie. You were going to stick your filthy dick inside her."

His head shakes weakly as he sobs, pleading with me. "No—"

Another scream erupts from his cracked lips when I ram the splintered end of the stake inside his rectum, shredding him to pieces. "Let's see how you like it."

The veins in my blood-splattered forearms pop as I violate him with the stake. I don't feel anything besides this blinding fury that burns me up from the inside. I'm so damn numb; nothing except my wife's tight pussy has the power to resurrect me from the ashes.

After I rip the blood and shit-soaked stake from his ass, I throw it down beside him. He's barely conscious as I carve into him with the knife, but that doesn't stop me from skinning him alive or removing his inner organs, one by one, and placing them around his body.

By the time Sinclair finally clears his throat with an arched brow, I've got Beaumont's heart in one hand after prying his chest cavity open. He jerks his chin for the others to leave, and they sidle out. Elijah smirks at me before disappearing out the door.

Sinclair approaches me with a careful air about him. "He's dead, Darian."

I stare at the carnage before me, unblinking and uncomprehending. I never lose control like this, never give in to the terrifying darkness, yet here I am, with a man's innards pooling around my expensive, polished shoes and his heart clutched in my palm.

Sinclair puts his big hand on my shoulder. "Cutting him into pieces won't bring your family back."

The heart trembles in my grip as I look him in the eye, lost and alone.

"It won't bring you answers."

When I still don't respond, he takes the heart and drops it back inside the pried-open ribcage before pulling me in for a hug and slapping my back hard. This isn't a bro hug. It's a real one, and I cling to him, clutching his suit jacket tightly and staring at an invisible spot on the wall. My eyes burn and sting, but no tears fall.

He pulls back and holds me by the shoulders. "Whatever you need, I'm here just like I was then. You hear me? You're not alone."

I think I nod. I'm not sure. The next thing I'm vaguely aware of is being led outside, away from prying eyes, and guided to a waiting car. Cecilia is not here yet, so I wait in silence, staring at my crimson fingers.

When she finally enters the car, she spots my blood-soaked appearance, and her mouth falls open. She starts to speak but wisely snaps her mouth shut and stays silent for the duration of the journey home.

Once we arrive at the house, she slides her eyes in my direction at the bottom of the stairs, but I don't have it in me to reassure her that everything is fine.

It's not.

Nothing is fine. She went through my laptop and was ready to hand the sensitive information to Beaumont.

*But she didn't,* a voice whispers in the recesses of my mind.

*But she was going to,* a different, more insistent voice counters.

"Go to bed," I tell her, shoving my bloodied hands into my pockets.

She hesitates, peering back at me one final time before she turns and ascends the stairs. It's obvious by her slumped shoulders that she wants me to talk to her about tonight, but I don't have the energy. Not now.

I wait until she's out of sight before entering the kitchen and making a beeline for the cellar. As I stomp across the small space, van der Meer's cruel chuckle greets me. Sometimes, I forget that his eyes have adjusted to the darkness after so many years locked up down here, forgotten, unloved, and left to wither away.

"It looks like you finally cracked, huh? Lost your iron hold on that self-control you cling to so dearly." He shuffles closer to the bars while I light the torch, and flames flicker wildly in the dim glow as he barks a harsh laugh. "Look at you, drenched in blood. How long did you keep him alive?

An hour? Two? All night?"

My jaw tightens as I drop the box of matchsticks to the floor.

"How does it feel to be a monster, Darian?" he asks, gripping the bars with filthy hands. "We're not so different, you and I."

"Shut up!"

My wet, blood-soaked, and cold clothes glue to my skin as I walk closer and stare down at him with all the fury, disgust, and hatred I can dig up from the trenches of my tired soul. He doesn't deserve to sully the air with his rancid breaths.

"Let me guess." His eyes gleam as he peers up at me. "My daughter is the reason behind tonight's bloodshed?" A rush of laughter disturbs the tense silence. "Only a woman can ruin a proud man like you, Darian Delacroix. It's the universe's cruel humor that it had to be my daughter."

"SHUT UP!" I roar, spit flying from my mouth.

If anything, he laughs even louder. Crueler. "Look at you. Do you think she'll ever love a monster like you?" Shaking his head regretfully, he presses his brow against the bars. "You're not even a monster. You're something worse. Something *weak.*"

*Weak.*

*Weak.*

*Weak.*

The word echoes in my head, and I crouch down, pulling hard at my hair as an intense throbbing pounds against my skull. "Shut up. Shut up. Shut up."

"You hid while your mother was being raped again and again and again."

"Please…stop."

"And now you're hiding from my daughter because

you're too afraid to let her see the real you." His yellow teeth barely hang onto his gums as he peels his lips back in a condescending, belittling smile. "You're *weak.*"

The way he enunciates the word makes my skin crawl with imaginary bugs. "I'm not weak!"

"Yes, you are. You couldn't protect your mother then, and you can't protect my daughter now. You would sooner hide" —he digs his finger into his temple—"in here than crawl out from your hiding place. You're the weakest of the weak."

Falling back onto my ass, I rock on the spot while shaking my head almost frantically to shut out his words.

*"Scream, whore. Let your husband hear how much it hurts. And your kid, too. Where is that little brat? You hid him somewhere, didn't you? HEY, KID! COME OUT, COME OUT, AND I'LL STOP HURTING YOUR MOM."*

*Muffled, "No, Darian, don't—"*

*A hard slap. "Shut your filthy mouth, slut!"*

"She bled on my cock, Delacroix." His sickening words drag me back from my memories. "And that was before my Commoners tore through her, too."

"Just tell me what happened to her after you took her away."

"You already know what happened. We killed her."

With a final hard tug on my hair, I look at him through the haze of unshed tears. "How did she die? Give me the details."

"So you can continue tormenting yourself?" He cocks his head curiously. "Isn't it funny how the same thing unites you and my daughter?"

Confused, I lower my hands.

"She's driven by the need for answers and revenge, just like you. *What happened to her father?* It's nothing more than a scratched record, and why she's here. Why she joined the Antichrist, and why she was at that party." He flashes another leery smile. "She has her daddy issues, and you have your mommy issues."

"Stop fucking talking." I almost shout the last word.

"Darian?" a soft voice comes from behind.

My eyes briefly close. Why did she follow me? I don't want to have to hurt her, but she gives me no choice by being here, seeing her father—

"Darian?" She flicks her eyes toward the cell and back.

"Weak," her father whispers in a mocking voice.

I ignore him and turn to my wife, who has paled and is glancing nervously between me and her emancipated father.

Fuck. I try to stand, but I'm too damn exhausted. Defeat rolls off me in waves as I slump back down and rest my arms on my knees. "Go ahead and hate me."

"Hate you?"

"For this." I wave a hand at the cell.

"See how she looks at you now," her father taunts in a low voice so only I can hear. "You think she'll forgive you?"

"Shut the fuck up!" I roar at him, and my wife flinches, inching backward.

Noticing, I stiffen.

Is she trying to leave? No. She can't leave me. She's my wife. *Mine.* Fucking mine.

Shooting to my feet, I block the exit. "I'm sorry. I should have told you… I should have…" Words fail me as her eyes fill with glassy tears, which soon spill over and trail down her cheeks.

"I don't even know why I didn't just kill him. I was angry and—"

"Kill who?" she asks, interrupting me mid-sentence.

Frowning, I look from her to her father, who shrinks back into the shadows with a taunting glimmer in his eye. "Your dad," I start, but snap my mouth shut when I see her confused expression.

Jabbing a finger in the cell's direction where her father's legs peek out from the shadows, I say, "Aren't you going to say something, Cecilia."

She swallows audibly as she wraps her arms around herself.

"YOUR FATHER!" I roar, making her jump and hug herself tighter.

"Darian…" Her voice is so weak I have to lean in to hear her. Nervously, she wets her lips. "My father is dead."

I rear back like I've been slapped. "Dead? No, he—" I look behind me, feeling lightheaded as I digest what she's saying, but Cecilia's hand on my arm brings me back to her. "He's right there."

"He died, Darian. Years ago."

# CHAPTER TWENTY-FOUR

CECILIA

## EARLIER THAT NIGHT

*"Hey, Cecilia." Sinclair catches up with me as I exit the estate, descending the steps to the circular driveway. Darian waits in the car, hidden behind tinted windows. I don't know what awaits me, and that makes me anxious.*

*I turn on the last step, tired and ready to admit defeat. Lauren smiles softly as she walks past me to her lift.*

*What could Sinclair possibly want? I've already fucked up royally tonight. What was I thinking?*

*Sinclair towers over me, standing a step higher, which makes him look impossibly tall—taller than he already is. He holds out the USB, so I reach for it, but he doesn't let go immediately. "How much do you know?"*

*His voice is clipped, but behind the sharp lash hides a softness, which stares back at me through his cautious eyes. My heart jolts, and I clutch the USB as he lets go. What isn't he saying? No one knows Darian better than Sinclair.*

*A cool breeze teases curls of hair across my cheeks. Reaching up, I slide them away.*

*Sinclair shoves his hands into his pockets and shrugs. "Well?"*

*"I know enough."*

*He simply nods, a rueful look flickering across his features. "Darian was only a young kid when your father and a group of Commoners raped his mother and killed his father in front of him while he hid in the closet."*

*My chest feels too tight, and while it's on the tip of my tongue to shake my head and deny his accusations, I know he's right. I saw the proof with my own eyes when I searched his laptop. Well, what little I could stomach.*

*"My father took Darian under his wing, but he was never the same. His night terrors led him to spend time in a treatment facility for a while." Sinclair's intense eyes sear into me, making me feel ten feet small. "As you might have guessed, the Exiled doesn't take too kindly to weakness, so my father kept Darian's whereabouts a secret from the King."*

*The USB burns in my hand as his words sink in. I feel an insane amount of guilt for searching through his laptop and invading his privacy.*

*"My father treated him like his own son, which is the only reason Darian survived. Of course, Darian would never tell you this himself because he's proud. It was hammered into him that night that it's dangerous to show weakness."*

*It feels strangely intimate to hear him talk about his friend like this. I'm Darian's wife, but he hasn't yet entrusted me with this information, which makes my heart ache.*

*"Listen," Sinclair says, wetting his lips and glancing at the car, the trees to our left and, finally, me. "There are truths about Darian you don't know yet, but when you do, just..."*

*He lifts his hand and rubs his mouth, clearly uncomfortable. "Don't hurt him more, okay? He's been through enough."*

*My brows draw together, and I open my mouth to speak, but what do I say to that? Sinclair is a man who usually smiles and has an easy charm, even if it's a camouflage to hide his hedonistic tendencies. And he wouldn't hesitate to slice my throat if he perceived me as a threat, so to see him this ruffled raises my shackles.*

*"Why are you telling me this?" I ask.*

*"Because you're the bleeding crack in his shell, and if you keep pushing, he'll break. I mean, fuck..." He points back at the large estate. "There's a chance it's already too late. You didn't see him tonight. What crawled out of him back there isn't a side of him I ever thought I'd see."*

*"What are you saying?"*

*"Darian suppressed his trauma by exerting control in every area of his life. Then you came along and now his carefully constructed control is seeping between his fingers like sand on a beach." He drops his arm, shoulders slumping as he runs a hand through his hair, ruffling the strands, agitated and frustrated. "For a long time after his parents were murdered, he couldn't remember that night, almost as if his mind erased it to protect him, a coping mechanism that got him through the day. The only time the memories would haunt him was at night."*

*"He remembers that night now," I point out as I recall how he stays up late drinking because he's unable to sleep, haunted by the past.*

*"Yes, parts of it," he admits almost reluctantly. "Darian sat in his father's congealing blood for several hours, trying to rouse him, before my father found him. His mind, the mind of a five-year-old boy, broke that day. And though he grew*

*into a man in a ruthless world of money and power, that boy never got over the trauma of witnessing his parents' murders. You have to understand that Darian carries tremendous guilt for not protecting his parents, especially his mom."*

*"He was only a child."*

*"He doesn't think that way." Sinclair's Adam's apple jumps on a swallow. "I see how you look at him."*

*My eyes widen with alarm. "Excuse me?"*

*"You're in love with him."*

*I gasp, but when I start to protest, he holds his hand up to silence the denial on my tongue. "Spare me the lies. Just be good to him. Darian's mind is…fragile."*

*"Why are you telling me this, Sinclair? I don't understand—"*

*"You're the daughter of his enemy." Reaching for my hand, he removes the USB, then holds it up for me to see. "You know the truth. Your father is behind the downfall of Darian's family, and the Exiled is behind the downfall of yours. The soul-destroying hunger for revenge brought you together, so tell me… Are you Darian's enemy or his ally? Because trust me, if you hurt him, I'll come for you, and I will kill you."*

*Sinclair hands me the USB, and I take it with trembling fingers and a bleeding heart. Next, he removes the Antichrist necklace I lost in my shuffle with Beaumont, fishing it out of his pocket.*

*He descends the last step, forcing me back, then turns me around to fasten the necklace around my neck. I hold my breath, unable to look him in the eye when he moves around me and tips my chin with his curled finger. "Are you a foe, Mrs. Cecilia Delacroix?"*

## PRESENT

My heart breaks at the confused look in Darian's eyes. This is what Beaumont wanted: to use Darian's greatest weakness for blackmail, a weakness that will see him killed in this cold, heartless world. If anyone finds out about my husband's struggles, he'll lose his Duke position and everything he has fought so hard for.

Darian grinds his teeth, listening intently to something behind him before turning over his shoulder and shouting "shut up" to the shadows in the empty cell.

I move forward, touching his cheek and coaxing his eyes back to me. His skin is cool to the touch. "It's okay," I whisper.

When his pained gaze drinks me in, my heart bleeds for him. I've never seen my husband this broken. The hurting boy who kneeled in his father's blood stares back at me through the eyes of this grown man.

If I could only reach into his past and soothe the hurt my father carved on his soul, but I can't erase the past. Nothing can. Darian's brokenness is caused by the blood flowing through my veins.

As tears glisten in his eyes, I stroke my fingers through his sharp stubble, feeling it rasp beneath my trembling touch. "It's okay that you don't remember."

"Don't remember what?" he asks, confused, as his brows pull low.

I shake my head once and push up on my tiptoes to press my lips to his, whispering, "It doesn't matter."

Cautious fingers land on my waist before he pulls back. "Aren't you angry?"

"Angry?"

"Your father? He—"

Silencing him with my lips, I cling to him like he'll fall to pieces if I don't glue him together with my love, somehow. My broken, perfect, beautiful man.

My ruined monster.

My fractured tormentor.

"I could never be angry with you, Darian."

That makes him chuckle, which acts as a band-aid on my splintering heart, holding it together when it feels like it might splinter. "My art collection respectfully disagrees."

"Well, you were an asshole."

His big arms wrap around me, and I'm enveloped with warmth, love, and fragile hope. My own heaven. Darian seems to have forgotten about my father, for now—the phantasm of the night haunting his nightmares.

I grip onto his bloodied shirt as he thrusts his tongue between my lips.

*"There are truths about Darian you don't know yet, but when you do, just... Don't hurt him more, okay?"*

*"Darian's mind is...fragile."*

My heart pounds, slamming hard against my bruised, sore ribs. I'm growing dizzy. Darian's love holds me in a brutal fist, squeezing me enough to hurt, enough to gasp for air, yet beg for more.

Somehow, his mind has effectively blocked out parts of his past and distorted his reality to keep him safe and in control. I don't know what goes on inside his head, but I know he's hurting, and I wish I could heal him, no matter how foolish that wish is.

I wrap my arm around his neck and kiss him deeper until I'm no longer aware of where he begins and I end.

*"Are you a foe, Mrs. Cecilia Delacroix?"*

I speak against his lips. "Come with me, Darian."

He slams his mouth to mine, kissing and nibbling, feasting on me like I'm the sun in his galaxy, and then he breaks the kiss, tearing his mouth away like it hurts him. "Where?"

*Away from here. Away from this cellar. Away from the ghost of my father's legacy.*

"Anywhere. I'll go anywhere with you."

Questions flicker in his eyes, but then he nods, entwines our fingers, and walks ahead, leading me out of the room.

*Look at me, Darian. Don't look at the cell.*

*I'm here. Your nightmares aren't real.*

He turns and walks backward to the exit. The torch burns lower then, and the fading light flickers across his face.

My skin tingles where our fingers connect, and I trap my lip between my teeth as he reaches for my other hand. But good things never last, not in our godless world, yet for a brief moment, as Darian's coarse, warm palm glides over mine, I let myself believe in the burning devotion in my husband's eyes.

Perhaps we could burn bright in a dark world. Maybe I could be the flame to his darkness and spark of hope in his nightmares. Maybe I can be the reason he finds his way back from the night.

I'm torn from my thoughts when the door slams open with a loud bang to reveal a large, burly man dressed in black, with his face covered in a hawk mask and a crossbow in his hand. He barges into the room and aims the weapon directly at Darian's back, then fires a shot just as I let out a scream.

Darian collapses to his knees, a pained groan filling the room while the arrow protrudes between his shoulder blades. The intruder quickly moves around him to reach me.

Panic floods my body, and I run in the opposite direction, but he's quicker and catches me by the hair. Terror claws at my clammy skin as I fight with everything I have to escape his strong grip, but it feels like fighting a brick wall. I know I don't stand a chance, yet I refuse to let him take me.

More masked men in black enter the room, quietly and methodically, as though this attack has been planned for some time. They haul Darian away, who barely struggles, while I cry and beg and squirm in my assailant's hold like a worm on a hook.

Once the men disappear down the hall with Darian in tow, Lauren enters the room, having changed into a black top and a leather skirt.

As she nears, I spit in her direction. "You fucking planned this."

I should have seen this coming a mile away. She warned me the Antichrist would be there tonight, and she told me they would come for us sooner or later, but I didn't take her seriously.

"You should show me gratitude," she says, grabbing my chin and inspecting my face while I pant hard through my nose, struggling against the constricting arms around me. "I could have left you here, imprisoned, but I'm a better friend than that, and you deserve more."

I jut my chin, trying to free myself of the sharp grip her nails have on my chin.

If my arms weren't trapped by the behemoth of a man behind me, I would punch her in the face. "Darian's hurt," I point out, and she raises a brow, a smirk playing on her lips, as if she finds my worry amusing. "He needs hospital treatment."

"He's a Duke, Cecilia, a disgusting pig, but you can't see that because you've been compromised and forgotten what we're fighting for." She inspects her nails and then lifts her gaze. "You opened your legs to that monster and disrespected everything we've fought for. All the people who've died fighting the Exiled. Why? So you could be that pig's whore?"

How dare she speak to me like that? She knows *nothing.* A blast of fury heats my cheeks. I spit at her again. At least it gives me a smidgeon of satisfaction to see her eyes flare with anger right before she backhands me so hard, the sharp sound bounces off the cellar walls.

Breathing harshly, I try to control the maelstrom of emotions pressing on my sternum—an agonizing mixture of fear, rage, and betrayal. They'll kill Darian or use him for leverage against the Exiled.

"I know you're not in the right frame of mind," she says with a heavy breath. "So I'll forgive you this time."

She turns over her shoulder, calling out for someone, then smirks at me as another man enters, carrying a cloth and a brown bottle of liquid.

As he hands it to Lauren, my eyes widen. "Chloroform?"

She shrugs and pours some onto the cloth. "We can't risk you screaming the place down. It's better this way."

"No, no, no," I cry, struggling in the man's firm grip. "Please don't do this."

"We're not going to hurt you," she replies, reaching for me.

I turn my head at the last second, but she sighs like I'm an unruly child and then grabs my jaw, pressing the cloth over my mouth.

Her eyes glimmer with a sadistic gleam as I hold my breath, refusing to inhale the sweet scent. "It'll be easier if you stop struggling. We're on the same side," she says.

My eyes widen in fear, and I try to shake her off with the bit of energy I have left, but my lungs burn.

Soon, my survival instincts kick in, and I inhale a greedy breath, struggling in vain as my vision begins to blacken at the corners.

I feel myself growing weak, held up by the man behind me, whose hot breath fans my ear. Lauren's voice swims in my head, sounding distant. "I'll see you soon."

# CHAPTER TWENTY-FIVE

DARIAN

*Why do mosquito bites itch? And why do mosquitoes only come out in the summer? Mommy says insect bites and scraped knees are a part of childhood, but I don't like that. I don't like the itching. Winter is better because I don't get bitten, and Santa Claus comes to gift me presents. Daddy doesn't like Santa. "Stop putting silly ideas into his head," he always says to Mommy, but she smiles that pretty smile, and he shakes his head and grumbles something under his breath, then softens when she kisses his cheek.*

*"Are you listening?" he says now, frowning as I scratch the latest bite on my arm. We're in the backyard, enjoying the late summer sun. Mom is inside, preparing food, the mouth-watering scent of bacon drifting through the open patio door. "Stop that. It'll get infected." He tips his stubbly chin toward the soda can he put on the tree stump at the edge of our yard. "That's your target, Son. Think you can knock it off? If you do, I'll give you the latest video game you were asking for."*

*My eyes go as wide as saucers. Daddy wouldn't let me*

*buy it before because Mommy said it was too grown up. "Really?"*

*This is better than the gifts Santa brings me.*

*"Really!" he says, then ruffles my hair with an affectionate smile before glancing toward the house. Mommy is still inside. Turning back, he slides his gun out from the back of his pants and hands it to me. "Remember what I taught you the other week? How to load it?"*

*"Yes," I reply, making 'pew, pew' noises as I aim the gun at the soda can, pretending I'm a cowboy in a Western.*

*Mommy likes that movie with the old man who chews on a cigar and says—according to Mommy—smart things like, "When a man's got money in his pocket, he begins to appreciate peace."*

*Mommy, seated cross-legged on the couch, once mouthed the words, and Daddy snorted, saying, "What a load of bollocks. If anything, the more money a man has in his pocket, the more he appreciates war," before rising from the couch and leaving the room.*

*I don't know what "bollocks" means. Mommy said it's a British word, because that's where Daddy grew up before his family moved here.*

*"Cyrus Delacroix," Mommy's stern voice says from the patio door, and Daddy groans tiredly under his breath, then winks at me as he straightens up. Mommy strides across the grass, still dressed in her pinafore, her hair messy atop her head. She's always pretty, my mommy. "I've repeatedly asked you not to teach him this stuff yet. He's too young."*

*Daddy puts his hands on his hips, his head slightly tilted down as he peers at Mommy through his dark lashes. "He needs to learn how to defend himself in case something happens. Hell Fire Night is coming up and—"*

*"No." Mom's firm voice stiffens my spine. "It's out of the question. He's only a child, Cyrus."*

*Daddy stares off into the distance, sweat beading on his brow, and then he puts his hand on my shoulder. "Go back inside, Son. Mommy and Daddy need to have a grown-up conversation."*

*I don't like their grown-up conversations. They rarely fight, but Daddy sometimes upsets Mommy when he says he has to be the man of the house and put his foot down. Sometimes, Mommy doesn't like those decisions and gives Daddy the silent treatment for days while stirring the pan or washing the dishes aggressively like they upset her too.*

*I glance at Mommy, but she's not looking at me. She is standing with her arms crossed and eyes narrowed on Daddy. After handing Daddy the gun, I walk back to the house. My arm itches, so I dig my dirty nails into the skin as I enter through the patio door.*

*"We live in a dangerous world," Daddy says to Mommy as I hide just inside the entrance to avoid detection.*

*Mommy's voice drifts on the summer breeze, a tired plea for my Daddy to listen for once. "I'm aware, Cyrus, but don't you want him to have a childhood?"*

*"What I want is for him to be safe. Unlike you, I don't pretend everything is fine."*

*"Unlike me?"*

*"Forget it." Daddy turns to walk away, but Mommy grabs him by the arm.*

*"Don't you dare walk away from me! We're talking."*

*Daddy's chest inflates with a heavy sigh, and he reluctantly turns around, crossing his arms over his muscular chest, the T-shirt straining at the seams.*

*"What's that supposed to mean?"*

*"It means I refuse to baby him like you."*

*"Baby him? Uh-huh. That so? I baby him?" Mom sucks on her teeth, almost trembling with anger.*

*"Yes," Daddy replies exasperatedly, unfolding his arms. "He'll grow up weak and unable to survive in this world. Unless you've noticed, he's the son of a Duke. One day, he'll be expected to follow in my footsteps. The others already make fun of us because Darian is too soft."*

*Daddy's words hurt more than when I fell off my bike the other day and scratched my knee up real bad. Mommy said I shouldn't ride downhill so fast.*

*I shrink away from the door, my chin trembling.*

*"Don't cry. Don't you dare cry," a voice in my head scolds. Daddy says tears are for the weak. We are men, and men like us don't cry. If anyone sees us cry, it'll be bad for us and Mommy.*

*"Has it ever occurred to you that not all wars are fought with weapons and hatred? Some are fought with the heart, Cyrus. Some are fought with love."*

*"Listen to yourself," Daddy scoffs, placing his hands on his head and barking a cruel laugh, a harsh sound I haven't heard my daddy make before. "Some are fought with love? Don't be ridiculous." Lowering his hands by his sides, he stares at Mommy for a long moment before leaning in. "There's no room for love in the Exiled. I'm teaching the kid to use a gun."*

*As he strides toward the house, I spin on my feet and run to my room. If Daddy finds me eavesdropping, I'll get my butt whooped.*

*Mommy doesn't speak to Daddy for a week. When I finally knock the soda can off the tree stump, I see her watching me in the doorway with a soft yet sad smile. Daddy swoops me up and runs me around the backyard while I pretend to be an airplane. I think I like summer and insect bites and scraped knees, after all.*

# CHAPTER TWENTY-SIX

DARIAN

*"Cecilia?"*

*Is it really her? A spark of hope ignites inside me. I barely dare believe she's here in front of me, unhurt.*

*I shake my head to clear the haze, but it's heavy, my chin lolling uselessly against my chest. She's so beautiful and bright it's almost blinding, like an angel in the darkness.*

*I croak her name again. My dry mouth feels like sandpaper, and a pounding headache throbs behind my temples. How long have I been out? Days? Weeks? Wait a minute? My eyes widen, and I squirm in the chair I'm tied to as I inspect the room, or rather, the wardrobe. "Where am I?"*

*I'm torn from my thoughts when Cecilia crouches in front of me and places her gentle hands on my knees with a tender look in her regretful eyes. "You need to be brave, Darian. Promise me that you'll be brave."*

*Her smooth fingers brush against my cheekbone when I fail to respond, and my attention flitters around the confined space.*

*She cradles my cheek in her palm and tilts her head*

*slightly as she studies my face. "You were brave once. You can be brave again, for me."*

*My eyes clash with hers. "Why am I in a wardrobe?"*

*Fear crawls over my clammy skin beneath my clothes, like countless little spiders with eight legs and pincers.*

*I thrash in my chair, suddenly overcome with the immediate need to escape. "I have to get out of here NOW. I can't be here. I can't—"*

*"Sshh," Cecilia soothes. "Be brave, remember." She's closer now, leaning up on her knees and pressing her lips to my brow. "You're not alone. I'm here with you."*

A bucket of icy water is poured over my head, and I shoot upright, spluttering and cursing as a sharp pain spreads out between my shoulder blades.

Within seconds, I'm shivering violently, my teeth are chattering, and I feel like I've been simultaneously doused in gasoline and set on fire and then dunked in a frozen lake.

"Good morning, princess."

A closed fist flies out and punches me in the cheek.

*CRACK.*

My head whips to the side with such force stars circle me like a damn cartoon, but whoever my tormentor is, he's not done. Another punch follows, this time in my gut, and I double over in my chair with a grunt.

My stomach rolls, nausea climbing up my throat, and he laughs as he grips my face, squishing my cheeks together with fingers that smell of unwashed cock and tobacco. "You don't look like such a big shot now, pretty boy."

"That's enough," a different voice says from the door. The man shoves me back and steps away, leering at Lauren on his way out, but she pays him no attention, arms crossed, as she stares at me just inside the door. "You look a little pale and cold, Delacroix." Stepping deeper into the small walk-in wardrobe, she glances around. "How do you like the setting? Are you comfortable enough?"

"Drop the fucking act," I growl, twisting my wrists against the restraints securing me to the chair. Lauren better pray I don't find a way to escape, because she'll be the first person I come for.

"Oh, baby…" She pouts as she walks up to me with a predatory gleam in her eyes and a sway in her hips that spells trouble, her unruly amber hair spilling over her shoulders.

When she reaches out to stroke my hair away from my brow, I flinch back, which makes her lips twitch with amusement. "So angry."

"Fuck you!"

She hums and skims her fingers through my sopping strands. I can't possibly lean back any farther. "How's your back? I wanted to leave the arrow in, but Greta saw to it that they patched you up."

"Quit the fucking small talk. Where's Cecilia?"

"Cecilia?" Her fingers pause in my hair, and she studies my beat-up face and shivering, no doubt blue lips before cupping my chin and dipping down to stare into my eyes. "Cecilia is dead."

I feel the blood drain from my face. "No…"

She's lying. She has to be. There's no way my wife is dead. I refuse to believe it.

Lauren fakes regret, her expression bleeding insincerity, and then she climbs onto my lap, hiking her short leather skirt up to her waist. "I'm sorry to be the bearer of bad news, Darian, but your precious wife was murdered." Leaning in, she trails her lips, sticky with lip gloss, across my cheek and whispers against the shell of my ear. "Murdered just like your mother."

"You're lying!" I struggle against the restraints, causing the ropes to cut into my skin.

Lauren moves back to study me. "You're not going anywhere, baby. Not until I'm done with you." Her words are accompanied by her hands fumbling with my belt, and I wish—oh, how I wish—I could wrap my fingers around her neck and squeeze until she's dead.

"So this is why you have me tied to a chair? You're in the mood for a little fumble in the dark?"

"Would it be so bad to have some fun?" she asks as she slowly pulls the zipper down while nibbling on her lip—a seductive tactic I'm sure works on a lot of guys. But not me. I'd rather join an orderly than touch this vile bitch.

"You're a Duke, Darian. The son of Cyrus Delacroix. The Exiled is in your bloodline. You see, for decades, we've gone about this all wrong, attacking you on Hell Fire Night and making you pay in blood, but that's like poking the bear with a needle pin. You just keep bouncing back like a virus, so it's time to change tactics. Play a different game." She leans in and sinks her teeth into my earlobe before sucking and licking. As she rolls her hips against me, she whispers, "What we need in our war is an heir."

Every muscle in my body stiffens with dread, and she laughs a breathy, cruel sound. "Cat got your tongue, handsome?"

"How will an heir help you in your war against the Exiled?"

"You're a smart man, Darian. Put two and two together. You know your world and the importance of bloodlines. An heir would be our greatest asset. Just think of all the resentment that would fester inside them and how we could use it to our advantage when they finally claim their place as a Duke.

Especially when they find out their father raped their mother."

I rear back, my jaw slack. "That's your flawed plan?"

"Oh, come on, Darian," she breathes, her voice tinged with suppressed laughter. "Don't look at me like that. Sure, it's a long-term plan, but they won't see it coming." She dips her hand inside my briefs, palming my dick, and much to my horror, it soon swells in her grip.

I break eye contact, clenching my jaw so hard that my teeth hurt.

"Oh, my! Cecilia said you have a big cock. For once, she wasn't lying."

"I'm telling you this now out of courtesy because you're her friend. If you know what's good for you, stop this now, or I swear I'll kill you."

"You won't kill me, Darian," she says, pushing my briefs down and freeing my cock. "You'll stay tied to this chair until you've served your purpose, and then we'll put a bullet in your brain and dispose of your body."

Grinding my teeth, I give her an indignant look. "So you think you can just waltz right into the Exiled in eighteen years' time and be welcomed with open arms?" I lean in closer and sneer. "They'll eat you alive."

"Maybe, but our child will have access to all that power, thanks to their bloodline and being the sole heir to the Delacroix fortune." Releasing my dick, she taps her lip with her shiny blood-red nail and pretends to think. "Which is now combined with the van der Meer's fortune, am I right? That's why you made her marry you, isn't it? Couldn't let all that money go to waste." Her eyes gleam when she looks at me again. "That's a big fortune, handsome. Makes me horny."

I grunt as she resumes stroking my length before shifting on my lap and placing me at her entrance.

"I promise you'll enjoy it," she purrs, smashing her lips to mine, but I refuse to kiss her back as I wriggle my wrists in a desperate last-ditch attempt to break free. Never did I think I would find myself here, tied to a damn chair, while my wife's unhinged best friend assaults me. I don't like to hurt women, but she better fucking run when I break free, because I'll kill her so damn slowly, even the reaper will grow bored waiting.

A flaming pain sears through my wrists, but I continue to twist and pull, letting out a grunt as she bites down hard on my bottom lip, drawing blood. When she moves back, it drips down my chin.

She's just about to sit on my dick when a different voice says, "Leave the poor man alone, Lauren."

We both stiffen, and Lauren's jade eyes harden. At the same time, relief floods through me, and I slump in the chair, resisting the urge to peek around Lauren to thank the intruder for their perfect timing.

"I'm a little busy here," she says without taking her eyes off me.

"This isn't how we handle things." The newcomer's voice is stern but motherly. "And it's not what we're about."

That does it. Lauren huffs a breath, climbs off, and turns to face the old lady in the doorway, who stares back at her behind her walker with enough authority to let me know she's in charge around here. She's short, with puffy white hair and a silk orange scarf around her head, tied around her chin. Her long, pleated purple skirt swishes around her ankles as she shuffles deeper into the room. I blink when I spot the purple gems on her walker.

This is surreal. Maybe the arrow in my back somehow caused brain damage, too, or maybe I'm sleeping and dreaming up crazy women and elderly ladies with blinged-out walkers.

"Hello, Darian Delacroix," she says, turning her attention to me and studying me from behind her frameless glasses perched low on her nose, seemingly unfazed by my now flaccid dick. "I haven't seen you in a very long time, not since you were a wee bairn in diapers."

My eyes flare at the Northern English saying for a small child. I haven't been called a "wee bairn" since my granddad was alive. I still remember him puffing on his cigar on the armchair while squinting at me through a cloud of smoke, with one of his soft smiles reserved only for me. He could be a formidable man, but I worshipped the ground he walked on.

Every time he visited, he'd bring me candy, which made Mom roll her eyes. She'd take them away from me and glance at my granddad with a reluctant smile before telling me I'd get them back after dinner.

One rainy afternoon, Mommy sat me down to explain that Granddad had joined the angels in heaven, and I cried for weeks.

"Yes, I knew your granddaddy," the lady says. "He was a good man behind that steel exterior."

I've heard the stories of how my great-grandparents emigrated to England to escape, but no one ever leaves the Exiled. Once you're in, the only way out is death. The Exiled caught up, and my granddad had no choice but to move back.

Greta turns her attention to Lauren and tips her chin in the direction of the door behind her. "Why don't you see if the others need help with something? Let me have a chat with the young man."

"Are you serious?" Lauren spits. "We can use him, Greta. He's our best shot at revenge. Actual *real* revenge."

"And you suppose stealing his sperm will further your agenda?"

"Not mine. The Antichrist's."

Greta's face remains impassive. "Admittedly, we've all suffered great losses, but this isn't the way. I won't let you bring an innocent child into this war to be used like a weapon."

Lauren turns red, her lips thinning as she glares at the old woman. "You think the Exiled shows mercy? They ruined us, Greta. Every one of us has suffered at their hands. We've all lost family members whose deaths were swept under the rug. Unless you've forgotten because of that dementia-ridden brain of yours, none of us have seen a speck of justice yet. The Exiled is stronger than ever, and we need to level up."

"Get the poor boy dressed," Greta orders sternly, ignoring her outburst.

Lauren glares at her for a moment, then makes an indignant sound before storming over to me and pulling my briefs and pants back up without meeting my gaze. When she's done, she stomps out.

Sighing, Greta shuffles over to me, and seconds pass, maybe even minutes, while she studies me from head to toe, making me squirm. "I hear things," she says finally.

My brows shoot up. "You…hear things?" I repeat.

"Telephone whispers, you could say, though more often than not, there's some truth to rumors."

"Okay? I'm clueless here, lady. Mind explaining what your point is?"

Her lavender smell scents the air as she leans over her walker and flicks my nose with her finger. "Rude boy!" She straightens up and gives me a disapproving look. "Don't they teach your generation to respect your elders?"

That flick hurt. I wiggle my nose, wishing I could rub it. "I'm sorry, ma'am."

"Don't you *ma'am* me, boy! I might be eighty years young, but there's life in these bones yet. Now…" She shuffles around, sits her butt on the walker, and rests her wrinkly hands on her thighs. "Rumor is that you're one of the good ones."

Now that makes me bark a laugh, but it soon dies when I see the serious expression on her face. This crazy lady isn't joking.

"Me?" I ask. "A good guy? No, you're mistaking me for someone else."

Greta narrows her eyes. "Ain't no other boy in the Exiled who'd dare marry the King's niece."

I grow completely still. Greta smiles knowingly. "Don't look so surprised." Tapping her ear, she winks. "I hear things."

"I don't know what you're talking about."

"That girl isn't just anybody, is she? She's the King's niece. And she was promised to Dalton, the King's son, before she was born. But you know what happened, don't you? Mr. van der Meer backtracked on the deal, so the King murdered him in cold blood. The King's sister, Mrs. van der Meer, took Cecilia and ran, but they were hunted. It wasn't a question of *if* the Exiled would catch up to them but *when.*"

Her wise eyes harden. "The King's son is a mean-spirited boy without a bone of empathy. He's also prone to fits of rage, and Cecilia would've been in for a marriage from hell. That's if she would have survived his beatings. But you found her first and stole her from under the King's nose, and it wasn't about the money, was it? Darian Delacroix doesn't need more pocket money. Nor was it a matter of pride like it is for the King."

"No, you had nothing to gain from this union except to silence your curiosity, maybe. But even so, if you married her to piss off the King, you wouldn't have kept her identity from the Exiled. You acted from the heart and cloaked your good intentions."

My head shakes. She's still talking, but her words sound echoey and far away. She's wrong. The King didn't kill Cecilia's father. He's alive. I have him locked up in my basement.

But Cecilia said…

I squeeze my eyes shut as a blinding zap of pain assaults my skull.

*"He died, Darian. Years ago."*

"No," I say forcefully.

Greta falls silent, watching me peculiarly as I open my eyes.

I wince as another stab of pain steals my breath. "Her father isn't dead. He's alive."

"Alive?" Greta sounds confused. "What do you mean, boy?"

"He's not dead," I say firmly, gauging her reaction. No one has ever believed me—not Sinclair, not Cecilia, not this lady. I even dragged Sinclair to the cellar, and he stared at van der Meer with the most bewildered expression, tinged with so much sadness, before he grabbed my shoulder and pulled me in for a hug, promising me that everything would be fine, that we would keep it a secret between us.

Greta looks at me like she's trying to understand—as though I'm not making sense. Her features soften with realization, and she dips her chin to her chest.

"You know," she says carefully, "I lost someone I loved too—my daughter. That sweet girl was the most precious thing in the world." She lifts her teary eyes. "A loss like that damages you. Sometimes, we suppress the things that hurt. Or we imagine ways to change the past. I sure do. And sometimes, it feels very real." Her voice softens. "On bleak days, I imagine I got my hands on the men who killed my daughter."

"Is Cecilia dead?" I ask, changing the topic, afraid of the answer.

My instinct tells me Lauren lied to hurt me, but a niggle of doubt lingers, and now it's all I can think about.

Greta's brows rise to her hairline. "Dead? No, boy, she's alive."

Thank fuck. Slumping with relief, I blink back tears and jiggle my knee—as much as I can with my ankle tied to the chair.

I don't know what I would have done if Lauren had told the truth. It shouldn't surprise me how deeply Cecilia is buried in my soul and how much I've come to care about her in such a short period of time. Lately, I've found myself looking forward to her smiles, dry humor, and the angry flare in her eyes when she doesn't get her way. I'd do anything to enter my house and find her throwing my artwork over the banister again or annoying me with her questionable taste in plants.

I flick my still-sopping hair out of my eyes, trying to control my chattering teeth. Greta notices. "I suppose we need to get you a warm blanket before you freeze to death."

"Or you can untie me."

"Not yet, boy. We're not done talking. You're still a flight risk until I know you can be trusted." She stands up on her old, rickety legs just as Lauren appears in the doorway and says, "You're needed in the office. It's urgent."

The old lady grabs hold of her blinged-out walker and makes her way to Lauren. "I'm watching you, young lady. If you touch the boy, I'll find out." She casts a glance at me, and then says, "Find him a warm blanket. He's shivering."

Lauren's jaw tightens, her eyes flashing with anger. If looks could kill, Greta would be a heap of de-fleshed bones on the floor. She stays silent, waiting until Greta has left before turning her hard gaze on me. "What's so special about Cecilia, huh?" Crossing her arms, she shrugs and walks closer. "She's nothing special beneath all that money and prestigious bloodline."

I don't bother with a response because her question is absurd at best. Cecilia is the damn sun in my universe, and she doesn't have to lure me in because I was hooked from the first moment I saw her polishing glasses in the cottage. The way she looked at me with her big eyes. I knew then that I had to have her, and I also knew I could never let the King's son sink his filthy claws into her and kill the fire in her bold eyes with his suffocating, cruel nature. Just the thought of him bruising her flawless skin with his fists made me want to go on a murder spree.

I didn't understand my violent emotions where Cecilia was concerned then, and I still don't. She's an enigma. Lauren doesn't hold a candle to her.

"Aren't you at least a little bit tempted?" Lauren asks as she slides her leather skirt higher up her thighs to expose her bare pussy, but I don't even spare the dark curls a cursory glance, my eyes on her face. "It can be our secret."

"Cover yourself up," I reply in my most dismissive tone.

She huffs and drops the skirt. "Fine. Be a bore." As she inspects her nails, she says in a tone that raises my shackles, "So maybe I can't touch you, but there are other ways to hurt you, Darian."

"Yeah? What's that? Good old waterboarding?" I'm back to trying to wriggle free of my restraints.

She looks up from her nails and scoffs. "Waterboarding? No, thank you. I like methods that are a bit more unorthodox." With that, she turns on her heel and walks to the entrance, hand hovering on the light switch outside. "You shouldn't have rejected me. Enjoy the dark, Darian. Try not to think of Mommy and Daddy too much."

The doors slam shut, and the light goes out, flooding the room with darkness.

My heart nearly jumps out of my chest, beating so hard that I'm starting to feel dizzy, and I quickly turn my head when I hear screaming outside. *My mom's screaming.* And masculine laughter. Lots of evil laughter.

I thrash in my chair, roaring so loud that my voice grows hoarse, but no one comes, and the screaming outside continues.

*It's in my head.*

*It's all in my head...*

# CHAPTER TWENTY-SEVEN

CECILIA

I'm not a nail biter, but in the last few days, I've chewed my nails to the wick while locked up in this claustrophobic bedroom. A single bed sits tucked away in the corner, a plain desk is pushed against the boarded-up window, and there's an adjacent bathroom with a toilet and a shower. I'm ready to start peeling wallpaper soon if they don't let me out or at least give me some information about Darian.

I woke up in here with my wrist cuffed to the metal bedframe. A young guy dressed in a Motley Crue T-shirt and gray shorts, with wiry chestnut hair and a small shaving scar on his chin, placed a plate of food on the nightstand and a glass of water. I asked him a million questions while rattling the cuff, but he said nothing and walked out. The same pattern continued for two more days. Last night, the handcuff was removed, so now I can pace the room.

What if Darian is dead? He was bleeding profusely when they dragged him out. I chew my thumbnail, ignoring the stinging pain of having already bitten it too short. Maybe Darian's injury looked worse than it was. I've never seen anyone get shot with a crossbow before.

My thoughts grind to a halt when the door opens, and Lauren steps inside.

She leans against it and studies me from head to toe, almost like I'm an insect she wants to squash, one she's had enough of. The distaste in her gaze surprises me, but before I can read into it, she scans the room. A leather skirt hugs her curves, showcasing her long, toned legs, and her tank top shows ample skin. She's tied her hair up in a high pony, which sways behind her now that she walks deeper into the small room and eyes the untouched food on the plate. "Not hungry?"

I'm too worried about Darian to eat. Just the thought of what might have happened to him knots my stomach. "Where's Darian?"

"Have you learned nothing?" she asks, walking past me. "You need to forget about him."

"Is he okay?"

She spins on her tall heels, studying me. "Darian is none of your concern. The Antichrist is."

"Please," I plead as my nerves run amuck all over again. "Just tell me if he's okay."

Her lips twitch, but she schools her expression quickly. "Darian is alive, for now. He was unconscious for a while but is awake and ready for interrogation."

"Interrogation?" My blood runs cold. I've been a part of the Antichrist for long enough to know exactly how they extract information from captured Exiled members, and it's not pretty. Sometimes, they blabber almost right away, but others are more loyal, and they're the ones you have to break to get to the kernel.

I shudder as I recall the harrowing screams echoing from the cellar throughout the years. Sometimes, they captured Exiled members on Hell Fire Night and kept them alive for months. Though the soundproofing is decent, it's not perfect.

"What are they doing to him?" I ask carefully as Lauren comes up behind me.

Her chest presses against my back, and she puts her mouth on my ear. "He's tied to a chair in a closet in the dark."

*They left him in a closet?*

My chest constricts, and I spin around. "Anything but that. You know what happened to him."

A cold smile touches her lips. "Why do you think we locked him in there? Torturing him the good old-fashioned way would never work, but this will break him wide open."

"You can't do this! He's terrified of closets."

"No," she says, inching closer. "He's terrified of the memories associated with them."

"Please," I beg, my stomach churning.

She can't do this to him. He'll break beyond repair. I saw the look in his eyes in the cellar when he spoke to his vision of my father. The way he looked at me when I told him my father was dead. He thought he was there. He genuinely doesn't remember parts of his past, and forcing him to relive the night they murdered his mother is beyond cruel. It's evil.

"Please," I repeat. "Don't hurt him like this. Don't force him to remember the fear and helplessness of that night. There's got to be another way."

She sighs like she's tired of me. "See, this is why you need to stay locked in here. It's a shame, you know. You could be out there fighting with us. Instead, you're trapped in a cage for your own good until you come to your senses." She tucks a lock of hair behind my ear. "Darian never loved you. You were a bargaining chip—a way to get back at the King, like a big juicy 'fuck you.'"

"You're lying," I bite out, moving away from her touch.

"Am I?" she asks as her hand drops. "Maybe I'm the only one who pays attention around here and doesn't follow blindly." She digs her finger into her temple. "I actually think for myself, and do you know what I found out by sticking around and listening to that old lady you worship so much?"

"Leave Greta out of this!" My voice is a low growl.

"You always thought too highly of that old hag. Where has she been all these months, huh? She sure took her fucking time rescuing us. Do you think she couldn't get to you? No…" Her chuckle is bitter. "She wanted Darian to fall in love with you so the Antichrist could use him in this war. She waited and let us rot."

I look away, my chest clenching uncomfortably. "You've never liked her."

"She's not a fucking angel, Cecilia, and this is war. Maybe Darian treated you well, but my time as a Commoner was not a fairytale filled with roses. I was repeatedly raped and beaten. No one came for me. Why? So that Darian could have sufficient time to fall head over heels for the perfect Cecilia van der Meer, the greatest tool this rebel group has ever recruited."

I gasp, blood freezing in my veins as she smirks.

"What? Did you seriously think they didn't know who you were when you sought them out, broken and hurt after your mother's fatal car crash, with nowhere else to go? Of course, they knew. Maybe they even killed your mother to force you into our fold? Ever thought of that?"

Tears prick and burn as I avert my gaze. "Stop it…"

"You've got to admit, it makes for a compelling plot twist. Anyway, that's neither here nor there. Let's get back to the topic at hand. I stuck around today and heard Greta tell your precious husband that she knew you were promised to the King's son. Come on, Cecilia, think about it. Can't you see the puzzle pieces falling into place? The van der Meers were like royalty in the Exiled before their great fall, and you were going to birth the next heir and continue the prestigious bloodline."

I shake my head as the first tear falls. "I don't want to hear this. You're being cruel."

"Cruel?" She laughs disbelievingly. "I'm being honest, unlike everyone fucking else. And do you know what else?" she asks as she walks to the door.

I'm too broken to look at her, my thoughts spinning in a million directions. It can't be true that the Antichrist orchestrated all of this. If Lauren is right and they knew who I was, it would mean they willingly sent their own members to their deaths, Lauren included, on Hell Fire Night because they knew I would walk right into Darian's path. *"Sacrifice a few for the greater goal."*

I feel sick.

But not as sick as when Lauren says, "You were right about one thing, Cecilia. Darian does have a big cock, and he fucks like a beast."

I surge forward, but it's too late; the door is already closed, and I bang my fists on it as I shout, "You fucking bitch!" I kick it, too, for good measure. "I should have known you wanted to get your fucking hands on him."

Spinning around, I storm over to the bed and rip off the mattress. The plate of food is next. I toss it against the wall, and the plate splinters on impact. Peas and potatoes fly everywhere, but seeing the destruction does little to wrangle my fury. I'm so sick and tired of being a pawn on someone else's playing board. It's been the same fucking story my whole life, from the moment I was conceived, and it never stopped.

I collapse in the middle of the floor. Did my husband sleep with Lauren? Why would he do that? Why would *she* do that? I always thought we were friends. No, she's lying. Darian is injured. Why would he fuck her when he's injured?

*Why wouldn't he?*

I force that intrusive thought far, far down as I rest my head on my knees. Now isn't the time to wallow in self-pity. I need to get out of here somehow. I'm no good to anyone locked up.

But maybe this is exactly where they need me. If I'm such a big asset to them—and they knew who I was all along—why wouldn't they want me where they can keep an eye on me? It makes perfect sense. They know I'm valuable to the King. He's incredibly difficult to get close to because of his high position within the society, so it wouldn't surprise me if they tipped him off in the hopes of drawing him out. But he's not the only one who'll come for us. Sinclair, too. There's no way he'll let anyone kidnap Darian without raining hell on the Antichrist.

"Oh my god," I whisper as the seriousness of the situation dawns on me. "I need to put an end to this."

---

You have to get creative when you have no weapons at your disposal. While using my femininity to manipulate a barely legal boy to let me out repulses me, it's not like I have any other choice unless I want Sinclair and the Exiled to kill the people I've lived with for years. These people are my friends, but so are Darian, Sinclair, and even his psycho son, Elijah. I'm stuck in the middle, fighting a war I no longer care for.

I don't care how my father died or what happened to him. Not anymore. It won't change anything to seek revenge. He'll still be dead and will have still murdered Darian's family.

My father is the reason Darian is struggling. He's why my

husband spent time hidden away in an institution for parts of his teenage years, battling against his demons.

How can I feel anything but disgust toward my own father for doing that to him? I'm tired. I'm just so tired of living in the past and letting rage pave the way for my future—a future that can only lead to death and destruction.

But how do we beat the Exiled? How do we stop a powerful secret society from hosting more Hell Fire Nights? I can't just walk away, either. I have a responsibility. Whether I want to accept it or not, my legacy is tied to the Exiled, and sticking my head in the sand isn't the answer. I've already spent years running, and look where that got me—right back here.

If it weren't for the Exiled's sickening rituals, my family would be alive. Darian's family would be alive, and he wouldn't have witnessed his mother being raped and his father murdered before his eyes as a young boy. Every member of the Antichrist wouldn't have suffered at the hands of powerful men at the top of society. Our loved ones would still be alive. The problem is, I no longer know who to trust. I'm a pawn on both sides of the fence.

Fuck, I'm a mess, and I don't know what to do.

The door opens to reveal the young man, who enters the room and scans the mess. I'm still seated on the floor, staring up at him, wondering if I have it in me to seduce him. The key must be in his pocket. Maybe I can fish it out if I straddle his lap.

Or I may need to harden my heart and do what needs to be done. I've seen how he looks at me, his eyes lingering on my body in my nightdress. It's unflattering, but he seems to like what he sees, so maybe I can use that to my advantage.

"I'm sorry," I say, looking sheepish and nibbling on my bottom lip. "I'll help you clean up."

He raises a brow in surprise but says nothing. In fact, he hasn't uttered a word since day one. He just…stares.

"I didn't mean to make such a mess. I was upset." I climb to my feet. "Being locked up does that to a person." Hesitating, I fix my eyes on him. "You must be new here. I haven't seen you before."

He makes a grunting sound, then disappears out the door again. I deflate, thinking I lost before I even tried, but then he's back with a sweeping brush and a bucket of soapy water.

He won't let me help, ordering me with silent puffs to sit on the bed after he puts the mattress back in place and starts to sweep. I watch him for a moment, trying and failing to ignore the guilt swirling in my gut. This guy seems nice, unlike Lauren. He's shy, keeping his eyes averted as much as possible, though every now and then I catch him watching me.

I can't do it.

I can't use this man for my own selfish reasons, but then I remember what Lauren said about my husband's cock, and a burst of anger rushes through me again. Leaning back on my elbows, I spread my legs, feeling the nightdress ride up my bare thighs.

The man pauses, growing as still and silent as the night. His throat jumps, and he averts his gaze just as quickly. Then he continues sweeping, a crimson hue coloring his cheeks.

I can't steal the key if he's over there. Somehow, I need to coax him closer.

"You're handsome," I say, the skirt shifting higher as I reach down to drag my fingers up my thighs. "You seem shy. I don't bite."

He's blushing even harder now. "I'm not supposed to talk to you."

My brows fly up at the sound of his low, raspy voice, and

he quickly averts his gaze before he turns around, but I jump off the bed. "Wait!"

Pausing with his back to me, he stays still. I can't tell if he's breathing or not.

"What's your name?"

"Thomas."

"It's nice to meet you, Thomas."

Turning over his shoulder, his eyes lock on mine for the briefest of seconds before he walks out, leaving me strangely affected by the encounter. I frown, about to sit back down, when something occurs to me. I never heard the lock click.

I run to the door and sneak into the quiet hallway with my back pressed to the wall. As I peek around the nearest corner, my bare feet padding on the floor, it dawns on me that I have no clue what I'm doing, and no plan. But it doesn't matter. I need to find Darian.

## CHAPTER
# TWENTY-EIGHT
### CECILIA

It's the strangest feeling tiptoeing through the hallways of my previous home. I lived with these people for years. They were my family and this used to be my safe space. Though perhaps my only true family was Lauren, Keith, and Carlo. We were the closest. Keith was like a father figure to me, maybe even a better father in many ways than my real one. Greta is a different story. She has her own agenda. We all know it. While she's at the helm of this rebel group, she's a mystery in many ways, and I need to keep my distance until I can trust her again.

I dart past the living room, careful to avoid the creaking floorboards. Laughter spills from within as grown men curse like sailors. A group of rebels watches a football game on the TV with their socked feet on the coffee table, which is littered with pizza boxes and empty beer bottles.

I recognize some of them by their boisterous voices alone. Antonio, a brute-looking man in his late thirties, sits in one of the two armchairs with his arm behind his head and a beer bottle balanced on his stomach. He was the member who taught me how to drive a stick.

Aria, a short-haired woman in her mid-twenties, with a fierce lion tattoo on her back, sits perched on the armrest, hollering at the TV as loudly as the guys.

She joined the Antichrist after members of the Exiled drove up beside her and her boyfriend in a flashy, top-of-the-range car. They hauled him into the trunk before driving away into the foggy night, leaving her behind, alone and scared, while their fading laughter drifted through the open windows. We all have a story with heartbreak at its center. It's what bonded us over many moonless nights.

I escape upstairs, my bare feet sinking into the red carpet. Voices drift through one of the closed doors, so I quickly run past, my heart thudding hard as I glance at the surveillance camera in the corner. I didn't exactly plan this impromptu escape, and it won't be long until they discover I'm gone. This might be my only chance to find him.

Call it intuition, but as I near the next bedroom in line, my chest tightens, and a strange pull urges me forward. Darian is in there. I know it even before I inch the door open to peek inside. There's no sign of anyone in the empty room. Why would there be? They've left him alone, for god only knows how long, in a wardrobe, just like that night when he listened to his mother's screams and cries for help.

Once I enter the room and close the door softly behind me, careful not to make a sound, I glance around at the sparse furniture and the potted herbs on the windowsill. As I walk deeper into the room, I almost trip on the curled corner of the plush rug on the floor.

"Shit," I curse, stumbling forward.

This is the primary bedroom. It used to be Keith's when he was alive, but I don't recall ever entering it until now. The walls are painted a dark gray shade, giving the space a modern feel. A large bed with crisp white bedding stands out against the walls, while simple IKEA nightstands on either side hold farmhouse-style bedside lamps.

A muffled sound comes from behind the closed wardrobe doors, and I rush forward to slide them open, gasping at the sight that greets me.

Darian's bloodshot eyes blink against the light as I enter the small space and fall to my knees before him. Sweat is beading on his brow and upper lip, his skin clammy beneath my touch.

A rush of relief spears through me as I palm his face. "Are you okay, baby? It's me, Cecilia."

"Cec—" he croaks, clearing his throat and trying again. "Cecilia?"

"I'm here, baby." I fuss over him for long, precious minutes we don't have, then set to work untying the ropes. Darian stares at my face as though I'm an apparition.

"Is it really you?" he asks.

My hands tremble violently, and I have to inhale a few deep breaths to steady the adrenaline rush of seeing him in this vulnerable state. Darian has always been indestructible and larger than life. Nothing could touch him. I'm furious, I realize, as I meet his gaze. Furious that anyone would hurt him like this. Furious that someone tried to keep us apart.

"I'll get you out of here."

"Cecilia," he says, and I stop trying to untie the rope around his ankle to wipe the tears from my eyes. It's hard to look at him because it makes me want to murder whoever did this to him. "I thought…"

The haunted quality of his voice grips my aching heart in a vise. I raise my gaze, struck by the sincerity in his. He lifts his free hand and cups my cheek, touching me with a reverence I've never felt before. "You thought what?" I ask.

"I thought I might never see you again." His chin wobbles

as he strokes his thumb through the salty tears on my cheeks. “I thought…”

“It’s okay. You don’t have to say it.”

He thought they were hurting me while he was tied to a chair and hidden away in a closet, unable to save me.

“I’m okay,” I reassure him as I finish freeing him from the chair, the ropes falling to the floor. “Come on, let’s get out of here.”

We exit the wardrobe, and I look back and take his hand. Darian pulls me to a stop and sweeps me up in his arms, his nose buried in my neck. “Are you sure you’re okay?” he asks, breathing me in. “I swear if they hurt you, I will—”

“No one hurt me.” I dig my fingers into the expanse of his back through his slightly damp shirt, confused for a moment as I ease back. “Why are your clothes wet?”

Before he can respond, my eyes widen as I remember his injury. “Your back… The crossbow… Are you okay?”

He reaches for my hand, and we cross the room. “I’m fine.”

“You don’t look fine,” I say, noting the dried blood on his shirt.

*It’s a lot of blood.*

He presses a finger to his lips in a silent command to stay quiet and then releases my hand to open the door carefully. I wait patiently while he sticks his head outside, my palms clammy with nerves. Someone will come to check on us soon. I’m surprised no one has sounded the alarm yet, though there’s a football game on the TV. They’re always laxer on game night.

When the coast is clear, we exit the room. Darian is surprisingly light on his feet for such a large man, and I admire his agility as we turn the corner in sync.

We hurry downstairs, descending the staircase as silently as we can. Darian pauses on the second to the last step, listening intently, and then we're on the move again, running across the hallway.

As we turn another corner, Lauren appears and whacks Darian in the head with a baseball bat. He falls to the floor with a sickening thud, and my heart stalls at seeing him incapacitated.

Lauren sneers down at him, teetering on her heels. "Why do you always get the good parts?" she asks me as she lifts her gaze. "Is it because you're a precious van der Meer? A runaway princess. Just because you were born into privilege, the rest of us should settle for less? Is that it? Well, I've got news for you, princess. The Antichrist wants nothing to do with your kind. You're the abomination we're fighting against. Just because you were let into our folds doesn't mean you're one of us."

"I don't know what you're talking about," I say, inching back.

"Sure you don't. The moment you were conceived, you were destined for grandeur. Isn't that so? You were meant to lead at the top with the next generation King." Nostrils flaring, she steps over Darian's unconscious body. "The future *queen.*"

"We were friends, you and I," I say shakily, hating how scared I sound.

"We were never friends."

One step closer.

I glance down at the bat in her hands, the end smeared with blood, and my throat jumps.

"I am done playing the role of your keeper. It's time we do this my way."

"Your way?" I gulp, inching away.

She stalks me, dragging the bat along the wall. "You marrying Darian and having his babies could have been a solid plan in our fight against the Exiled, what with such fine breeding, but you had to go and fall for him like a fucking fool." She cocks her head to the side. "And now you're a liability."

"Let's talk about this, Lauren."

She stops and laughs. "Talk?"

"Yes… Please, I'm begging you, whatever is going on inside your head, it's not true. I'm not your enemy. Nothing has changed."

Her smile takes on a dark edge. "Nothing has changed?" she asks, spinning around and walking back to the body. "Then you won't mind me killing him? He's an enemy of the Antichrist, right?" She raises the bat above her head, about to strike his skull, and looks at me. "I bet he won't be so pretty when his head is bashed in like a melon."

"No!" I rush forward before I can think clearly, and a victorious smile twists her mouth.

"No?" she asks, bat poised to strike. "I thought you said nothing had changed. So you're a liability, after all."

She sets off after me, and I let out a terrified gasp as I flee down the hallway, but I don't make it far before Antonio appears out of nowhere and blocks my path. "In a hurry somewhere?"

I glance behind me to see Lauren dragging her bat along the wall, a manic grin contorting her facial features.

"It's over, princess," she taunts. "Your precious Greta isn't here to save you this time."

Hope flares as Ari walks around the corner and takes in the scene, her short hair swept off her puckering forehead.

"What's going on?" she asks, glancing from Lauren and the bat to Antonio, who blocks my only escape route.

"It's a misunderstanding," I rush out, at the same time Antonio says gruffly, "She escaped the room."

Ari's brows shoot up, and she looks genuinely surprised. "Thomas abandoned his post?"

"Who knows," Antonio replies, his eyes on me. "The boy sprouts an erection at the slightest thing, so it wouldn't surprise me if our little girl here used that to her advantage."

His knowing smirk makes me sick to my stomach. I try to escape past him again, but he grabs me by the shoulders and shoves me so hard that I fall to the floor. "Stay down, bitch."

I scramble away and press myself against the wall. From this angle, he appears even taller and bigger, and I realize I can't escape past him without a weapon.

Ari studies me. "Is it true that you're in love with the Duke?"

I look from her to Lauren to Antonio and back to Ari. "Eat horseshit, all of you."

Antonio bursts out laughing. "Horseshit? I like that. Very original."

"You think you're so fucking brave, huh?" Lauren says as her heels click on the floor.

She puts the bat beneath my chin, tilting it up, and I swallow as my heart drums an irregular beat. "You're ours now, princess, and we don't have to pretend to like you anymore. You're nothing but an Exiled slut."

I feel tears trail down my cheeks as she smiles cruelly, and my gaze flicks to the others, seeing the hatred sparkling in their eyes. For years, I considered them my family. I trusted them. We planned our revenge on the Exiled together. We were fighting for a common cause *together.* But it's obvious now that they never cared about me. None of it was real. Did Keith and Carlo hate me, too? Did they pretend to care for me? Was it all a lie? Did the Antichrist use me as a pawn from the very beginning?

"Don't look like such a kicked puppy. I promise we won't hurt you and your precious boyfriend—*much.*" Lauren's honeyed voice cuts through my warring thoughts.

She raises the bat to swing it at me, but before she gets the chance, Darian appears behind Ari and wraps his arm around her neck.

It all happens so fast. One minute, his eyes meet mine over Ari's shoulder, and the next, a sickening snap fills the room. He launches himself at Antonio next, and I use the moment of surprise to throw myself at Lauren's legs. She topples to the floor with a yelp, and we tussle for the bat.

"You fucking bitch," she says, kneeing me between my legs as I try to secure her wrists. Then she rolls over onto her stomach, reaching for the bat, but I grip her by the hair and slam her face into the floor, breaking her delicate little nose with a loud crunch.

"Fucking gross," I mutter, launching forward to grab the bat.

Lauren looks up, cupping her bleeding nose, her eyes filled with anger. In a swift move, she takes off her heel and drives it into the back of my bare calf.

I cry out as white-hot pain sears through my leg, leaving me whimpering and breathing heavily.

Lauren laughs as she stands up and collects the bat. "Looks sore," she says, nodding toward the heel stuck in my leg.

As I look over my shoulder at my calf, a cold sweat breaks out on my forehead. There's blood everywhere, smeared across the hallway floor like a scene from a horror flick. I roll over, careful with my injury, and yank the heel out.

*Fuck, that hurt.* I try to breathe through the sharp pain, but it's so severe that I struggle to focus.

Antonio has gained the upper hand.

He is straddling Darian now and laying into him with his fists.

Lauren swings the bat with a manic look, striking me in the shoulder. A loud crunch fills my ears as I collapse to the floor, writhing in pain.

"That's enough," Lauren says to Antonio before she delivers another hard blow to the back of my thigh. "We need him alive—"

A silenced pop rings out, and Lauren topples to the floor, staring up at the roof with a bullet hole between her manicured brows. Surprised, I look up to see Sinclair haul Antonio off my husband and knee him hard in the face before he aims the gun at his head and shoots him dead with a cold look that sends shivers rushing down my spine.

Frozen to the spot, I'm hauled to my feet by Elijah, who picks me up in his strong arms and carries me out past Darian. My eyes widen when I see his barely recognizable face, and I beat Elijah's broad chest, ordering him to put me down, which he does reluctantly.

Ignoring the throbbing pain in my leg and my dislocated, possibly broken shoulder, I collapse between Darian's spread legs and cup his bruised face. Both eyes are almost swollen shut and blood pours from a deep gash on his forehead.

"Darian…" My voice trembles as I swipe my thumbs through the slick crimson on his cheeks. "Please, look at me."

Sinclair puts his hand on my shoulder, causing me to stiffen. "We need to leave."

I jerk free. "I'm not leaving him here."

"Of course, we're not fucking leaving him here." With a nod toward Elijah, I'm once again picked up like I weigh nothing more than a feather. I don't know why I fight. Sinclair is my husband's friend and possibly his only ally, but my instincts override my common sense. I squirm in Elijah's arm, beating his chest while demanding that he take me back to Darian, and he grumbles something under his breath about how I'm paying for the dry cleaning.

# CHAPTER TWENTY-NINE

CECILIA

Muted orange streetlights fill the car in waves as we drive down the highway on our way to get medical help. Darian is passed out in the back, but at least he's breathing. I keep looking over my sore shoulder to check.

Elijah demanded to find his own way home after dumping me unceremoniously in the front seat with no care in the world that I nearly passed out in pain, and now he's no doubt terrifying some unsuspecting woman in his blood-soaked clothes. The guy has a creepy serial killer vibe about him.

I'm leaning with my head against the window, wincing in pain every time there's a slightly uneven surface on the road. My injured shoulder feels like it's been doused in gasoline and set on fire. Not to mention my throbbing leg and the bleeding injury in my calf.

Tilting my head, I study Sinclair.

Shadows cling to him tonight as he rests his elbow on the window, staring unseeingly at the dark road ahead, his other hand hanging over the steering wheel. He notices me watching and frowns, then rubs his fingers over his full lips as if deep in thought. With a sigh, he drops his hand. "I guess you have questions."

"You can say that again." I try to keep my voice light but can't stop it from shaking. "I don't know who I am anymore. Those people back there…" I drift off, my heart clenching painfully. "I thought they were my friends."

"You can't trust anyone in this world," he replies darkly.

"Not even you?"

"Especially not me."

I stare at his side profile as the seconds tick past. "Where do your alliances lie, Sinclair? The only time I've seen you truly care about anything or anyone is when your family is involved. Maybe I'm going out on a hunch here, but I think Darian is part of your family, blood-related or not."

His eyes slide in my direction as a corner of his mouth lifts. "You're right," he replies, checking the rearview mirror. "Darian is like a younger brother to me. After he lost his family, mine took him under their wing, and I've been there to look out for him ever since." Curling his fingers around the steering wheel, as though he needs to anchor his emotions, his smile slips. "He used to be a happy kid before that night, but…uhm…"

He wets his lips, brows creased in concentration. "He was never the same again. My father took him to see a psychologist, but there wasn't much they could do for him. Darian retreated into himself. Don't get me wrong; he was by no means weak, but the night he lost his parents changed him. As he grew older, he swore to seek revenge, to kill your father himself, but politics aren't that straightforward in our world. Van der Meer held a lot of power. My father warned your husband against doing anything stupid until the time was right. Not to make the wrong enemies. In the meantime, Darian worked hard to climb the ranks over the years."

Sinclair blows out his cheeks, his chest deflating on a deep sigh. "He was finally ready to kill your father that Hell Fire Night, but the King got to Mr. van der Meer first."

Eyes wide, I lift my trembling hand to my mouth.

"I didn't think much of it. Mr. van der Meer was dead. His wife had gone on the run and took you with her. But Darian kept discussing revenge like your father was still alive."

"What happened then?" I ask.

"Not much," he answers, but I don't miss the tick in his jaw. "Darian threw himself headfirst into the Exiled. By now, he was a respected and feared Duke, like his father, but it was all…" Sinclair seems to search for the correct word. "Robotic. His heart wasn't in it. While the other Dukes live and breathe the Exiled, Darian merely tolerates it." He looks at me then, his blue eyes roaming over my face as another wave of orange streetlight fills the car. "I have no doubt he'd leave the Exiled in a heartbeat if the right incentive presented itself."

My heart thuds harder, and I turn to look at Darian over my shoulder.

His chest is still moving.

Relieved, I face forward, clutching my injured shoulder. "I don't want him to defy the King because of me."

"It's a little too late for that," he replies, chuckling. "He put a target on his back when he made the rash decision to marry you. It's only a matter of time before the King discovers your real identity and makes an example out of him, if he hasn't already figured it out. No one has defied him like that since your father had the guts to go back on their deal."

"I can't believe he promised me to the King's son before I was born."

Sinclair frowns, glancing at me. "Are you serious? You're the daughter of not one, but two Dukes. Of course, you'd go to a high bidder."

I choke on my breath. "A high bidder?"

"You're so naïve," he responds, not quite containing his amusement, but then he sobers, gripping the steering wheel. "Shortly after Darian moved into his new house, I caught him talking to the shadows in the cellar."

I stay silent, sensing he has more to say.

"According to his psychologist, it was his mind's way of protecting him from reality. Somehow, the phantasm of your father allowed him a sense of control, something he lacked the night his mother was raped and murdered."

"Did you not tell him it wasn't real?"

He grinds his teeth and checks his mirrors. "He had it under control. You don't know Darian the way I do. Trust me when I tell you he was improving."

"So what changed?"

"You did." He says it so easily, my breath catches.

"Me?"

Sinclair hums an agreeing sound as we enter a filter lane. "Before you, Darian was a vault. His emotions were locked up so tight that he was barely human, but then you crashed into his life and pried him open."

*Crashed into his life?*

"Excuse me? He forced me to marry him."

*No one held a gun to his head. He could have me killed that night. Instead, he chose to marry me.*

"He did it to stop the King's son from sinking his claws into you. Trust me, you got the better end of the deal."

"I don't get it. Why would he do that?" *It makes no sense. Why would he feel a sense of loyalty to me?*

"Beats me," Sinclair says, slowing to a stop at a roundabout. We watch a silver Mercedes drive by while Darian's labored breathing fills the small space in the back seat. "Let's just say, Darian was a very impulsive kid before his parents' murders." Rolling his head on the headrest, he looks at me. "The night he married you was the first time I'd seen him act impulsively since we were young."

A blush creeps up my neck, and I break eye contact. Sinclair can't be right. Why would Darian risk his position in the Exiled and his standing with the King to keep me safe?

"I think you intrigued him when you bulldozed yourself onto the property under the pretense of belonging to the cleaning crew. It was a very bold and reckless move and sure to catch the eye of a man in power."

He gives me another pointed look before entering the roundabout, and I shrink a little in my seat, embarrassed by how naïve I've been. How could I think I could just waltz right in and go unnoticed?

A thought occurs to me. "Do you think the Antichrist used me? Lauren said they knew who I was when they recruited me and did it intentionally to use me in their war."

"Honestly," Sinclair replies as the streetlights become far and few between, the stretches of darkness growing wider, "I don't know." Shrugging, he gives me an apologetic look.

I chew on that for a while as my gut twists uncomfortably. "Where do I go from here?"

I don't belong anywhere. I can't go back to the rebels after Sinclair killed their members, not that they'd want me anyway; I'm just a weapon in their war, and I refuse to be a pawn anymore.

But I also can't stay with Darian if it puts him in danger.

"I don't like that look in your eyes," Sinclair says. "Whatever you're thinking, stop it. It'll do you no good to run away. Darian will still have a target on his back, no matter what."

"Are you sure about that?" I reply, growing larger in my seat. "It's me he wants. No one else except my husband, you, Elijah, and a few trusted others know I'm the van der Meer's sole heir. The King is out there searching for me. He doesn't know I've been hiding under their noses."

Sinclair scoffs. "You shouldn't underestimate him. It wouldn't surprise me if he knew by now. The rebel group probably leaked your whereabouts."

"Why complicate it, Sinclair? Darian is only safe if I'm not around. It's only a matter of time before the King finds out I'm here. It's dangerous for me to stay." I nibble on my bottom lip, my thoughts a jumble of scattered pieces trying to fall into place. "If he wants to find me, he can. So what is he waiting for?"

Sinclair stares into the darkness ahead, frowning like he wants to grab me by the hair and jostle me like a piggybank to get at my thoughts. "He probably already knows you're here, and he's biding his time, waiting for you to run away and leave yourself unprotected," he answers reluctantly, almost thoughtfully. "Perhaps he's banking on it. And you would be just stupid enough to do it to keep Darian safe."

We lock eyes in the darkness, the lights on the dashboard the sole illumination.

"You know Darian will catch you if you run."

"He underestimates how good I am at hiding. After all, I did it for ten years."

"No offense, Mrs. Delacroix, but you underestimate what a good hunter your husband is."

---

TIME HAS SLOWED to a near crawl. Something about hospitals defies natural laws. Out there, in the real world, hours feel like minutes, sometimes seconds. But here, at my husband's bedside, the seconds slither by painfully slowly. I've barely slept since we arrived weeks ago, refusing to leave his side. At one point, a nurse draped me in a blanket.

Except for the bruises to his face from the beatdown, Darian suffered a small brain bleed, which required emergency surgery and a stint in the ICU. His doctor remains hopeful for a full recovery, but there are no guarantees, and all we can do is wait.

Wait for my husband to heal.

Wait for him to be strong enough to be roused from his induced coma. For now, he needs to rest.

I've lost count of how many sunrises have woken me up from my restless slumber while I've been curled up awkwardly in my chair or sleeping with my head on Darian's mattress, his hand clutched in mine. I've also lost count of how many times I've witnessed the sun dip behind the trees outside the building to mark the end of another day.

Sinclair arrives daily to check on Darian, looking tired and paler than usual, his concerned eyes raking over my withering form. "Have you eaten something?" he always asks, and I respond with a faint shake of my head as I continue staring out the window. Nothing else is said, but I feel his disapproval.

Before he leaves, he likes to bark orders at the overworked, underpaid nurses to bring me a hot meal. Other times, he'll appear at my side with a wrapped sandwich.

"You should go home and get some sleep, Cecilia," he says tonight as he eyes my husband's breathing tube and the beeping monitors.

When I don't respond, his eyes land on me. "You need more than an hour's sleep here and there. I'll stay."

"I'm not leaving him like this," I respond, sounding dead even to my own ears.

Sinclair frowns, and I worry for a second that he'll haul me over his shoulder and carry me home. It seems like his M.O to boss women around, but if he so much as tries to move me from this chair, I'll fight him tooth and nail. I'll scream the place down.

"I'm not leaving," I repeat in a firm tone. "Don't make me."

Sinclair studies me in the muted light from the bedside lamp, which offers the sole illumination. "You know Darian will have my head if I don't look after you while he's gone, right?"

"No offense, Sinclair, but I'm a big girl. I can take care of myself."

"When was the last time you showered? Slept? Ate a proper meal?"

"I could use a fly swatter right about now," I grumble, rubbing my eyes. "Your concern is heartwarming. It is. But don't you have like a hundred bat plants to look after? I heard they flourish if you talk to them."

Much to my surprise, Sinclair laughs, and if I didn't feel like death warmed up, I could appreciate the sweet sound. When was the last time something made me laugh?

Leaning forward in my seat, I reach for Darian's hand, careful not to disturb the cannula, and kiss his knuckles.

Tears moisten my lashes as I linger with my lips on his warm skin, which smells of faint antiseptic like everything in this room.

"Does the King know?" I ask, lowering his hand to the mattress.

"No. No one knows you're here. Dr. Grant can be trusted."

I smile weakly. Sinclair swipes his suit jacket from the armchair on Darian's other side and shrugs it on, his tie askew. "I trust you're not a flight risk, Mrs. Delacroix."

My eyes roll even as my lips twitch. "Not until I know he's safe."

Sinclair walks around to my side and puts his big hand on my shoulder, squeezing tight. "Give me a call if you want a break. Your husband would want you to sleep."

"Go home, Sinclair."

With a final squeeze, he leaves the room, and the tears I couldn't let fall while he was in here finally spill over. I reach for Darian's hand and bring it to my lips once more, kissing his palm. My heart throbs against my bruised ribs, my eyes drifting to the feeding tube and the wires attached to him. I hate anyone seeing him this vulnerable and unable to defend himself.

"I love you, Darian Delacroix," I whisper as I place his palm against my cheek, leaning into his touch, noting the bruises on his cheeks. "I should have told you sooner."

# CHAPTER THIRTY

## DARIAN

"Darian?" A squeeze of my hand.

I feel like I'm being pulled out of a cold lake, drifting higher and higher through murky water.

I finally resurface, blinking against blinding brightness while a doctor shines a light in my eyes. "Welcome back, Darian," he says, pocketing his flashlight and smiling at someone in the room.

My mouth feels scratchy and dry like a desert. No amount of swallowing helps. An incessant beeping noise filters in and out of my consciousness. I try to lift my head, but someone shushes me and says, "You need to take it easy, honey."

"Honey?"

Through my haze, I recognize Sinclair's amused baritone.

"What am I supposed to call him? Asshat?" a female voice snaps.

I know that voice. It's the voice of an angel. Fuck. What kind of drugs did they give me?

"Darian, baby, can you hear me?"

I roll my head on the pillow, trying to adjust to the bright lights.

Soft fingers stroke my cheek, while the most entrancing, expressive eyes I've ever seen gaze down at me. I pause as I notice my heart rate picking up on the monitor. "Cecilia?"

"Hi, honey."

Sinclair snickers, and she shoots him a brief glare before her green eyes capture me again and soften. Leaning down, she presses her forehead to mine. "You scared me."

"I'm sorry," I croak, reaching up to stroke my fingers through her cascading locks. "What happened? Are you hurt?"

She eases back and studies my face. "I'm better now."

I turn my head to see Sinclair watching us with an unreadable expression. He notices me looking, and I raise my fist for us to do our secret handshake we used to do as kids.

Chuckling, he bumps his knuckles to mine one last time. "You gave us a fright. You know you can't die on us, right? No way in hell am I looking after your feisty wife. My home already resembles a botanical garden or a damn jungle. The last pussy I brought home asked me if I was into *Tarzan* cosplay."

"Let me guess, you rolled with it?"

"Hell yes, you think I'm going to turn down an opportunity like that? I had a fake vine installed on the roof and everything. You should have seen her swinging in her little leopard bikini."

"Gross," Cecilia mutters, but she's smiling, and it's the most beautiful smile. In fact, my gaze lingers on her mouth long after she stops.

"Of course I wasn't so lucky," Sinclair grumbles. "When I tried to swing, it snapped, and I almost broke my tailbone."

"That explains why you couldn't sit comfortably for a week," I say, laughing despite my sore throat, and we share a smile before he clears his throat and jerks his thumb toward the door. "I'll go speak to the doctor and get us drinks."

Cecilia wipes tears from her cheeks as he walks out, hoping I won't catch her crying. I reach for her small hand, interlacing my fingers with hers. "I'm sorry if I scared you."

"No…" She shakes her head. "You have nothing to apologize for."

"I'm the reason behind your tears. I don't ever want to be the reason you cry."

One minute, she's seated, and the next, her plush mouth is on mine. I tangle my fingers in her hair, thrusting my tongue between her sweet lips.

She tastes of heaven and my tailor-made addiction, of life and reasons to fight.

We break apart, her heavy gaze flicking between my lips and my eyes. I bump my nose against hers and whisper, "I didn't dream a lot, but when I did, it was of you."

She beams, her eyes twinkling with happiness, and we kiss again to the soundtrack of the heartbeat monitor and fading conversations in the hallway. Cecilia moans into my mouth, causing my cock to twitch at the sound despite my current state. When I break away, I'm breathing heavily.

Fuck me. This woman drives me insane. I could be at death's door and still want to fill her up and make her scream my name.

She bites her lip to stop grinning. "If you hadn't woken up from a coma mere minutes ago…" Her voice takes on a flirtatious edge. "I would climb on top of you and ride that fat cock of yours."

*Little tease.*

I groan, my dick aching at the playful smile on her lips and the filthy promise behind her words. "I'm fine. Look at me. I'm practically brand new."

She pats my cheek, smiling even wider. "Be a good boy and rest up, and I might reward you later."

"Fine. I'll entertain this game of yours for now," I reply with sigh, "but as soon as we leave this place, I'll show you who's in charge."

"Ooh," she teases, leaning in to hover with her tempting lips inches from mine. "So bossy."

I grind my teeth, equally loving and hating how she has the upper hand. I like to exert dominance, to make my subject bend to my will, yet here I am, ready to do just about anything to make her happy. The way she's smiling at me is sexier than any skimpy little outfit she could wear. If I believed in fairytales, I'd call her a siren because my dick just needs me to simply lay eyes on her to stand at attention. It's almost humiliating.

"I think," she starts, taking pity on me, "that you deserve a treat."

"Yeah?" My heart rate accelerates.

"Yeah," Cecilia whispers, reaching down and plunging her hand into her joggers. She watches me closely as she fingers herself. "After all, you did kill someone for me and nearly got yourself beaten to death."

"I would die for you any day," I reply, eyes riveted on her slick fingers when she pulls them out from her joggers and sucks them clean.

My heart sinks with disappointment, but then her lips are on mine, and I lose all train of thought when I taste her arousal on her tongue. I kiss her harder, groaning into her mouth. No other woman tastes as fucking sweet as her. No other woman drives me this crazy. I'm famished.

"Let me eat your cunt," I beg—yes, beg—pulling her back to my hungry mouth when she tries to move away. "Let me fuck you with my tongue."

"Baby," she says, her voice breathy with laughter. "You've just woken up from a coma. You need to rest."

"No…" I frantically shake my head. "Who told you that? Dr. Boring out there with the silver goatee? Ignore him and his ridiculous advice. He's just trying to get me killed. What I need is your pussy in my face."

Cecilia pulls away with a blush coloring her cheeks. Her eyes sparkle with happiness as she sits back in her chair.

She's too far away for my liking. If I had it my way, she'd never leave my side—she'd have a permanent seat on my face or dick.

"Think of it as an incentive to get better."

I flop my head back down dramatically. Sinclair enters the room with coffee in takeaway mugs and an old book tucked into his belt. He hands Cecilia a mug and gives her a warning look, which makes me frown and try to decipher their silent conversation. It's useless.

Then he turns to me and smiles, tossing a weathered paperback onto my stomach. I pick it up and read the title, looking at him questioningly. "*Kama Sutra*?"

"Funny story. I found this cute little bookshelf in the cafeteria for used books. One of the elderly ladies serving coffee beamed when I complimented the wallpapered shelves. Then she scurried over on her eager little legs, surprisingly fast for a pensioner, and handed me the book. I took one look at the title and thought it could be perfect for your book club."

"You complimented the wallpaper?" I can't quite keep the disbelief out of my voice.

Sinclair simply smirks, slamming his hand down on my shoulder and jostling me hard enough to make my head spin. "It's good to have you back, man. Now do some reading and rest so we can get you out of here. Your girl will start to stink up the place if she doesn't have a shower soon."

Cecilia flips him off, and he winks as he walks to the door, then he turns with his hand on the frame. "I mean it, Darian. Rest up."

---

"Dammit." A deep sigh, followed by thick silence. "Are you sure? I can't be in two fucking places at once."

I've been snoozing on and off most of the day when Sinclair's voice wakes me up. He's over by the large windows with his broad back to me, his shoulders tense as he pulls his hand from his pocket to rub his brow. Outside, night has fallen and the full moon outside bathes him in a silvery hue.

"She'll bite my head off if she finds out I have her shadowed. She won't care that it's for her own good." He snorts at whatever the person on the other end has to say. "You clearly don't know Darian very well. If he were ever to find himself pussy whipped, it was always going to be by a woman like Cecilia. She's headstrong and doesn't take his shit." His eyes meet mine over his shoulder. "Look, I've got to go. Don't lose sight of her, but tell the others to be discreet." Hanging up, he pockets his phone.

"Where's my wife?" I ask, my throat dry and scratchy.

Sinclair strides over to me, takes a seat in the chair, and hands me the glass of water on the nightstand. I gulp it down, some spilling onto my chin. After placing it back beside the bedside lamp, I settle and look at him expectantly.

"She's gone home to shower and sleep."

I'm already pining for her. It's pathetic at this point how much I love having her by my side at all times, but maybe I need to give myself some slack.

"Who was that on the phone?"

Sinclair's eyes darken before he runs a hand down his tired face and sits forward with his elbows on his knees. Restless energy pours from him in waves as he hangs his head. "The King knows you have her."

"Fuck…" My voice is low as a sense of dread moves through me.

"He'll come for you," Sinclair says, lifting his heavy head, eyes brimming with regret. "I don't know what to do here, Darian. I've got our most trusted Commoners shadowing Cecilia and two men stationed outside this room, but you know he won't stop until you're dead."

"Well…" I stare up at the ceiling. "We both know I can't go back."

There's no returning to the Exiled now. I could only hide Cecilia in plain sight for so long before the King figured it out. This was always going to happen sooner or later.

The scent of fresh linen surrounds me as I roll my head on the soft pillow to look at Sinclair. His shoulders slump as if the weight of the world is weighing him down. Bloodshot eyes gaze at me through dark lashes, and he jiggles his knee for a beat. "Fuck, Darian… We're screwed. What are we going to do?"

"*We're* not going to do anything."

His face pinches, about to retort, but I can't bring him down with me. This is my mess and my mess alone. I know he's loyal to me, just like I will always be to him, but I need him to put his own safety first for once.

Realization dawns on him, and he straightens, growing larger and wider. "Don't you fucking dare, Darian! First her and now you?"

"Her?" I ask, confused, but he shoots to his feet and tugs hard at his ruffled silver hair while pacing the room.

He jabs a finger in my direction. "We've been friends

since the fucking womb. Do you really think you can push me away now? Fuck you, Darian. Fuck you to hell and back." A bitter look comes over his face, his jaw tight, as he runs his hand over his stubble. "Why did it have to be her? Couldn't you have fallen for some sweet little Duke's daughter with soft thighs and nothing in her brain? Why the van der Meer's daughter?"

I open my mouth to reply, but he makes a throttling motion in the air, pretending to shake sense into me. "Don't answer that. I know far too fucking well why you fell for her, but dammit, you couldn't have thought with your brain for once instead of your fucking genitals? We wouldn't be in this mess if you didn't stick your dick inside Dalton's property and then put your ring on her finger."

"What did you mean when you said, 'first her'?"

Pausing, his brows pull low.

I shoot upright. "She's going to run." I'm out of bed in the next second, pulling off wires and making for the door.

"Are you fucking nuts? You're not in shape to leave yet. You suffered a brain bleed, you fucking moron." Sinclair wrestles me back, and I curse that he's bigger and stronger than me when it matters. If I weren't so weak, I could give him a good fight, but even I can admit I'm not in good shape.

He shoves me down. "Don't move, or I'll shackle you to the bed."

"I'm not one of your fuckbuddies."

In the next second, he's punching me square in the jaw, then shakes out his fist, cursing under his breath. "You deserved that."

I wiggle my sore jaw. "You've got a mean hook on you."

Adjusting his circular glasses, he smiles weakly and flops into Cecilia's chair. "Fuck," he breathes, looking defeated, rubbing his brow.

"I can't let her leave. I need to find her before she runs."

"She hasn't run *yet.*" He sighs. "You're not in the shape to leave. Will you please just trust that I've got this under control?"

I hate to admit that he's right. I can barely stand upright, never mind chasing my wife. Although it's a blow to my ego to admit defeat, maybe now it's time to trust my best friend. "I've never seen you like this before," I admit as I adjust the bed into a seated position, the soft whirring filling the room.

He lowers his hand, eyes averted. "What can I say? I've been under a lot of stress lately."

"I remember it all now."

His eyes snap to mine.

"When I was tied up in that wardrobe. It was like…" My brows knit. "All these memories came flooding back, like a four-dimensional movie I couldn't stop. Before then, it was just nightmares, snippets, but this…" I swallow around a thick lump in my throat, my chest tightening and making it hard to breathe. "I remembered it all. Every single painful detail."

Sinclair scoots forward on his chair, his long legs stretching out in front of him, crossed at the ankles. His creased suit jacket pulls around his shoulders, and his loosened black tie sits at an angle, yet he's never looked more alert.

I shrug.

While we're friends through thick and thin, it's still hard as fuck to admit I'm full of flaws. Flaws that make me human, but flaws nonetheless.

"Can I be brutally honest?" I ask, unable to look him in the eye.

"Of course."

Dragging my lip through my teeth and allowing the bite

of pain to ground the strange ache growing in my chest, I gaze into the distance while Sinclair gives me space to formulate my thoughts.

"I feel like the benefits of this friendship are a one-way street, you know? Like I'm just siphoning and stealing and dragging you down." I look at him then, letting him see the pain in my eyes. "You've always been there to pick me up when I…can't." Shrugging helplessly, I drop my gaze. "And, erm, I'm sorry… I'm sorry I've never been strong enough to be there for you when you need it."

Sinclair sighs, leans back in his seat, and stares at me for a beat before a deep breath inflates his diaphragm. "I almost wish you didn't remember that night now." His voice carries a hint of humor. "Look," he says, tapping the armrest, "you have nothing to apologize for. You're not dragging me down. I'm not good with this"—he gestures between us—"sharing emotions malarkey. But you know I've always got your back, just like you have mine, and if we have to take on a damn secret society and raise a little hell, then let's do it." Sitting forward, he holds out his fist, and I bump my knuckles to his.

"So you remember everything, huh?"

"Unfortunately, yeah…"

"Cecilia's father?"

"He's dead." I cringe, looking away. "I can only imagine what Cecilia thinks of me." A weak, bitter laugh rumbles in my chest. "I bet she can't wait to run as far away from me as possible."

"Don't make me punch you again." Sinclair flexes his fingers and then forms a fist. "Because I will if you spew shit like that one more time. Your wife is crazy about you. Today marks her first time leaving your side since you entered this hospital."

Despite the shame heating my cheeks, his words fill me with hope. “You said you have her shadowed?”

“Of course. She won’t be able to run far even if she tries.”

A smile curves my lips. “I almost kind of hope she tries.”

Sinclair scoffs. “You always liked a good hunt.”

“Where’s the fun if the prey doesn’t put up a fight?”

He hums thoughtfully, then stands and pats my shoulder. “I need to arrange a safe place for you and Cecilia. Can I trust you to stay in bed and not run after her before you get the all-clear from the doctor?”

“Are you serious? If she runs away, I’ll chase her whether I’m dying or not. Trust me, I’m a way faster runner than the reaper when I want something.”

He crosses his arms and widens his stance. “I will cuff you to the fucking bed if you so much as move a damn muscle before the doctor says you can.”

“Why don’t you go ahead and punch me now.” I point to my jaw. “Right here. Go on.”

Unfolding his arms, Sinclair rolls his eyes behind his glasses. “You’re like a damn child, you know that?” He strides across the room, tossing over his shoulder, “I have to make a few calls and put the fear of God into your wife so she doesn’t get any stupid ideas of running away before you’re healed up and ready to chase.”

“Fine, take away all of my fun,” I call out after him as he leaves the room, but then I smile, feeling lighter than I have in years. I’m on the King’s shitlist, but if I’m honest, it was only a matter of time. This outcome was long overdue. In the end, it’s all worth it to have her.

## CHAPTER THIRTY-ONE

CECILIA

*The bedroom door flies open with a loud bang, causing one of the picture frames to crash onto the floor. Mom rushes inside and pulls a packed suitcase from underneath the bed. Her frantic eyes land on me where I sit on the rug in my pajamas, surrounded by my dolls, each with their own teapot. I should be asleep. Mom has already read me my bedtime story and kissed me goodnight, but she doesn't seem too upset to find me awake or even frazzled by the mess on the floor.*

*"Come on," she says, holding her hand out, the other clutching the suitcase's handle. "Pick a doll. We need to leave."*

*I scan my dolls, and they all look at me expectantly. "Where are we going?"*

*"We're going on an adventure," Mommy replies, then gestures for me to take her hand. "We need to leave now, sweetheart."*

*Unsure, I look at each doll and reach for Molly. She's my favorite because of how shiny her brown hair is. Though it's dirty now because that annoying boy, my cousin Dalton, dropped her in a puddle last week when he visited with my uncle.*

*I don't like his dad. He's scary. And my daddy doesn't like him either. After he left, Daddy called him a string of bad words. Mommy clamped her hands over my ears, but it was too late. Besides, I could still hear him say, "I don't give a fuck about the King's contract. I tore it up in front of him."*

*We exit the house in a hurry. Mom drags me along faster than I can walk, strapping me in the car before settling behind the steering wheel and turning the key in the ignition with trembling fingers.*

*"What's wrong, Mommy?" I ask as we drive down the street.*

*She looks in the rearview mirror. "Nothing is wrong, sweetie."*

*"Is Daddy not coming with us?"*

*Mommy suddenly looks sad. I don't like it when she cries; it makes me upset, too.*

*"No, sweetie. Daddy won't be coming with us this time."*

*"Why?" I ask, patting my doll's hair.*

*"Because," Mommy says, staring at the dark road ahead, a lock of blonde hair framing her face, "Daddy went to see the angels in heaven."*

My iPhone lights up on the motel bed, vibrating on the burgundy comforter. Darian is phoning me. I should switch on the lights and unpack my suitcase, but something stops me. Call it instinct, a sixth sense, or maybe muscle memory from being on the run for years. It was almost too easy to escape Sinclair's watchful eye. When I informed him I was heading home to shower and sleep, he didn't even look up from his phone. He just said, "Sure. Don't run away."

So what did I do? I ran away after one of the Commoners took me back to Darian's estate.

Ever since I was a little girl and Mom drove us off into the night, all I've known is how to run from danger. It's what I'm good at. After Mom passed away in a car crash, I became an expert at staying under the radar until I was so tired of running that I decided to face the danger head-on. What was the worst that could happen? I wasn't living.

I didn't want to leave Darian. I'd never wanted anything more than to stay, but the longer I did, the more danger I was putting us both in.

If the King hasn't already figured out who I am, it's only a matter of time. When he does, he'll make an example of Darian, like he did to my dad. I can't let that happen.

If I love Darian, I have to let him go, no matter how much it hurts. The Exiled runs in his blood. It's his family.

I have to set him free.

Maybe we'll meet on the battlefield one day on another Hell Fire Night.

Glancing from the phone to the window, I round the double bed and cross the floor. Heavy curtains block the view of the parking lot outside, the flowery fabric faded over time. As my fingers inch the worn material aside, a muted glow from a streetlamp fills the room. Nothing looks out of place. Three cars, surrounded by low-hanging mist, sit parked beside each other, facing the reception. They were here when I arrived: two sedans and a rusty Chevrolet.

Still, something isn't right.

There! A curtain twitches in one of the windows across the parking lot. I know, I just fucking know, my husband and Sinclair's men followed me here. I should have known it was too easy to escape. No Commoners were where they usually are as I left.

Sinclair and Darian know exactly where I am. When they're ready, they'll collect me like a cash prize.

"Not on my watch, you fuckers," I say as the curtains fall shut.

I should have known Sinclair had me shadowed the moment my husband woke up. He knew my intent and believed that allowing me to think I was free was preferable to dragging me back. This way, he could keep an eye on me and report back to my husband without physically shackling me to my husband's bedside.

I'm almost impressed, though I'm not surprised.

"I suppose I can't bring you with me," I say to my phone as I shove my wallet into my back pocket. My suitcase will have to stay behind too. I don't trust Sinclair not to have ordered his men to put a tracker inside it. It's also a nightmare to drag everywhere, especially now that I need to make a stealthy escape.

My eyes land on my iPhone again. I really shouldn't do anything reckless, but dammit, I want to. He shouldn't have underestimated me.

*No, walk away, Cecilia, while you have a head start. Don't blow your advantage. They think you're in here, clueless.*

Fuck it.

I pick up the phone and dial Elijah's number since that will allow me a few extra minutes I won't have if I phone his father.

He picks up on the second ring, breathing into the phone without saying a word, like a psychopath.

I look at the screen, confused for a second. Sure enough, the call is connected.

Pressing the screen to my ear, I say, "Listen here, you little psycho, tell your daddy and my husband that if they want to trick me, they'll have to do a lot better." I hang up and toss the phone on the bed before bolting for the windows on the other side.

After sliding up the frame, I climb out and run like a bat out of hell with its ass on fire. But I'm not stupid. They'll think I'm running toward the woods behind the property. That's where they'll go.

Instead, I sprint toward *their* room and crouch outside the window. This is the last place they'll think to check, because why would anyone in their right mind hide in the enemy's lair?

I would. I'm not of a sound mind right now. I'm pissed off, exhilarated, and running on enough adrenaline to power a city.

The scent of dew drifts from the wet grass as a late evening breeze cools my damp neck. I peek through the window. The room is empty.

Elijah didn't wait around to set the alarm.

A chorus of masculine voices echoes across the parking lot, a swath of men in black swearing up a storm. I almost snicker as I push open the window and climb inside. Did they think I was that naïve? That I wouldn't know they had me followed?

I crash to the floor with a hard thud, groaning as I roll onto my back on the threadbare carpet. I'll be safe here tonight. They won't return now that I'm officially on the run from their bosses.

I'll catch a few hours of sleep and reevaluate in the morning. There's a chance they'll keep an eye on this place tomorrow in case I'm still hiding somewhere, so I'll need to be careful when I sneak out.

I stand up and cross the room, observing Sinclair's men through the window as they converse in terse tones before loading up their guns and proceeding to kick open each door, much to the horror of startled motel guests. One man is thrown out buck naked with a terrified woman in tow while they search the room.

As I knew they would, they bypass this one and go straight for the one next in line before giving it the all-clear. Their voices soon fade away, and the men searching the nearby forested area return.

"Someone is getting fired in the morning." I snicker.

Three black Range Rovers with blacked-out windows pull into the parking lot to collect the men. Two men stay behind, as I suspected they would, and I watch as they turn and make their way back.

*To this room.*

"Fuck," I whisper, frantically glancing around for somewhere to hide.

My eyes land on the double bed.

It'll have to do.

I throw myself down and roll underneath, disturbing dust bunnies large enough to frighten long-legged spiders. The door opens, and gruff voices fill the room. "I don't understand why we have to stay. She'll be far gone by now. This is ridiculous."

"It's the boss's orders," one of the men says, the taller of the two.

His black cargo pants rustle as his large combat boots sink into the thin carpet. He walks over to the window and moves the flowery curtain aside with his gun. "I'll keep an eye out of this window. You do that one."

The other guy huffs and puffs as he crosses the small room. "She won't come running back." Instead of taking his position at the window, he sits on the springy mattress, his mud-caked boots too close for comfort. "If she does, it won't be for a while." His deep voice drips with enough innuendo to make my eyes widen.

*No fucking way.*

"I don't know," the man by the window says as he abandons his post. "We'll get in trouble with the boss."

"The boss isn't here." The mattress squeaks as the guy on the bed crawls across it. "No one will find out."

*This isn't happening.*

"Want me to suck that big cock of yours?"

I roll my eyes as the other guy crawls onto the bed. The sound of a zipper being lowered fills the silence, and then it's heavy breaths, gagging, and slurping noises.

Just when I think they're done, the springy mattress begins to squeak rhythmically, almost bumping my nose with every violent thrust, while the bedframe bangs against the wall. I have to turn my head to the side to stop from getting squashed.

This is how I die, crushed to death by two fucking men. Their wild, rough tryst dislocates enough dust from the mattress to make me waft the air, and my nose soon tingles as I fight the urge to sneeze.

I squeeze it hard as every muscle in my body stiffens. Luckily, my quiet sneeze is drowned out by the ruckus above—the carnal sounds of slapping skin, a banging headboard, and groaning.

It goes on forever.

Their boss will definitely be pissed. Very fucking pissed.

Have I ever seen Sinclair pissed? I'm sure it involves guns and torture weapons. If they're lucky, it's my husband they have to deal with. He's efficient and quick, but where I'm concerned, I'm sure he'll make them eat their own organs.

My back cramps. I think I fell asleep at some point.

Silence finally falls, and they return to their posts, thankfully fully dressed, though the peace doesn't last. Hours later, I'm startled awake by shouting, panicked voices. The door flies open, and gunshots ring out.

*POP. POP. POP.*

Sinclair's men collapse to the floor on each side of the bed, their dead eyes staring at nothing as dark red blood soaks through their T-shirts.

I cover my mouth with my clammy hand to muffle my surprised yelp, but it's too late. A pair of shiny, expensive leather shoes stops in front of the bed.

The newcomer's black trench coat creases on the floor as he crouches down and rests his leather-gloved hands on his knees.

"Hello, Cecilia," he says, peeking beneath the bed with a curved, dark smile. "It's been a while since we last met. Well, *formally* met. Let's ignore the fact that you were at the latest fundraiser. I didn't know your real identity back then. Darian was tight-lipped on the details." My stomach sinks as his eyes take me in. "Look at you, cousin. You're all grown up."

# CHAPTER THIRTY-TWO

DARIAN

Handling a weapon is second nature to me. I could do it blind and still nail a bulls-eye every time. My father taught me how to load a gun before I mastered my shoelaces. Mom never approved, but my dad refused to budge, spending hours target practicing with me. Now that I think back on those summer afternoons, they're the best memories of my dad.

But a gun won't do now that my anger resembles a volcano about to erupt. I need something sharp. Something that'll hurt like a motherfucker.

Sinclair enters the basement, looking sharp in a black tailor-made suit. He eyes the naked, sweaty man strung up like a slaughtered cow from chains attached to the rafters. I've already roughed him up with my fists a few times, my knuckles cracked and bleeding, but that's foreplay compared to what's coming.

"I can't shake you these days," I say as I inspect each sharp tool on the metal table. "Do you miss me already?"

"Well, you did threaten to murder the terrified doctor with

his own stethoscope if he didn't agree to discharge you before you were ready."

"My wife was kidnapped. I can't stay in bed all day while her captors touch what's mine. It's rather disrespectful of them if you ask me."

"Have I ever told you that you can be a scary motherfucker when you get in these moods?"

"What moods?" I ask, inspecting a sickle probe.

"You're looking at that tool, Darian, like you want to pop his eyeballs with it. It's pretty self-explanatory."

I hum an agreeing sound. "When in Rome."

"And then there's the language you use when you've passed the line of pissed off into nuclear angry. You almost sound like a duke from centuries past."

"While this has been a pleasant chit-chat, Nathaniel, I have a man to prep for the reaper."

"I think I'll stay for the entertainment."

With a scoff, I cross the grimy cement floor to where one of the King's Commoners dangles like a worm on the hook, his toes barely skimming the rusty metal drain. Locks of sweaty, blood-streaked blond hair stick to his damp forehead and his right eye is swollen shut.

"You know," I say as I round him with slow, measured steps. "I almost feel sorry for you. How old are you? Twenty-four? Twenty-five? I would feel inclined to let you go if I didn't have it on good authority that you were involved in the kidnapping of my wife."

Just the mention of it has my blood boiling all over again.

"I don't take well to others touching what's mine."

"No one raped her," he rushes out, swaying on the spot. "No one touched her."

"But you did put your hands on her. How else did you take her away from me? See, here's the thing. No one so much as puts their fingers on my wife's body unless, of course, they want to lose their digits. By the time I'm done with you, your fingers will serve as birthday candles for my wife's next celebration, and your hands, well, I'm sure we can find some use for them."

"He's not lying," Sinclair pipes up, enjoying the fear in my victim's eyes. "Mr. Beaumont thought he could get away with touching her, and he ended up cut into pieces."

"I never hurt her," he says as sweat beads on his brow. "I would never hurt a woman."

I laugh. I can't help it, but then it dies in my throat, and I shove the sickle probe deep into his ear canal, making him scream like a dying, wailing animal. Liquid seeps from his ear, mixed with blood, as he continues crying and blubbering.

"It doesn't feel so good having your eardrum pierced, does it?" I taunt, yanking the tool back and ripping his ear. "You have good teeth, so I'm sure you know this tool is used to remove plaque, but it has other uses, too."

Behind me, Sinclair chuckles, but I'm not here to entertain him. I'm here to purge the restless fury growing inside me and demanding to be set loose on vermin like this strung-up man who thought he could take my wife from me.

She's mine.

No one fucking else's.

"Where did you take her?"

"If I tell you, you'll kill me."

"Newsflash, pup, you're dead either way, but it's entirely up to you how much pain you want to experience before you meet your maker." In a swift move, I shove the sharp tool into his nostril, so far fucking up that tears spring to his eyes before I hook it and pull hard, shredding and causing significant damage to his nose.

"Tell me where she is," I demand when his agonized

screams finally die down, "or I'll set to work on your gums next."

"I don't know where she is."

Seconds pass while I suck on my teeth in mild annoyance as the man desperately tries to find purchase with his toes on the floor. Ridiculous. Out of all the people I could capture and torture, it had to be this pathetic fool who is barely old enough to order beer.

Bored out of my mind, I spin on my heel, wondering what it will take to get him to sing. My wife is out there somewhere in their filthy clutches, probably scared out of her mind. I swear if anyone has so much as left a mark on her skin, I will eat their innards for dinner.

Sinclair laughs behind his fist as I skim my fingers over the tools before collecting a set of pliers and walking back over to the bleeding man. I grab his jaw and pry it open with my bruising grip, wrestling with him until I have his front tooth secured in the pliers.

His terrified eyes lock on mine briefly, and I don't know what he sees there, but I hope it's the devil himself.

It takes effort to pull a tooth, but it's satisfying as hell to see the long, twisty roots pop out of the gums, though I don't care much for the grotesque noises or the endless screaming. For once, I don't wait before giving his next front tooth the same treatment, yanking, pulling, and wiggling while he thrashes in the chains.

Inspecting the milky tooth under the fluorescent flickering light, I pull a disgusted face before walking around him and spreading his ass cheeks with two gloved fingers. He barely fights me as I insert the two teeth into his rectum, shoving them knuckle deep and wiggling for good measure because why not? He'll soon find out firsthand how much enjoyment I get from his pain and humiliation.

"How many teeth do you think I can fill your ass with before you finally talk?" I look over the sobbing man's shoulder and ask Sinclair, "How many teeth do humans have?"

He shrugs, his arms crossed. "Most adults have thirty-two teeth."

"Interesting. I'm a bit bored with pulling teeth, though. It's such standard torture, don't you think? My friend here"—I wave vaguely in Sinclair's direction as I round the trembling prisoner—"he's the senior dentist. I'm more of an… intern."

"Do I even want to know?" Sinclair says as I pick up the electric hand mixer.

"Probably not," I reply, hunting for the extension lead and plugging it into the nearest socket. I spin around to face my best friend with the mixer in the air. "Are you judging my methods?"

"Well, no." Sinclair looks away so I don't see him smothering a laugh. "It's just… In all my years, I don't think I've ever seen anyone bring an electric hand mixer to an occasion like this."

"Seriously?" I scrunch up my nose. "Don't you ever have intrusive thoughts when you whisk up pancakes or something?"

"What kind of intrusive thoughts?"

"I don't know… Like what would happen if you shoved your hand in there."

Sinclair blinks at me, his face blank. "Can't say I do, no."

"Huh." I shrug.

"But go ahead, whisk a confession out of him."

"Har. Har," I reply, experimenting with the settings. The whirring sound makes the man whimper behind me, and I slowly spin on my heel with what I'm sure is a manic look on my face.

Maybe the brain bleed did more damage than I thought because, for the first time I can recall, I'm enjoying myself. "Let's try this again, shall we? Where's my wife?" I enunciate each word as I take slow steps closer. "Tell me, and you can spare yourself a lot of pain."

"Liar," Sinclair coughs into his fist behind me, and I glance at him over my shoulder with a 'what the fuck?' look.

"Why don't you leave if you aren't going to be helpful," I suggest.

He holds up his hands. "I'll behave, teacher. I promise."

Grumbling under my breath, I turn back to the man who needs to tell me what I want to hear this instant before I lose my damn mind. Every second counts.

"Final chance. Where's my wife?"

When I bring the whisk dangerously close to his face, his eyes blow wide, the whirring sound loud and threatening.

"They took her to some warehouse."

"Where?" I growl.

"I don't know."

"Liar," Sinclair pipes up again, just to piss me off.

Inhaling a deep, steadying breath, I turn to face him so slowly that it feels like I've aged a decade by the time we lock eyes. "Don't you have somewhere better to be? A tight pussy to fuck, perhaps?"

"Not at this present moment in time, no." He matches my dead tone, but I don't miss the slight twist at the corners of his mouth. He's always been an infuriating fucker when he wants to be.

"Well then," I grit out with a fake-ass smile. "Shut your mouth and let me drill for oil in this man's Uranus."

He barks a laugh. "By all means, go ahead. Let off steam."

As I swivel back around, the chained man panics, swaying back and forth with the effort of moving away from me. "No, no, no. I don't know anything, okay."

"That's unfortunate for you," I say as I drop into a crouch behind him.

He screams and wails and sobs when I shove the whisk into his rectum, my thumb hovering over the switch. "I've been very patient with you today, but unless you talk, you'll soon find out that patience isn't my virtue. Your boss has my wife, which makes me the most dangerous man on the planet. I'm not pissed, okay? I'm beyond enraged. The correct wordage doesn't even exist in the human language yet. So unless you want me to make rectum mash of your asshole to go with your meatballs, I suggest you tell me where your boss took my wife."

"Oh, God," he chokes out, trembling violently, his remaining teeth chattering. "Okay, okay." Sucking in a breath, he lisps, "They took her to the abandoned warehouse near the burnt-down cigarette factory. You know, the one on the news a few years back."

Sinclair shakes his head as he laughs quietly, rubbing his forehead. He knows what comes next. He knows what I *need.*

With a flick of my finger, the mixer whirrs at an alarming speed as blood and shit gushes from his rectum and onto the floor. I push deeper, a red haze taking over me. If the angels could scream, I'd be in heaven now.

# CHAPTER THIRTY-THREE

## CECILIA

They keep me in a human-sized cage in an abandoned warehouse, a large, open space, with nothing except this cage and two bored bearded men seated on upturned crates. The sickly scents of [illegible], damp leaves, and cannabis prick my nose. They're men of few words except when I rattle and kick the rusty bars, which makes them holler and sneer. One of them even cups his junk and makes a lewd gesture with his fingers and tongue despite Dalton giving him strict instructions not to touch me.

Once a day, they drag me out of the cage to relieve myself in a bucket in the corner. It's humiliating and demoralizing, but they enjoy that, judging by the twisted gleam in their eyes as they watch me pull my pants down and crouch over the bucket, careful to hide my modesty.

Then I'm hauled back and tossed inside the cage. If I'm lucky, they slam the cage door shut and return to their crates, but there have been times when they followed me inside and cornered me against the bars.

Reminding them of what the King will do if they touch

me always works. They soon back off, spitting in my direction as they leave the cage.

I'd lie if I said it didn't rattle me. It does. I'm always left trembling as I settle back in the corner, where I can keep an eye on them while they smoke their weed and watch me like I'm a snack they want to sink their teeth into.

Something has to change soon. Someone has to come for me. How long will they keep me locked up like this? This is twice now I've been kidnapped, but I doubt it'll work in my favor if I try to seduce the guards this time.

A shiver runs through me when I think about it.

What does Dalton want? Money? Is he holding me hostage while he blackmails Darian? Surely not.

I've lost count of how many days I've been locked up, when cars pull up outside, their engines rumbling.

"If it isn't my favorite cousin," Dalton says, a gust of fresh, damp air blowing in behind him as he enters the warehouse. Two hulky, bald men in black pants and shirts flank him, and I wonder briefly if they go everywhere with him or if he's taking extra precautions lately.

Some part of me wants to believe it's the latter, that maybe Dalton and my uncle fear my husband's retaliation, but a different part of me knows the King's son can't go anywhere without bodyguards. He was born with a target on his back.

"I hope you find the cage comfortable. I had it installed just for you."

Dressed in pressed pants, a pristine white shirt, and a black trench coat, with a fine mist of rain on his shoulders, Dalton looks like he stepped off the pages of a fashion magazine.

As he crosses the room, he takes off his leather gloves

and slips them into his pocket. "I'm sorry it has taken me this long to see you. I've had some urgent matters to deal with."

He stops in front of the cage and studies me disapprovingly from head to toe. "So this is what all the fuss is about?"

Silence fills the warehouse. One of the men lights a cigarette, watching me through the curling smoke.

"Cecilia," Dalton says, notes of impatience bleeding into his tone. "Look at me."

I reluctantly swing my gaze to him, and he steps closer. "This is who was promised to me?" He turns over his shoulder. "Did any of you touch her?"

Their heads snap to attention, and they hold their hands up. "No, sir."

Seconds pass as he narrows his eyes on my tormentors, and then he orders them to remove the bucket in the corner of the room because it reeks. They scurry into action, crashing into each other and almost falling on their asses in their rush to please the King's son.

Dalton's attention returns to me, his cold eyes falling down my body and leaving a slimy chill behind. He juts his chin, silently commanding the others to open the cage. One of the men appears like a genie, fumbling with a set of rustling keys, while the other Commoner carries the stinking piss bucket outside.

"What are you? A fucking imbecile?" Dalton barks, unimpressed, as the man drops the keys.

The moment he picks them up, Dalton snatches them out of the man's hands and unlocks the creaky door.

It's the most ominous sound I've heard. I can't threaten my cousin with his father. My uncle probably condones this.

As he enters the cage, my eyes widen in alarm, but there's nowhere to go. He's blocking the only exit. The cage was small before he entered, but now I feel truly cornered and helpless.

I dart my gaze behind him as he drinks me in, but before I can see what the others are bringing in from the car, he walks closer and traps me with his hands on the bars on either side of me.

"You really are a pretty little thing, aren't you?"

The scent of fresh rain and the outdoors clings to his trench coat, and rain droplets dampen his windswept blond hair. He studies me closely, intrigued, as he roams his eyes over my face. "I don't see it," he says. "The family resemblance, I mean."

Letting go of the bars, he fingers a strand of my hair. "Maybe it's the blonde?"

My throat jumps on a swallow as he lets go of the lock to trace the backs of his knuckles down the column of my throat.

His thin lips quirk menacingly. "You're scared of me."

"You sound happy about that." It's a challenge to keep my voice steady, and my skin crawls when he hums, sliding his fingertips over my collarbones.

"I like it when women fear me."

"I bet," I grit out.

I sound braver than I am, and he can see right through me, judging by the knowing glint in his eyes. His touch travels lower, his thumb trailing over my sensitive nipple through my clothing, and then he cups my left breast, observing my reaction closely. I try so hard to remain strong, but my chin trembles as tears gather on my lashes.

"Darian stole something of mine," he says in a low, chill-inducing tone. "Something of great importance."

Overhead, rain patters on the steel roof as the clinking of chains rustles in the background. Dalton continues massaging my breasts, his eyes darkening further when my tears spill over.

"Your virginity was promised to me," he drawls as he trails his fingers lower, and I suck in my stomach. "I don't like thieves."

"Darian didn't take my virginity," I reply boldly. "I gave that away as soon as I found out about the contract between our parents."

Seconds pass, and then Dalton's hand flies out, quick as a flash, and he grabs my jaw, ramming the back of my head against the bars. "You're a little whore, aren't you?"

"No," I sneer, baring my teeth, "I just knew I would rather die than offer you my virginity."

For a moment, I think he might punch me, and I prepare for the impact, but then he steps back and smiles coldly. "You won't be so brave soon, cousin."

As he exits the cage, he orders his lackeys to fetch me.

One of them approaches with a smirk, ducking his bald head as he enters the small space. I panic and kick at him, but he overpowers me with his height and strength.

"You little slut!" He backhands me hard and then grabs my hair, pulling me out despite my struggles. Once I'm out, he drags me to a wooden cross on the floor and shoves me down. Fear washes over me as I squirm and scream, but he keeps me pinned on the cross.

The other man clamps his dirty boot down on my wrist, a hammer dangling from his hands, and then his cracked lips peel back into a sickening smile to showcase his sharp canines as he wiggles the large nail in the air for me to see.

"Wait," Dalton speaks up, and relief floods through me with such force that I can barely suppress a sob.

"Strip her naked first."

"What? No!" I flail, mortified, as the two men rip at my

clothes, copping a feel with their greedy hands. Dalton smirks with his head tilted sideways and his hands in his pockets.

This is all a game to him.

When I'm naked, and my clothes are in tatters on the floor, he kicks my panties out of the way and widens his stance. "Your mother did this to you when she took you and ran. She knew there was no way out of the Exiled. She knew and still took her sweet little daughter and ran away."

One of the Commoners appears with ropes, then ties my wrists and ankles to the cross while I wriggle and pant desperately.

"And then there's the question of your husband, of course." Dalton sounds conversational.

The fourth man puts a tripod down and directs a camera at me.

Dalton slides his hand from his pocket and rubs his mouth, deep in thought. "Did he really think he could keep you hidden from us? It was a reckless move to steal you from beneath our noses and parade you around like some prized horse." He wiggles his finger in my direction. "Admittedly, the eye masks at the fundraisers helped hide your identity, but it was never going to last. My father had been looking for you for a very long time. Can you blame him? A devoted uncle, searching for his niece."

I spit in his direction, and one of the guards smacks my face with such force that my face whips to the side.

Dalton's smirk grows, and he gestures to the camera. "I hope you don't mind being the star in our home movie."

I lift my head, my cheek throbbing. The camera is aimed right at me, capturing every moment of this nightmare.

"We have to send a message to traitors. This is what happens if you betray the Exiled or try to work against us in any way. We won't tolerate uprisings." He crouches at my feet and lets his hungry gaze feast on my naked breasts and pussy. "It's also a message for your husband. How long do you think it'll take him before he comes to your rescue?" His hand slides over my foot. "He'll be filled with so much rage. So much fury. I can almost taste it."

Dalton stands and stares down at me. "When he comes, my men will be ready for him." He juts his chin to the men, and my body breaks out in a vicious cold sweat. I scream and thrash, fighting with everything I've got, but it's useless against four large men.

A large nail digs into my palm, and I scream in agony when he slams it down with a hammer. All I know from that moment onwards is excruciating, blinding pain.

Pain so agonizing, I soon drift in and out of consciousness.

# CHAPTER THIRTY-FOUR

## DARIAN

As I speed down the country road, my vision zeros in on the horizon in the distance until it blurs into nothing.

My long fingers curl around the leather steering wheel, and I push down harder on the accelerator, but I'm already flooring it. Despite my dance with death, my heartbeat remains calm and steady, like a glassy lake reflecting the trees outside.

Each pounding heartbeat thuds like a kick drum. What I feel now is beyond anger or rage. I'm emotionless—an empty void of unleashed darkness with one goal in mind.

Complete destruction. Aim and kill.

One quick glance at the speedometer has a small smile tugging at the corner of my mouth. If I make the slightest mistake now, take my mind off the target for even one second, I'll be snuffed off this planet in a heartbeat.

My phone rings in the passenger seat, the phone vibrating across the leather.

*Sinclair.*

Always the voice of reason in my muddled mind.

I press answer on the steering wheel.

"This is fucking madness," he says, his voice filling the car when the call connects. "You'll kill yourself."

I stare at the mirage ahead, glimmering in the distance. "The only one dying is the King."

"I can't let you do this, Darian. Not like this. I know you're angry, but we need a plan before we attack."

My gaze flicks to the climbing speedometer again, and my breaths grow shallower until I barely feel its whisper on my lips. Sinclair wants me to turn back and formulate a plan of attack, but I don't have precious seconds to spare. I'm bringing my wife home, no matter what it takes or what nightmare greets me.

"Darian!" Sinclair's sharp voice snaps me back from my thoughts, and a frown creases my brow.

When I flick my eyes to the rearview mirror, he's hot on my tail. "Go home, Sinclair."

His deep, resigned sigh fills my car and then he says, "You forgot one very important thing."

The horizon stares back at me, a speck in the distance. "What's that?"

"I have your Bugatti, and it's a fuckton faster than your car."

I can't help but laugh when he pulls out and speeds past me, maneuvering the car with an ease most professional racers would covet. He whizzes by like a bullet, flying down the road before pulling the handbrake and spinning the car around like a suicidal madman until he faces me.

"Crazy motherfucker," I chuckle as I slam on the brakes, the tires squealing loudly on the road.

When our cars finally come to a standstill, we stare at each other through the windshields, high on adrenaline and breathing like bulls, road dust swirling around us.

"Are you going to move your car?" I ask, resting against the headrest.

"Are you going to use some common fucking sense?" he counters, his voice filling the car through the speakers.

I chuckle. "Nope."

"Then no, I think I'll stay parked right here."

Smacking the glovebox, I retrieve my gun, ensuring he can hear it click before I exit the vehicle, walking toward him with the weapon drawn. "Move your fucking car, Sinclair."

Instead of responding, he grins behind the steering wheel and shakes his head. Then he opens the door, slams it shut, and walks toward me. Women of all ages have always loved this side of Sinclair, his masculine cockiness and lack of fear. He's an arrogant fucker, and if I didn't respect him so much, I would've shot him by now.

"What good do you think you'll be to your woman if you're dead?"

"Now is not the time for chit-chat. Move out of my way."

"You know, I always admired you for being a strategist, but all it took was one warm, tight pussy for you to become so fucking blinded, you'll get both of you killed." Before the words have left his mouth, he wrestles the gun from my hand and swipes my feet from underneath me.

Surprised, I hit the ground hard, the breath knocked from my lungs.

Sinclair is about to empty the gun of bullets, when his phone vibrates in his pocket.

With a brief glance at me—coughing on the ground and clambering to my feet—he pulls it out and taps the screen.

"Shit," I grumble, straightening up. "I think I broke my back."

"Where's your phone?" Sinclair asks carefully as he pockets his.

Something about the change in tone has me stiffening, and I eye him for a second before darting to the car to retrieve my phone, but he anticipates my move and tackles me.

"What the fuck?" I shove him off me, but he launches himself at my back and we wrestle for reasons I can't fucking figure out.

"What the hell is wrong with you?" I growl, refraining from punching him in the face as we roll into the ditch. "Ow, fuck! What the hell are we doing, Sinclair?"

Shoving off me, he jumps to his feet and runs for the car. Confused as hell, I pop my head up from the ditch, watching him grab my phone from the passenger seat.

He tosses it to the ground and stomps on it, looking as frazzled as I am.

I climb out of the ditch, dirt and sticks stuck in my hair, and throw my hands out. "What was that for?"

Sinclair's attention lands on me, and he does a double take as though he forgot I was here. Then he walks closer, hesitantly, peering into the distance. "I need you to listen to me carefully."

Frowning and out of breath, I wait for him to continue while he rests his hands on his hips. When he doesn't, I gesture impatiently, "Yes?"

"You can't freak out. Something bad has happened. Something really fucking bad—"

My eyes widen, but before I can storm back to the car, he puts his hand on my shoulder. "Darian, I need your head in the game. Okay? You're not thinking straight."

Releasing me, he removes his phone from his pocket and makes a few calls. Meanwhile, I eye the cell with my nerves on fire, debating if I should steal it from him to see what he's hiding. But maybe he's right. I'm already volatile. I need to keep my head on, and I'm already doing a piss poor job of that.

"What happened to a plan of attack?" I ask when he hangs up.

With his chin on his chest, he rubs his eyes, his other hand on his hip. "Time's up."

When he looks at me, I feel my face drain of color. He breaks eye contact, strides to the Bugatti, and leans back on the hood. Shoulders slumped, he hangs his head in defeat.

Is Cecilia dead? Is that what he's not telling me?

Fear, unlike anything I've experienced, sinks its hooks inside me, and the anger from earlier drains away until I'm as tired and broken as Sinclair.

I cross the road and sit beside him, staring into the distance beyond my car and the tire marks on the asphalt. A cawing bird disturbs the silence, taking flight from a nearby tree.

"I know I said it before," Sinclair says, watching it circle above. "There's no going back—not for you or me."

"You don't have to come along. This is my fight," I reply with a heavy breath. He looks away from the sky and studies my face, then he wraps his arm around my shoulder and points a finger at the approaching blacked-out Range Rovers. "Here comes the cavalry."

They park up behind my car, and Elijah opens the driver's door and steps down on the cracked road, his signature smirk revealing the dimple on his cheek. "Let's get your woman back, Delacroix."

---

It wasn't safe to park too close to the warehouse, so we parked farther down the road, close enough that we could make a hasty escape, but far enough away not to draw attention.

I look out behind the tall trees, relieved when the desolate warehouse appears, the metal rusty after years of neglect. Tufts of dry, yellow grass line the building, and tall fir trees stand guard around the abandoned structure.

I share a terse look with Sinclair. Behind us, we hear sticks snapping as Elijah approaches, dressed in all black. "Something is wrong," he says.

His father nods and studies the building.

"It's too quiet," I reply, noting the absence of cars.

"Come on," Sinclair says as he sets off walking, and we follow behind.

Elijah is a steady, formidable presence at my side. Just like his father, he's got his head screwed on tight when he needs to. Me? I feel like I'm falling apart, layer by layer, as the large structure looms ahead.

I try to force down the insistent fear that wants to render me useless, but something is terribly wrong. I feel it in the air.

Gray, ominous clouds gather overhead, crows caw in the distance, perched on the roof, and the air smells of an impending storm.

We walk up to the entrance, weapons drawn. Sinclair puts his ear against the surface and makes a few hand signals before slowly opening the door. After a final nod, he steps inside. I follow, hearing the crunch of dried leaves underfoot. Elijah comes in next, holding the door open for the man behind him.

Sinclair puts his arm out to stop me, and I raise my gaze to see a Commoner tied up on the floor, beaten unconscious, by the looks of it, but alive. A note written in blood is stapled to his shirt, and I crouch down and rip it off.

*"Darian, enjoy your gift."*

Elijah frowns when I hand it to Sinclair. Behind us, the other men look around the vast empty space.

"She's not here..." My voice shakes as I feel something break inside me—the small sliver of hope I had left.

Sinclair drops the note, allowing it to flutter to the ground, and looks at me. His brows pull down when a drop of red splats on my shoulder, and I swallow, feeling the warm liquid on my fingers as I touch it. We share a worried glance before looking up.

"Holy mother of God," Sinclair breathes, and all hell breaks loose around me.

"We need something to get her down. NOW!" someone shouts in a panicked voice that sounds muted and far away.

Suspended from the roof, crucified, Cecilia's beautiful hair cascades from the upside-down cross, her naked body whipped and covered in dried blood.

The floor opens to swallow me whole, and I feel myself endlessly falling and spiraling until there's nothing left but an unquenchable desire for revenge.

As she's lowered to the floor, I fall to my knees beside her broken body while they remove the ropes and call for medical assistance.

"I'm sorry," Sinclair says, squeezing my shoulder while I feel for a pulse in her neck.

"She's not fucking dead," I spit, refusing to lose my wife, refusing to let the fucking Exiled break me a second time. They've taken too much already. They're not taking my wife, too. She will survive this, and I will bathe in their blood and burn the entire society to the ground. I don't care what it takes.

Their reign ends with me.

Sinclair crouches beside me, stroking her blood-streaked hair away from her brow, a wretched look on his face. "Fuck,

I'm so sorry," he says again, and fury explodes inside me like a supernova as I stare at the bloodied nails in my wife's pale hands.

I launch myself at the tied-up, unconscious Commoner on the ground, lift his head off the floor, and smash his skull against the concrete until there's nothing left—until my fingers are slick with his blood and brain matter.

With an agonized roar, I hop to my feet and kick his dead body. I kick the living shit out of his remains for my mother, for my wife, for every helpless woman who's fallen victim to the King and his reign. Some of the men try to stop me and calm me down, but I shove them away before stomping on his bleeding corpse.

How the fuck could the King do this to his niece. His own flesh and blood.

To the woman I love.

"We have a pulse. It's weak, but we have a pulse." I'm torn away from the broken body, and Sinclair jostles my shoulders, his face blurring in front of me. "She's alive, Darian."

I whip my head around. Paramedics have entered the room. Paramedics we can trust.

Because we're on the run now.

Fugitives on the run from everything we've ever known.

Sinclair's big hands clamp down on my tear-streaked cheeks. "She's alive."

---

In the few months I've known my wife, we've been through hell and back, yet here we are, still fighting.

Well, she's healing, and I'm fighting.

Always fucking fighting for her.

Standing by her hospital bed in our secret location, the sun streaming in through the window, I stare at the fading bruises on her face. One day soon, I'm going to avenge each mark on her body.

She hasn't woken up yet, and I'm grateful for every moment she stays asleep and lets her body heal from the ordeal she has suffered through.

Every time I think about what they did to her—nailing her to a cross, whipping and beating her pale skin before suspending her upside down from the ceiling—the putrid hatred inside me expands.

In a way, it's good. I'll need it to survive what's to come. But as I stroke my finger over her bandaged hand, I wish I could go back in time and take it all away.

I should've killed the King when I had the chance.

Why didn't we take him out years ago? What was I waiting for? He doesn't have a soul, never mind a heart, and he proved as much when he killed his own brother-in-law for refusing to sell his daughter.

We're all collateral damage in this war, our hearts blackened and tarnished from the heartbreak we've suffered at the hands of greed for power.

"How is she doing?" Sinclair asks from the doorway.

"She'll heal. There might be some nerve damage in her hands and feet, but she'll survive, and that's what matters. The same can't be said for the King and his son."

"You know this was a warning, right?" he says, approaching the bed. "A declaration of war."

I raise my dead glare; my wife's bandaged hand is the only thing keeping me grounded.

"Trust me, I'll make him regret the day he looked at my wife wrong."

Sinclair nods, glancing at Cecilia. "You will need to keep your head in the game."

I listen to the sound of the heartbeat monitor for a moment before I lean down and press my lips to her forehead. When I straighten, I say, "Whatever it takes to keep her safe."

"Good. Because I have a plan." Smiling mischievously, he holds out his hand. "Head in the game?"

A smirk curves my lips, and we do our secret handshake from youth. "Let's kill the King."

"And burn the Exiled to the ground."

# EPILOGUE

CECILIA

## ONE YEAR LATER

As I trace my fingers over the intricate detailing on the oil painting, my eyes catch on the pale scarring on my hand. There will come a day when I can look at my scars without a knot forming in my throat, but I'm still a long way from healing emotionally. At least we're safe for now, living in a new house, far away from the Exiled's clutches, while Darian and Sinclair are the head of their new society.

"Are you going to throw that?" Darian's deep timbre downstairs has a spark of joy bubbling up inside me, but instead of spinning around and beaming like he's the sun in my universe, I bite back my smile and hum.

"Will you be mad if I do?"

"Why don't you try me?"

My smile slips free, and my lip escapes the confines of my teeth. I turn on my heel and step up to the banister.

Looking as handsome as the day I first met him in a shirt

and dress pants, Darian stares up at me from the bottom floor with so much admiration it takes my breath away.

His dark hair is interspersed with more gray strands than a year ago, and the smile lines around his eyes are more pronounced, yet he's more attractive than he's ever been.

Maybe because he smiles freely now.

Yes, he has his dark moments, especially in our war against the Exiled, but he's also happier.

"Maybe I should," I tease, walking my fingers along the wooden banister with a flirtatious smile, and then before he can reply with a witty remark, I turn back around and lift the large painting off its hooks. It's a lot heavier than it looks, and by the time I'm precariously balancing it on the railing, Darian is biting back an amused smile.

"You're a lot stronger than you look for such a short woman."

I scoff, pretending to be offended. "How dare you call me short? I'll have you know, I'm five foot two.

"Impressive," he says.

"I'm only short to you because you're so tall." I sound petty, but Darian just chuckles and rubs his brow.

"Are you throwing the painting or not?"

I debate it for a moment. It would be a shame; it's a pretty one, probably my favorite in this new house. "I like this one," I say with a sigh.

Darian's eyes twinkle beneath the chandelier's soft glow.

"Why don't we keep this one," I muse.

As I go to place it down, it slips from my fingers and crashes to the floor by Darian's feet, splintering on impact.

"Oh shit…" I press my hands over my mouth, staring wide-eyed at the mess, then at Darian, who slowly lifts his gaze. When he raises a dark brow, laughter bubbles up from my chest.

I can't help it; the look on his face is too funny.

"Oops." I roll my lips to prevent them from curling.

"Oops?"

"For once, I didn't mean it."

Darian inhales deeply. "Looks like I'll have no choice but to punish you."

"Oh, please," I laugh, "like it's any trouble."

Now it's his turn to laugh, the sound dark and husky. He shakes his head and studies me with a smirk so sinfully delicious that heat settles low in my core. "You're right," he says with a simple shrug. "It's my pleasure to chase you down and spank your little pussy."

He pretends to look around, but I know what's coming even before he runs up the stairs, making me squeal with excitement. "Where are you going to hide, Mrs. Delacroix? There's no library here."

After I throw open the door to our bedroom, I dart inside, but before I can close it, he shoulders through and kicks it shut behind him.

I stop dead in my tracks, staring at the countless red roses covering every surface. And bat flowers—so many ugly little alien flowers amidst the red petals.

His warm chest lines up with my back, and he shifts my hair aside to place a tender kiss on my shoulder. "Have I ever told you that you're the light of my life?"

"Darian," I whisper, my voice trembling.

As I turn around, I gasp at the sight of Darian kneeling with a ring box in his hand. The most beautiful diamond ring I've ever seen sparkles up at me, and his eyes hold a vulnerable, boyish look.

"Mrs. Delacroix," he says, "I never gave you the proposal you deserved. When we first met, you married me because you had no choice. I want to give you that choice."

He swallows hard, looking up at me with such hope that my heart speeds up. "I love you. I love you with every heartbeat, every breath, and every smile you bring to my lips. There is no other woman like you, and I should've known the first time I saw you polishing glasses that you were going to bulldoze your way into my life and make me feel things I never thought possible. You fought for me when I didn't deserve it and loved me in a dark place where no one had reached me."

"Oh, Darian," I whisper as I wipe my wet cheeks, but more tears fall.

"I don't regret stealing your freedom, not when it brought you to me," he says. "But I regret not giving you the wedding you deserve, the flowers, the dress, the celebration. You deserve each and every dream of yours to come true, and if you let me, I will give you them all, no matter how big or small. There are no limits to your happiness. I never offered you a choice to pick me when we met, but I'm begging you now. Pick me, Mrs. Delacroix. Choose me. Will you be my forever? My wife? My best friend and my lover?"

Chewing on my lip, I consider his words. "So if I decide to walk away, you'll let me?"

His throat jumps on a thick swallow. "Yes."

"You're giving me a choice, Darian Delacroix?"

A muscle clenches in his cheek as fear creeps into his eyes, but he nods once. "Yes, baby, I want you to be happy. I've never let you have your freedom before, and I can't live with myself if you're here because you're caged. So if you want to walk away, I won't stop you."

My eyes drop from his sincere gaze to the ring, and tears trail down my cheeks as I sift my fingers through his soft, dark hair. "I don't feel caged, Darian. If anything, you set me free."

When he continues kneeling with that hopeful look in his eyes, I drop to my knees, too, and cup his stubbly cheeks. "The answer is yes, Mr. Delacroix. I choose you."

He gives me a boyish smile, his fingers trembling slightly as he removes my ring and replaces it with the new one. I watch his Adam's apple bob as he reaches into his pocket and pulls out a necklace. "I also have this. I'd like you to wear it, if that's okay?"

I eye the heart pendant before rising to my feet and spinning around, moving my hair away from my shoulder. "It's beautiful."

"It was my mother's," he says, his breaths fanning my neck as he stands up and secures it. "She gave it to me that night."

As his touch lingers on my skin, my heart thuds harder. I glance at him over my shoulder, and his eyes fall to my mouth. "I will always keep you safe. You know that, right?"

I finger the heart pendant and feel my chest ache with tenderness.

His mother once wore this necklace—her last gift to him. Now, he wants me to have it. "We keep each other safe, Darian."

His fingers trail through the strands of my hair, and I lean back against his chest, looking out over the roses.

A thought occurs to me. "Were the bat flowers your idea?"

He snorts, which makes me smile. "You're kidding, right? It was all Sinclair. You're family now, he said. And family looks after each other."

"Darian?"

He hums contentedly.

"We're already married, so how can we do it again? I'm not divorcing you."

"We can still have a celebration."

Turning in his arms, I wrap my mine around his neck. "I like that idea."

"Yeah?"

I kiss him. "Very much."

"Good," he says, sweeping my hair away from my brow and kissing the tip of my nose, lips, and cheek. "Are you ready for your punishment now?"

"I thought you had forgotten about that."

A wolfish smile spreads across his face. He lifts me like I weigh nothing before he tosses me onto the bed and removes his shirt.

Giggling, I bounce on the mattress, surrounded by luxurious cushions and silk, watching my handsome, fearsome husband strip out of his clothes.

"Come here, wife," he says, climbing on after me and circling his fingers around my ankle. "Let's spank that pretty pussy."

With a quick yank and a salacious grin, he pulls me down the bed to the soundtrack of my peals of laughter.

*The End.*

**What's next?**

**For more of Darian and Cecilia and the war against the Exiled, check out Nathaniel Sinclair's upcoming book *Unholy* by Kinsley Kincaid.**

**A special thank you to Ms. Kincaid for letting our words crossover and entrusting me with her characters.**

# ABOUT THE AUTHOR

Harleigh Beck is an international bestselling author of dark romance and erotic horrors. She lives in a small town in northeast England with her hubby and their three children. When she's not writing, you'll find her head down in a book. She mainly reads dark romance and horror, but she also likes the occasional rom-com. She has more books planned, so be sure to connect with her on her social media for updates.

Printed in Great Britain
by Amazon

63256611R00201